THE
SE

Over the years David Jones has collected together a vast library of letters written to his magazine. Many were published, some were cut (for space or legal reasons), and some never saw the light of day. Far more raunchy and realistic than the average erotica title, they made quite a collection. Finally David decided to choose the best of them and get them published – which they were in two best-selling books.

Now – for the first time – New English Library are publishing them all together in one plush volume.

Also in paperback from New English Library

Summer School
Sex Thief
Submission
Naked Lies

The World's Best Sex Anthology

Edited and compiled by David Jones

NEW ENGLISH LIBRARY
Hodder & Stoughton

This collection volumes published in paperback in 2001
by Hodder and Stoughton
A division of Hodder Headline

A NEL Paperback

10 9 8 7 6 5 4 3 2 1

British Library Cataloguing in Publication Data
A CIP catalogue record for this title
is available from the British Library.

ISBN 0 340 76924 6

Printed and bound in Great Britain by
Mackays of Chatham PLC, Chatham, Kent

Hodder and Stoughton
A division of Hodder Headline
338 Euston Road
London NW1 3BH

The World's Best Sexual Fantasy Letters: Volume One

INTRODUCTION

Fantasies are what inject the life into most of our sex lives. At dinner parties, when the food is cleared away and the coffee, port and brandy are served, the subject, sooner or later, turns to sex. And one of the most frequent, and most popular, of sexual topics is, inevitably, where does real sex stop, and where do fantasies begin? There have always been two distinctly opposing views about fantasies. There is the one that says the best advice is to keep your fantasies as exactly that, for once you have turned them into experiences, they will lose their magic. And then there is the opposing view that says that the only worthwhile reason for having a fantasy is to be able to look forward to turning it into reality. And enjoy doing just that.

The trouble is, of course, that one man's sexual fantasy can be another man's complete sexual turn-off. But herein, perhaps, lies the magic. Many young men and women, at the outset of their sexual experience, find the thought of performing either cunnilingus or fellatio distasteful. Literally. Whereas most sexually mature men will leap at the opportunity. Many older men actually complain of the lack of opportunity to indulge in oral sex. My own view has always been that taught to me, years ago now, by a delightful young woman called Ann Summers. Which is that, whatever two people do together in their sexual relationships is perfectly acceptable, *provided* that both of them want to do it, and that no physical or mental harm results to either. I accept that there are people who consider that sex in anything other than the missionary position is abnormal, and that to them those of us who like to experiment with our sexual partners are the worst kind of deviants.

Be that as it may, in a career in men's magazine publishing as a journalist, editor, and publisher, spanning over thirty years, my experience was that the readers' letters columns were always a mainstay, a linchpin, of the textual content of all the magazines upon which I ever worked.

These included Paul Raymond's *Men Only* and *Club International*, back in the days when they quite properly assumed that their male readers had partners of the opposite sex, at least for some of the time, rather than the – to me – seemingly single-minded preoccupation with single-handed sex that appears to obsess whoever edits their columns these days.

We also, back then, published the finest writers and artists that money could buy, to produce and illustrate the features, fiction, reviews and interviews that were as essential a part of the magazines as were the girl sets. Strangely, it is a fact that in the 1970s and 1980s, we paid more for the words and pictures than those magazines do today. And I think it shows.

Frank Norman, Wolf Mankowitz, Irma Kurtz, Jeffrey Bernard, Daniel Farson, Molly Parkin, George Melly, Sandy Fawkes, the late Kingsley Amis and his son Martin Amis, all wrote for me in the United Kingdom. Ralph Steadman, James Marsh and George Underwood used to illustrate fiction for the magazines, as did Brian Froud and Brian Grimwood. Fluck & Law, the originators of *Spitting Image*, built models that we photographed for humorous features, long before they'd even thought of *Spitting Image*. Tom Hustler and Patrick Litchfield photographed for us. So did David Parkinson and Geoff Howes. In the United States, William Burroughs, Clifford Irving, Andrew Sarris and F. Lee Bailey were regular contributors, amongst many others. Perhaps the audience today is different. But I don't believe so. Today, magazines like *GHQ*, *Esquire*, and *FHM* still perpetuate that old, up-market, quality approach to men's magazines, showing respect for the intelligence of their readers. Thank God someone does.

In the United States I eventually ran Paul Raymond's flagship American magazine *Club*, whose circulation went from four hundred thousand copies a month when I took it over from my old friend Tony Power to one million, two hundred thousand copies a month under my editorship. I also ran another magazine from the same stable, one that attempted to be all things sexual to all people sexual, and that was entitled *Club Quest*. It almost succeeded. I treasure the copies that I still have.

Back here in Britain, I subsequently took over the European editions of *Penthouse*, of *Forum* and of *Variations*. Not forgetting, of course, *Omni*, then the world's best science magazine for laymen, edited in those days by Professor Bernard Dixon, the ex-editor of *New Scientist*.

Forum, of course, started its life in England, as did *Penthouse*. It was originally the brainchild, back in the late 1960s, of Professor Albert Z. Freedman, who still works with Bob Guccione in the United States (where *Forum*'s current associated publisher and editorial director is a protégé of mine, V. K. McCarty). Al had the intelligence to see that the correspondence columns of *Penthouse* could spawn a magazine offshoot of their own, and thus was *Forum* born. In the past, the UK version has had many distinguished names upon its editorial staff, including – after Al Freedman – Philip Hodson, Anna Raeburn, and the late Roger Baker, the respected author of what is still the definitive book on drag. Sadly, he died recently.

Over the years, the main difficulty with publishing readers' letters – and, most particularly, readers' fantasy letters – has always been the question of space. Almost every reader's letter published in men's magazines, anywhere in the world, upon whatever topic, is edited down from its original length. With fantasy letters, this is often to the detriment of the letter. And to the disappointment of the reader. It is simply a sad fact of magazine editorial life. Now, New English Library is publishing two volumes of the world's best fantasy letters – of which this is the first – collected from over the years, and which permit – for the first time ever – the best of these letters to be published in their original, unedited, full-length state. An historic event! Enjoy.

David Jones. Hampstead, London. 1996.

ALICE IN KNICKERLAND

I love to look at young girls walking in the street, sitting on buses, or travelling on the Underground, and wonder to myself what kind of underwear they are wearing. I fantasize about their knickers, and try to decide, by looking at their faces, what they might be wearing. Are they wearing tiny little silky G-string-style knickers? Perhaps in black, with little red lace bows? Or have they got on bikini-style knickers, with high-cut sides and low-cut fronts? Maybe in pink? Or maybe they are wearing totally transparent white nylon lace knickers that show their pubic hair and their little pink cunt lips through the front?

In my daydreams, I order the girls into my bedroom, one at a time, and they lift up their short skirts and show me their knickers. Of course I reach out and stroke and feel their pussies through their knicker crotches, and I remark on it when the knickers are wet from the girls' pussy juices. If they're really wet, I make the girls take them off, and I make them hold their damp knicker gussets up to my nostrils, so that I can breathe in the delightful smell of cunt. And while I'm sniffing their knickers, I'm fingering their wet cunts.

It's a sort of competition, really, and in my fantasy, depending upon the style of knickers worn and the amount of dampness between their legs, and the specific aroma of their pussy, they will either be rejected, in which case they simply leave, or they are selected, in which case they are short-listed for fucking – and other sexual acts – later on. Sometimes I fantasize that a girl might be wearing a pair of old-fashioned knickers. You know, the kind that schoolgirls wear. Navy-blue, heavily textured, woolly ones. And I put my fingers underneath the leg elastic, and slip them into their pussy, which is always wet and warm, and very accommodating, and then I masturbate them. Do you think this is a peculiar fetish?

A. J. Stroud, Glos.

Absolutely not. Whatever turns you on.

KNICKER KICKER

My husband has always been a dyed-in-the-wool knicker fetishist, from long before we ever got married. The vulgarly sexy tart's knickers that he buys me on every possible occasion – birthdays, Christmas, St Valentine's Day, and so on – mean far more to him than they do to me, and for that reason I'm beginning to wonder if it's me he wants to fuck, or the knickers. Black is obligatory. Black satin, black nylon, black lace. Cami-knickers, French knickers, teddies. You name it. Rather like Henry Ford's cars, I can have any colour I like, provided that it's black. In one way I don't mind. I'd much rather that he bought the knickers for me than for some other woman. But on the rare occasions when I've either chosen to wear a different colour, or have refused to wear black, or suggested that I take my knickers off before we get into bed, he doesn't seem to be able to get it up. I simply can't win. No black knickers, no sex. It seems vital to him that our fucking has to begin with him sucking my pussy through my knicker crotch. If he isn't allowed to do this, he doesn't get an erection. Or he doesn't even attempt to make love. What shall I do?

P.A. J. Lincoln, Lincs.

Make love, not war. It may be irritating, but I think you're stuck with it. At least he's not into rubber *knickers. His preoccupation with black underwear is what fetishism is all about. My dictionary defines fetishism as '. . . the irrational worship, or reverencing, of an inanimate object, for its magical powers . . .' If it magics up his hard-on, it can't be all bad, can it?*

NIX TO KNICKS

I very recently began my first live-in love affair. I'm twenty-three and have just come down from university, where I read psychology. I'm not a virgin, but nor am I very sexually experienced. I appreciate that I have a lot to learn about life, but at least I thought that my theory, with regard to sex, was fairly well grounded. My boyfriend is five years older than I am and has lived with a number of girls before me. I do love him, but I find some of his habits strange, to say the least.

He's very up-front, and tells me all about his fantasies. He says that the idea of prostitutes excites him, but he also says that he's never had one. The main problem is that he wants me to dress up as one and perform certain sexual acts that I basically find distasteful. He wants me to wear crotchless knickers and peep-hole bras – two items of underwear of which I was ignorant until he recently brought them home. I'm not totally against wearing them. If it gives him pleasure, then why not? They seem, in themselves, harmless. But then he wants me to take these knickers off and masturbate him with them while I talk dirty to him. This seems to me to smack of his having a knicker fetish. Is there anyone else out there who has been through this experience? Is he simply going through a phase, or is this something that could stay with him throughout his life? I'm disturbed that he's basically sexually immature.

L. C. Ipswich, Suffolk.

You're right, he is *sexually immature. And, yes, he* is *a knicker fetishist. And, yes, the chances are that he will retain these preferences throughout his sexual life. Please see my comments in answer to the letter above.*

PANTIE FREAK

I just adore women's intimate lingerie. In my home town, I can't keep out of the lingerie departments of places like Marks and Spencer's, for example. When I go down to London, my friends want to go to the Tate, or to the National Gallery, or to see some show or other. All I want to do is to go to stores like Dickens and Jones, or Ann Summers, and look at sexy knickers.

And whenever I fuck my girlfriend, the most exciting part of all, for me, is pulling her knickers down. I just love it. I love the feel of the soft, silky material under my fingers, and I love the scent that lingers around the gusset of her knickers. If I ever become rich, I shall pay young girls to let me pull their knickers down. I'd love to actually tear them off. Rip them off. I sometimes dream of sniffing girls' knickers without their owners knowing what I am doing, and then I wake up with a huge boner. I read the advertisements in girlie magazines offering women's worn knickers for sale, and I'm tempted to send off for them. But I strongly suspect that they would simply keep my money, and I wouldn't get any knickers. Do other male readers have this penchant for ladies underwear?

S. E. Carshalton, Surrey.

In a word, yes.

LADIES' CHOICE

I'm a girl who's happily into sex (with the opposite sex) but it never ceases to surprise me that my girlfriends don't seem to fantasize about men as much as I do. Your columns are always full of male erotic fantasies. May a mere female be allowed to voice her favourite fantasy? Thank you.

I love to imagine that I'm a royal princess and that I'm at some well-attended charity dinner. I spend the earlier part of the event, before the actual meal, selecting the male whom I'm going to take back home with me afterwards. I do this by reaching out and feeling the men's cocks in a perfectly straightforward manner whilst I'm talking to them. When I find one that feels as if it will stiffen nicely, given a little TLC later on, I tell the guy that he is to accompany me back to my luxury home at the end of the evening, and that this is a royal command. There is no question of his saying no, or pleading a headache!

In my fantasy, I start to feel the man up in my limousine on the way home. I quickly undo his fly and pull his gorgeous cock out into the open, where I begin to masturbate it up to a full erection. When it is fully erect, I lean down and begin to give him head. Not to the point of ejaculation, but simply as an exercise in controlled oral sex. If you think about it, it wouldn't *do* to come in a royal mouth, would it? I mean, not on our first date. I use my lips and my tongue, as well as my fingers. Sooner or later the man always says something like 'I simply don't believe that this is happening to me,' or (my favourite one, this) 'I never imagined that one of the highest in the land would give the best blow job in Christendom.'

When we get back to my place, I take him straight into my royal bedroom, where I have thoughtfully arranged for a bottle of vintage champagne to be left on ice. I get him to open the bottle and pour two glasses and, after a sip, I command him to take the royal knickers down. This involves him kneeling in front of me. I then hoist the royal skirt, and he slowly pulls down my naughty black bikini knickers, revealing my curly royal blonde – and highlighted – pubic hair, in the midst of which pinkly nestles the royal slit. It is, of course, by now oozing royal pre-come juices, and I sit down on the edge of the bed, spread the royal legs, and command him to suck the royal pussy. I always make certain that I've taken my knicks away from him, and put them away somewhere safe. Well, just imagine what a tabloid would pay for an opportunity to photograph the royal knicks! David Mellors's Chelsea strip wouldn't be in it. They'd probably run them as a special royal scratch-and-sniff centre spread.

Speaking of which, the royal legs are still spread, and our manly volunteer is by now sucking and licking the royal clit. After I've come a few times, I command him next to lie on the bed, where I wank him a little just to make certain that he's good and stiff before I lower myself slowly down onto his pole – and fuck him senseless. I'm never sure, in my fantasy, how to thank the object of my desire that particular evening. Offering him my knickers as a souvenir is obviously out, for the reasons stated.

Eventually, I get out my Polaroid camera. First, I toss him off until he's good and stiff again, and then I take a photograph of his erect cock to add to my rapidly growing collection. Queen Victoria's gamekeeper would have loved it. Then I spread my legs wide again, hold my cunt lips open with my fingers, and tell him to take a picture of the royal gynaecological apparatus. When it has developed, I check it out, to make certain that there is nothing in the photograph to identify my apparatus as actually being mine, and then I give the picture to the man as a souvenir. 'Remember,' I tell him, 'that a lot of the crowned heads of Europe have been down there between my legs. And now so has yours. To say nothing of your cock.' And off he goes, as chuffed as anything. When he's gone, I often ring my philandering husband. Just to ask him if he's actually getting any. Usually, he just puts the 'phone down. Fuck him.'

S. F. Pewsey, Wilts.

You forgot to say that you always give your guests a knighthood, in the interests of safer sex.

GIVING A TOSS

I'm using your columns to ask, if I may, whether there are any other young girls like me (I'm eighteen and a half) who have an obsession about masturbating. Themselves, that is. I like to fuck, and I think I probably get more than my fair share, but I'm still as horny as hell almost all of the time.

In the office, I'm constantly slipping into the loo and slipping my fingers into myself to bring myself off. If there's no one in my office, I'm regularly to be found with my fingers up my knickers, wanking myself slowly to orgasm. My boss opened his connecting door unexpectedly the other day, and found me playing with myself. *Ooops*, I thought. 'Excuse me,' I said to him. 'I had an uncomfortable itch.' Well, it was true, really, wasn't it? On buses, I always go upstairs and take a back seat so that I can attend to my aching pussy without anyone noticing. Failing that, I always carry a largish shopping bag which I can put on my knee and use to cover up my manipulative sex.

When I'm in the bath, I simply lie there wanking away, having orgasm after orgasm, to my heart's content. The moment I've finished, I want to start again. Am I ill? Do I need to see a doctor? Or a psychiatrist? I was lucky enough, last St Valentine's Day, to get quite a selection of Valentine cards from admirers. It occurred to me then that perhaps my fingers should have sent one to my pussy. What's your advice?

(Name and address supplied.)

Let your fingers do the wanking. We all do it. It's not a problem.

ANAL RETENTION

My fantasies are all about fucking girls in the arse. It's something I've never done, but in my fantasies beautiful girls come up to me in the street, at parties, on public transport, and say things like, 'Hi. My name's Andrea. Are you doing anything right now?' And I say, 'Why do you ask?' And then they say, 'Well, you'll probably find this fairly disgusting, but I love anal sex, and my current boyfriend won't fuck my arsehole. He thinks it's dirty. I wondered maybe if I could come home with you, and if you'd bugger me silly when we get there?'

Of course I agree. I call a cab, we get to my place, I offer them a drink, and then we go into the bedroom. They say, 'Don't bother to undress me. I'll just bend over this chair and pull my skirt up, and you can pull my knickers down. Then we'll get at it.' And then I say, 'Have you got any lubricant? You know, K-Y jelly. Something like that.' And they say, 'No. But anything will do. Vaseline. Butter. Olive oil. Lard. Anything greasy.' And then they pull their knickers down, take their arse cheeks in their hands, and pull them apart, showing me the shiny, pink inside of that beautiful little brown arsehole. I dash off into the bathroom, grab a tin of Vaseline, go back into the bedroom, and carefully and lovingly anoint that puckered little centre of anticipated pleasure with the care of someone repairing a delicate antique.

Then the girl says, 'That feels good. I'm well greased, and I'm ready for you. Bugger me now. Please.' And she stands up, turns around, undoes my flies and takes out my

John Thomas, which she squeezes and pulls until it's fully erect and throbbing in her hand. Then she'll kneel down, take it in her mouth, and just simply suck it, very, very gently, for a few moments. And next she takes it out of her mouth, stands up and bends over the chair again, pulls her arse cheeks apart again and says, 'Let me feel it up my arse, baby. But slowly at first. I haven't had my arsehole stretched for a very long time. Too long. So take it carefully. If I say "Stop," then stop. Immediately. OK?' 'Don't worry about a thing, my darling,' I say. 'Just leave everything to me.'

I take my swollen prick in my hand and I guide it carefully to the dead centre of her lovely, forbidden arsehole, pressing my cock up against its soft, puckered skin. Then I slowly begin to ease my cock in, and she says, 'Oh, God. That's good. Oh, darling, that feels so good. That's lovely. You're buggering me. I love it. Bugger me harder.' And I obediently thrust my tool harder up her arsehole, she relaxes her anal sphincter, and I slide deeply into her. She feels warm, and soft, and wet, and tight. I begin to fuck her properly. I'm in her up to the hilt, and she's beginning to move against me, thrusting her buttocks backwards against me. I can feel the suction as she begins to work her arse muscles up and down the full length of my cock. My balls are slapping against her cunt. I can't believe that my dick is where I've wanted it to be for so long. Up a girl's anus. And the bum of a really pretty girl, at that. Not that I care. I'd fuck a slag right now, so long as it was up her arse. I wonder, while I fuck her anally with long, strong strokes, if perhaps I should ask her to marry me, while I have the chance.

She is grunting and muttering to herself as I bugger her, wriggling her arse, and then she reaches behind her, takes the base of my cock in her hand, and begins to wank me into her rectum as I thrust in and out of her. I can smell the acrid scent as my tool thrusts deeply up her arse – and at that moment she lets go of my cock. Putting her hand between her own legs, she begins to frig herself, her fingers busy at her clit, bringing herself to orgasm as I begin to feel my own ejaculation gathering deep in my groin.

I look down at what I'm doing. Here's this lovely young woman, her short skirt up around her waist, her white nylon knickers pulled down below her knees. I can see a dark stain at the cotton lining of her knicker gusset as I look down, confirming that she was sexually excited at the thought of what we were going to do when we arrived, as we sat in the taxi on the way here. In my fantasies, the girls are always as randy as I am at the thought of anal sex. They may not think of anal *rape* as excitedly as I sometimes do! But then, if it was going to be rape, they wouldn't be here in my fantasy anyway, would they?

Maybe that's a thought for another fantasy. Right then, I am distracted as I feel my ejaculation rising suddenly, spurting through my cock and into the girl's arse, jetting up inside her. She squeezes me with her rectal muscles as she feels me coming inside her. She shouts out and frigs herself feverishly as I orgasm into her, joining me finally with long, shudderingly enjoyable vaginal convulsions. 'Oh, my God,' she shouts. 'I'm coming. I'm coming as you spunk up my arsehole. I'm coming as you bugger me. Oh God. I love it. Do it again. Fuck my arsehole again. Now, baby. Now. Please.' I stay up her until every last spasm has been extracted from my rapidly shrivelling dick, and I finally pull out of her.

'Thank you, darling,' I say. 'That was wonderful.' She stands up, turns around, and puts her arms around me. 'Wonderful?' she says. 'What do you mean, wonderful? It was fucking marvellous. We'll do it again, just as soon as you're ready. Is there anything you'd like, as a little sexual treat, while we're waiting? Is there anything that your other girls won't do for you? Would you like me to suck your cock? Strap a dildo on, and fuck *you* up the arse? Anything?' She grins at me as she hugs me.

'You've just done the one thing I seriously fantasize about,' I tell her. 'None of the girls I know will let me even put my finger up their arse, never mind allowing me to actually bugger them. But if you're serious . . .' She interrupts me. 'I'm serious, darling,' she tells me. 'Anything you want. Absolutely anything. You can fuck me when I've got my period. I'll wank you with my tits. You can come in my mouth. Anything. You only have to ask.' I feel embarrassed. I've never actually asked any girl what I am about to ask this girl. 'Could you . . . would you . . . give me a wank?' I ask her. 'You know . . . a plain, old-fashioned J. Arthur. One off the wrist. I'd love that.' She laughs. 'Oh, sweetheart,' she says. 'What a lovely request. I thought wanking had gone out of fashion. It'll be my pleasure. I was the champion school wanker when I was in the fifth form. They used to pay me fifty pence, which included showing them my pussy – no touching, mind you – and letting them sniff my dirty knickers whilst I wanked them. They used to queue up around the back of the gym, waiting for me to toss them off. Just come here, my darling. I'll give you the wank of your dreams. With the greatest of pleasure.'

She bends down, pulls her knickers all the way down her legs, and off, and then hands them to me. 'Let's do it in proper fifth-form fashion,' she says. 'You've probably looked up more pussies than I've had hot dinners, but I bet it's a very long time since you sniffed a girl's knickers. Have a sniff of those. From the way I was wetting myself coming here in the taxi, thinking about you buggering me, I wouldn't mind betting you that they smell pretty sexy. The real aroma of sexually aroused cunt. All the fifth-form boys used to get was the scent of over-wanked teenage pussy. And there *is* a difference.' She laughs.

'What else should we do to bring back all those happy

memories? Oh, yes. Of course. I know. You should feel me. Starting with my tits. Shouldn't you?' She takes a deep breath, standing there in front of me. 'They're a lot bigger than they used to be, but they're still not exactly blockbusters,' she says. 'But have a good feel. I used to wear a bra in those days. We all did. It made us feel grown up, even if we didn't really have any tits. These days I don't. Wear a bra, that is. Which perhaps ought to make it a little bit more interesting for you. What do you think?' She comes and stands up against me, taking my flaccid cock in her hand. I reach up, and take her right breast in my own grasp. Her breast is warm, and soft, and firm, and I can feel her nipple hardening beneath the thin material of her blouse.

'You had a far more sophisticated education than did I,' I tell her. 'I never touched a breast whilst I was at school. Nor looked at a pussy. Nor sniffed a pair of knickers. I did all those things at college. I fucked girls too. But I was in my twenties. All I did before that was think about it. And wank, of course. But for myself. By myself. I used to buy *Men Only*, and jack off looking at the pictures. So what you're going to do for me is something of a first. Quite an historic first, in fact.' 'How lovely,' she says. 'I'll do my best to make it memorable for you. I promise. But you were a bit backward, you know. When I was growing up, I gave many a wank to men who wanted to fuck me, simply because it was an easy way out.

'They didn't actually care, as long as they got their rocks off. And then it was a sort of tradition that I grew up with. If I had my period, I'd give a man a wank. Or if I simply didn't feel like a fuck, I'd do it. I know it seems lazy, and I know it would drive any feminist potty. But it simply was the accepted thing in the world that I lived in, in those days. I mean, if a man's got a hard-on, and he wants to fuck, it's only going to take a few seconds to wank him off. It's no big deal. But if you just flatly refuse him, you're probably going to lose a friend. You've heard of date rape?' I nod. 'There wouldn't be such a thing as date rape, if only more girls had the sense to give a man a quick one off the wrist at the end of the evening. It takes all the stress and passion out of the event. No one is offended. Nobody's hurt. What's the worst that can happen? You get sticky fingers.' She laughs again. 'No big deal, eh? Now come here, my darling, and I'll show you what a serious wank is about.' She starts to move my foreskin slowly up and down, and as she does, I go on feeling her breasts through her blouse. They are small, but nicely full and well-shaped, and both her nipples become rock-hard with my manipulation of them. I know before she starts that I shall come very quickly once she begins seriously to masturbate me. And I do.

'There you go, baby,' she says, as I spurt my semen all over her hand. And that is where my fantasy usually ends. When I open my eyes, the girl of the day (or night) has disappeared, of course. Along with her receptive arse and her masturbatory expertise. But it is always fun while it lasts. One day, perhaps, it will come true. I sincerely hope so.

L. P. W. Dublin, Republic of Ireland.

That's one fantasy that is probably better kept as *a fantasy. It's still illegal in the UK for a man to have anal sex with a woman. But between consenting males of legal age, it's OK. Strange, isn't it?*

LESBIAN LOVE

I've always wanted to experience the classic male fantasy – that of watching two girls making love together – and I recently began talking to my new girlfriend Sarah about this dream. To my surprise, she told me that there had been a period in her adult life when she had been into other women, sexually, and that she still found some women sexually attractive. If I was serious, she said, it wouldn't be too difficult to contact one of the lesbian women she knew from that time and arrange a demonstration for my benefit. But she warned me to think about it carefully and seriously before agreeing to it.

There was the obvious danger, she said, of my being jealous of her having sex with another woman. That was something that I must admit hadn't occurred to me. And the second thing she wanted me to consider was, she said, the fact that not all lesbian women are, as she was – and still is – bisexual. If I felt like joining in at any stage (usually part of the classic male fantasy in this situation) I would need to know beforehand that the other woman in the threesome was agreeable to that kind of relationship. If she wasn't into it, it was positively *verboten*.

I took her advice to heart and gave due consideration to her warnings. After deliberation, I felt that I could cope with all the points that she had raised, and my overwhelming wish was still to be able to be a voyeur at a lesbian love-nest. Some weeks later, Sarah came home one Friday evening and told me that she had contacted one of her friends, and that the friend had agreed to allow me, as Sarah's husband, to be present while the two girls made love. Any participation by me was to be by general agreement at the time. There was no automatic agreement, but neither was a sexual threesome forbidden in advance. Sarah had agreed that the session would take place at the woman's home, since various items of equipment that might be used were difficult to transport. I felt my prick stiffening at the thought. A week later (a week of intense sexual excitement and anticipation for me, and one during which my sexual activity with my girlfriend reached a new peak), at six on the Saturday evening, we arrived at Sarah's girlfriend's place. She had a flat in a large, converted house in a residential suburb of North London. The house had walls thick enough to ensure total privacy.

Sarah's friend answered the door and welcomed us both in. She was an attractive woman of about twenty-three or twenty-four, with short dark brown hair, long legs, and a good figure. Sarah introduced her as Margie. She led us down a short hallway and into her living room. There was plenty of light, but it was of low intensity. There was music playing softly – gentle, romantic music. Margie had opened a bottle of red wine, and she poured glasses for Sarah and for me. She raised hers to both of us. 'Lovely to see you again, Sarah darling,' she said. 'And good to meet you, Charles,' she said to me. We all drank. 'Shall we get on with it before any of us loses our nerve?' Margie asked Sarah. Sarah agreed. 'Why don't you sit over there, Charles?' Margie suggested, indicating a sofa that was placed diagonally across from the fireplace, with its matching twin opposite.

I settled down quietly on the sofa, my glass of wine on a small table beside me. 'Shall we have a drink the way we used to, darling?' said Margie to Sarah. 'Oh, yes. That would be nice,' Sarah said. They were both standing together in the middle of the space between the two sofas. Margie took a mouthful of wine from her glass, but I noticed that she didn't swallow it. She put her mouth to Sarah's, and they kissed. As they kissed, Margie passed the wine from her mouth to Sarah's, and Sarah swallowed it as they continued to kiss. It was intensely erotic. And it was certainly something that Sarah and I had never done. I got an immediate erection.

Sarah then did the same thing in reverse: she passed a mouthful of wine from her mouth into Margie's. Margie drank it, thirstily. They then put their glasses down on a side table, and began to undress each other. They were kissing and hugging, in between starting to take off each other's clothes, which extended the time that it took for them to get down to their undies. Margie was wearing a short black leather skirt, which only just covered her bum, and a tight black T-shirt. This basic outfit was finished off by black nylon stockings or tights (I couldn't see which, at this stage) and black high-heeled patent leather court shoes. Sarah had on a navy blue wool suit, with a shortish skirt (but not as short as Margie's!) and underneath her jacket she was wearing a white blouse. She had on (I knew, because I'd seen her put them on) black silk stockings, held up by a suspender belt, and she was wearing highly polished navy blue leather court shoes.

Sarah undid the zip at the side of Margie's skirt, and she then knelt down on the floor and pulled the skirt down around Margie's ankles. Margie stepped out of it. She next took off her own T-shirt, pulling it up over her head and throwing it onto the floor. She wasn't wearing a bra of any kind. Her naked tits were fantastic. I noticed that her nipples looked fully erect. Patently she had the hots for Sarah. She was wearing thin, pure white cotton bikini panties, with lace inserts at the sides, and more lace all around the waist. (I believe that 'broderie anglaise' is the proper name for this kind of decoration.) The cotton was so thin that I could see her dark brown pubic hair through it. Her black nylon stockings, I could now see, were of the hold-up kind. Self-supporting, in fact. Sarah took off her own suit jacket, and Margie quickly relieved her of her skirt, showing that Sarah, too, was braless, and revealing to my gaze her pretty black lace suspender belt, with its long, thin, black suspenders holding up her silken stockings, and her matching sexy black silk French knickers. Her stocking tops were heavily patterned, as is the fashion of today, according to her. Sarah is a natural blonde. She shaves her pubic hair, which I find a tremendously erotic pleasure. I could suck her shaven pussy all night.

So there they were, two pretty girls, naked from the waist up, and wearing only panties, stockings, and shoes, with one of them – Sarah – also wearing a tiny suspender belt. As I watched, Margie put her hand between Sarah's legs and began to rub her fingers up and down Sarah's crotch. Sarah responded immediately by doing the same with her long, slim fingers, excitedly rubbing the translucent material between Margie's legs. Her white cotton knickers soon became stained with whatever liquid was now flowing generously from her aroused cunt.

They continued to kiss as they rubbed each other's pussies through the crotches of their knickers. After a while, Margie pulled her face back from kissing Sarah and looked into her eyes. 'Oh, darling,' she said. 'I have to kiss your lovely cunt now. I can't remember when I last sucked your lovely bald little cunt, but I must do it again. Now. Please. Don't keep me waiting.' I knew exactly how she felt. Sarah didn't say anything right then, but she smiled at Margie and, standing back for a moment, she pulled her black lacy French knickers down her thighs, down her long, slim legs, and took them off. She left her suspender belt and her stockings on, went over to the sofa opposite the one that I was sitting on, and lay down upon it. She didn't even glance at me, but she lay back, spread her legs, began to finger her hairless pussy lips, and said to Margie, 'Come on then, Margie darling. I'm ready for you. Wet and willing. Come and suck me.' She was frigging herself quite hard as Margie came and knelt down on the carpet in front of Sarah's spread legs.

Margie pulled down her white cotton knickers, and, looking at me for the first time since the two girls had started touching each other, she grinned at me, threw me her knickers, and said 'There you are, Charles darling. Toss yourself off into those.' I caught them and held them up to my nose, inhaling deeply. They smelt divine. Of unadulterated, beautiful clean cunt. I was tempted to do as Margie suggested, but I was fascinated by the sight of Sarah's fingers busy at her shaven pussy. Her cunt lips were full and fleshy, and palely pink. They obtruded far more out from her plump pudenda, in its complete hairlessness, than they would have been seen to do had she had a strong pubic growth. Her outer lips were pulled back, showing her full inner lips at their most succulent. I wasn't exactly jealous of Margie, as she knelt down, and took Sarah's pussy lips into her mouth, but I would have been happy to do exactly that which she was doing at that particular moment. Instead, I put Margie's knickers up to my nostrils again and breathed in her lovely cunt smell. At least I could enjoy the scent of cunt, if not the taste. It was fascinating for me to watch Margie's pink little tongue lapping my Sarah's bald, pink cunt. She was doing a terrific job with it. As a bit of a specialist cunt-lapper myself, I could tell that she was thoroughly enjoying what she was doing. And certainly Sarah was having a grand time.

She was lying right back, her legs spread wide, her eyes shut, moving her hips to the rhythm of Margie's tongue while she used both hands to play with her nipples. From where I was sitting, I had a tremendous view of Margie's lovely little bum. I could see her hairy cunt. Inside her dark brown hairy little pubic nest, her lips were much smaller than Sarah's. Sort of neater. Tidier. Know what I mean? But still extremely kissable. And fuckable, of course. Given the opportunity. I wondered for a moment what the chances were, and then I thought, the hell with it. Enjoy this while you can. Whatever happens, happens.

Looking once more at Margie's bum, I could see her tiny, pinky-brown arsehole, tucked in between her arse cheeks, about an inch above her pussy. It was tightly clenched (as most arseholes are) and classically puckered. I itched to ease my middle finger deeply into it. That's something that girls' arseholes do to me. Do they have that effect on you? Her lovely bum was framed by her shiny black hold-up stockings, with her sexy, lacy patterned tops. I love that part of girls' stocking tops where there is a plain band of heavier weight nylon between the patterned top and the basic leg part of the stocking. It's the bit you always want to slip your hand up and stroke and feel when you see a girl in black stockings and a really short skirt. She's probably bending over something, and you can see this lovely, darker stocking band, and – if you're lucky – a bit of tightly-stretched knicker crotch. That aside, Margie's buttocks were moving lecherously as she moved her head up and down Sarah's slit, and she was simply asking to be raped. In both entrances. At that point I was distracted by the fact that Sarah started to orgasm, which she did with the maximum amount of thrashing about on the sofa upon which she was lying, and also with the maximum amount of noise. It occurred to me for a second or two that she never came as loudly as that when *I* was fucking her, but then I realized that I had never been an audience on those occasions but had always been very much part of the act. So it wasn't a fair judgement. That's my story, and I'm sticking to it.

Margie leaned back and stretched as Sarah's multiple orgasms died slowly away. Then she stood up – not glancing in my direction, or saying anything to Sarah – and went to a cupboard at the far end of the room. She opened the door, reached inside, took something out, shut the door again, and came back to our end of the room. This time she did look at me. 'Have you ever seen one of these, Charles?' she asked me, holding the object out to me. 'It's one of the reasons why I prefer girls to boys.' She laughed. 'You meet a better class of prick, if you see what I mean.' I took hold of it, to discover that it was a large pink rubber dildo. A lifelike, knurled, extremely phallic, double-ended dildo, with a leather harness at one end. Its dimensions were indeed impressive. It was certainly larger than any live male penis, erect or otherwise.

'Mmmmm,' I said, slightly self-consciously. 'I do see what you mean.' It was at that moment that I realized that Sarah had just seen what Margie and I were talking about. She sat up. 'Oh, Margie, darling,' she said. 'You're going to fuck me. And with that dildo that we bought together in Soho. Oh, darling. How lovely.' 'I wondered if you'd remember it, darling,' Margie said, grinning at me. 'Especially since you've been getting the real thing recently.' Sarah *almost* blushed. But not quite.

Whilst we all laughed, Margie was greasing the dildo with some kind of emollient out of a tube that she had taken out of a near-by drawer. She then inserted one end of it slowly and carefully into herself, holding her labia apart with the fingers of one hand, while she fed the rubber prick up her love-hole with the other. I could see how it stretched her: she grimaced slightly as she worked it up and down a few times, after which she relaxed, smiled, and began to do up the leather harness around her thighs and waist.

Sarah at this stage was lying back on the sofa, her legs splayed, playing idly with herself as she watched Margie intently. When Margie had satisfied herself that she had adjusted the dildo straps to her complete satisfaction, she walked over to Sarah, the dildo standing up rampant in front of her, and handed Sarah the tube of lubricant. 'You grease your end, darling,' she said. 'And then you'll know for certain that it isn't going to hurt you.' Sarah took the tube, and squeezed some of the jelly-like substance out onto her fingers. She then carefully anointed the rubber prick, stroking and rubbing it as if masturbating it. I found the sight of her doing that strangely erotic. Almost as if she were masturbating the rubber tool. The low lights in the living room reflected off the knobs and whorls of the now well-greased weapon, and Margie gave Sarah a small towel on which to wipe her hands. Neither of the girls said anything at this stage, but Sarah lay back, her legs apart, her knees drawn up. Margie knelt between them and fed the other end of her dildo up Sarah's pussy. Sarah groaned, holding her pussy lips apart as the tool entered her. Whether with pain or pleasure, I wasn't too sure. Perhaps both.

My immediate reaction was the thought that if this was what Sarah was accustomed to being fucked with when she first met me, then it was something of a surprise that she managed to get off at all when I fucked her. I've never felt under-endowed in that department, and I've not had too many complaints. But the dildo that was now enthusiastically fucking Sarah, its rhythm building rapidly as Margie moved her hips faster and faster, was something that I could never, physically at least, compete with. But – unless Sarah was a past-mistress at faking orgasms – we enjoyed a happy and fulfilled sex life. We fucked long and hard, and frequently. Sarah was now groaning almost continually, and as I watched, Margie leaned down and began to kiss her passionately.

The sight of the two naked girls on the sofa, bucking and writhing in their lesbian ecstasy, their tongues thrust down each other's throats, Margie's fingers tweaking and pulling at Sarah's engorged nipples, and Sarah now inserting a finger up Margie's arsehole as they both began to orgasm, was terrific.

I wanted to leap on the two of them, sucking and fucking at every available orifice. But there was no indication from either of them that they even knew that I was there, so, with considerable effort, I simply sat there watching, storing up mental images for the next time that I was fucking Sarah. And then, suddenly, it was all over. The girls lay side by side for a while, not speaking, but holding each other, and then, eventually, Margie suggested that they go and shower, which they did. When they came back, they were fully dressed, made-up, and chattering away about supermarket prices. That was the sum of their lesbian sex for the evening and, after another glass or two of wine, we all took off for a meal at a local restaurant. On reflection, I did enjoy the experience. Very much. Whether or not I shall ask if it can be repeated, I don't yet know. Certainly my sex with Sarah has been even better since that evening.

C. D. Earls Court, London.

Sounds like the best of both worlds to me.

KNOTTY PROBLEM

My boyfriend and I have known each other for almost a year now, and over that period of time, it has become evident – quite slowly – that he is seriously into bondage, and also, to a degree, into sadomasochism. My problem is that I don't know to what specific extent he is into S&M. Up until recently, I didn't mind him tying me up. In fact, I quite enjoy it. I love the feeling of submitting to him, sexually. But I'm not at all into pain, or real S&M of any kind, and I'm worried now that if I continue to let him tie me up, the time will come – even if it isn't intentional – when he'll be overcome by his sadistic tendencies, and hurt me. I've tried discussing it with him, but he clams up the moment I get onto the subject. It's not any great love affair, but we like each other's company, and the sex is good, apart from this particular worry. What is your advice?

K. A. L. Croydon, Surrey.

If he won't discuss it with you, find yourself a new boyfriend. Better to be safe than sorry.

SPANKS FOR THE MEMORY

At the age of thirty-seven, I've discovered an avenue of sexual activity that is entirely new to me, and which I never thought I would ever even experience, never mind enjoy. I've become addicted to being spanked. It started off, strangely enough, in Kingston, Jamaica. I recently divorced my husband of twelve years. Whilst our sex life was perhaps, at best, acceptable, it was finally destroyed – as far as I was concerned – by the fact that he was consistently unfaithful to me. Mostly with prostitutes. But actually with anything to hand. Or perhaps that should be with anything to cock. There's a lot of it about, as he always told me. However, be that as it may, I was always faithful to him. Looking back, I realize that I was probably very stupid.

Either stupid to be faithful to him, in the face of the continuing evidence of his unfaithfulness, or stupid to remain married to him for so long, in such unhappy circumstances. Happily, that is now all in the past. I am currently living with a man whom I met whilst staying in Kingston, where I went to spend the last Christmas holiday with friends who live there. John is divorced, three years older than me and, like me, he lives in London. He is a successful solicitor, with a great sense of humour. We like each other a lot, and have fantastic sex. But not long after our first night sharing a bed together, he grabbed me as I took off my dress, which left me wearing just knickers and my hold-up stockings. I don't need to wear a brassiere. He then put me – quite forcefully – across his knee, and started to spank me. 'You've been a very naughty girl, Diana,' he said. 'I'm going to have to punish you.' And he began to spank me on my knicker-covered bottom, with just the flat of his hand. I have to be honest and say that it was more of a statement than a serious spanking. Hurt it didn't. But what it did for his cock made the next part of the evening particularly enjoyable. However, my initial reaction was one of extreme indignation. Who the fuck did this creep think he was? And naughty? What sort of naughty?

I was trying to do a number of things at once. I was trying to wriggle off his lap, but I was firmly held in position there by his left hand. I was trying to look up at him as I shouted at him, telling him exactly what I thought of him and his 'punishment'. 'You're being even naughtier now, Diana,' he said. 'I'm going to have to pull your panties down, and spank your bare bottom.' And so saying, he did exactly that.

He pulled my knickers down to just below my knees, and then he spanked my naked buttocks. His hand stung my naked bottom just a tiny bit, and I wriggled and screamed, with real tears running down my cheeks. More from anger, I realize, looking back, than from actual pain. But slowly, as he spanked away – quite gently, really – I began to realize that my pussy was getting wetter and wetter, and that actually I was beginning to feel seriously horny. 'Oh, John darling,' I said to him. 'That's very exciting. You're making me feel very sexy. You're going to have to fuck me very soon. And fuck me properly. With your great big stiff prick, all the way up my tight, wet little cunt. Oh, I love it. Please don't stop. Please go on spanking me. Please.' I could feel that my pussy was getting wetter and wetter as he spanked me, and I was worried that I was going to make a sticky mess on his trousers, but he didn't seem bothered. 'Your bottom's getting all red as I spank you,' he said to me. 'I'm going to have to stop spanking you, and start *massaging* your naughty bottom. We don't want to cause permanent damage, do we?'

'Sod massaging my bottom,' I told him. 'Get out your great stiff prick and fuck me. Fuck my tight little cunt. Or fuck my tight little arse. Or would you rather that I sucked your swollen cock in my mouth, until you shoot your spunk down my throat? Or would you like me to toss you off as you spank me? I'll do anything for you. Anything. Just don't stop spanking me. Spank me, wank me. Anything you want to do to me. I love you spanking me. I love you wanking me. I love you fucking me. I love it when you fuck my mouth, and come down my throat. I just love it. All of it.' 'That's very generous, Diana my darling,' he said. 'I think I will go on spanking you for a little while, then, if that's all right with you.' He hadn't stopped stroking my buttocks ever since he'd actually stopped spanking me. I loved the feel of his firm, hard palm on my bottom. He stroked and rubbed and felt my posterior for what seemed like fifteen minutes, but it was probably a lot less.

'Do you like anal sex?' he asked me. 'It very much depends upon who's asking me,' I told him. Quite honestly. 'If they've got a huge prick, like yours, the thought of it tends to make me a bit nervous. But if it's someone I can trust, with a rather smaller cock than yours, they can fuck me anywhere they like. At least, they certainly can if they've wound me up first, as you have, by spanking my naked bottom.' And so he fucked me. Deliriously. But not up my arse. That'll come later. I hope. Now he's talking about buying a cane. I love it. Whatever next, I wonder? Yours,

D. P. Henley-on-Thames, Oxfordshire.

You've obviously got to the bottom of your sexual pleasures. Enjoy.

CANE AND ABLE

I'm just an ordinary reader of your excellent magazine, and I enjoy reading the letters in your correspondence columns about your readers' fantasies, their sexual problems, and their sexual successes. I'd love to tell you about my biggest sexual fantasy, in the hope that one of your male readers might get in touch with me, and join in with me in acting it out. Will you indulge me? Please? Then here goes.

I've always had strongly sexual dreams about being used. In every possible way. What I think I mean is that I want to be someone's sexual slave. I want a man to say to me, do this. Now. And I will want to do it. And I will want to please him. Shall I give you some examples? OK. I'd love a man to say to me, 'Sit down in that chair, pull your knickers down, and masturbate yourself until you come. When you've excited me by doing that, then you can masturbate me until I come.' Or, even more deviously, I'd love a man to say to me, 'Bend over, pull your skirt up, pull your panties down, and then reach behind you and stretch your arse cheeks apart. I'm going to bugger you. When I've spurted my load up your bottom, then I'll sit down and you can suck my cock clean.' I want to be sexually humiliated, you see. Is there anyone out there who understands that? Another part of the same fantasy is that I would like a man to see how many ways he could use me, sexually, to continually bring himself to orgasm. It is something to which I would love to give my enthusiastic attention. In no particular order of priority, he could, one, fuck me. Two, I'd toss him off. Three, he could have anal sex with me. Four, he could fuck my breasts. Five, I'd suck him off. Six, we'd start again at the beginning.

There are a number of other things that I've only either read or been told about that I would love to try, even though I know I wouldn't enjoy some of them. But if they turned my man on, I wouldn't object. These include, one, giving, or being given (I don't feel strongly about either option) an enema. Two, pissing on, or being pissed on by, my partner. As with enemas, the idea doesn't appeal very much, but from the Scandinavian magazine pictures that I've seen of both these options, some people seem to enjoy it. Sadomasochism doesn't appeal. At all. But if some guy wants to get his rocks off by putting clamps on my nipples, I'll try anything once. (Provided that he fucks me afterwards of course). I'm not into being caned or whipped or spanked, either. But you can do it to me, or I'll do it to you, if you really want that. And if you promise to love me forever, afterwards. OK?

K. W. Bromley, Kent.

Hey, slow down, baby. You don't have to go to those lengths. Really you don't. Just take it easy. OK?

NO BOUNCE

I've got this rubber fetish. At least, I think I have, in that I'm turned on by the very idea of my girlfriend wearing latex garments. Skirts. Bras. Knickers. Stockings. Arm-length gloves. Dresses even. But I can't persuade her to actually wear anything made of latex. I've bought quite a selection of this type of thing, but she simply refuses to wear any of it. I'm reduced to masturbating over them – or with them – when she's not around. She says that what I want her to do is perverted. What do you think?

A. O. Cardiff, Glamorgan.

I think you should respect your girlfriend's wishes.

QUICK CHANGE

I love to see women undressing. Preferably without them knowing that they are being watched. I discovered this when I happened to be on the woman's fashion floor of one of London's bigger department stores with a girlfriend, and she went into the changing rooms to try something on. I waited just outside, like a number of other husbands and boyfriends, and quickly discovered (we all did!) that, because the curtains weren't properly closed, we had an excellent view into the changing room itself. It was one of those stores that had one large communal room, rather than a number of separate closets, offering an excellent if slightly restricted view of a number of women in various stages of undress. Including, of course, my girlfriend. I found it extraordinarily erotic to see a pretty young woman walk past me, fully clothed, into the changing room, and then watch as she first took off her suit jacket, then her skirt, revealing herself in only tights, knickers and a bra, while she then tried on the dress she had been carrying. This activity was repeated continually as I stood there and watched. A number of the girls were bare-breasted. There were even a couple of girls wearing stockings with suspender belts. There was an interesting variety of underwear, from the strictly functional – plain white cotton – variety, to the truly exotic. There were kangas, French knickers, tiny bikinis, frilly, lacy, sexy panties. The prettier the girl, generally speaking, the plainer her underwear. Whilst we men outside the entrance were all watching for all we were worth, none of us spoke to the others about what was happening.

I didn't tell my girlfriend about this delightful interlude when she finally emerged, for fear that the revelation might prevent her from providing me with another opportunity in the future. But the episode has, in fact, changed my life. Whereas before this happened I was like any other bloke in that, yes, of course I have always enjoyed watching my girlfriends undress, I have now become a real voyeur. I seek out opportunities to see strange women undressing. Often, these days, I go into London's West End and hang about outside women's changing rooms in stores, as though waiting for someone. It's surprising how often I succeed in obtaining glimpses of undressed women. And my fantasies all revolve around secretly watching women undressing. I am a night-watchman at a girls' boarding school. Or the caretaker at a women's rowing club. Or a teacher at a girls' physical training college. Or I'm a voyeur, a Peeping Tom, spying on ballet dancers as they change into or out of their tutus. Or I'm at a swimming bath, peeping into the women's changing rooms, spying into individual cubicles. If I'm lucky, I sometimes catch a woman playing with herself, her fingers busy up her knickers, tossing herself off. I particularly enjoy it if she sucks her fingers when she's finished. I'd like to suck them for her.

A favourite fantasy is that I get to spy, quite by chance, on a pair of lesbian lovers, who slowly undress each other as they kiss, and who feel up each other's sexes through their knickers, wanking each other off while they are still kissing. Eventually, of course, they peel each other's knickers off (and in my most favourite fantasy, the gusset of their knickers is always so wet that it sticks in the girls' pussies, and is slowly and carefully pulled out of there by each partner). Then they feel each other up with their fingers, exploring, stroking, frigging, until one will pull the other down onto the floor, or onto a sofa, or a bed – depending upon where they are –

and then they start to suck each other off.

I often vary the ending of this particular fantasy. Sometimes the girls just fuck each other with their fingers and their tongues. Sometimes I have them frigging each other with one or other of all those penis-substitute variations that one reads about girls using. Milk bottles. Candles. Cucumbers. Carrots. Occasionally they use vibrators on each other. And, naturally, some of them use dildoes. Sometimes strap-on single ones. Sometimes double-ended ones (so that they can fuck each other at the same time). Naturally enough, I'm beating my meat all the time that I'm watching these delightfully dirty young ladies at their private sex games, but in the very best of these fantasies, where there are two girls, (i) I happily actually let the girls know that I have been watching them, and (ii) they turn out to be bisexual – yes, both of them – and they are always delighted to let me join in with them. Ain't life wonderful?

Sometimes I fuck one of them whilst the second one helps me. She might, for example, hold her friend's labia apart for me as I thrust my swollen cock up her friend's cunt. Or if I'm into anal sex on this occasion, she'll pull her friend's buttocks apart for me as I thrust into the offered, opened anus. Or she might simply French-kiss me, using her agile tongue to excite me, whilst I fuck the other girl doggy fashion. Another favourite is when one of the girls wanks me off into her friend's mouth. These variations, with a couple of really co-operative bisexual lesbian girls, are endless. Think about it.

W. P. S. Hull, Humberside.

I will. I hope your night-watchmen are getting good overtime rates.

DYKE'S DELIGHT

I love to read your letters columns, but I strongly suspect that the vast majority of them represent reader's fantasies. And there's nothing wrong with that. But I thought that it might make a pleasant change for at least some of your readers if, as a young, pretty (I'm told) practising lesbian, I told you what it *really* feels like to make love to girls. So here goes. But first of all, may I please get one thing straight? I don't pretend to speak for all lesbians. Only for myself. I'm the so-called butch half of my relationship. To me, that simply means that I'm the instigator. The male, if you like. And the point that I want to make is that I have never used a dildo, or a vibrator, or a penis-substitute of any kind, in my entire life. Sex for me and my partners is entirely oral, or manual.

I've actually never even seen a dildo. Nor have any of my girlfriends. I think girls fucking each other with penis-substitutes is a mostly male fantasy. Strange, isn't it? I mean, women don't fantasize about men fucking false vaginas. I know they exist, but did you ever know anyone who used one? Like men, I find that pretty lingerie turns me on, and it's always fun for me to buy sexy underwear for my girlfriends. And like men, it's fun, occasionally, to buy really vulgar undies. Tarts' knickers. You know the sort of thing. Red satin, crotchless knickers, with lots of black lace. And then you bury your face in the exposed pussy and suck and lick your way to heaven!

As a lesbian, I've always loved sucking pussy. But it has to be clean. So a bath or a shower together is often the starting place for sex, *chez moi*. I love to soap my girlfriend's pussy and slide the soap right inside her, rapidly followed by my agile, clit-finding finger. I don't seriously suffer from penis envy, but the one thing that I *do* envy men is the ability to have an erection. It's such a magnificent statement of sheer, unadulterated lust. Of desire. It says I WANT TO FUCK YOU in a way that a woman can't. Yes, of course, I know that we show similar feelings by getting our pussies all wet. And I get wetter than anyone I know. But it's not in the same league as walking around with a rampant cock. So we've been through the pretty knickers bit, and I've told you that I like to suck pussy. Freshly washed pussy. What comes next. Oh, yes. Actually doing it. Some men are very expert at cunnilingus. I've been sucked off by a few expert gentlemen in my time, I have to admit.

And when a girl is fortunate enough to meet a guy who likes sucking pussy, she's on to a good thing. No doubt about it. I speak from experience. I haven't always been gay. Nor am I, necessarily, always gay now. But – in my admittedly limited experience – a lot of men won't suck cunt. They love girls to take their dirty, unwashed cocks in their mouths and suck them off. But they won't suck cunt. The thought horrifies them. It's dirty. Disgusting. If girls are made of sugar and spice, and all things nice, they quote, why do they taste of kippers? Har har. Clean cunt doesn't taste of kippers. Take it from me. It tastes of elixir. Sexual elixir. Come and taste mine. Any time.

So, as the evening wears on, when I'm with a new girlfriend, I get more and more excited. We have dinner. Somewhere romantic. I keep trying to touch her. No. Not touch her up. Not yet. Just touch her. You know. A hand on her elbow. An elbow brushing against her breast, as I take my coat off. A hand on her knee, to make a conversational point. And then, after dinner, I love to dance. Yes, of course we go to gay places to dance. I want to be able to relax, just the same as you do. I want to be able to put my arms around her, in the semi-darkness, and stick my tongue down her throat, and dance with my thigh between her legs, grinding it against her sex, and feel and squeeze her buttocks while we dance, just the same as you do. There's not *that* much difference between what you and I like to do, you know. I want to wind her up. Get her feeling sexy. Wanting me. I want her pussy to be wet, just the same as you do. And then I want to take her home in a cab, with my arm around her waist. I probably won't kiss her in the cab, as you would, because London cab drivers are notoriously chauvinist. But I might stick my hand up her skirt, and gave her a quick feel, if the cabbie's not looking in his rear-view mirror.

And then it's pay off the cab, in through the front door, up into the bedroom, and knickers round your ankles, just like Adam Faith used to demand in *Budgie*, all those years ago. And then it's down onto the bed, onto her back, spread her pretty legs, press my lips against her wetness, and lick the divinely tasting fluid that is emanating from her pretty little cunt. And she'll raise her hips up right off the bed as I suck her. She'll writhe, and moan, and say, 'Oh God. I like it. Oh, yes. Oh, Jesus. Oh, darling. Oh, I'm coming. Oh fuck. I'm coming now. Oh yes. Oh, please. Oh, God.' And she'll grind her cunt against my lips as I suck and tongue and lick.

And I'll keep on sucking her, but at the same time I'll slide my forefinger down inside her wet little pussy, and I'll find her clitoris, and I'll masturbate it until she's practically screaming for mercy. But I won't stop, even when she asks me to. I'll keep on, and on, and on. Until, eventually, she'll have a giant orgasm. Which she'll love. And after she's recovered from that, she'll suck my pussy until I'm ready to faint. And she'll be feeling so randy, by this time, that she'll keep going all night. Because, like I said earlier, while I'd love to have a rampant penis, wouldn't *you* like to be able to go on fucking for ever? Without ever needing to stop? Because that's what me and my girlfriends do. We go on sucking all night. And playing with each other's pussies. Who needs cock? Yours very respectfully.

W. T. Bolton, Lancs.

It sounds like a lot of fun. Or should I say a slot *of fun? Good luck.*

RELUCTANT HEROES

Can anyone out there tell me why so many men don't like oral sex? I love to suck pussy, and my girl, Mandy, loves me doing it to her. I can happily suck her off for hours at a time. But she tells me that I am very much in the minority. She says that most men aren't into cunt-lapping. Apparently there are many men who think that the idea of kissing and licking a girl's sexual organ is a disgustingly dirty thing to do. She said one man even said to her, 'How can you possibly expect me to do that? You might just as well ask me to lick your arsehole.' I'm certainly not averse to *that*, but pussies are my favourite.

Let's examine, for a moment, some of the alleged reasons why men don't like to suck pussy. One: some men say that women's vaginas smell nasty. Not if they're clean, they don't. So if in doubt, wash it out. That can be good fun in itself. In my experience, I have never actually gone down on a girl who smelt unpleasant 'down there'. I always wash my cock before a heavy date. I'm sure girls act similarly. But what could be the worst that could happen? If you went down on a girl in the evening who simply hadn't had an opportunity to freshen up since leaving home that morning, well, I guess that you might get just a tiny whiff of urine. I actually find that aroma sexually exciting. I guess it's a matter of association. I know where it comes from, and where it comes from is one of my most favourite female places. I believe that all men love having their cock sucked. It's the same thing, isn't it? I'll bet there's many a man who has had his cock sucked at the end of a hard day at the office without being able to wash it first. So what?

Two: the kind of man who will complain of the smell of the cunt he's sucking will probably also complain about the taste. Me? I love it. It's my favourite flavour. Sexually aroused cunt. Fantastic. I wish they made cunt-flavoured mints. I'd suck them all day long, to remind me what I was going to suck all *night* long. And of course my fantasies are all about sucking pussy. I can't look at a woman in the street, or in a pub, or a restaurant, or anywhere, come to that, without wondering if she likes her pussy sucked. And whether she realizes that she is close to/opposite/standing beside one of the world's great pussy eaters. And I always wonder if her pussy is wet or not.

In my fantasies, I lean across and whisper in her ear that I'd like to suck her pussy, and she gets very excited and makes an excuse to get away from whoever she's with. She meets me outside, and we go off together – usually back to her place – and I watch her undress, which these lovely girls always do very slowly. When they're down to their knicks, I take over, and I kneel down in front of them, and pull their knickers down, very, very slowly, revealing first their pubic hair (or, oh Jesus, sometimes the complete lack of it). And below their plump little pudendas, of course, come their outer labia. You will know as well as I do that no two women have identical pussies. They're all different. And I love the excitement of slowly revealing a new one, in all its erotic glory. I just kneel there, and take in its beauty. The colour of the pubic hair. Thick, blonde, curly pubic hair. Long, strong, straight black pubic hair. Curly black pubic hair like steel wool. Soft auburn pubic hair. Wispy, young, sparse pubic hair. Sometimes, as I said, the beauty of a shaven pudenda, the flesh creamy and soft in its immaculate nakedness. I have to reach out and touch it, feel its smooth baldness. And then, down below, the outer lips, guarding the inner labia. A million different patterns. Almost non-existent lips. Swollen, fleshy lips. Long droopy lips. Little short, tight, thin lips. It is, of course, another mouth, and the varieties of lip are as extensive as they are with the facial kind. I trace their outline with my finger.

As I'm kneeling, my face will be only some six inches or so away from the object of my desire. I look for the tell-tale dribble of colourless, sticky mucus that will tell me that its owner is anticipating the entry of my tongue between her cunt lips. I always have to reach out and part the outer labia with my finger tips. Gently. Lovingly. Revealing her inner secrets. That close, I can also inhale the strong scent of her. Aroused pussy. Pussy aching to be sucked. And – eventually – fucked. For, with me, the one leads, as inevitably as night follows day, to the other.

By now I will be highly sexually excited myself, and my erection will be strong and firm. I will probably have undone my flies, allowing my cock to thrust out and up, freeing it from its restraining clothing. I will almost certainly interrupt the proceedings here and stand up to quickly disrobe, throwing my clothes into a corner so that I may, as quickly as possible, return to kneel before the altar of my sexual desire. I will now thrust a finger carefully into the shining pink centre of my mistress's vagina, parting her lips like the petals of some rare, highly scented, satiny-smooth orchid.

She'll be warm, and wet, and tight. She'll gasp at the unexpected intrusion of my finger, which I'll thrust into her as deeply as I can, burying it into her up to the knuckle. Sometimes I'll be able to feel the entrance to her womb with the tip of my finger. At other times I won't come anywhere near it, for the depth, or length, of a woman's cunt is as varied as is the size and length of a man's cock. I love some of the variations that my examination will by now have revealed. What am I saying? I love *all* the variations that will by now have been revealed. But some particularly. Naturally black pubic hair dyed blonde always excites me. Whilst I love a shaved pudenda, I also love hirsute pudendas, covered thickly by a long-haired, springy pubic bush. I find that very sexually exciting. And I just adore hairy female arseholes. But that's another story. I understand the need, but I am not overly fond, of the fashion model's tendency to cut her pubic hair back, leaving a symbolic tuft of hair immediately above the entrance to her vagina.

I worship big cunt lips. The kind that look like miniature spaniel's ears. Or pink butterflies, perhaps. And I never fail to be surprised at the amazing range of colours in which pretty pussies come. From the palest pink to the darkest blue-black. And every variation of shade in between. And all with matching nipples! At this stage in my fantasies, I usually use both hands and put them between the girl's legs, pressing her thighs apart slightly, indicating that I wish her to spread them for me which she then always does. I next reach behind her and clasp her generous buttocks, squeezing them. I pull her towards me, lean forward, and kiss her directly on her vaginal lips. Softly at first. Lovingly. Gently. Then I lick her copiously oozing slit, starting at the bottom, and I lick it upwards, slowly and delicately, revelling in the taste and flavour of her effluent. It tastes good. Delectable. Nice.

Then I stand up, my erection proudly rampant before me, take her by the hand and lead her over to the bed. She lies down and spreads her legs wide, pulling her knees up to allow me free access to her sex, and I lie beside her, my head down between her legs. And I begin. I make her come. Over and over again. Until she is sobbing with sexual pleasure. I kiss her, suck her. Manipulate her clitoris with my fingers. Masturbate her. Wank her. She orgasms. Again and again. Her orgasms build and merge. Build and merge. Until her womb is erupting in one all-consuming, all-embracing, continual orgasm that has her whole body shaking, and now she is pleading to be fucked. 'I want you inside me,' she says. 'In my cunt. I need your cock. Inside me. Now. Fuck me, darling. Please. Now. Fuck me. Fuck me. Fuck me.'

And I get myself up from my prone position, turn myself around and thrust my prick up her tight, wet, welcoming hole. And I fuck her. Seriously fuck her. Fuck her brains out. And she comes again. Only this time, I come with her. I jet my hot semen up her, and we orgasm together, clutching each other, holding each other, our bodies shuddering as we unite in our mutual climax. I'm in heaven. A heaven that began with oral sex.

P. D. Ipswich, Suffolk.

Helped, obviously, by a flight of angels, who took you for a sucker.

JUST GYMSLIPS

I've always been turned on by the idea of sex with young girls and, whilst I have obviously never indulged in underage sex, I get a lot of my sexual pleasure by persuading my wife to dress up in a variety of youthful, girlish outfits. First of all is, of course, the ever-fancied, ever-fanciful navy blue gymslip. Ours comes from an Oxfam shop, and is the genuine article. It is very short, and fully pleated. Beneath this she wears a basic, plain white blouse, and a very small pair of navy blue cotton knickers. To these she adds black nylon stockings, sometimes held up by a black satin suspender belt, and on other occasions she will wear self-supporting stockings. She plaits her long blonde hair into two schoolgirl-type plaits, secured with ribbons, and the outfit is complete.

She will be wearing this when I come home from work, and will spend much of the time preparing and serving our evening meal giving me lots of opportunities to see her knickers and that lovely bit of naked thigh between her stocking tops and her knicker edge. She will sometimes come and sit opposite me, her legs wide apart so that I can see her knicker crotch, and pretend that she doesn't know what she is showing. I particularly like this when I can see the moisture darkening the already dark blue material between her legs. When I can't stand it any more, I leap at her, and feel her up, and she pretends to scream, and tries to stop me from feeling her between her legs. She loves to play at being raped, and I enjoy fucking her as she pretends to sob her little heart out.

At other times, she will deliberately be 'naughty'. At first,

I will threaten her with a spanking. She (who loves a little mild 'discipline') will of course go on misbehaving until I take her, put her across my knee, pull down her navy blue knickers, and spank her on her bare bottom. I love to watch it getting redder and redder, and I keep at it until she is pleading with me to stop. Another favourite 'uniform' is that of the Girl Guides. This we got from a theatrical costumier. I expect you can imagine the kind of games we play when my wife is wearing this one. And the final outfit is one she designed herself. It's what she calls her 'Teenage Tart's' outfit.

It comprises a skimpy, extremely tight, very short pair of gold satin hot pants, worn with a white, almost transparent bra top, about two sizes too small. She wears these items with the kind of self-supporting stockings that come just up over the tops of her knees, or else with black nylon stockings with seams. Too much make-up and a wad of gum that she chews enthusiastically complete the picture. I can have any kind of sex I like, but I have to pay for it. I don't often fuck her in this outfit, since she insists that I wear a condom, which I dislike. I usually settle for a blow-job (for five pounds) or a quick one off the wrist (at three pounds). We both enjoy the fun we have with these dressing-up, make-believe games.

D. H. Norwich, Norfolk.

Continue to enjoy.

PROFESSIONAL JEALOUSY!

I am a Professor of English at a women's college at one of the older universities, and I write to tell you of the pleasures offered by a number of my female students. As part of the regular system, I take them in small classes of two or three – tutorials – as well as in larger groups. Sometimes, two of the three girls due to see me together may not turn up, for one reason or another, and I am left with just one student. This happened to me recently. I was having the girl read to me from one of the required texts, and she was doing very well when she put the book down, came over and stood beside me (I was sitting on a chair behind my desk as I usually do). She leaned over the arm of the chair, unzipped my fly, reached inside, and pulled out my flaccid penis. I have to say that I in no way tried to resist her. 'This will be much more fun,' she said, and she began to masturbate me. She was absolutely right, of course.

She is an attractive young woman. About twenty-two or twenty-three, with bold, firm, high-standing breasts, and given to wearing short skirts that show off her lovely long legs to perfection. My cock quickly became fully erect: she then knelt down beside my chair and took my erection into her mouth, where she sucked and wanked it until I came in her mouth. She didn't pull away, but swallowed my juices with seeming enjoyment. When she had finished, I thanked her, and put my cock back inside my trousers, after which we resumed the tutorial. Everything went normally until the end of the session, when she came and stood in front of me and stroked my cock through the front of my trousers. 'If you'd like to fuck me, I'll happily come to your rooms in the evening,' she offered. 'I'm on for every kind of sex. Normal. Oral. Anal. You name it, I like it.' As you can probably imagine, my cock stood immediately to attention again, and I said that yes, I'd like that. How would seven o'clock on the following evening suit? 'I'll be there,' she said. 'I'll look forward to that.' *Not half as much as I will*, I thought. And then she left.

That following evening she arrived, as arranged, at seven o'clock. She smiled as I opened the door. Entering my rooms and shutting the door behind her, she carefully turned the key in the lock. She then came to me, took my head in her hands and pulled my face down to hers, at which point she started to French-kiss me. Her tongue probed mine and we exchanged wet kisses until we both needed to stop for breath. During this exchange, I could feel her full breasts pressing against my chest, and I began to get an erection. 'Shall I do a striptease for you?' she asked, and I said that would be fun.

She was wearing a black skirt, with a white blouse and a black woollen cardigan. She took off the cardigan, then the blouse, exposing her naked breasts. She took hold of her nipples, which were bigger than any I had seen before, and began to pull them, playing with them, and twirling them in her fingers. 'Do you like big breasts, Frank?' she asked, using my Christian name for the first time. 'Have you ever sat astride a girl and let her wank you between her lovely, big, soft breasts?' I admitted that yes, I did like big breasts. They have always excited me. And no, sadly, I have never experienced the joys of what I believe is called a French necklace. 'We'll do that later, if you'd like to,' she said. She then turned around, so that her back was towards me and, unzipping her skirt, she wriggled it slowly down her hips, then down her thighs, and finally down her legs, until it was in a heap on the floor, at which moment she stepped out of it. She stayed bending over for a while longer.

I loved the time that she spent bending over and pulling the skirt down: her black lacy knickers were stretched tightly over her full buttocks which I could clearly see revealed against the translucent material of her knickers. The crotch of this flimsy item was also pulled tightly up into her groin, although I could only imagine what it was so coyly covering, since the cotton lining prevented me from seeing anything more. She was also wearing black silky stockings with lacy bands around the tops, which seemed to keep up of their own volition. I think they probably had some kind of elastic around the tops.

As she stepped away from her skirt, she stood there in front of me, naked from the waist up, with just her knickers and stockings and black, high-heeled shoes on. She said, 'Do you like what you see, Frank?' I said, 'Very much, my dear. Very much.' 'It's all yours, darling,' she said to me. 'It's all yours, to do whatever you like with.' I couldn't believe my ears. I mean, I'm not a young man. I'm fifty-three. And I've not had that many women in my life. Three, to be exact. And here was this beautiful young woman offering her body to me, quite voluntarily, to do with as I pleased. It was a dream come true. She looked at me, and smiled. 'Shall I take my knickers off now, Frank darling?' she said. 'Or would you rather take them off for me?' I felt desperately embarrassed. Of the three women in my life, I had never actually seen any of them totally naked, whether in daylight or electric light. Sex had always been an under-the-covers-with-the-light-out activity, and I had never even seen a bare breast, clearly, for any length of time.

'Er, you take them off, please,' I said, hoping that my embarrassment didn't show. And hoping too – although I knew it was not possible – that she could not see my erection, standing out against my fly. This time she stayed facing me, and she very slowly pulled her knickers down, humming the old classic stripper's song as she did so. You know the one. I think it's actually called 'The Stripper'.

I had to laugh. She was making sex so much fun. As she revealed first her pubic hair (which was thick and black and curly) and then her pubis, and, finally, the lips of her sex, she did the classic American stripper's bump-and-grind routine, shaking her hips and wriggling her bottom, her breasts thrust forward. When she stepped out of her knickers, she was left standing there in just her black, silky stockings. It was, I think, the sexiest thing I had ever seen in my life. She crumpled her knickers up in her hand into a little black silken ball, came over to me, and pressed them against my nose. 'Sniff, Frank,' she said. I drew in a deep breath. They smelt entirely of sex, with overtones of heavy scent. 'What do you smell, Frank?' she asked me, continuing to rub the knickers against my nostrils. 'Er, I'm not sure,' I said, not liking to use the words that came to mind. She laughed again. 'That's cunt, Frank,' she said. 'Unadulterated, nicely wet, sexually stimulated cunt. Feel.' And as she spoke, she took my hand and placed it between her legs. She moved my fingers around amongst the hair that I first felt, until they came to her sex. It felt warm, and very wet. She rubbed my fingers up and down against her wet sex, and then she pulled my fingers up in her hand again, and placed them against my lips.

'Taste that, darling,' she told me. I put my fingers in my mouth. Tentatively at first. Then with enthusiasm. I don't mind saying it now, but right then, I was embarrassed to say that I'd never had oral sex of any kind. I realize now that I'd probably never had what most young people these days would call real sex of any kind. But I'm learning. The wetness on my fingers tasted like elixir to me, and I sucked at my fingers until every last trace had been licked off. 'Would you like some more, darling?' she asked. I nodded. 'Let's go into the bedroom, and make ourselves comfortable,' she said. I led the way through to the bedroom where the girl undressed me in an unfussy, methodical way. When I was naked, she lay back on the bed and opened her legs. She took my hand in hers. 'Let's start gently,' she suggested. 'There's no hurry.'

'First of all, I don't know whether or not you know my Christian name, but it's Pamela. OK?' 'Of course,' I said. I knew she was P. Clarke, but I didn't know – hadn't taken the trouble to find out – that the 'P' stood for Pamela. 'Put these two fingers together,' she commanded, closing together my forefinger and my middle finger. She spread her legs even wider. 'Now, I'll help you to put them up inside my pussy,' she said, and she followed her words with the actions, helping me to slide the two fingers into her. 'Have a little feel around in there, darling,' she suggested. I did as I was bidden. It felt lovely and tight. And warm. And very wet. I could feel sort of ribs in the lining surrounding my fingers, and I could feel a sort of bump at the end. The bottom. I'm not sure of the proper terms.

As I moved my fingers about, she squirmed and wriggled quite a bit, and said things like, 'Ooh. Yes. Mmm. Nice. Lovely.' And so on. After a while, she asked 'Do you know where my clit is?' 'Er, no,' I said. It was true. I knew *what* it was, but I didn't know precisely *where* it was. It is, I'd been told, the hub of all female sexual pleasure. The nub against which a man is supposed to rub his cock, thus stimulating the clitoris, and bringing the woman to orgasm. I'd read all the books, but I'd never had this kind of conversation with a woman.

'Give me your finger again, darling,' she said. 'Just the forefinger this time.' I did as I was told. She took it, and slid it into her waiting pussy. She moved it about for a moment or two, and let it finally come to rest on what felt like a small, raised bump. 'Can you feel that?' she asked me. 'Yes,' I said, moving my finger around. 'If you mean that little bit that I'm touching now.' 'The very place,' she said, laughing. 'Now then, sweetheart,' she said. 'Pay attention. If you stroke and rub that little thing that you can feel there – but gently. Carefully. Then,' she said, 'Then, you'll feel it grow. Become erect. Just like a tiny cock.' I must have looked puzzled. 'No,' she said. 'Don't give up. You haven't tried yet.' I tried to relax, and when she had taken her hand away, I felt for, and found, her clitoris once more. When I got there, I spent all the time in the world stroking it. Very, very gently. Moving my finger around and around in small circles. And, magically, I suddenly felt it growing beneath the pressure of my finger. 'Oh, yes,' said Pamela, breathing heavily. 'Mmmm. Oh, Yes. Good. I like it. That's nice. Oh, God. I'm coming. I'm coming now.' And as I continued to massage her clitoris, she actually came. Noisily. I felt as pleased as a teenager.

'Terrific,' she said, sitting up on the bed. 'I'm the one that's supposed to be teaching you, and you're doing things for me. That was terrific. Thank you. Now then, what would you like me to do to you? Like I said before. Anything, absolutely anything at all. Just tell me.' There were so many things that I would have liked her to do to me – and me to her – that I couldn't prioritize any single one. I stayed silent, not knowing what to choose. 'Shall I run through a few possibilities?' she asked. 'You know . . . just to warm you up?' 'Please do,' I told her. 'There's so much that I'd like that I can't make a decision.' She grinned at me. Just like the Cheshire Cat. 'Look, Frank,' she said. 'We've got all the time in the world. There's no hurry. We can do absolutely everything that you want to do. And then we can do it all over again. And again. It's not a problem. Just tell me what you want.'

I took her at her word. 'I want to lie on top of you, right now,' I told her, 'and slide my cock right up your lovely wet cunt. And then I want to plain, old-fashioned fuck you. Out of your senses. And out of my mind. That's all I want. But

I've been wanting it all my life. How does that sound to you?' 'If that's what you're after, sweetheart,' she replied, 'then that's what you shall have. Come to Mama.' She beckoned me nearer to her. She lay right back on the bed, and opened her legs wider than I would have thought possible.

I knelt down between her thighs, my rampant cock jutting out at a proud angle. She took hold of it and guided it down, in between her legs. I pressed downwards, to thrust it into her, and she raised her buttocks, seemingly anxious to receive it. Once inside her, she seemed to suck me in, rather like a vacuum cleaner. I could positively feel the suction. She felt tremendous. As I tried to become accustomed to the feelings in my cock, thrust deeply into the pussy of an extremely attractive young lady, I wondered at the circumstances that had brought me here. But my real wonderment came from the sensations that were permeating my entire sexual apparatus. They were the most wonderful that I had ever experienced.

I didn't know what sex was all about, prior to the fucking that I was getting right now. Earlier in my life, it had been like rape legalized by marriage. But Pamela was freely mine, and I could do what I liked with her. Or so her own rule book said. I grabbed her buttocks, squeezing them, and began my long climb up to ejaculation. 'Go for it, baby,' Pamela whispered in my ear. 'Fuck me. Fuck me silly. You've got your huge cock up my cunt, and I'm enjoying it. All I need, soon, is a great wad of your spunk up me. I love spunk. I love to drink it. Suck it out of your cock. Come into me. Now, baby. Now. Fuck me now. Please.' Even as she spoke, I was spurting my ejaculate into her womb. I was so embarrassed at having come so quickly that I apologized to Pamela. 'Don't worry about a thing, Frank,' she said. 'Just leave it in there. We'll have you on the go again in minutes.'

And it was exactly so. That evening and night, I did

everything with Pamela that I had ever fantasized about. I fucked her mouth, her vagina, and her rectal orifice. She, apparently, was enjoying teaching me, and I was more than happy to learn. I finally fell asleep, exhausted, with Pamela by my side. When I awoke the next morning, she was gone, but she had left a note saying, 'See you this evening. Love, P.' The day dragged slowly by, but the evening finally arrived. I had an erection simply thinking about what I was going to do to Pamela when she eventually knocked at my door. Imagine my surprise when, having accepted my offer of a glass of sherry, she told me that she was indeed there for me to do anything sexual to her, or with her, that I wished, but that there was something that she felt she ought to get clear first. 'Of course, my dear,' I said. 'What is it?'

She then spent some time explaining to me that, in return for her sexual favours (which, to be fair to her, she said would be available on a daily – or should that be nightly? – basis, and would, as before, include anything that I wished) she would expect a guaranteed First Class Honours degree at the end of her three years. I was flabbergasted, naturally, and I quickly explained to her that, unfortunately, there was no question of my being able to agree to such a suggestion. My professional ethics simply would not permit an arrangement of that kind. She was sorry to hear that, she said. Because after she had left me in the early hours, she had taken a taxi to a friendly doctor who, by prior arrangement and accompanied by a nurse, had given her a thorough physical examination, including the taking of oral, vaginal and anal swabs. These, through DNA 'finger-printing' techniques, would immediately identify me.

She would, she went on, be perfectly prepared to swear on oath to the college authorities that I had forced her to have sex with me, against her will and under threat of failing her in her examination prospects. She also reminded me that anal sex with a woman was illegal in Britain, and that anal rape was much frowned upon, and heavily punished by, the courts. As she sat there telling me this, she pulled her skirt up and her knickers down. She opened her legs, affording me an attractive view of one of the three parts of her anatomy that had given me so much pleasure the previous evening. 'All you have to do to avoid all that unpleasantness, Frank,' she said, 'is to agree to my suggestion. And then this is yours to play with. Right now. And every day. Whenever you want it.' She looked down, fluttering her eyelids and, I swear, blushing slightly. 'And the other parts, of course,' she said. 'Whenever you want them.' I remembered the joy of buggering her. My rigid cock sunk deep between her bum cheeks. Her anus dilated, its puckered circumference stretched tight by my swollen shaft. And I gave in. I agreed.

She slipped out of her chair, unzipped my fly, took out my cock and, just before she took it in her mouth, she said 'Oh, Frank. I knew you'd see it my way.' And then she sucked me off.

J. L. H. Norwich, Norfolk.

Here endeth the second lesson!

BOTTOMS UP

I love to read the mixture of true stories of sexual exploits and descriptions of individual sexual fantasies printed in your columns as related to you by your readers. I wonder if you would care to read about one of mine? Which of the two types this story is, I shall leave you to judge for yourselves. I recently spent ten days in New York on a business trip, staying at the Plaza Hotel, on the south side of Central Park. You will know that this is one of the city's top hotels. I lunched and dined at some of the better-known New York restaurants, as a guest of my hosts, and I loved all of them. They included Windows on the World, Le Cirque, Palm, P. J. Clarke's, and The Tavern on the Green.

But, much as I enjoyed this hospitality and the chance to see (and eat in) some of the most famous restaurants in the world, what I really wanted to do was to get myself down to Greenwich Village, and suss out one of the New York S&M clubs that I had heard so much about. And then my opportunity finally arrived. I had a free evening, to spend as I wished. So, thinking that the Plaza's concierge probably wasn't the man to ask about S&M clubs, I bought a copy of *Screw* magazine from a bookstall, and ran my eye down the club listings.

I ended up at a basement address on the Lower West Side. It didn't look much from the outside and I almost turned away. But I thought nothing ventured, nothing gained, and rang the bell. It was opened by a very pretty girl wearing classic dominatrice gear: black leather basque, net stockings, black patent leather high-heeled shoes, studded wristlets and anklets. She wore a top hat over her long auburn hair, and she carried a vicious-looking whip. 'Hey, Mac,' she said, opening the door. 'Come in. What can we do for you?' As she shut the door, I heard a terrifying, high-pitched scream echoing hollowly from somewhere out at the back. The girl smiled at me, and held out a hand. 'I'm Victoria,' she said. 'Let me take you through to the bar. Just follow me.' We were standing in what was simply a hallway. It was well decorated, expensively carpeted, and hung with some good contemporary art dealing with sexual subjects. Mostly S&M subjects, reasonably enough.

I followed Victoria through to the bar, which was impressively large, and manned – if that's the word – by two barmaids, dressed like Victoria but without the top hat. There were four other people on my side of the bar. A couple, who seemed to be together, and two men dressed, like me, in business suits. 'What can I get you?' Victoria asked. 'We have most things. Alcohol is on the house. These two girls are Linda' (pointing at the nearest girl, who smiled back) 'and Frances' (pointing at the second girl, who raised a languid hand). 'Either of the girls will pee into a glass for you. Or into your mouth, if you prefer. And in private, of course. That we charge for.'

She looked at me, expectantly. 'Thanks,' I said. 'I'll take a Scotch on the rocks, with branch water.' Victoria passed my request on to Linda, who brought a large Scotch on the rocks, with a small bottle of water, and a Seven-Up for Victoria. I wondered if it had any vodka or gin in it. 'Cheers,' said Victoria. 'Cheers,' I said, opening the water and putting some into my Scotch. 'Now then,' said Victoria, 'shall I run through what's available, or would you prefer to tell me what you're looking for?' I took a long slurp at my Scotch and water. 'I'm looking for a pretty girl to spank,' I told her. 'I'd like to tie her up – or have her tied up – spank her, and then fuck her.' Victoria grinned at me. 'Oh, what a pleasant change for someone to ask me for something normal,' she said – rather ironically, I thought. 'That's no problem. Finish your drink, then we'll go together and you can choose your girl. OK?'

'It surely is,' I told her. I had begun to pick up one or two conversational New Yorkisms. Like 'surely', and 'momentarily'. We both finished our drinks. Victoria stood up and I followed her. We went through the bar, to a door on the far side. As Victoria opened the door, that dreadful scream rang out again. 'That's coming from the torture dungeons, downstairs,' she explained. 'I guess it takes all sorts.' I didn't say anything. I tried not to think about it. She finally led me through a door at the end of a corridor into a tiny room, which had what was obviously a one-way mirror in the centre of the opposite wall. It was a big mirror, and it gave a good view of a large room, furnished with easy chairs, sofas, and tables. There was a small hatchway on the far side of the room, which seemed to be dispensing drinks and snacks.

What was attractive about the room, for me, was the fact that it was occupied by around twenty or so beautiful young girls. Victoria looked at me. 'How serious is your spanking?' she asked me. 'And it's vital, to save a lot of trouble later on, that you answer me truthfully. You can thrash the living daylights out of someone, if that's what you're after. But it's vital that I know beforehand. If you're only going to play at it, then tell me now.' That was easy. 'I'm not seriously into pain at all,' I told her. 'I just love spanking bare bums. Or bums covered with tightly-stretched knickers. Bums in all their taut, globular beauty. I love the feel of firmly fleshed buttocks under my hand. I love to spank, but really only very lightly. But it *does* excite me if the girl cries. Or, at the very least, pretends to cry. And that's it. I'm not into caning, pain, blood, or anything seriously unpleasant.' Victoria smiled at me. 'Well, that's very easily set up,' she said. 'For what you're looking for, any one of those girls you can see through there will be up for it. If you had wanted to use a cane, or a whip, and draw blood, then I would have had to point out to you the girls who will accept that kind of treatment. Of which there are quite a few,' she added. 'But not *all* of them.'

I began to look at the assembled girls. They were all remarkably attractive. And they were all young. I don't suppose there was one there over the age of about twenty-five. Most were in some form of lingerie. One or two were completely naked. None was fully dressed. As I looked around the room, my eye was caught by a tall, lithe, long-legged redhead. She was at least five ten, five eleven, with legs all the way up to her shapely bottom, which itself was lusciously full and firm. She had what I'd call a spanker's arse. It just cried out to be chastised. Her strikingly auburn hair was long, almost down to her waist, and although she was wearing white, semi-transparent panties of some kind, they were of a sufficiently thin material for me to be able to see quite clearly that her pubic hair matched her long tresses.

'That's the one, Victoria,' I said, pointing. 'That one over there. The tall girl, with the long auburn hair.' Victoria smiled. 'Oh, what a terrific choice,' she said. 'You'll enjoy her. That's my younger sister. Her name's Prudence. Pru for short. You'll love her. She gives great head.' Victoria turned and looked at me. 'And she loves to be spanked,' she said. 'I'll go and get her ready. I'll get her to dress in some kind of sexy lingerie. After that, it's up to you. OK?'

'OK,' I said. 'Come with me,' said Victoria. 'I'll show you to a room.' We set off into the softly-lit depths of the building. She handed me a sort of small, menu-like card. 'This is our price list,' she said as we walked along. 'The company prefers me to ask you at this stage how you are going to pay. Travellers' cheques and most credit cards are acceptable. As is cash. We give a small discount for cash. Details are on the bottom of the card.' I looked at the price list. The prices certainly weren't cheap. But then, one didn't expect them to be. Good-quality perverse sexual services with pretty, amenable young girls come highly priced in the world's major cities. 'I'll pay by credit card,' I told her, 'if that's acceptable.' 'Absolutely,' said Victoria, holding out her hand. 'May I take it now? I'll run off a blank form which you can sign as you leave. I'll bring your card back right away.'

I got out my wallet and handed over my platinum card. If she was impressed, she didn't show it. 'Thank you,' she said. She stopped, and opened a door. 'This is your room,' she said. 'Make yourself comfortable. Pru will show you where everything is. Have fun.' And she was gone, shutting the door behind her. I looked around the room. It was large, and well furnished. There was a king-size bed at one end, a bathroom with toilet, bath and shower at the other end of the room, and a small bar with a padded leather top just off to the left. I wandered over to the bar, opened the door of the fridge, and took out a bottle of champagne. It was vintage Veuve Clicquot. Good stuff. I looked around, found a couple of glasses, and opened the bottle. I poured a glass and carried it with me as I continued my trip around the room. There was a small panel with three rows of buttons on one wall, but there was no explanatory text anywhere near them. Looking around, I couldn't see anything which connected to them. Air conditioning, perhaps, I thought.

Just then there was a tap at the door, and it opened without waiting for my answer. It was Pru. 'Hi,' she said. 'I'm Prudence. Call me Pru. And you're Geoffrey. And you're British.' She came over to where I was standing, holding out a hand. You might have thought that we were at a Buckingham Palace garden party, except for the fact that Pru was naked from the waist up and wearing only the briefest, pale-lemon-coloured pair of satin bikini panties, and net stockings with a small, pale-lemon suspender belt. On her feet she was wearing black pumps. We shook hands. 'Champagne?' I asked, indicating the bottle on the top of the bar, next to the empty glass. 'Oh, wow,' she said. 'Champagne. Yes, please.' I poured her a glass, and handed it to her. 'Cheers,' she said. 'I gather I've been a naughty girl.' 'Oh,' I said, not thinking. 'How's that?'

She gave me a slightly old-fashioned look. 'Well,' she said. 'I'm told you're going to spank me. On my bottom. With your hand. So I must have been a *very* naughty girl. To be spanked on my bare bottom. Are you going to take my knickers off?' she asked me. 'Or do you want to spank me with them on? I may wet them, if you do. One way or another.' She laughed, and took another swig of her champagne. 'Keep them on, Pru,' I said. 'At least for the moment.' And then, 'Tell me,' I asked, 'What is that panel for over there, on the wall? The one with the buttons?' Prudence put down her glass and moved over to the panel. 'I understand that you want to tie me up, before you spank me,' she said. I nodded. 'Then you'll want to use one of these,' she said, pressing one of the rows of buttons.

A panel on the wall opposite us slid up, revealing a sort of triangular cell containing a wooden whipping post, complete with leather restraints for wrists and ankles. It was the kind that, when you have strapped your victim to it, they look rather as though they have been crucified, but with their backs to you, leaving back and buttocks available for whatever pleasures you have in mind. She left it in position for a few minutes, whilst I took in its details. I could see that it was well padded, and wasn't, in itself, going to cause its victims any actual pain.

'Or this,' said Pru, pressing another button. The triangular cell swung around, disappearing as another, similar unit came into view. This was a different version of the same kind of thing. A wooden frame, again with restraints, over which your victim would be strapped, but this time very much with her (or his) buttocks presented up in the air, for your delectation and attention. 'And finally,' said Pru, pressing another button, 'here is your choice of implement.' As the last of the three units swung around, I could see that it was equipped with every kind of pain-causing whip, cane, paddle, and riding crop, and even with a couple of cat-o'-nine-tails. There were also nasty things like nipple clamps, electric probes, branding irons, pincers, and the like. It seemed that some of the club's customers took the application of pain seriously. I looked at Pru. 'Actually, Pru,' I said to her, 'I don't really need any of those things. Not the whipping posts, nor any of those nasty weapons. When we're ready, I shall simply put you across my knee and spank you with my bare hand. And then, of course, fuck you. That's all today is about. It's not about causing *real* pain. It's about make-believe. That you've been a naughty girl means that you must be punished. I shall punish you. You will cry. Punishing you, and making you cry, will give me the kind of erection that will then make you very happy. It's the opposite of a vicious circle. It's a happy circle.'

Prudence laughed. 'It sounds like a lot of fun,' she said, draining her glass. 'Shall we start?' She went over to the bed. She was every man's walking sexual fantasy, with her gorgeous body dressed simply in her panties, suspender belt and stockings. I had a serious erection just looking at her and thinking about what was coming next, so that I had difficulty in getting my trousers off. When I was finally naked, I sat on the edge of the bed, took Pru's hand, and pulled her towards me.

'Naughty girls get their bottoms smacked, Prudence,' I told her. 'You've been very naughty, and I'm going to spank yours.' 'Oh, please don't spank me,' she said, beginning to sniffle. 'Please don't spank my bottom. Please don't.' I ignored her, and pulled her down across my knees. I placed my hand on the rounded globe of one buttock, and stroked it through the thin satin of her knickers. It felt warm and smooth beneath my hand. I massaged it, and squeezed it, and then I slid my hand up under the elastic of her knicker-leg and stroked her naked flesh. My fingers ran down into her anal cleft, just touching the puckered flesh of her anus in passing. I could feel her pubic hair, and I allowed my fingers to drop down between her legs, where I felt a wet warmth issuing from her secret place.

'That's very naughty, Prudence,' I said. 'You're practically wetting your knickers.' I pulled my hand out from underneath her knickers, and slowly pulled the flimsy item down her thighs. As I pulled it down, I could see that the white cotton gusset lining the satin crotch of her panties was stained dark with her juices, and as I gazed at it, the delightful aroma arising from it reached my nostrils. I breathed in deeply. She smelt of fresh melons, roses, and just a touch of tropical lime. I left her knickers there where they were, halfway down her thighs, the crotch well positioned to continue allowing its scent to reach me, and stroked her now fully exposed buttocks. I could at last see the soft auburn curls of her pubic hair thickening as they disappeared down towards her sex.

I massaged and rubbed and squeezed, until I felt ready to start spanking her. I raised my hand, and she said softly – almost whispering – 'No. Please. Please don't hurt me. Please don't make me cry.' I brought my hand down, sharply. Her buttocks quivered as my hand made contact, and she burst into tears. They were either real, or she was an impressive actress. I looked down, and I could see the imprint of my hand, fingers spread, rising pinkly on her buttocks. I raised my hand yet again, and slapped her once more, this time on the other buttock. I waited until the imprint started to appear, and then I continued with the punishment. Her buttocks slowly turned from pink to red, and her tears progressed from soft sniffles to what seemed very like the genuine article. She interrupted her crying to speak to me, her voice thick with emotion. 'Oh, please, sir,' she said, 'please don't spank me any more. I'll be a good girl, sir. I'll do all those things you want me to. I'll suck your thing for you. I'll play with it, the way you like me to. But please stop spanking me. I'll do anything you want, sir. Anything.'

I found the thought of what Pru was actually saying to me extremely erotic, and I pulled her off my knee, turned her over onto her back, pulled her knickers all the way down her legs and off, and straddled her, my rigid member standing out before me. She looked up at me with her tear-stained cheeks, grasped my prick in her hand, and guided it between her legs, where I sank it into her. She was wet and slippery, and took me all the way in, up to the hilt. She was hot, tight, and very wet. She was everything any man has ever dreamed of. She was sexually exquisite. Her pussy throbbed, and worked itself around my male muscle as if it were a hand, masturbating me. I felt my ejaculation rising rapidly. I could hear her calling me 'sir' as I spanked her. I remembered the obscene things she had spoken of, and I came, luxuriantly, splendidly, into her receptive, hard-working cunt. 'Oh, yes,' she said, to my surprise, as I pumped my semen into her. 'That's nice. That's really nice. You can come and spank me any time, mister, so long as you promise to fuck me like this afterwards.' What more can I tell you?

P. K. New Cavendish Street, London, W.1.

Not a lot. New York, New York. What a wonderful place. Like the song says.

TONGUE TWISTER

I wonder if I may use the facility of your columns to make a complaint? To make a stand, as it were, for all my sisters out there who may have the same problem that I suffer from? I'm a fairly normal nineteen-year-old woman, who has had – and is still having, thank God – her share of men. I've met all sorts.

I've given as good as I've got, and I've got – up until now – as good as I've given. I don't have too many hang-ups. I'm not into water sports. That's a bit too specialist for my tastes. I'm not overly keen on being fucked up the arse, although your letters pages tell me that I'm missing a lot of fun there. I'm not against it in principle. It's just that in my limited experience, I've found it painful. I don't believe that sex of any kind should hurt. But perhaps I've been unlucky. I'm willing to try again, with any man who loves me enough to take it gently. But that's by the by. My complaint is that I love to suck cock. I'm really into oral sex. I can come with a beautiful, preferably large, cock in my mouth. I don't even have to touch my pussy. But my Jewish boyfriend of the moment tells me that he isn't into oral sex. Either way. He says it's dirty.

I've read a lot of letters in your columns, over the years, putting forward the thought that sucking pussy is disgusting. Sadly. But I've never before come across a man who doesn't want his cock sucked. I mean, in my book, that makes my boyfriend a real cocksucker, if you'll forgive the expression. I started off, as most young girls do, before we are ready to experience real sex, by giving my very young boyfriends a slow, loving wank at the end of a pleasant evening. I was a virgin in those days, as were most of my girlfriends, and although I didn't want to lose my virginity, I wasn't against giving as much sexual pleasure as I was able, within those limiting circumstances.

From there on, over a period of time, I progressed from what eventually became mutual masturbation (when the boys eventually got to the stage where they realized, however reluctantly, that girls like to have orgasms too) to mutual oral sex. And finally, of course, to adult sex. I have no sexual inhibitions whatsoever, apart from those I've already mentioned. But I was left at the end of the day, with an all-consuming desire to suck cock. I would almost pay money for the privilege of taking a swollen, gorgeously erect penis in my mouth, and tonguing and licking and sucking it until it spurts its owner's come down my throat. Fantastic!

So why on earth doesn't my present boyfriend enjoy that which (again from your letters columns) I read that a small percentage of women refuse to do, on the grounds that they think it's dirty? Or degrading. Or using them like prostitutes. I gather that the world is much fuller of men who would like a nice girl like me to – what do you want to call it – give them head, go down on them, suck them off, French them? You can call it what you like, as far as I'm concerned. Just show me a man who wants his cock sucked. And if he wants to suck my pussy in return, who am I to stop him?

K. O'G. Newton Abbot, Devon.

We'll forward your mail on to you.

THANKS FOR THE MAMMARIES

Years ago, when I was younger, men standing around in pubs over a pint or so of beer would ask each other whether they were tit men, leg men, or arse men. The answer indicated which of those three delightful sectors of female anatomy appealed most to the person being questioned. It implied, I always understood, a question of aesthetic beauty, rather than specifically of sex, although I may be wrong here. Nowadays, one never hears the question. Have we become so blasé about our relationships that we no longer categorize our chosen area of admiration? It would seem so.

I have always been a breast man, ever since working in Africa as a youngster. Before my arrival out there at the age of twenty, the number of ladies that I had seen close to *sans* vests was very few. Suddenly – and joyously – I was thrust into a society where women wore little other than a row or two of beads around their loins. It seemed, after a while, the most natural thing in the world. When walking through the bush and passing some local beauty on a jungle path, one would murmur 'Good morning' or 'Good afternoon' in the local language (usually Mende) whilst assessing her exposed bust for entry into the office competition on return to base. The categories, as I remember them, were (not necessarily in order of merit) bee stings, pears, spaniels' ears, super-duper droopers, and block-busters. If it were possible to take a photograph without causing embarrassment, one did. This was usually a clincher in the competition – or not, as the case might be – but, regrettably, it was not often possible. I remember that the rainy season was a particularly happy time. I submit that there is no more stimulating sight than a fine pair of young, black, firm, well-shaped breasts with pointed nipples, running with rainwater, the nipples dripping like miniature drainpipes. A secondary consideration (bearing in mind that one was also oneself wet through in these circumstances, if better dressed) was the fact that the rain was warm.

The years that I spent in Africa were extraordinarily happy ones. The people were charming, the countryside beautiful. It also gave me the experience necessary to enable me to give the lie to an oft-repeated rumour, back here in the United Kingdom, that black males are better endowed sexually than their white brothers. From years of walking along riverbanks in Africa in the mornings and seeing both African males and females at their ablutions, I am pleased to be able to report that, in that respect, black males are exactly the same as white males. They come equipped with every variation of male organ size, from the impressive to the insignificant. Just as we whites do.

C. L. H. Bournemouth, Dorset.

But do they play a better tune?

HAIR OF THE DOG

Am I unusual in loving hairy women? I just adore women with a plethora of hair. I love unshaven armpits, unshaven and/or untrimmed pudendas, hairy arseholes. The whole bit. There are only two exceptions; I am not fond of women with moustaches, nor women with hairy legs. But give me a girl with a luxuriant pubic growth, and you'll see a happy man. Nuzzling my nose into a nest of hirsute pubic locks brings muff diving into real perspective for me. I love to lick a bushy armpit, suck a bewhiskered rectum, kiss a nipple surrounded by soft, wispy hairs. Am I alone in this pursuit of the hirsute?

S. St. P. G. Andover, Hants.

You sound like any normal eager beaver to me.

BROTHEL CREEPER

I've never actually been to a brothel. In fact, although I live in England's capital city, I've never been able to discover such an establishment. Maybe they are but figments of overworked, feverish imaginations? Relics from Victorian memories? Or superseded, perhaps, by the individual ladies advertised on the cards stuck to the insides of telephone boxes throughout the city?

But the thought of brothels dominates my fantasies to such an extent that I am moved to write to you and relate my feelings to your readers. In every fantasy of mine, the door is always opened by a pretty girl in a French maid's uniform. The classic bit. You know: short black skirt. White apron. White blouse. Black stockings, black suspenders, black knickers. White mob cap. Black high-heeled shoes in patent leather. She smiles at me, and opens the door. I walk into the passageway, and feel up underneath her skirt as I pass her by. The crotch of her knickers is wet, and I finger her cunt through the moist material. She says, 'Ooh, that's naughty. But I like it.' And she shows me into a waiting room. On the walls are pornographic photographs and paintings of pretty girls performing every possible kind of sexual act you can think of, and one or two that may not have occurred to you. There is always one of a girl who has a cock up every orifice. One up her pussy, one up her anus, and one in her mouth. In addition, she has two more cocks – one in each hand – which she is masturbating. Then there is one of a girl who is simply the filling in a sexual sandwich.

She is being fucked and buggered at the same time.

There are always lots of pictures of girls bound into sexually receptive, or painful – or both – positions. Hands are usually bound or manacled behind the back, and the girls are usually bent over a variety of whipping posts, offering access to their so-called private parts, although anything less private than what is represented in some of these pictures is difficult to imagine. Mouths are frequently tightly gagged. Then there are explicit photographs of girls masturbating themselves. Sometimes simply with long, carefully manicured fingers. Sometimes with huge over-sized dildoes. And then there are the illustrations of girls sucking girls. You know what I mean. Cunt sucking. And fucking each other with strap-on dildoes. Or double-ended ones, so that they both get off at the same time.

And then there are the flagellation pictures. Girls being beaten. Whipped. Thrashed. Spanked. Slippered. The girls are often pictured with raised weals criss-crossing their thighs and buttocks. If not naked, they are inevitably pictured with tight, silky knickers pulled tautly over full bottoms. There are girls being whipped by men, and girls being whipped by girls. Very thin girls, being raped by men with very fat cocks. Girls being raped by brutal, phallic monsters. The girls' mouths are open in long, silent screams, and any men in these pictures always have enormous, swollen erections. Then there are the one-on-one oral sex scenes. Men with their cocks forced all the way down girls' throats, with the girls patently gagging at the exercise. There are always a few shots of girls sucking two men off at the same time. That doesn't appeal to me at all, but I know a few chaps who support this approach. And of course there are photographs of men sucking girls' cunts. The girls lie back, their eyes closed in utter sexual gratification, their legs spread wide, their hairy pussies (or bald pussies, depending upon the artist's or the photographer's predilection) open wetly under the ministrations of attentive male tongues.

And don't forget the fetish pictures. Some of them real photographs. But more often the work of imaginative artists. There are women wearing every kind of rubber, latex, leather and patent leather items of clothing that you can think of. Skirts. Dresses. Brassieres. Knickers. Gloves. Stockings. Women wearing latex gloves, masturbating men. Women bound with intricate ropes and knots. There are women wearing every possible kind of lingerie, from the frankly sexual to the femininely sweet. From the virginal, simple, plain white, to the tartish, open-crotched, open-nippled, fantasy brothel wear. It's either very exciting, or it's very boring, depending upon what your sexual proclivities are. But, being brothels, there is something for everyone. Variety, as they say, is the spice of life. Just then, the door to the room that I am in opens and an attractive woman of around thirty comes in and introduces herself. She is French, she is called Jeanne, and she is, of course, the madam. We talk of payments. I produce a credit card and hand it over, and Jeanne leads the way out of the room and down a corridor, where she opens another door which turns out to open on a large room full of gorgeous girls.

'Take your time, m'sieur,' Jeanne says to me. 'There is no hurry. Have a good look around, and choose the woman that you fancy. She will ask you what sexual act or acts you wish her to perform, or which you wish to perform upon her, and she will tell you whether or not they are within her repertoire. Not all the girls do everything. Some girls specialize. Others do not like, for example, being physically beaten. Some do not perform oral sex. Some prefer not to have anal sex. But they will all tell you, quite plainly, what they are prepared – or not prepared – to do with you.' She handed me a printed card. 'Here is a list of your prices. They are fixed. They are not negotiable. Do not let any of the girls hustle you into doing something that you do not want to do, or into choosing them if you are not sure that they are what you are looking for. Call me if you need me. Otherwise I will be back in a while, to see how you are getting on. Au 'voir, m'sieur.' She left me there, surrounded by pretty girls.

Some were naked. Some were fully dressed. Very elegantly so. Others wore varying degrees of undress. All were fantastic. There were blondes, redheads, girls with black hair, girls with brown hair. Amongst the naked girls, I could see that there were girls with shaven pubes. I particularly fancied a redhead with a bald pussy. I made a mental note. She had beautiful, pointed, firm breasts, an arse that would have given the Pope a hard-on, and the loveliest green eyes. She saw me looking at her, and she came over and spoke to me. 'Hi,' she said. 'My name's Monica. What's yours?' 'Hallo, Monica,' I said. 'I'm George.' 'Well, George,' she said. 'Look no further. I'm the greatest fuck you've ever had in your life. Are you looking for anything special. You know, kinky? I'm into pretty straight sex, myself.' I looked at her. 'No, nothing kinky,' I told her. 'A little fellatio. A good fuck. Maybe a wank.' 'Here I am, George,' she said. 'I give terrific head, and my hand-jobs are sensational. And I fuck like a dream. A dirty dream,' She laughed. 'Let me think about it, Monica,' I said. I moved away. She smiled at me as I left. I gave her full marks for that.

I was also attracted to a tall, black-haired girl, who looked foreign to me. Italian, maybe. She had a slightly olive-coloured complexion, and her hair was thick and lustrous. She was wearing a figure-hugging leotard. You know the things. Almost a one-piece bathing suit. This girl was tall, long-legged, with a fabulous figure and a lovely smile. I went over to her. 'Hallo,' I said. 'I'm George.' 'Hallo, George,' she said, in the softest of Irish accents. 'I'm Bridget.' How wrong can you be, I asked myself? 'Are you looking for anything special?' Bridget asked. 'I saw you talking to Monica over there. She's a lovely girl. She's a friend of mine.' I suddenly had this wondrous idea. I looked deep into Bridget's beautiful blue eyes. I told her what I'd told Monica. About fellatio. And fucking. And being tossed off. And then I said, 'But do you and Monica do a lezzie act? I mean, you know, a show? An exhibition? Just for me? I know Monica said she was pretty straight, but don't most of you lovely girls put on little pretend-lezzie shows for people like me?' She looked at me for a while, without saying anything. Then she smiled and said, 'We do that. In fact, Monica and I were rehearsing ours only yesterday. Let's go over and talk to Monica together.' We walked back across the room to where Monica was standing. She smiled at Bridget.

'So you've picked Bridget, then?' she said. 'And a very good choice too. She's a lovely girl.' 'No, no, shhh,' said Bridget. 'Listen. He hasn't picked me at all. Or, rather, not *just* me. He's picked both of us. He wants us to put on a girly show for him. Do you fancy that? You know? Like yesterday?' Monica giggled. I didn't see anything particularly amusing about what had been said, but patently Monica had. 'Well, does he now?' replied Monica. 'Well, now. I think we could manage that,' she said. 'Leave it to me. I'll go and find Jeanne, and set it up. You stay here and talk to George.' At which she left, naked as she was, through the main entrance door. 'Is this your first visit here?' Bridget asked me. I suppose it was fractionally better than, 'Do you come here often?' To which, had she asked me, I would have said 'I hope to.' Ha ha. Ah, well.

Just then Monica came back through the door. 'We're in Suite Seven,' she told Bridget and me. 'If you'll take George up there and show him what's what, I'll go backstage and start to get things ready. Will you join me there?' 'I will that,' said Bridget. Monica stood on tiptoe and gave me a kiss on the cheek. 'Thank you for choosing Bridget and me,' she said. 'You won't be sorry.' She left, once more, and Bridget turned to me and took my hand. 'Follow me,' she said. She guided me out of the room, along a short passage, and up some broad, well-carpeted stairs. At the top, the corridor led off in two directions. We took the corridor to the left. It was rather like walking down the corridor in an expensive block of flats. The walls were painted cream. The carpet was a dark green, and thick. The lights were bright. Every twenty yards or so there was a door, and each door had a number. Otherwise, there was no character. No ambience. No sound. We stopped outside a door bearing the number seven. Bridget pressed a button, and the door swung open. Silently. She entered, and beckoned me to follow her. We were in a smallish hallway, with two doors leading off. One of them was open. As we passed the shut door, Bridget said, 'That's the bathroom, when you need it.' 'Thank you,' I said.

The room we entered was nicely, expensively, comfortably furnished. It was a wide, long room. In the centre of the space there were two large sofas, facing each other, whilst the floor in between them was padded and covered with what looked like a silken sheet. It was, to all intents and purposes, a large bed, but one obviously intended for people to perform upon. There was a large, traditional double bed up at the other end of the room. There were side tables, easy chairs, and a small, well-stocked bar, with a sink and a refrigerator. The entire ceiling was mirrored. There were spotlights trained onto the padded area.

'This is where Monica and I will do our thing for you,' said Bridget. 'If you feel like joining in at any time, feel free.' As she spoke, she was peeling off her leotard, and in seconds she was naked. Her breasts were beautiful. She had huge teats. I looked at them, completely mesmerized. She stepped right up close to me, and took my right hand in hers.

Her naked breasts pressed hard against me. She put her lips up against my ear, put my hand between her legs, and said, 'And speaking of feeling free, feel *this*, darling.' I did. I thrust two fingers deep into her moist slit. She wriggled appreciatively. She was wet. She was tight. She was warm. And she was raring to go.

Her other hand found my swelling cock and she began to massage it through my trousers. She put her lips on mine and thrust her tongue into my mouth. After a few moments of heavenly sexual anticipation, I pulled my mouth away from hers. 'Hold on, sweetheart,' I said. 'If you go on doing that, it will all be over before you've even started.' I pulled my body away from hers as I spoke. She grinned at me. She looked as if she was about to say something, but right then Monica came in through the door. 'Getting to know each other, I see,' she said. She was still naked, but this time she was carrying a largish holdall. She dumped it in a corner of the room, away from the 'stage'.

'OK, boys and girls,' she said. 'Let's get George here comfortable, and then the show will commence. What can I get you to drink, George?' 'Scotch and water, please, Monica,' I said. 'No ice.' She went over to the bar, and came back a couple of minutes later with an unopened bottle of The Famous Grouse, a cut-crystal tumbler, and a carafe of water. 'Here you go, George,' she said. 'Help yourself. Cheers.' She and Bridget went over into the corner where the holdall had been dumped. Monica picked it up, and the two girls went through to the bathroom. I kept my eyes on Bridget as she walked past me. Her pubic hair was indeed thick and luxuriant, as I had guessed. I remembered that it was only a few moments since I had been standing there with her naked, my two fingers up inside her cunt, her tongue in my mouth. My penis swelled at the memory. I poured myself a large drink, and settled back on the sofa. Bridget popped her head around the door.

'Are you ready, sweetheart?' she asked. 'Ready as I'll ever be,' I replied. 'Hey, why don't you get your clothes off, darling?' Bridget said. 'First of all, you'll be more comfortable.' She grinned at me. 'And secondly, you'll be ready for anything,' she said. 'OK?' 'OK,' I said, and I stood up and quickly undressed. I felt faintly embarrassed, sitting there with half a hard-on. But then I thought what the hell? And I relaxed. Some music suddenly began from somewhere. Softly at first, and then building slowly. It was very sensual.

The two girls appeared out of the bathroom. They were wearing crotchless black satin knickers, which revealed Monica's shaven pussy and Bridget's hirsute one. They also were wearing black satin bras, with holes which allowed their nipples to jut through. Bridget's giant teats looked eminently suckable. As did both their pussies. Monica had the holdall in her hand, and she put it down at the edge of the padded arena.

Bridget lay down on her back on the area, her legs apart, her knees drawn up. Monica lay beside her, and began to massage Bridget's pudenda through her thick growth of black, curly, pubic hair. Soon – as I had – she found Bridget's pink, wet slit and she thrust just one finger deeply into it. Bridget made a noise somewhere between a moan and a deep, rich purr, and opened her legs even wider. Monica stopped her fingering, pulled her fingers out of Bridget's honeypot, and, kneeling up for a moment, she pulled Bridget's black satin knickers down her long legs and off. Bridget sat up for a moment, reached behind herself to undo her bra, and took that off. Whilst she did this, Monica put a hand out, pulled the holdall nearer to her and looked for, and found, a large vibrator. She kept this in her hand, and I assumed – wrongly, it transpired – that she was going to use it up Bridget's vaginal orifice. But no.

Still holding the vibrator in her right hand, Monica

positioned herself so that she could lower her head between Bridget's legs. She started by kissing her cunt, then licking and sucking it, and finally she treated her colleague's sex to an enthusiastic combination of all three. Clear liquid soon started running down Bridget's thighs. After a little while, Monica let go of the vibrator, and I assumed that she had changed her mind about using it. As I watched, she slid a hand beneath Bridget's buttocks. Bridget obligingly raised them slightly, to permit Monica's hand free access, and I was surprised to see Monica's middle finger ease its way through Bridget's thick growth of anal hair, and into her tightly clenched anus.

Bridget let out a gasp, as if this intrusion was as much of a surprise to her as it was to me. However, Monica continued with her cunnilingus as she finger-fucked Bridget's anus, and Bridget soon began to pant, after which she started to move her hips up and down in an extremely explicit fucking motion. Then, almost before I realized it, she was screaming and moaning, and tossing her head from side to side, her hips working double time, as she succumbed totally to Monica's ministrations, and underwent an enormous, almost continual, series of orgasms. I thought that might be the end of at least that part of the show, but neither girl showed any sign of getting up. Instead, Monica reached out for the vibrator and, pulling Bridget's legs wider apart, she started to ease it up the other girl's rectum. I could see that Bridget was thrusting her hips and buttocks downwards, endeavouring, it seemed, to help the vibrator all the way in, and quite quickly it was fully in position. Only the tip of the very end – the end incorporating the on/off switch – could be seen, sticking obscenely out of Bridget's arsehole.

At that point, Monica switched the device on. 'Oh, God,' screamed Bridget, almost immediately. 'Oh, Jesus. Oh, fuck. Somebody fuck me. Please. Oh, God. Please, God.' Monica raised her head, looked at me, and then raised a quizzical eyebrow. 'The lady wants a fuck,' she said. 'Do you fancy a fuck, right now? She's good and wet, I can guarantee.' My prick stood to full attention at the very thought. The idea of fucking this gorgeous, nubile, randy young woman with a live vibrator buzzing away up her anus was too much. I practically leapt up off the sofa and stood there, looking down at Bridget's lewdly spread legs, her magnificent pubic growth, and her wet, pink slit running down the centre, immediately over the humming vibrator. I was not entirely sure what to do next.

Monica came to my assistance. 'Here,' she said, standing up. 'Let me help you.' She took a hand, and pulled me over towards Bridget until I was standing between her open legs. 'Now kneel down,' she suggested. I did as I was told. She took hold of my tumescent cock and guided it down to the outside of Bridget's saturated cunt. 'Now push forward. Slowly,' she said. Again, I did as I was told. She was still grasping my erect cock and, as I pressed forwards and downwards, she fed it into Bridget's hot, wet sex. Then I was literally sucked in. It was as if Bridget had switched on some kind of suction pipe in her pussy. And over all, over and above the noise of the vibrator stuck up Bridget's arse, I could feel its actual vibrations, transferring themselves through Bridget's rectal passage to her pussy, and through her pussy to my cock. Fantastic!

Despite the temptation to just lie there and let it all happen to me, I began to move my hips in the classic fucking motions. It felt fabulous. I was in no hurry, and I fucked away slowly, wanting these wonderful sensations to last forever. But there was more to come. As I fucked Bridget, Monica had stripped off her bra and knickers, and she now came and lay beside Bridget, naked, her open legs on a level with my face, her shaven pussy right beside my mouth, its lovely gash shining wetly from within her pinkly open labia. 'Why don't you suck my beautiful bald pussy while you fuck Bridget?' she asked. I couldn't think of a single reason why not so, without in any way interrupting my rhythm, I leaned down to my left and began to suck at Monica's smooth-lipped cunt. She smelt of clean, sexually excited young pussy.

It was open, and wet, and it tasted delightful. It was as smooth as the proverbial grape skin, and I sucked and licked at it with wholehearted erotic pleasure. As I fucked and sucked, I reached up with my right hand and began to knead Bridget's enormous left-hand teat. It swelled and grew in my hand, and Bridget began moaning again. Monica turned her head to the left, where it was more or less on a level with Bridget's head, and she reached over and pulled Bridget's face towards hers. She then started kissing Bridget on the lips, which favour Bridget returned with enthusiasm. I wondered if Bridget could taste her own vaginal juices on Monica's lips, remembering how Monica had been busying herself down at Bridget's sex, and I wondered whether, if she could, she found the thought of that as sexy as I did.

The sight of the two girls French kissing each other, their tongues deep in each other's mouths, their eyes shut, their breath impassioned, whilst I fucked the one and sucked the other's cunt, was almost too much, sexually, to bear. I thought that I might explode from sheer sexual fulfillment. And all the time, the soft buzz of the vibrator in Bridget's anus sent a sexual message to all our brains. As well as to my cock.

Bridget pulled away from Monica's mouth. 'Oh, God,' she moaned. 'I'm going to come again. Oh, God. Oh, yes. Oh, I'm coming. I'm coming now. I'm being fucked, and I'm coming now. Oh, Jesus. Oh, yes.' And with her final shout, she writhed and twisted as her orgasms took over her whole body, and she moaned and cried out and then, as the orgasms died away, she fell silent. Monica leaned up, reached down, found the end of the vibrator, and switched it off. She withdrew it carefully, and placed it on the edge of the padded area. 'Well, that's one lady well serviced,' she said. 'Now, how about me? I haven't been fucked yet, you know.' She lay down, a few feet away from Bridget, and opened her legs. She looked over at me. 'And you haven't had your cock sucked, and you haven't had your hand job yet. What an idle couple of tarts we are. Whatever next, I wonder?' she said, smiling at me. 'Get yourself over here at once.' She looked fantastic. Her long, auburn hair was lying spread around beneath her head and shoulders like the aura around an angel's head. Her green eyes looked somehow translucent. Her lips were wet, and she kept licking them. Slowly. One finger of one hand was idly playing with her shaved pussy. It had disappeared up to the first knuckle of her finger and, as I watched, she slowly pulled it almost out, and then thrust it down deep inside herself again.

'Mmmm,' she said. 'Reminds me of something. I'm not sure what.' She grinned a lazy grin. 'What do you want first?' she asked. 'Or, perhaps I should say, what would you *like* first? A slow wank? A quick fuck? Or perhaps you'd prefer a quick wank and a slow fuck? Or would you like to suck me while I fellate you? I told you that I give great head, didn't I? And I do. You don't have to suck me, of course. But I've been watching you. You like girls with shaved pussies, don't you? And you love to suck shaved pussies, don't you?' I nodded. 'I knew you did,' she said. 'I can always tell. Come over here, for God's sake.' She patted the padded carpet beside her.

'Am I allowed to change my mind?' I asked her, getting up and walking over to her, and then kneeling down beside her. She reached out and took my throbbing cock in her hand. She sat up, leaned forward, took my knobhead into her mouth and began to masturbate me. She smiled at me over the top of my cock. She gave wondrous head, as she herself said. She was the best fellatrice that I had ever had the pleasure of, as they say. She must have spent her childhood blowing eggs. When I had asked her if I might change my mind, I was playing with the idea of anal sex with her. But her expert fellatio completely distracted me – in the nicest possible way – and the added invitation to suck her delightful, smoothly shaven cunt was too much to resist. 'Let's use the bed, Monica,' I suggested. 'It'll be more comfortable.'

I pulled out of her mouth, albeit reluctantly and, taking her by the hand, I led her over to the bed. I lay down on it, my cock standing proudly erect up between my thighs. 'Kneel over me, Monica,' I suggested, 'so that you can sit back on my face, and suck my cock in comfort.' She did as I asked and threw a leg across me, grasping the base of my cock and taking it in her mouth again as she slowly settled herself comfortably down on my mouth. I looked up as her bald sex lowered itself down towards me. And then her sex was upon my mouth, and I thrust my tongue inside her as my lips closed over her labia. As I sucked her, I had a close-up view of her shaven anal cleft and her tight little anus. Someone must shave that for her, I thought, as I sucked happily away. Probably Bridget. I would have loved to shave it for her. Her cunt was running wet with her juices, and she tasted strongly of sex. She had that extra, tangy, slightly musty odour that redheads always have, giving them a subtle, underlying, marginally acrid flavour. I always find it particularly erotic, and sexually very stimulating.

As I kissed and licked and sucked, Monica began to wriggle her hips, thrusting strongly down onto my hard-working mouth, and I guessed that she was building up towards an orgasm. I began to pump my cock up and down, relishing the sensations she was giving me through the obviously practised use of her lips, mouth and tongue, and I felt my own ejaculation starting somewhere deep down. Her buttocks were smooth and soft, and I clasped them in my hands, squeezing them sensually. As I did so, the thumb of my right hand brushed over her puckered rectum, and I watched it clench, then relax as it reacted to this encounter. Fascinated by its almost automatic response, I drew my forefinger gently down across its brownish-pink diameter, and saw the same instant reaction. I next pressed my finger gently into its centre, and found it dry to the touch, and resistant to my attempted entry.

I spat a gob of saliva onto my finger, then rubbed it over her anal circumference, spat another gob, and pressed into her again. This time my finger slid inside her on the saliva, and once I was inside, she seemed wet, as if from her own internal anal lubricant. 'Mmmm,' she said. 'That's *naughty*.' I was still busy sucking at her sex with my mouth, so I didn't reply to her. It didn't seem necessary, somehow. I insinuated my finger slowly farther and farther inside her anus. She felt hot up there, and the deeper I got into her, the wetter she seemed to be. She was gloriously tight and I shut my eyes, imagining my cock where my finger was. I wished I *had* changed my mind, earlier on.

My cock spasmed in Monica's mouth at the very thought, and my anal fantasies brought my ejaculation spurting down Monica's throat, rather like a miniature geyser. She used her hand to masturbate me as she sucked and swallowed my semen, and I finger-fucked her briskly anally, while carrying on sucking her off, as I continued to shoot my come into her mouth. And then, finally, it was all over. She had literally sucked me dry, and she had a series of increasingly shuddering orgasms as I concentrated on my cunnilingus. When we were both finished, she rolled off me and kissed me, wetly, on my mouth. 'Oh, God,' she said. 'That was fantastic. Terrific. Thank you. Truly. Thank you.' 'My pleasure, darling,' I said. And I meant it. Bridget was still lying on the floor where we had left her, but she was turned on her side, watching us and smiling. 'Well,' she said. 'You two certainly looked as if you were enjoying yourselves.' 'We were,' we said, together. And then we all three of us laughed. I never did get my hand job in that particular fantasy, but I'm sure it will happen sooner or later.

J. L. Maida Vale, London.

Brothels certainly exist, that's for sure. But it doesn't sound to me as if you seriously need one.

GYM WILL FIX IT

I recently joined a mixed health club. Unlike a number of these clubs, mine is open all day, every day, to whoever wishes to use it. Provided, of course, that they are members. There is no question of the male and female members being separated, or of each sex having set hours. There are also both male and female instructors, and every member can choose the instructor of his or her choice. These facts have brought a new sexual pleasure into my life. First of all, I have suddenly become aware of the sexual attraction of a woman's body as it is working out. I now am almost hypnotized by the sight of a woman *in extremis* in a gymnasium. In a sweat-stained, clinging top, her nipples standing out brazenly against the moist cotton. With perspiration running down her trim thighs, from beneath her skimpy, athletic shorts, or from under the elasticated edge of a tightly-fitting leotard. I get stimulated by the scent of a woman who is sweating after exercise. I can smell the sweet, liquid effusions from her armpits, her thighs, and her groin, and the mixture of these is extremely sexually exciting to me. I love to look at girls' crotches as they strain at the various machines in the gym, the thin cotton of their exercise clothes drawn tightly into them, often outlining the shape of their vaginal lips, so tautly are they pulled into the womens' groins. On extra-special days, I may be fortunate enough to see a moisture stain darkening this private area. I often get a hard-on, watching a girl on an exercise bike, imagining what the hard leather bicycle saddle is doing to her clitoris as she pedals frantically away, her eyes on the mileometer, measuring her efforts.

Having spent some days when I first joined simply sitting around and watching the action, I selected a female instructor to work out an exercise programme for me. One whose lush body particularly appealed. She is short – about five-two – but has a fabulous figure. Large, firm, well-shaped breasts, with nipples that stand out beneath her T-shirts or work-out tops like erect thimbles. Her thighs are generous and the space between her legs, emphasized by the tautness of the thin material at her crotch, hints at a generous pudenda and large pussy lips.

I love to watch her on one of the gym's rowing machines, for as she comes forward after the end of each of her 'draws', with her legs fully splayed and with her hands fully forward on the 'oar', I like to imagine that in this position her labia are firmly outlined against the gusset of her skimpy shorts. I also enjoy standing beside her, whichever of the machines she is demonstrating for me, and watching the sweat gather and then trickle down the cleavage which separates her thrusting breasts. My instructor is called Melanie and recently it became fairly obvious that she was beginning to fancy me, a situation that brought me much anticipatory pleasure. The indications included leaning against me when demonstrating particular items of equipment, thrusting her gorgeous heavy breasts into me at every possible opportunity, and leaning down over me when I am seated on some piece of equipment so that I am blessed with a view of her breasts in free fall, unencumbered as they are by any kind of brassiere.

On one particular evening, I booked a session with her at the last possible time in the evening – eight-thirty until ten-thirty, as a matter of interest – and was delighted to discover, as we finished, that we were the only two people left in the gymnasium. There were others – members and instructors – in the showers, the changing rooms, and the bar, but we were alone in the actual gymnasium area. When we finished, we were both wet through with perspiration and physically exhausted. As I got up from one of the rowing machines, Melanie grabbed me, put her arms about me, and gave me a big hug. 'I don't know about you, Peter,' she said, 'but I'm knackered. What I need is to go and lie down somewhere.' She looked up at me, a smile on her face.

'What a good idea, Melanie,' I agreed. 'That's exactly what I need too.' She detached herself from me. 'Follow me,' she said. I followed her through a door at the side of the gym marked 'Private Staff Only', and we went through into a corridor, off which were a number of doors. Melanie took a bunch of keys out of the pocket of her shorts and unlocked one of the doors. Once inside, she locked it behind us, and then she grabbed me again. This time, she had one hand between my legs, stroking my cock. 'Oh, God, Peter,' she said, breathing hard. 'I've been lusting after you for weeks. I thought you didn't fancy me. I want you to fuck me. Now. Feel me. Suck my tits. Suck my cunt. Fuck me with your huge tool. Take me. Rape me. Do anything you want with me. Please.' She pulled my head down and kissed me fiercely, her tongue working away in my mouth, whilst she started to massage my cock through the thin material of my shorts. It stood politely to attention for her.

Suddenly she let go of me, pulled away, and tore off her shorts and T-shirt. 'Take me now,' she said. There was a small pile of exercise mats stacked over on one side of the room which was plainly a storeroom. Melanie lay down on the mats and opened her legs. 'Now, Peter darling,' she said. 'Fuck me now. Please.' What can a chap do? In any case, my erection was so hard, it was becoming painful. I tore my own clothes off and lay down between her legs. She took my cock and guided it into her cunt. She was very wet. And as tight as the proverbial duck's arse. I slid in, and she began using her vaginal muscles on me. 'Oh, darling,' she said. 'Suck my tits while you fuck me.' I did as I was bidden, and as I sucked her nipples fully erect, she worked her hips, her cunt muscles and her buttocks as I fucked her.

In what seemed like moments, she was coming all over the place, shouting out her pleasure, and bucking like a horse that's just trodden on a snake. I was concerned that someone might hear her and wonder where the riot was. As she lay there, shuddering with yet another orgasm, I came into her, jetting my semen up her in long, strong spurts. 'Oh, yes,' she groaned, bucking yet more wildly. 'Oh, Jesus, yes. Oh, God. You're shooting your spunk up me. Oh, God, God, God.'

It was tremendous stuff, and we subsequently spent some hours doing all the things that Melanie had initially suggested, and one or two that she hadn't originally thought of. My sexual excitement was kept on the boil by the all-pervading aura of fresh sweat that surrounded us both, as well as by her nubile enthusiasm and her seemingly boundless sexual energy. When I finally called pax, we spent a further jolly time together in the women's showers (the entire club was, by then, completely deserted) and by the time we had finished carefully soaping each other's orifices and protrusions, we must have been the cleanest two people in town. We have, since then, carried on with our mutually satisfying affair, but we now work ourselves up sexually as we work out together. We then shower and take ourselves off to either Melanie's place or to mine, where we work off our sexual fantasies on each other until we fall asleep, exhausted, in each other's arms.

P. W. Bromley, Kent.

Seems like you've worked it out for yourself. Congratulations.

THE BOTTOM LINE

I am a young woman who first started butt-fucking when I was still in college in New York State. I was introduced to this pleasure by one of the members of the college football team, and I've never looked back. I admit that I was nervous at first, but with loving care, and a generous amount of K-Y jelly, I quickly became an enthusiast. Harry was a gentle, patient teacher who took me through the various stages, one at a time. Maybe it would interest those of your readers who have not yet explored this satisfying aspect of sexual relations if I took them through the whys and wherefores?

First of all, both parties should be sure that they want to try anal sex. If one partner is forcing the issue, or if one partner is agreeing for all the wrong reasons, then it will almost certainly not work well. Rule one: be familiar with each other's anal parts. Look. Touch. Feel. Explore. Familiarize yourselves beyond any possible embarrassment, until each other's rectum is as exciting, and as enticing, as each other's penis and vagina. Two: always, *always* use plenty of sexual lubricant. K-Y jelly is ideal. Failing that, anything greasy is better than nothing at all. Butter, margarine, olive oil, lard are usually around in most people's kitchens. Cold cream, Vaseline, any kind of greasy unguent. Soap, as a last resort. But if you haven't got a lubricant of any kind, forget it until the next time. Trying to fuck a dry arsehole will cause pain to both parties.

Three: begin anal penetration first of all with something small. A finger. A vibrator with a small anal probe. Lead up slowly to full penile penetration. Four: be certain that both parties are comfortable with the actuality, before commencing penile penetration. Five: do it very gently. Six: if your girl says stop, stop immediately. Seven: be sure you know whether anal sex with a female is legal in your state. Despite relaxed homosexual laws in most states these days, anal intercourse with a female isn't legal everywhere. Hank was a gentle teacher, like I said. He encouraged me to plan my introduction to butt-fucking carefully. When the agreed evening arrived, we dined out at a favourite neighbourhood restaurant. Afterwards, when we got home, we opened a good bottle of wine and went to bed in the normal way that we did as the culmination of any pleasant evening. Hank spent time on foreplay, as he always did, but for obvious reasons, this night he concentrated on my anus. Touching me there. Stroking. Kissing. Licking. Until I felt fully relaxed. He then greased me thoroughly with K-Y jelly, after which I greased the full length of his penis, and then, finally, we were ready.

I was quite well worked up by this time, and was aching to be fucked. Hank got me on the bed on my hands and knees, my legs well spread, and began by inserting his finger up my anus. I was by now well accustomed to him doing this and it excited me, made me even randier than I was already. Then came the moment of truth. I could feel the head of his penis against my rectum, at which point he suggested that I reach behind me and hold his penis around its base. This was intended to give me confidence that I was in complete control.

Looking back, I don't now believe that I was, but it was a very reassuring gesture at the time. All the time this was going on, Hank was talking me through it. Slowly bolstering my confidence, reminding me that all I had to say at any time was 'Stop' and he would do exactly that. Having checked that I was finally ready, he began to press the head of his penis carefully up my arse. I had been practising dilating my anus for about a month before this evening, and I now used my muscles to dilate my back entrance as he pressed slowly against it. Suddenly, with minimal effort (and no discomfort at all) he was inside me. It felt very exciting. Very sexually stimulating. 'Oh, terrific, Hank,' I almost shouted. 'Now fuck me. Fuck my asshole. Do it to me. Now. Please.' He needed no second bidding, and began to thrust further into me, until I could feel his balls against my cunt, and I knew he was in me up to the hilt.

'OK, sweetheart?' he asked. 'Are we ready for take-off?' 'OK, honeybun,' I told him. 'Have your evil way with me.' He began to move in and out of me, increasing his tempo rapidly, until he was fucking my butt seriously. It felt good. Really. I could feel an orgasm building, although there was absolutely no contact, of course, between Hank's cock and my clitoris. It was more a mental thing, in that the feelings that his penis was producing in my anal passage were sexually both exciting and stimulating, I think it was the *thought* of what he was doing to me, rather than any direct result of the presence of his penis in my anus, which finally brought me to orgasm. These days, I either masturbate myself to orgasm as I'm being fucked in the arse, or I get my partner to do it for me. Either way, I'm guaranteed a truly satisfying sexual experience. Men love it, after they've got over the initial shock of a woman suggesting that they bugger her, because of the enjoyable tightness of any girl's asshole.

Since that delightful introduction to butt-fucking, it has become an essential part of all my subsequent sexual relationships, and I have had the intense pleasure of introducing a number of men to their very first experience of butt-fucking. I thoroughly recommend it to all my sisters under the skin. Have fun!

P. I. New York, New York.

It certainly sounds fun. I only hope your enthusiasm doesn't bottom out.

PARTY GAMES

I was lucky enough to meet a really pretty girl at a party given by friends recently. Things started off fairly light-heartedly with her. I happened to be wearing a rather tight pair of jeans, since girls tell me that they find my bum attractive in tight denim and I've never been one to ignore a possible edge over the competition. Tight jeans also allow me to bulge at the front a bit, you know where. I'd just arrived, I'd greeted my host and hostess, and I was sipping my first drink and looking at the talent when this lovely girl comes up to me and says, 'However do you get into those jeans?'

I've been asked that question before and I'm well prepared so, quick as a flash, I say, 'Well, you could always offer to buy me a drink, for a start.' Some girls take a while to get there, but this little doll saw it straight away. She loved it, and fell about laughing, after which we got chatting and it wasn't too long before she'd accepted my invitation to find somewhere to eat together after we left the party. After a while, we agreed that it was time to go and eat. I think we both wanted to sit down somewhere on our own and find out more about each other. There was a definite, very positive, mutual attraction.

The party was in Chelsea, and we found a pleasant little restaurant in a quietish back street, just off Flood Street. One where we could take our time, enjoy our food and each other's company, and not be rushed to make room for another tableful of customers. The girl's name was Jenny. She told me that she was twenty-three, single, uninvolved with anyone right now, and lonely. She smiled at me as she said the bit about being lonely, and I thought, hallo. Play your cards right, and you could be onto something really nice here, my boy. So I played my ace card. I told her where I lived. It almost never fails. At the end of the meal, I said to Jenny, 'Do you fancy coming back to my place for a drink? It's not far. I live on one of those houseboats off Cheyne Walk. Just around the corner.'

Looking back, I think she would have come back with me wherever I lived. But it's amazing the number of girls who would normally turn down that kind of an invitation the first time you meet them who'll almost take their knickers off before they get there once you tell them that you live on a houseboat.

I don't know how many of your readers know London's Cheyne Walk, but there are two groups of houseboats moored there alongside the road: a largish group of smaller boats, and a smaller group of larger boats. Mine is one of eight larger boats. It's actually a tank landing craft converted into three flats and mine is the stern flat, meaning that I am in the back end of the boat, away from the road, sticking out into the River Thames. It's a lovely place to be. This was a summer evening, and it's totally restful and relaxing, after the hustle and bustle that commences the moment you set foot ashore. Well, Jenny happily dropped her drawers, as most girls do in those circumstances. It's got nothing to do with me, and everything to do with the romance of the river. And, of course, actually being on board a ship which is moving up and down gently on the water as other craft go by. At low tide, she settles down on the mud, but when the tide is in, you can shut your eyes and imagine yourself at sea anywhere in the world that you would like to be. I poured us both a glass of wine, put some romantic music on the hi-fi, and sat next to Jenny on the one sofa. The slight disadvantage of houseboats (apart, of course, from the large, modern, floating caravan kind) is that they are not exactly spacious. But in this instance, I was delighted to be as close to Jenny as I could get. And she seemed similarly inclined.

In no time at all, we were off the sofa and down on the soft fitted carpet of the main cabin, easing each other's clothes off. Jenny had short, medium brown hair, cut like a little close-fitting hat, surrounding a diminutive face. It suited her. It made her look like a little cherub. She had brown eyes, long brown lashes, and she wore dark red lipstick. As I unbuttoned her blouse, to reveal small, pretty braless breasts, she was unzipping my jeans and reaching down inside for my cock. Her short brown leather skirt took no time at all to remove, leaving her in transparent brown seamed hold-up stockings, and a pair of pale-green satin knickers, embroidered with beige lace, that only just covered the subject. I let go of Jenny for a moment, and stood up and peeled off my jeans myself. There was no way, tight as they were, that she was going to be able to get them off me on the floor. But they had certainly served their purpose.

My prick was jutting out like a small truncheon as I slipped the jeans off over my ankles, and as I divested myself of my boxer shorts Jenny reached up and took hold of it. She then pulled me gently towards her and took its throbbing helmet into her mouth. Her lips were soft and wet, and her tongue was warm. I almost came then, as she began to work at me, but I managed to control myself. I eased myself down onto the floor beside her, without needing to pull out of her mouth, and I began slowly to pull her knickers down. I noticed, as they came down her thighs, that their cotton gusset was damp with her juices, which I took as an indication that she was wanting to be fucked. And soon.

I got her knickers properly down and off over her ankles, and she lay back and spread her legs while still fellating me.

Open, her legs revealed her inner feminine secrets. She had a neatly clipped small bush of quite luxuriant pubic hair, the same medium brown colour as that on her head. Down below this trimmed area, she was completely shaved, revealing her plump pink fleshy labia running down the centre of her pale soft white pudenda. It seemed something of a sexual compromise. A sort of half-woman, half-girl approach to sex. But there was nothing girlish about her actions. Jenny liked her sex, and she didn't mind who knew it. She was obviously very experienced, and she took enormous pleasure from everything that she did.

She sucked cock like an angel. Or at least how I imagined an angel would suck cock. Which was slowly, imaginatively, and with great enjoyment. She fucked like the proverbial stoat, giving as good as she got, and she enjoyed her seemingly endless orgasms both loudly and strongly. I can't remember how many times I came before I had to call a halt to our endeavours, but it was certainly a world record for me. She had ways of getting my cock back up again that I'd never even thought about. She stayed for a memorable night, sharing with me my rather narrow bunk. We had no sleep at all, and I strongly suspect that we kept most of our quasi-nautical neighbours awake too. That night was the beginning of possibly the best sexual relationship I ever had in my life. And it wasn't only the sex. Jenny was amusing, intelligent, good company, understanding, and loving. She was even a fabulous cook. She was everything that a normal male could wish. After three weeks, I was seriously beginning to think of marriage. Me, the original confirmed bachelor. And then, one evening on the houseboat, it all fell apart.

Jenny and I had pretty much avoided any kind of discussion about previous lovers. I think we both agreed, without needing to discuss it, that there wasn't any future in that kind of a conversation. At our reasonably young age – I'm twenty-seven – we're bound to have had a number of previous sexual adventures. Everyone does. So I didn't know at that time that my immediate predecessor had been a rock-band drummer who was seriously into S&M. And drugs. And booze. So he'd get drunk, down the tablets, get out a leather strap, and beat the shit out of Jenny. When you looked at her back and buttocks, you could actually see the faded scars. Bastard. But until she told me what they were, I just assumed that her skin on those areas wasn't quite as perfect as it was everywhere else. Why should I ever think that they were scars from beatings? But the saddest thing of all was that Jenny had come to like it. She'd finally given up the drummer, thank God, because the drugs and the booze had made him impossible to live with. She was eventually frightened for her life, she told me. But she'd come to enjoy the beatings.

We were lying on my bunk on the houseboat one summer evening. We were naked and we'd been necking happily like a couple of teenagers, when Jenny had rolled over onto her side, looked me straight in the eye, and said, 'Will you beat me, please, David?' I thought I'd misheard her. 'Will I what, darling?' I said. 'Beat me,' she said. 'You know. With your belt. On my bottom. Beat me. Please?' 'Don't be silly, sweetheart,' I told her. 'I can't do that. I'm not into it. I've never beaten anyone in my life.' I thought for a moment. 'Well, no. Make that, I've never beaten a *woman* in my life. I've never physically hurt a woman in my life. Ever. I'm just not into it,' I said. 'Well, I am,' Jenny said. 'Why?' I asked. She was silent for a long time. And then she told me about the drummer.

'At first, I just used to cry,' she told me. 'But after a while, I really got into it. It made me feel sexy. It might simply have been the association of ideas. I mean, it turned him on. And after a while, like Pavlov's dogs, I came to associate being beaten with being fucked. And eventually, I got to expect it. Then to accept it. Then to like it. And finally, to *need* it. I need it now. Beat me, darling, and you'll see what it will do for me. I'll get wetter than you've ever known me. And randier than ever. And I'll fuck you like there's no tomorrow, as they say in the bad jokes. Except that this happens to be true.'

I lay there for a while thinking about what she had just said. Closing my eyes, I tried to imagine her lying there, getting a wet pussy while the drummer beat her. Trying to envisage the blood. Because, to get scars, you've got to draw blood. While I was thinking, she put out a hand and held mine. 'It'll hurt me more than it'll hurt you,' she said, trying to make light of it. I think she knew, as I did, that suddenly it was all over. That the idyll had become an embarrassment. To be fair to myself, I did try. I got up off the bunk and went and found a good, strong, wide leather belt. Jenny turned over onto her stomach. I looked at her beautiful bottom, and I thought of all the things that I had already done to it, and some of the things that I had fantasized about doing it. And I'd never even considered beating it! I raised up the belt in my hand and gave it an exploratory *swish* through the air. It didn't do anything for me at all. But if this was what Jenny wanted, then so be it.

I laid the belt across her naked buttocks, and then I took a rather half-hearted swipe at her. It echoed throughout the small cabin with an awful *thwack*. Jenny shuddered as the belt hit her. 'Harder,' she said. I tried again. This time, I think it probably did hurt her. I kept going, but I couldn't get any kind of enthusiasm for what I was doing. As I kept at it, Jenny's bottom began to turn pink, and then red. But there was no question of blood. Indeed, there was no question even of the odd weal. I simply wasn't hitting her hard enough to produce those kinds of injury. Suddenly, Jenny rolled over onto her back, and then stood up. 'For God's sake, David,' she said. 'It's not too much to ask. Give me the belt.' I gave it to her, wondering if perhaps *she* was going to hit *me* with it. But no. She turned around, and started beating the bed. Viciously. With all her strength. After half a dozen strokes at full force, she handed the belt back to me. '*That's* what I'm after,' she said. 'Do you think you can manage that?' Her voice shook with emotion. Whether it was anger or passion or what, I wasn't sure.

I looked at her and shook my head. Sadly. 'No, Jenny, darling,' I told her. 'I'm sorry, but I can't manage that. It just isn't my scene. It actually turns me right off. I'm sorry.' We both spent the rest of the evening in sulky silence, and we didn't make love when we finally went to bed. After that, I didn't call Jenny, and Jenny didn't call me. Three months later, a girlfriend of hers rang to ask if she could come and pick up the few things of Jenny's that were still with me on the houseboat. I said yes, naturally. When she came, she was pleasant enough. She said that Jenny had taken a job in Italy, and that she was leaving London at the end of the month. I never saw or heard from her again. Have any of your readers managed to overcome an initial, genuine dislike of flagellation, and come to enjoy it? I feel I may have thrown away my one real chance of happiness.

D. T. A. Chelsea, London.

Like the song says, the party's over. I don't believe that there was any real alternative. I'll pass on any letters that I get on the subject.

FLASH OF INSPIRATION

I work in a bank, but not as a bank clerk. I'm not in contact with the general public who come into the bank. I sit in a general office with a number of other people – men and women – at desks arranged around the edges of the room, leaving the centre of the room empty. I sit opposite a young girl whom I rather fancy, except that she's in her early twenties and I'm well into my forties. She started work here about six weeks ago now. She seems a perfectly normal girl, and is always pleasant. But never more than that. She doesn't seem to show any serious interest in any of the other men, even the younger ones, and never speaks of a boyfriend, or boyfriends. But to the point.

After she had been there a few days, I noticed that her desk was missing the usual 'vanity' panel across its front, offering me a splendid view of this young girl's pretty legs. She wears rather shorter skirts than do the other women in the bank. From my position directly opposite her, I can hold up a piece of paper – a letter, or anything, really – and pretend to be reading it, whilst actually enjoying looking at the girl's shapely legs. This has become something of an obsession. But the really interesting thing is that whilst the girl – Jane is her name – shows absolutely no indication of being aware of my interest, I think you will agree that the following details prove that she is not only aware of but also actually enjoys my attention.

At first, all I could see were her legs with her short skirt coming down to perhaps three or four inches above the knee, thus revealing a few inches of lower thigh. Fun, but nothing to get overly excited about. Then one day I noticed that she had crossed her legs beneath the desk. Something she had never done before, to my knowledge. The interesting thing about this was that this position afforded me a brief glimpse of underskirt, or petticoat. And then, only a couple of days later, whilst I was holding up a document in order to look at what was becoming a daily pleasure, Jane simply opened her legs. Another first.

I swear she never looked up herself from her work, and couldn't have known that she was affording me such joy with her (as I thought then) involuntary exhibition. For with her legs apart, I could see a glimpse of white knicker. The bit stretched tautly between her legs, down the front of her crotch. I have to admit that I sat there with a throbbing erection, praying to God that I wouldn't need, for any reason, to stand up whilst thus embarrassed. Since then, I now have the daily pleasure of being shown what colour knickers young Jane is wearing. She has an extensive lingerie wardrobe, in every colour that you can imagine.

My own particular favourite is white, after which I think black comes second. Beige is nice too, for I can almost imagine that she isn't wearing any knickers at all. But yesterday! Ah, yesterday. She opened her legs to me first thing yesterday, and I could see that she was wearing white knickers. My firm favourites. Shortly after having spread her legs so generously, Jane received a telephone call. There is too much noise in the room for any of us to hear what any of the others may be talking about on the telephone, what with phones ringing, computer printers buzzing and clicking, and the general hum of conversation. So I have no idea whether her conversation was about business or pleasure. But I could hardly believe my eyes when, as I watched, she slipped her right hand down below the desk, up under her skirt, on underneath the elastic of her knicker leg and there, in full view, she began to masturbate herself!

She continued to look down at her desk as she spoke into the telephone, and no one walking past her or looking at her desk from anywhere in the room other than directly opposite her, would have had the faintest idea what she was doing. But as I watched, both amazed and fascinated, I could see the increasing rhythm of her fingers moving under her knickers and then, finally, the sudden slump of her shoulders as she – presumably – came. I almost came myself as she withdrew her fingers from her pussy and then put them in her mouth and sucked them. After which she looked directly across at me, and smiled. Do you think that, if I invite Jane out for a drink after work one day, she will accept? I don't want to spoil what has become a daily delectation. But then, if the girl is willing to put on a sexual display especially for my benefit (or so it would seem), surely she wants to take this situation to its logical conclusion?

P. W. Wellingborough, Northampton.

I wouldn't bank on it. Maybe you should wait until she does a Sharon Stone for you? On the other hand, faint heart never won fair lady. Let us know what happens.

A TOUCH OF EASTERN PROMISE

My fantasies centre entirely around Eastern and Oriental women. I've never had the pleasure, as they say, but in my dreams I always begin by entering a brothel somewhere in the Far East. I sit down at the bar, where I am served by pretty Thai girls, stripped to the waist, their tiny pointed breasts brushing against my hand as they lean over my table to give me my drink. They are very young, and heavily made up, which I find sexually exciting. They smell delightfully of heavy perfume, and they simply exude sex. I am not in a hurry, and I lean back in my seat and enjoy my drink as I look around me. Oriental music is playing softly and as I sit there I notice that there is a stage at the far end of the room. I get up from my chair, and go and sit nearer the stage. If there is a show, I want to be as close to it as possible. As I watch, the music rises to a crescendo, the curtains part, and a master of ceremonies announces that the show is about to begin. Apart from the MC, the girls behind the bar and me, there is no one else in the room. It doesn't seem to matter. The Oriental music changes dramatically to a European rock beat, and a chorus line of six girls runs onto the stage. They begin a sort of Asian Radio City Music Hall ensemble number, the main difference (apart from the number of girls involved) being that these girls are wearing shoes, stockings, gloves, hats, and nothing else. As they high kick, they split their beavers, as our American cousins say, showing off pretty little pink-lipped cunts, surrounded by black, wispy pubic hair. As they finish their number, I applaud loudly, along with the MC and the bar girls, and they dance off.

One of them comes back almost immediately, and begins to do all sorts of conjuring tricks, mostly of the kind in which she makes things disappear up her pussy. She even smokes a cigarette and blows smoke rings out of her cunt. Honestly. After a while, realizing that I am the only customer, the girl comes and kneels on the stage right in front of me. She is maybe a foot away from me. She leans back on her heels, and pulls her outer labia apart with her fingers, showing me the pale pink interior of her shiny, wet little pussy. It is, like all of her, very small, and I begin to get a hard-on, thinking how tightly it would fit around my swelling cock. 'You like?' she asks me. 'I like,' I tell her. 'You want to lick it?' she asks. 'Sure, baby,' I say.

I lean forward, and as she continues to hold her pussy lips apart I lick and tongue her pink inner hole. It tastes of a combination of pussy and urine, a blend which I find strangely erotic. 'You like to jig-a-jig me?' the girl asks. 'Up here on stage. No charge.' 'You're kidding me,' I say. 'No. No kid you. You come up here, fuck me. No charge. No money. Buy me drink after, if you like.' 'You're on, baby,' I said. I got up out of my seat, and climbed up a small ladder that I could see at the side of the stage. The girl walked towards me.

She was even smaller, standing up in front of me, than she had appeared as I looked up at her on the stage. She smiled at me, and then reached out and unzipped my fly. She stood close to me, and pulled my cock out of my trousers. 'Hmmm,' she said. 'Not bad. Better than Japanese man.' She massaged my cock. Wanked it, really, is a better description. Not unreasonably, it quickly became fully erect. 'Usually now,' she said, 'at this stage in show, I ask audience how they like you to fuck me. Then take vote. You know? Fuck mouth? Fuck cunt? Fuck arsehole? Fuck hand? Anything. Doggy fashion. Straight up and down, like mum an' dad. Anything.

No audience, so you choose. How you like fuck me? I looked at her. She was gorgeous. 'Very, very slowly,' I said. She doubled up with laughter. She patently hadn't heard it before. 'Oh, yes,' she said. 'Very good. OK. You fuck me very slowly. But where?' I reached down, and insinuated my forefinger slowly up her pussy. 'Here, darling,' I said. She really *was* tight. Like a mouse's earhole. She was still wanking my cock. Frankly, I would have been more than happy to stand there, my finger up her pussy, her small, cool hand wanking me expertly, until the inevitable happened, and I came in her hand. But it was not to be.

She let go of my cock, to my chagrin, and slowly pulled my finger out of her pussy. Then she said, 'Lie down on floor now, please. Is clean. No make clothes dirty. Then I fuck you. You like? OK?' 'No problem, baby,' I said. I lay down on the stage, my erection thrusting upwards stiffly through my open fly. The pretty little Thai girl straddled me and then took hold of my cock again. She slowly let herself down onto me, guiding my prick up into her as she did so. She was delightfully soft, and warm, and wet. And yes, you've guessed, she *was* very, very tight.

I nevertheless slid into her all the way, without the slightest hindrance, and she began to fuck me. She moved her body up and down the length of my shaft, and at the same time she used muscles in her cunt that I didn't know women had. She literally massaged me with them. I swear that she used her pussy like a hand, grasping me, pulling my foreskin up and down, squeezing me, masturbating me into her with her expert, well trained, very practised pussy muscles. In no time at all, I was pulsing my semen up into her, and groaning aloud at the pleasure which she was giving me. She leaned down and kissed me on the mouth, her small tongue wet between my lips. 'Good?' she whispered in my ear. 'Good, baby,' I groaned, overcome with unspeakable, exquisite sexual pleasure. 'You buy me cold beer after show,' she whispered. 'Then, afterwards, I fuck you properly. Slowly. Make you come many times. You like that?' 'Oh, baby,' I said. 'Yes. Yes, please. I'd like that.'

She kissed me once more, and slowly pulled herself off me. My cock came out of her with a sort of sucking noise, so strong was the suction from her pussy. 'Go back to your seat, now,' she said. 'The show must go on.' We laughed together, and I did as I was told. Once seated, I remembered to tuck away my now flaccid cock, and zip up my open fly. The rest of the show passes pleasantly, but the only thing that I am thinking about is that I am waiting to fuck this delightful young girl, in the privacy of her own room, and that I will be able to take as long as I like, and to take her any way that I like. And that is exactly what I do, all night, in my fantasy. I hope, one day, to turn it into a reality.

T. K. A. Wrexham, Clwyd.

We wish you well to wear it.

OH, MISTRESS MINE

I got into an interesting conversation recently with a male friend of mine on the subject of choosing the ideal mistress. As a woman, I take the view that an ideal mistress would be young, beautiful, sexy, and always available. To which one could add such ideal things as not being jealous (of a wife, perhaps), not greedy, financially (for any proper mistress has to be paid, if only in the sense of supported, i.e. rent, utility bills, clothes, food, holidays, etc.) and – most importantly – she has to be satisfied with the amount of time that her lord and master is prepared (or able) to devote to her.

My friend agreed with all of these attributes bar the first two: that she should be young and beautiful. Nubile, yes, he said. Sexy, certainly. Available, of course. But neither too young, nor too beautiful, for the reason that he would very soon find that he had unwanted competition for her hand (metaphorically speaking). Anyone young and beautiful, with time on their hands, was bound, he said, to become involved with other men, even if it were only one man. A lover, of (perhaps) her own age. What my friend didn't know was that I *am* a mistress, and have been now for over three years. I am kept by a married man, who tells me that he loves his wife and children (two boys and a girl), but that the fun has gone out of his sex life. His wife is pushing fifty, as is he, and no longer, he says, enjoys sex.

But he loves her, and likes her, and finds her a charming, amusing, and happy companion. I'm twenty-five, and I love sex. He says I go like the nine-ten from Paddington. I know that I am simply here for fucking. I accept that. At least for now. My man is very up-front about our relationship, and he doesn't pretend that his wife doesn't love him any more, or that he has any plans for leaving her. Ours is a business relationship which we both enjoy. It's not a hard life. I live in a nice flat in W1. I don't want for anything, and I don't need to work. All I have to do is to keep Wednesday evenings free for him, and occasionally other times by arrangement. And then I do the sexual things which his wife no longer finds fun, like suck his cock, let him fuck me anally (which I love) and so on.

For the record, I do not have any other lovers – either privately or professionally – although I have had offers. What do your readers think? Which view do they take? I expect that your male readers may agree with my male friend, and your female readers with me. I'd love to know.

P. De C. London, W1.

We invite readers of both sexes to write in with their ideal choice of either (a) a young and beautiful mistress, or (b) a not so young and not so beautiful mistress. We'll keep the score, and let you know, Miss P. De C. Personally, we're with you. In our opinion, a man who isn't confident that he can keep the competition away from his mistress doesn't deserve to have one. (Editor's note: for the record, the votes came in fifty-four per cent for a young and beautiful mistress, and forty-six per cent for the alternative.)

KEEPING HER HAND IN

I was moaning a few weeks back to my friend Jean, in the office, about being a cricket widow, what with the summer county games, the Test Matches, and then the World Cup, and I was telling her how I get my husband's attention by giving him hand jobs in front of our television set. She seemed greatly amused by this confession at the time and at the end of the week, when Friday came, she invited me to join her in our office local for a drink before going home. By the time we got to our second drink, she brought up the discussion of earlier in the week, about my giving my husband a wank in front of the TV, and pleaded with me to give her more details. This surprised me, since we have never discussed sex of any kind ever before.

In fact, to be honest, I have always seen Jean as being rather strait-laced. But she wanted to know absolutely everything about these events. How, specifically, did I grip my husband's cock with my fingers? Could I demonstrate my grip on her thumb? (I did!) Was he circumcised, or not? How long did it take him to come? Did he go on watching the cricket while I was wanking him? Did I do it quickly, or slowly? (Meaning the speed of my strokes up and down his member.) Was talking dirty part of the session, or did I wank him in silence? She seemed obsessed with the subject of my masturbating my husband, but I nevertheless gave her as much information as I was able.

Over the next few weeks, every time that there had been cricket on TV the previous day Jean would ask me how my masturbatory sessions had gone with my husband and I would tell her that all had gone well. About two weeks later – again on a Friday – Jean invited me for a drink after we finished work, and when I agreed she almost immediately got onto the same old subject. Eventually – more to tease Jean than in all seriousness – I said that perhaps my husband and I should invite her over one weekend when there was a cricket match on, and she could watch us. She said yes, she'd love to do that, and then we changed the subject.

That Friday night I told my husband, Frank, about the conversation, and he was greatly amused by it. He also said, however, that if I seriously wanted to bring Jean over to watch us at our indoor sports, he didn't mind in the least bit. In fact, I think he got quite excited by the idea. So the following Monday, I invited Jean to supper with us the next Saturday, reminding her that there was a whole day of Test cricket on the box that day. I invited her for a drink at about six, which meant that there should be at least an hour of cricket before the end of the programme. When Saturday came, we all three of us sat on a sofa in front of our TV set, watching the cricket and drinking. I sat with Frank on my right, and he had Jean on his right. After a little while, I put my drink down and casually unzipped Frank's fly. Jean watched as I pulled his rapidly expanding cock out of his trousers and began slowly to masturbate him. She was absolutely fascinated and she leaned over towards Frank so that she might have a really close view of me pulling his pud. I talked her through what I was doing and then I took my hand away from Frank's cock, suggesting to Jean that she try her hand at it, as it were. Her eyes nearly popped out of her head, but she nevertheless took hold of him and began to wank him. Bearing in mind that she told me later that this was the first time she had ever given a man one off the wrist, she did pretty well, and it wasn't too long before Frank was shooting his spunk in the air as she wanked him to a climax. I think the excitement of a different woman's hand on his dick may have had something to do with it!

Fortunately I'd had the sense to have a box of tissues to hand, and I caught his ejaculate before it stained anything or anyone. Frank went off to wash himself, and then we all sat down to supper. After supper, I suggested to Jean that Frank was probably now back in a state where she could practice some more, if she so wished, and she said that yes, she'd like to, so we all repaired back to the sofa. The cricket by this time was finished, of course, but no one seemed too bothered by it.

Frank pulled his cock out with great enthusiasm and Jean began her ministrations again. Not to be left out, I slipped my hand up my skirt and began to rub myself off through my knickers, as I watched Frank being jacked off by Jean. I brought myself off very quickly, and, almost without thinking about what I was doing, I moved over to kneel in front of Jean. Then I slid my fingers up under her skirt and up inside her knicker leg. I quickly found her wet gash. She spread her legs for me, without saying anything. I immediately found her clit and began wanking her off while I did myself again with my other hand in my own knickers. We all more or less orgasmed at approximately the same time, and a great time was had by everyone. You won't be surprised to hear that we have already set a date for the next session.

P. W. St Albans, Herts.

So, eventually, everything came to hand . . .

GETTING INTO GEAR

I'm the only chauffeuse that I know, although people tell me that there are other girls driving limousines about in Bristol. I own and drive my own car, and I've built up a good business in the three years that I've been at it. I drive a beautifully maintained old Daimler, and I do a lot of weddings, as you can probably imagine. I do, of course, get propositioned a lot. Perhaps I should say here that I'm twenty-six, five foot seven, slim, with a good figure, and I love sex. I can also say no when I want to, and that's most of the time actually. But let me tell you of a rather special occasion recently when I was more than happy to say yes!

I was booked by the manager of one of the city's larger hotels to collect two of his guests arriving at Bristol Airport. I was given their names, and a card to hold up at the arrivals gate, to identify myself to them when they arrived. They were both in their early thirties, I would guess, and they were both pretty good-looking. They seemed as pleased to see me as I was to see them, and when I delivered them at their hotel, they took one of my business cards and promised that they would use me for any journeys that they made during their stay in Bristol. I didn't have long to wait, for they telephoned me late that afternoon, and hired me for what they described as an 'open-ended evening'. I was free, so I was delighted. When I picked them up at seven p.m., they said that they would first of all like to go to a decent restaurant. One that I would recommend. I took them to one of Bristol's better restaurants – one owned and run by one of the famous, original, old Bristol sherry shippers – and they insisted that I joined them for their meal. It was a great success, in that they were delighted with the food on offer, and I enjoyed both my meal and their company.

They both turned out to be Londoners. They worked for the same company, a firm of auctioneers, and were friends as well as colleagues. They didn't discuss their marital status, but I would guess that they were both married. The more particularly so from the way that the evening developed. They spared nothing over dinner, buying fabulous wine, and they were as generous with their hospitality as anyone I have ever known. After dinner, when we got back to the limo, they announced that they wanted to go to Bristol's best strip club. Driving business people around, you get to know where everything is in your own city, and, having translated 'best' as 'horniest', I took them to a club down by the docks that was infamous for the explicit sexuality of its show.

They again insisted that I accompany them, and so I got to sit through a strip show that met their every requirement. The girls were young and pretty. It was raunchy. Not to say, frankly, disgusting. Girls were sticking vibrators up their pussies, and switching them on. Openly masturbating themselves. (And I do mean openly. You could see the pink.) Taking off their knickers and holding the moist crotches under their clients' noses, for them to sniff the aroma of wet pussy. The audience – including my two punters – loved every minute of it. When we finally left, the two of them could hardly walk for the size of their hard-ons, and I guessed that the next request would be for high-quality, immediately available women.

I was right, but I didn't exactly reckon on what that could mean. 'How much will you charge us to fuck you?' asked Jimmy, the more vocal of the two. 'I know we could have got laid back at the strip club, but there was nothing there to compare with you. How much? For both of us?' I looked at them. They seemed in control of themselves, and they looked as if they could accept a no, if that was what I was going to say. But to my surprise, the strippers had turned me on too, and I fancied both of these men.

'Let's not fuck about, chaps,' I said. 'Let's say five hundred pounds. Cash. For that, you can have me any way you want me, for as long as you like.' 'Done,' said Jimmy. He reached into his pocket, pulled out a wad of fifty-pound notes, and counted off ten. 'There'll be a good tip, of course,' he said, 'for work well done.' He got into the back of the limo, undid his fly, pulled out his rampant cock and said, 'Suck that.' I love being dominated and I knelt on the floor in front of him and began to fellate him. He was circumcised, and the purple helmet of his swollen cock stretched my mouth. As I was sucking him, I felt the other guy's hands underneath my jacket, clutching at my breasts. He felt them, squeezing my nipples hard. They obligingly became erectile beneath his fingers, after which he released them and slid his right hand up under my skirt and into my knickers, feeling for my snatch. He found it quickly, and immediately discovered how wet it was. 'Oh, baby,' he said. 'You're good and ready for me. Here comes Old One-Eye.'

I felt him unbuckling his trousers and then suddenly he was right up me, fucking me from behind. His tool felt enormous and it was doing delicious things to me. After a little while, I took Jimmy's cock out of my mouth just long enough to look over my shoulder and say, 'Play with my clitty. Please.' He did as he was told and put a finger down between his cock and my pussy wall. He immediately found my clitoris, which he began to manipulate. He'd done it before, I could tell. I like a man who knows his way around a girl's pussy. It shows that he cares. I managed a few small, sneaky orgasms before he realized, and then I felt the biggy building.

Then he began to fuck me harder, more urgently, and I knew that his ejaculation was beginning too. I began to wank Jimmy's cock into my mouth with my expert fingers, in addition to sucking it, and he very quickly came, his cock pulsing and throbbing, spurting his thick, creamy seed into my mouth. I swallowed it all. I love the taste of come, and as he ejaculated it brought on my own orgasm, which was transmitted through my pussy muscles to the other guy's cock, instantly bringing him off too, so that all three of us were bucking and moaning as we erupted into each other. It was terrific.

That, of course, was just the beginning. By the time the two of them had finished, both Jimmy and the other guy – whose name, I discovered, was Lionel – had fucked me, and they had taken it in turns to suck my appreciative pussy. Jimmy had also fucked me anally. It took him forever, since he'd come twice before that, and I loved every long, slow, lingering, gorgeous minute of it. I just adore the feeling of hot come spurting up my rectum. It's *so* sexy. If any of you girls out there haven't tried it yet, you should. I guarantee that you'll love it. And, finally, I sucked Lionel off. When we had eventually all recovered, we got ourselves together, dressed ourselves, and I got back behind the wheel of the limo, with the two guys sitting in the back. When I dropped them off back at the hotel, each of them gave me a hundred pounds tip, and a big kiss. I took them both to the airport the following morning, and they swore that they would be back again just as soon as they could arrange it. I can't wait. They can auction me any time they like.

D. H. Bristol, Avon.

Sounds as if you drove them wild with excitement!

MOUTHING OFF

I would much appreciate the opportunity to be able to tell your readers about my new girlfriend. Annette is eighteen, and that singular sort of woman – in my experience – who just loves oral sex. She can't give me head often enough. Every male's fantasy! But it didn't start like that. We met in a local pub here in Gloucester. I was with three other male colleagues, from work, and she was with a group of girls from her office. She seemed quite shy at first, but she reacted very naturally and pleasantly when I singled her out and devoted my whole attention to her. One thing led to another, and we started going out. I didn't rush things and eventually, after about a month of visits to the movies, meals in restaurants and visits to the pub, we started having sex together. Looking back now, it seems strange to remember that she was actually shy about undressing in front of me. She was fine once she was naked – she had few inhibitions about her body – it was simply that she was embarrassed to be watched whilst she undressed. The first time that I sucked her pretty little pussy, she loved it. She was entranced. She came almost continuously, and while she was certainly not a virgin when I met her, no one had ever sucked her pussy for her before.

But when I first suggested that she might suck my cock, she was literally horrified. She was, admittedly, young, and she wasn't *that* sexually experienced. But her distaste at the thought of performing fellatio was a surprise to me. I didn't press the issue, and the rest of our sex was so good that it wasn't a big problem. As we grew to know each other better,

Annette's enthusiasm for sex grew too. I continued to suck her pussy, and she continued to enjoy it. Then I began to masturbate her. I would deliberately choose to do this during daylight hours, for at night Annette was happier with the lights off when we fucked.

Then, one day, I asked her to masturbate me. Again in daylight. This too was something that she had never done before. (To my surprise. I thought all girls started off their sex lives by masturbating boys, and being masturbated by them.) She seemed to enjoy doing this for me, and she giggled with surprise and delight when I shot my semen all over her agile little fingers. It excited her so much that she masturbated me back to full erection as quickly as possible, and then she leaped upon me and fucked me – and herself – to rapid orgasm. The next time that we had sex, Annette started off by playing with my cock and, leaning down over it, she examined it, very closely. I was happy to explain the rudiments of how a cock works. I showed her where it was sensitive to friction, and then I pulled back the foreskin, and displayed my swollen purple helmet to her. I then encouraged her to masturbate me again, slowly, until once more I spurted my come over her fingers. For the first time, she looked at me, grinned, and put her fingers in her mouth. 'Mmmm,' she said, after a moment's consideration. 'That tastes rather nice. It's not actually nasty at all. What a nice surprise.'

She then bent down and, taking my now flaccid cock in her mouth, she slowly sucked all the come off it, and from out of it, which she swallowed with evident enjoyment. Naturally enough, the feel of her soft mouth and lips around my prick for the first time ever, having been wanting her to do exactly that for so long, soon had it fully erect again, and in no time at all I came once more, this time in her mouth. I did nothing but lie back and enjoy what was being done to me. I didn't take her head in my hands, or begin to fuck her mouth, or do any of the many things that a more experienced fellatrice might reasonably expect.

Her enthusiasm for oral sex stems from that day. Now we almost always start our sex with her fellating me. She prefers that, she tells me, to our *soixante-neuf*ing each other. She loves me to suck her pussy, and she now loves to suck my cock, but she likes to separate these two activities. Her favourite way of fellating me is to have me sit on one of the two easy chairs that we have in our bedroom, naked, my legs spread wide for her. She then kneels – also naked – on the floor in front of me, and takes my cock in her fingers, wrapping them around the base of it, and pulling down my foreskin, so that my cock-head is fully exposed to her oral ministrations. It excites me as I sit there, with my swollen prick just inches away from her innocent lips. She smiles at me, and licks her lips in anticipation of what she is about to do. My cock throbs in her hand. She squeezes it.

Then she slowly exposes her wet tongue and, looking up at me all the time, she takes my full length deep into her mouth, closes her lips about me, and begins to suck. She tongues me, and pulls me in and out of her mouth, her head bobbing faster and faster as she gains momentum. And then, after a while, she will deliberately stop and slowly pull my cock, wet now with her saliva, out of her mouth, and blow upon it. A delightful sensation, but every single nerve in my blood-rich, throbbing penis is screaming for her to put it back in her mouth again.

As I watch, she pushes two fingers up her pussy, wiggles them about, and withdraws them. She holds them up and shows me how wet they are. 'Would you like to suck the pussy juice off my fingers, darling?' she asks me, all innocently. 'Yes, please, darling,' I say, and she puts her fingers in my mouth and waits while I suck every last vestige of her love juices off her fingers. 'Now I'm going to wank us both off together,' she tells me. 'Or, more accurately, I'm going to suck you off until you come in my mouth, and I'm going to wank my pussy with my other hand. With any luck, we'll come together.' She grins up at me. 'Here we go, sweetheart.' She takes hold of my cock again, this time with her left hand, and takes it into her soft, warm, wet mouth. She starts sucking and licking immediately. As I watch, she puts her right hand down between her open legs and begins to play with her pussy. At first, she simply thrusts two fingers in and out of herself, but quite soon she has isolated her clitoris and is massaging that for all she is worth. Then she takes my prick out of her mouth, looks up at me once more, and says, 'I want you to come in my mouth. I want to feel your hot spunk spurting down my throat. And then I'll come with you. OK?'

'OK, baby,' I said, trying not to show my surprise. Here was this young girl, who not so long ago was horrified at the suggestion that she take my cock in her mouth, kneeling naked in front of me, my erect prick deep in her mouth, having just said that she wanted me to shoot my ejaculate down her throat and make her come. She sucked, and licked, and wanked me at the same time with her hand, while her other hand was mightily busy between her legs. It was an enormously sexually stimulating sight, watching my rigid prick, wet with her saliva, disappearing in and out of her lips. Saliva was running out of the corners of her mouth, and she was becoming really worked up as she began to feel her orgasm building somewhere deep down near her womb. She began a sort of strangulated moaning, the sound distorted by the fact that her mouth was full of my cock, and I could see and feel that her orgasm was about to start. I knew that the very moment I began to ejaculate, she would orgasm. I took her head in between my hands, and she looked up at me. I began, very gently, to move my hips in the smallest possible fucking movements, and as I did so, I ejaculated deep into her mouth.

She moaned as I spurted into her mouth, and she immediately came herself, her body shuddering, her shoulders shaking, her mouth trembling. After that occasion, there was no holding her. Patently, the thing that had been putting her off oral sex was the thought of my ejaculating into her mouth. Now that this phenomenon held no fears for her, the problem disappeared. She simply couldn't suck cock often enough. Many evenings, she now prefers to spend the entire time giving head, without any thought of actually getting fucked. She has gradually improved her technique, until today I would enter her into any oral sex contest, and be more than surprised if she didn't win outright.

These days, when she is in the mood, she asks me to fuck her mouth. She loves to lie on her back, her legs wide apart, and have me kneel over her and literally fuck her mouth. She has become accustomed to the fact that I like to suck her pussy whilst I do what she wants, and now allows me to do so. I always ask her to keep her knickers on at the beginning of one of our mutual oral sex sessions, since it has always turned me on to suck pussy through girls' knickers. For me, there is something tremendously sexually exciting about sucking pussy through thin silk or nylon material. The feeling of warm, wet, fleshy, swollen vaginal lips beneath the coolness of wet fabric, is a guaranteed turn-on, and Annette has become accustomed to my fetish.

Nowadays, she takes my prick in her hand and feeds it into her mouth. I then start to move my hips, slowly at first, and then faster and faster, until I am seriously fucking her mouth. As I get more and more aroused, she starts to jack me off into her mouth, until finally I spurt my come into her in great long pulsating gouts. At the same time, I will masturbate her clitoris as I suck her pussy, and she too will come, bucking her wet, swollen pussy up against my mouth as she orgasms wetly. Long gone now are the days when she thought oral sex was disgusting.

J. T. L. Gosport, Hants.

It sounds as if she's seriously paying lip service to your needs.

TWO'S COMPANY

It's always been a fantasy of mine to be fucked by two men at the same time. My husband has always known this, but I never thought that he would actually do anything about it. How wrong could I be! On my birthday recently, he took me to one of New York's few surviving swinging sex clubs. We had both eaten a sumptuous dinner previously, at the Cirque de France, and had consumed sufficient beautiful wine, followed by liqueurs, to be in the mood for anything. On arrival at the club, over on the West Side, we sat at the bar for a while, and watched the dancing.

It wasn't long before an attractive young man came over and asked my husband if he might ask me to dance. My husband told him that he would be only too pleased, since he himself wasn't one of the world's great dancers. That was a lie, in fact. My hubby dances like a dream. However, so did the young man I was now dancing with, and it wasn't long before I could feel his erection thrusting stiffly between my legs as he guided me around the floor. My immediate reaction was to get very wet myself. It was the first time in years that I had felt a cock other than my husband's between my legs. After the young man returned me to my husband at the bar, he – my husband – suggested that we perhaps move on, to see what amusement we might find somewhere else, and asked the young man – Joe was his name – if he would care to join us. To my surprise, Fred, my husband, then drove us back to our apartment. We live on the East Side, in the low eighties, in a modern high-rise apartment on the twenty-eighth floor. When we got home, my husband told me that if I fancied Joe, he was happy for me to get fucked by the two of them, thus fulfilling my long-held fantasy. It was to be a birthday present. I looked at Joe, and Joe looked at me, and we both said, more or less at the same time, 'No problem!' We moved into the bedroom, and undressed in what must have been – for me – world record time.

I'm twenty-four, and have a good body. I'm dark-haired, with long legs (which I love to spread for my hubby), a great ass, and good tits with over-sized nipples. Fred is twenty-nine, and he's pretty fit. He's six foot tall, slim, and has a giant schlong. It was one of the things that most attracted me to him when we first met. Getting fucked by Fred is like being fucked by a stallion. My wanting to be fucked by two men at the same time in no way reflects on Fred's ability in the sack. Not to my mind.

Once naked, I lay on the bed and watched the two men undressing with some interest. Both had full erections, and Joe's cock was every bit as large as Fred's. Joe turned out to be twenty-seven and single. And then, suddenly, I had two pairs of hands all over me, feeling me up, squeezing my tits, massaging my butt. The men soon settled down to sucking my now fully erect nipples and someone – I didn't know who – had a finger up my ass. The fingers up my pussy, I soon discovered, belonged to Joe. I was wetter than I had ever been in my life before, as I took Joe's circumcised cock into my mouth and began to suck it, whilst I took Fred's uncircumcised cock in my right hand and began to jerk him off. Joe found my clit with consummate ease, and in no time I was writhing on the bed and moaning with ecstasy at my first orgasm of the evening. Joe had his tongue halfway down my throat by now, and I could feel Fred applying K-Y jelly to my asshole, so I knew what I was in for there. And then, as Fred spread my ass cheeks and began slowly to ease his huge schlong up my asshole, Joe swivelled around, his cock once more in my mouth, and got himself into a position where he could eat my pussy whilst I sucked him off.

Since Fred's cock by this time was all the way up my asshole, my right hand was free, and I began to jerk off Joe's cock at the same time as I sucked him. In no time at all, he exploded into my mouth, and I had the truly sensual pleasure, for the first time ever, of swallowing the hot come of someone other than my husband. This excitement, plus Joe's expertise at eating me out, brought on my second orgasm of the evening. Seconds later, Fred spurted his hot seed violently up my asshole, increasing the intensity of my orgasm tenfold, and then all three of us were, for the moment, sexually replete. We all disentangled ourselves, the one from the other, and took time out for a short break. Fred went off to the bathroom to wash his cock. I got up and went through to the sitting room, where I freshened up our drinks and took them through to the bedroom. Quite soon, the men finished their drinks and turned their attention back to me.

Fred seemed in a generous frame of mind, and was obviously allowing Joe, as our mutual guest, the first choice of whichever orifice in my body appealed the most to him. He chose my pussy, and decided that he would like to fuck me doggy fashion. I consequently knelt on all fours, thrusting my ass up in the air and offering it to him. He grabbed me around my waist, thrust himself into me, and began to fuck me enthusiastically. This particular position didn't leave a lot of opportunities available for Fred, so I suggested that he lay on his back, his cock stiffly erect beneath my face, and allowed me to suck him and jerk him off. This he seemed happy enough to succumb to, and for a while I maintained that position, one very large schlong fucking my pussy from the rear, whilst I masturbated the other one into my mouth, and sucked and licked it in my best fellatrice manner.

Your women readers will know that it is not easy to blow a large cock. Smaller ones are much easier. A cock that stretches your mouth to its limits doesn't leave a great deal of room for subtle use of your lips or tongue. Which is why, with both Fred and Joe, I used my fingers as well. It is, in my opinion, the only occasion in sexual games where a girl would prefer to work on a smaller cock. Joe was doing a great job fucking me from the rear, but this isn't the best position for any woman to be fucked from, simply because, in that position, contact between the man's cock and the woman's clitoris is minimal. Consequently – since my own right hand was busy with Fred's cock – I looked over my shoulder at Joe and said, 'Play with my clit, baby, please.'

I'm pleased to be able to tell you that it was no sooner said than done. He knew exactly where my clit was, and precisely what to do with it, and within seconds I was enjoying yet another orgasm. My vaginal contractions brought on Joe's ejaculation, and whilst all this was happening, I increased my masturbation of Fred to such a speed that he immediately shot his hot semen into my mouth and, once more, all three of us were satisfied. We went on for some time after that. The novelty of the situation for all three of us excited and stimulated our sexual responses far beyond what was normal, and the man kept changing places and orifices, until I finally fell asleep, exhausted but happy. When I awoke the following morning, Joe had gone, and we haven't tried to contact him since (nor he us). But I continue to thank Fred – nightly – for the greatest birthday present ever. And I have made up my mind that when his birthday arrives, in approximately three months' time, I shall return the compliment and have a threesome set up for him, this time with me and another girl! The youngest, prettiest girl I can find.

R. C. New York, New York.

Wish him 'Happy' Birthday from us.

TYING ONE ON

Although I'm a one hundred per cent dyed-in-the-wool male submissive, bondage and humiliation are not exactly my wife's favourite bag. She's frankly a straight-up-and-down, like-mum-and-dad girl. But, happily, she loves me enough, and is broad-minded enough, to indulge me on occasions. I particularly enjoy it when, to punish me, she forces me to eat her pussy for long periods. Last weekend, she told me that she was pretty pissed off with my behaviour generally, and that she was going to punish me. She ordered me into our bedroom and ordered me to strip. She then ordered me to lie on the bed on my back. When I had obeyed, she blindfolded me and then bound my wrists and ankles to the four corners of the bed frame. For a while, I could see and hear nothing, and the next thing that I knew was when she started pinching my nipples into nipple clamps. She screwed them down hard, and they were quite seriously painful so I soon had a rock-hard erection. Then I felt her undo the bindings on my wrists and ankles: she ordered me to turn over and lie on my stomach, after which she tied me up again. There was silence again for a while, and then I heard a *swish*, and almost at the same time I felt the burning sting of a cane across my buttocks. Then she began to cane me properly, *thwack* after *thwack* landing on my backside until I was crying out in pain. But I loved every minute of it. My wife asked me if I wanted her to stop, but I said 'No', and she continued thrashing me until I was pleading for mercy. Finally she stopped and undid my blindfold. She then took my painfully erect penis in her hand

and quickly masturbated me to the best climax I can remember having. When it was all over, I thanked her, humbly, and she told me to watch my step in future, or she'd have to punish me again very soon.

J. T. H. Limerick, Republic of Ireland.

You're bound to be pleased, you might say.

NAUGHTY KNICKERS

As I grew up, all the way through boarding school (Cheltenham Ladies' College) and university (London University) I thought that I was a fairly normal young woman. I started having sex when I was nineteen, which was about when most of my contemporaries started doing the same thing. And up until then, I had worn the kind of underclothes that were practical, rather than sexy. You know the kind of thing? I mean, plain cotton Sloggis. Practical. Comfortable. Plain colours. Reasonably priced. Easy to launder. All of those things. And then, one evening, in a pub off Gower Street much used by university students, I met David. David is a university lecturer, and is thirty-four and married, with three children. He is also cock-happy (perhaps *cunt*-happy is a more accurate description) and fucks everything in sight, given half a chance. I was delighted to give him all the chances he needed, for I found him amusing company, great in bed, and his wife and family were his problem, not mine.

He was teaching European Politics, which I wasn't taking, so we didn't have a problem there. He was – to me – innovative in bed and quite an appreciative, gentle lover. On about our third week together, we got back to my furnished room in Belsize Park after a few at the Haverstock Arms, down the road, and he produced a small parcel. He was stripping off as I unwrapped it, and he got into my bed preceded by the most enormous erection. I was dying to follow him and take it in my mouth, but I felt duty bound to open the present. Which I did, to find inside two pairs of what looked like extremely expensive, pure silk, very lacy, beautifully embroidered knickers. The kind rich men buy in Harvey Nichols, in Knightsbridge, for their mistresses (which, I have always believed, is why everyone calls them Harvey Knicks). One pair was primrose yellow, the other a bright royal blue.

'Darling,' I said. 'They're really beautiful. Thank you.' 'Put them on, sweetheart,' he said, 'and come to bed. My pleasure is in taking them off. Eventually.' I didn't know what he meant by that 'eventually', but I very soon found out. I put the pale yellow pair on. They felt fantastic, and the rub of the soft silk against my pussy was highly erotic. I was very touched. In more ways than one! As I got into bed with David, he threw back the covers, the better to get at that which he wanted to get at. Spreading my legs, he buried his face between them, and began to suck my pussy through the soft silk of the knickers. It was a delightfully sexy feeling, and as he sucked me I took hold of that magnificent erection and returned the compliment. David sucked and licked and tongued as if he had never put his head between my legs before. (He had. Often!) The sensation seemed that much improved by being strained, as it were, through the expensively silky material.

He next gripped my buttocks, one in each hand, and pulled my whole groin up that much harder against his mouth, until I came in an enormous, almighty orgasm that racked my whole body, down to my very toes. It was, for me, the best oral sex ever.

Finally, he started to ease the new knickers down my legs, very slowly, obviously enjoying what it was doing for his libido. He finally pulled them off over my ankles and, instead of dropping them on the floor, as I expected, he pressed the crotch of them – where they were now quite sodden, by a mixture of his saliva and my pussy juices – against his nose. He then breathed in an enormously deep breath which he held for a while and then let out, very slowly. 'Mmmm,' he said. 'My favourite perfume. Wet pussy. Do you mind if I take these away with me when I go?' I thought for a moment. Why on earth would he want to take away a pair of knickers that he had just given me? I couldn't think of an answer. 'Sure, baby, if that's what you would like to do,' I told him. 'But why?' He grinned at me. 'So I can keep them in a drawer in my office and, when I'm on my own, I can take them out and sniff the scent of your wet little pussy and toss myself off while I think about you,' he said. 'OK?' I had to laugh. He was so up front. 'That's quite a compliment, if I think about it,' I told him. 'Now fuck me. Please.' Looking back, I now know that David was particularly well endowed, but after the oral session through the crotch of my new knickers, he seemed even larger than usual, and he fucked me to a standstill.

I did my best for him too, his excitement creating excitement in me. I wrapped my legs around his back and crossed them, and then I locked them together, pulling him down hard onto me as he fucked me into oblivion. I fell asleep after this excellent performance and when I awoke, David had gone. Back to his wife and family, presumably. The pale yellow knickers had gone too. But I still had the royal blue pair.

David rang me the following evening and arranged to meet me at the Haverstock Arms once more. He arrived breathing heavily and couldn't get his drink down quickly enough before he asked me, 'Are you wearing the blue knickers?' 'No, darling,' I told him. And then, when his face dissolved into what I can only describe as a caricature of disappointment, I said, 'I'm not wearing any knickers at all. And my pussy is so wet that the liquid is running down my thighs. Does that make you feel happier?' I swear he walked the short distance from the pub to my rooming house on three legs. When we got there, I stripped off at high speed and lay on my back, my legs apart, and then I waited, patiently, while he took his clothes off. 'I'm so wet, baby,' I told him. 'Why don't you lick me dry? I'd like that.' He buried his head between my legs once more and sucked and licked until I think I was even wetter than when he started, but we both enjoyed what he was doing. He loved the taste and smell of pussy juice and was always telling me that he couldn't get enough of it. I was feeling lazy that evening, and enjoying just lying there being sucked, so I didn't suck him, I just took hold of his erect cock and wanked it slowly as he sucked me. I had a number of orgasms before David stopped sucking me and, kneeling up, urgently thrust his stiff cock up my pussy and gave me a very serious seeing-to. All this, and I've still got the royal blue knickers in reserve. Aren't I the lucky one?

K. G. Belsize Village, London.

Sounds like you're taking him for a sucker. . . No, seriously, yes, you are *a lucky girl. And David is a lucky guy.*

GOING PUBLIC

My particular bag has always been sex in public places. Not always necessarily out in the open. Last week, for example, I was with my boyfriend in a Mexican restaurant in Soho. I guess we'll never be able to go *there* again. We were enjoying our food, and our conversation, which was getting more and more blatantly sexy until we were both about as horny as could be, and I said to my boyfriend, why not? Moments later, we were locked into the restaurant's only lavatory – it served both men and women – fucking like rabbits. There wasn't a lot of room, but it *was* a lot of fun. The thought of being caught by a member of the restaurant staff added spice to the occasion. It was all over almost as soon as it started, we were so hot when we began, but we both came long and strong, and together. It was the best fuck all week. What we didn't know was that all four of the restaurant's waiters were lined up in the passage outside, listening to the urgent sounds of our sex. As we opened the door, intending to sneak back to our table, they all four gave us a round of applause.

We have fucked on the landings of the emergency stairs at Underground stations. The excitement of wondering whether or not we'll get caught by someone who uses the stairs, rather than the lifts, makes up for the discomfort of what inevitably has to be a knee-trembler.

We *have* been passed by other people. Twice. On both occasions, they pretended that we weren't there. We've never fucked in a public telephone box, considering them far too obvious. Everyone and anyone who has nowhere to go uses telephone boxes. We try to be more creative. Museums and art galleries are fun, although you have to keep an ear cocked for the attendants who tend to creep about, looking for people who are misbehaving. We haven't actually been caught (yet!) but I *have* been in a situation where I've had to hold my handkerchief over my boyfriend's ejaculating penis at the moment of truth and pretend to be kissing him in order to disguise what we were really doing, due to the unexpected arrival of an attendant in one of the galleries at the Victoria and Albert Museum. The National Portrait Gallery is a favourite place. It has a myriad smaller rooms – particularly on its upper floors – where members of the public seldom seem to venture. Even the attendants rarely patrol up there.

Hyde Park, Kensington Gardens, and the gardens in various inner London squares are all good places in the summer, except for the facts that, one, they tend to become rather overcrowded with other couples doing the same thing, and two, these days, they get very full of vagrants, alcoholics, the homeless, and other unfortunates. Some of the upper floors of the Festival Hall, in the mornings, are good places for public copulation, but they're obviously non-starters in the evenings. Women's changing rooms in West End stores are both exciting and challenging, but you need to be extremely careful. The basement of C&A at Marble Arch is an excellent and less challenging venue than many of the grander stores. Big, expensive hotels, like the Savoy, for example, or the Ritz, offer excellent opportunities, if you know your way around. After years of arranging private functions in West End hotels, I know where all the smaller function rooms are. It's easy enough to see whether or not they are in use, since this fact is always displayed publicly, usually in the reception area. The older hotels are the best, because of their old-fashioned buildings. Places like the London Hilton, in Park Lane, are useless, due to their contemporary design.

The Serpentine, in Hyde Park, is an excellent place, again in the summer, provided that you enjoy underwater sex. The girl has to wear a bikini, enabling her to stand in the water up to her waist, and pull her bikini bottom down. The man, of course, simply pulls down his trunks, and *voilà*, you're in business. (It always reminds me of Fatty Arbuckle, the old Hollywood silent-movie actor, who ruined his career by allegedly raping a teenage girl with a champagne bottle. As an alcoholic, he was vehemently against drinking water. 'Fish fuck in it,' was his loudly proclaimed objection to its assimilation.) Come summertime, I now feel a common bond with the Serpentine's fishy inhabitants.

I've heard tales about sex on aeroplanes. Who hasn't? The Mile High Club, and all that. But despite a considerable amount of flying, both within the UK and overseas, with and without partners on the flights, I have never made out on a plane. I've been masturbated to a climax, beneath the cover of a blanket, and have returned the compliment. I have given blow jobs, on more than one occasion, in similar circumstances. But I have never enjoyed cunnilingus or full sex on an aeroplane, ever. Sadly.

But my favourite venue of all is almost any box at the Royal Albert Hall. During a concert, of course. One can indulge in sex of most kinds in most theatre boxes. From mutual masturbation whilst apparently sitting up, paying attention to whatever is going on upon the stage, to abandoning the performance and giving one of one's own on the floor of the box. I have done both, and everything in between. I have knelt between the open knees of my lover as he sits up at the front of the box and given him a fine blow job. I have then changed places with him and been handsomely sucked off as I sit there, my long, evening skirt bunched around my waist, my knickers around my ankles, and my lover's tongue up my pussy. Delightful! One does need to be very careful about not making the kind of noises that one usually makes when achieving orgasm. It can be very distracting for the actors upon the stage. I know. I've moaned out loud whilst being sucked off at the theatre. All I could do was to try and turn it into an apologetic cough. I think I succeeded.

One needs to be careful too with one's timing when indulging sexually in theatre boxes. One has to be certain that the lights aren't going to come up for an interval, to reveal to those seated in the circle, and in boxes in higher tiers, oneself with one's legs spread wide, one's skirts about one's waist, and one's lover shafting away enthusiastically. I did that once, to my intense embarrassment. But I *did* get a round of applause from those able to see what was going on!

P. V. Battersea, London.

Are you offering shares?

NOTHING BARRED

Bars are probably more popular today than at any time in our history. They are even more popular now – and there are more of them now – than in the so-called Swinging Sixties. Since I'm a professional barman, that's got to be good for me. I wonder if I've ever served you? If I have, all you would remember is that you got your drink – or drinks – quickly, efficiently, and with polite pleasure. I love my job. But one thing you probably don't know about barmen is that, by and large, we get more pussy than our male customers. Does that surprise you? It happens to be true. How? It's simple, really. When you work behind a bar, you can't get away from it. So you're at the beck and call of anyone who cares to pull up a barstool and engage you in conversation. Male or female. And you would be amazed to know how many pretty girls are stood up in any bar on a given evening.

When they first come in, they won't even talk to you. They order a drink, and keep themselves to themselves. When they start looking at their watches, you know that their partner is late. When they start checking the time with you, you know that they're *very* late. And many of them stick it out to the bitter end. They can't actually believe that they've been stood up. So, by the time the bar closes, the chances are that they've absorbed far more booze than is their normal custom. They're angry. And they're maybe a little drunk. And they're feeling a combination of disappointed and randy. Over the course of the evening, the barman – provided that he's polite and sympathetic – becomes more and more attractive to them.

If not physically, at least emotionally, in terms of being pleasant. A friend in need. And then, at the end of the evening, if handled carefully, these girls are anybody's.

I'm the head barman in a bar just off Curzon Street, in the West End of London. Being head barman gives me priority over any of the other bar staff with any spare crumpet that may be around. It's an expensive bar, and the male customers are mostly well-to-do businessmen, with a sprinkling of show-business people. Actors and actresses. TV people. Publishers. That sort of thing. And the young, single girls who meet their dates there are mostly what we used to call good-time girls. They're not on the game. Not really. But they like money, and luxury, and being taken to expensive restaurants, and then on to a casino, maybe. Or to a fashionable nightclub or discotheque. After which, they're usually more than ready to drop their panties.

One or two of them are probably actual mistresses, and I exclude them from this conversation. They are, at the very least, having their rent paid, and are almost certainly given a living allowance. If they're stood up, they know that it's part of the arrangement. Perhaps their boyfriend's wife arrived unexpectedly at the office, just as he was about to leave to meet his mistress. They aren't going to fuck any barman, anywhere. It would be more than their job's worth. But the rest of them, by the time they've downed half a dozen champagne cocktails, or gin-and-tonics, they're probably raring to go. You have to approach them carefully. 'I'm afraid we're going to close in ten minutes, miss. May I order you a taxi?' One last look at their watch, and a cross little voice, covered up quickly by a painfully forced smile, says, 'Yes, please.' You wait until the bar is actually closed and then, 'Where shall I ask the taxi to take you, miss?' They usually say somewhere or other in the West End or nearby. Living close to the action is vital with these girls. Wherever it is, (provided that it isn't a million miles away) you say, 'Actually, miss, I've got my car outside, and I'm passing through X on my way home. May I offer you a lift?' The thought of saving the cab fare, plus having some company on the drive home, usually appeals.

Along the way to Bayswater, or Maida Vale, or the Edgware Road, or wherever, the chances are that they'll lean against you, and put their head on your shoulder, and tell you how unhappy they are. You're full of sympathy, of course. When you get to the block of flats (it's always a block of flats: it's the anonymity that appeals) you say, 'Hang on a minute, miss. I'll just see you to your door. It's much too late for you to be out on the streets by yourself at this time of night.'

You say this even if all she's got to do is cross the pavement from the car. They always accept. Who wouldn't? And you make certain that you accompany them all the way up to whatever floor it is that their flat is on and stand there while they unlock the front door. After which, they will always turn round to give you a thank-you kiss. This is where you take the only chance that you take all evening. You grab them and kiss them back. Hard. What the hell. You've got nothing to lose. They're never going to tell their boyfriend, your customer, back at the bar. It's almost guaranteed, I tell you. And the moment they start kissing you back, you slide them inside the door, close it behind you, and slip your fingers up their skirts and into their panties. Some of them have strange ideas about sexual loyalty. 'I've never been unfaithful to X,' they say. 'I love him. So you can't fuck me. But you can suck my pussy while I suck you off/give you a wank.' None of which I ever refuse. Would you?

Last night's was called Caroline. I've seen her in the bar a good few times, and she's always been nice to me. She seems to be in there usually with different men each time, rather than with the same one all the while. Last night was the first time that I've known her to be stood up. I've always fancied her, so I kept refilling her glass – she was drinking white-wine spritzers – without charging her. It's easy enough to do in a largely cash bar, if you know your way around. Which, of course, I do. Caroline chatted to me all evening, and so I didn't bother with the taxi spiel. I simply offered her a lift, which she accepted with alacrity. As soon as we drew away from the pavement outside the bar, she had one arm around my neck and the other one was unzipping my trousers. She put her hand inside and began to squeeze and pull my dick. She didn't actually take it out of my trousers, but she said, 'Are you going to come in for a drink, when we get there?'

Not fucking half, I thought. 'Thank you, miss,' I said, all respectful-like. I had to concentrate so as not to come in her hand as I was driving her home. It's not that often that I have a twenty-year-old girl playing with my cock as I drive along. She lived in Ennismore Gardens, just off Kensington Gore, so we were there in no time. What with Caroline's hand on my dick and the sight of her short little skirt, which had ridden up, exposing her shapely thighs encased in shiny, nylon, flesh-coloured stockings – or tights, perhaps, I couldn't see *that* far up her legs – it was just as well it wasn't too far to drive. I found a parking space and as I locked up the car she opened the front door to one of those enormous old Edwardian houses that so elegantly grace that part of London. Inside, I could see that it had been divided up into flats – one flat per floor – and there was, thank God, a lift, since it turned out that Caroline lived on the top – the fifth – floor.

Caroline began stripping off as she got out of the lift. By the time she had unlocked the door to her flat and closed it behind us, she was down to what were now apparent as self-supporting, flesh-coloured shiny nylon stockings, a tiny pair of crimson bikini panties and that was it. Everything about her said, 'Fuck me.' My erection said, 'Any time.' As she disrobed, she simply dropped each item of clothing where she stood. 'Drink, darling?' she asked. I said 'Yes, thank you. I'd love a Scotch.' 'Ice?' she asked. 'No, thanks,' I said. 'I'm so wet,' she said, in the same tone of voice that she might have said, 'I'm so tired' or 'I'm so bored'. I couldn't think of anything to say.

'Do you like to suck pussy?' she asked, as she poured a generous scotch into a crystal tumbler. 'Do I,' I said, as she handed me the glass. She went out of the room, presumably into the kitchen, and came back with a matching crystal jug of water. 'Say when,' she said, as she poured water into my glass. 'When,' I said. She poured one for herself. 'Cheers,' she said, raising her glass. I raised mine back. 'Cheers,' I said. She might have been standing there fully dressed, such was the aplomb with which she was carrying on. 'So,' she said, having taken a long pull at her glass. I hoped that it wouldn't react badly with all the white-wine spritzers she'd been drinking. 'You like to suck pussy, mmmm? But how about sucking *wet* pussy? Does that bother you? Mine's extremely wet, and getting wetter. It's telling me that it needs some of that lovely big cock I was playing with in the car on the way home shoved up it. But it needs sucking first. What do you say?' 'The wetter, the better,' I told her, sincerely. 'I love the taste of pussy. It's like nectar to me.'

'Oh, great,' she said. 'Then we can start straightaway.' She put her glass down on a nearby table, selected a large easy chair with a moderately high seat, and said to me, 'Shall I take my knickers off, or is that something you would like to do? Some men get a great rush out of taking girls' knickers off.' 'I'd love to,' I said. 'It always excites me.'

She stood there, smiling at me, as I knelt in front of her, my nose just inches away from her scarlet-silk-covered snatch. I could see her wetness staining the crotch of her knickers, and I could see the shape of her outer labia moulded in the silken material. I reached out a finger and felt her between her legs. She felt fleshy and moist, even through the material. 'Mmmm,' she said, wriggling as I touched her up. 'Don't stop. I like it.' I love girls with big, fleshy pussies. The kind that fill your mouth when you suck them. 'Hang on a second,' I said, and I stood up and almost literally tore my clothes off. She looked at my rampant cock. 'Oooh,' she said. 'Naughty. I like that too.' I knelt in front of her again, and, putting a hand on each side of the waistband of her knickers, I began to ease them down over her hips and buttocks, and then down her long thighs. I did it slowly, exposing first of all a thick expanse of soft, curly blonde pubic hair, obviously dyed to the same tint as that which crowned her head. Then, because I had been pressing my fingers into her snatch earlier on, through her knickers, I saw that the cotton-lined crotch was caught up inside her pussy, so that, although I was pulling them down, the gusset was reluctant to follow the rest of the garment. A truly sexual sight.

Reluctantly, I pulled a little harder, and the gusset slid out of her wet quim with a tiny sucking noise. I then slid her panties all the way down her long legs and held them as she stepped out of them. I caught a glimpse of elongated wet pussy lips, their interior aspect shining pinkly, and then she stepped back and sat down on the armchair that she had chosen. She spread her legs and lay back. 'It's all yours, baby,' she said. She put her fingers down and opened up her pussy, pulling her long outer lips apart. 'Feel free,' she said, and laughed. 'And kiss free, lick free, and suck free. And then we'll fuck free.'

It was only then that I realized that Caroline was just the littlest bit drunk. I hoped that she wouldn't have any regrets in the morning, but this wasn't my night for playing Goody Two-Shoes, putting her to bed and tucking her up carefully without taking advantage of her. I began to take advantage of her immediately. She smelled and tasted divine. She was patently no stranger to cunnilingus, and she obviously enjoyed it, from the writhing about and moaning and groaning noises that she was making. She began to orgasm almost immediately, and I don't believe that she stopped all the time that I was tonguing and sucking her. We both had a ball, for sucking pussy is seriously one of my favourite things. She was noisy with it too, shouting out from time to time things like 'Oh, my God, I'm coming again', and 'Oh, yes, baby. Oh, yes. I'm coming now. Oh, God', and then, finally, 'Oh, Jesus, fuck me, fuck me, fuck me'.

Jesus Himself not being to hand, I decided to stand in for Him. I rose, pulled Caroline up out of her chair, picked her up in my arms and carried her out of the lounge, looking for the bedroom. It wasn't far. The first door on the right, down the passageway. The only thing I noticed about the room as I entered was the king-size bed against the opposite wall as I went in. I laid her down on it. She opened her legs immediately and began playing with her pussy.

I always think that's one of the more stimulating sights, and I stood there for a little while, just enjoying watching her playing with herself. Caroline was a beautiful girl. She had full, firm young breasts, with small, dark pink nipples which right now were standing out, fully erect. Her stomach was flat, her hips narrow, her pudenda surprisingly generous, bearing in mind how slim she was everywhere else. I couldn't see her buttocks, since she was lying on them, but I had noticed, whilst she was walking about in the sitting room, that they were firm, taut and well-shaped. I wondered, for a moment, if she liked being fucked in the arse. She was clad only in her shiny nylon stockings . . .

I remembered why I was there. Because Caroline wanted to be fucked. Her fingers were still busy as I knelt between her legs. I watched her diligent digits for a few moments, whilst I could still keep my hands off her. She had her forefinger deep down inside herself, massaging her clitoris. Her eyes were closed and her mouth was open. Saliva was seeping from the corners of her mouth, in small trickles. She was breathing heavily, and she looked the epitome of fuckable female pleasure.

I took my cock in my right hand, used my left hand to pull her fingers away from her pussy, and thrust myself into her. 'Oh, my God,' Caroline said, opening her eyes in what looked like disbelief. 'That's what I've been waiting for. Cock. Seriously hard, rigid, beautiful, lovely cock. Hot cock.' She began to move her hips, slowly at first. She closed her eyes again. She sucked me into her vagina, and then she began to do wondrous things to me with her vaginal muscles. You've heard of pumping iron? This lady was pumping another kind of iron. My cock. I nearly died. From pleasure.

I began to try and return some of what she was doing for me. I thrust and withdrew. Thrust and withdrew. My cock really was hard, thanks to her, and it swelled even more within her tight, moist cunt, filling it completely. I grew inside her, distending her vagina, filling it, making it contract around my shaft, until, very quickly, she began to orgasm, her vagina contractions bringing on my ejaculation. And then we were both shouting, and gripping each other, and coming into each other, with loud, animal-like noises. 'Oh, yes,' she said. 'Oh, Jesus, yes. You're fucking me. You've got your huge cock up my cunt. You're fucking me. And I'm going to come. Now. Now. I'm going to come. Oh, JESUS. I'M COMING. NOW. YES. NOW. OH, GOD. YES. NOW. OH, FUCK. OH, JESUS. GOD, HELP ME. OH, YES. YES. YEEEEEEESSS.' After that we went on all night. She couldn't get enough, and I was sufficiently excited and more than happy to try and fulfil her needs. Happily, there were no regrets in the morning. Caroline is now on my regular fuck list. Maybe that will make some of you think before you jilt another young lady in a bar? But please don't change your habits.

P. W. Camden Town, London.

No holds barred, eh? Good luck.

TIGHT FIT

At the age of twenty-eight, I have – for some few years now – been secretly pleased that I'm the proud possessor of a large cock. I've never actually measured it, but all the girls whom I fuck tell me that it's the largest that they have ever had the pleasure of, if you follow me. They can't all be telling fibs. But recently, I have discovered that a large cock isn't always a good thing. You see, I've recently become a devotee of anal sex. And the one thing that most girls don't like up their tight little arseholes is a large cock. A lot of girls don't like *any* size of cock up their arse. But even those who *do* welcome a rear entry tend to be disapproving of a *very* large cock up there.

For me, the first time I was invited to ram my penis up a young lady's rectal passage I knew that this, sexually, was for me. I was in seventh heaven. But the young lady concerned spent most of the time that I was anally fucking her screaming, and she has never allowed me to repeat the event. So you can imagine my intense pleasure when, after work one day, I picked up a young Welsh girl in a bar near my office. She was what anyone would normally call petite. She was about five foot three or four, and with a small – but nicely shaped body. We got on well from my first approach and she happily accepted my invitation, at the end of the evening, to accompany me back to my place. All went as expected, but the interesting thing was that she began to show me some things about anal sex that were quite new to me. As is my wont, I began with a loving, caring, and quite intense session of pussy sucking. I love oral sex, and I find that, if one has brought about enough orgasms in a woman earlier on, then she is much more likely, later in the evening, to agree to anal sex. That's my experience, anyway.

This turned out to be the case on this particular evening, and Annabel (as was her name) was no exception to the general rule. When I gently suggested a little rear-entry sex, she was not only agreeable, she was actually ready, willing, and able. She had a gorgeously tiny, puckered, hairy little arsehole, and as I entered it, it seemed – to me – to be unusually pliable. As I looked at it, before I had even touched it, never mind attempted to enter it, she began to dilate it and then contract it. As I continued to watch, she went on with these exercises: each time she dilated it, her entry hole expanded and got larger, until she said, looking over her shoulder, 'OK, honey. It's ready for you now. It's all yours. Fuck me up my arsehole.'

As I slid into her, with the ease and pleasure of entering a well-lubricated cunt (none of the screaming and angst of my previous anal shafting experience) she began to open and close her sphincter muscle around my rampant cock until – it seemed like only seconds later but actually it was much longer than that – I shot my load up her beautifully tight little anus. We continued to fuck all that night, alternating between her cunt and her arsehole. At one stage, I was slipping in and out of the one, and then in and out of the other, switching backwards and forwards, until finally I spurted my come up her bottom. Her ability to open and close her anal sphincter was the most exciting thing, sexually, to happen to me in my entire lifetime.

S. P. A. Inverness, Scotland.

Sounds like you got to the bottom of the problem.

SHADOWS BETWEEN HER LEGS

I've always wanted to be a bondage girl. You know the kind of thing? Like the photo sets you see in girlie magazines sometimes. Tall girl (that's me) with long legs in black silk stockings. Held up by a black silk suspender belt. Very sexy. Patent leather 'fuck me' high-heeled pumps. Black knickers. Very *small* black knickers. And a studded leather collar around my neck. In the early pictures, my hands are bound behind my back, and there are shackles on my ankles, connected by a short length of chain. There are close-ups of my naked breasts. Close-ups of me peeling my knickers down, showing off my pubic hair. And in the final picture, on that page, I'm dropping my crumpled knickers on the floor by my feet. No cunt shots yet. Only pubes. Over the page, you get a terrific close-up of my arse. It's a lovely arse, if I say so myself. The kind where you want to pull my bum cheeks apart and ram your stiff cock up my darling anus. And then there's a tit shot, showing my erect nipples. Dead sexy. Next come close-ups of the crotch of my knickers, drawn tightly into my pussy, so that you can see the shape of my pussy lips beneath the silk. Then the camera pulls back and you see my crotch from further away, framed by the tops of my black silk stockings at the bottom of the picture, by my black suspender belt at the top, and by the long, thin, black suspenders running down my thighs at each side. Centrally, the photograph features (yes, you've got it!) my knicker-clad crotch.

In the next shot, I'm peeling the top of my tiny knickers down, revealing my pubic hair, and the final picture on that page is taken from my crotch looking up, with my breasts jutting out above, capped by my erect nipples, and my face smiling down from over the top of my breasts. There is no real continuity to these shots. For example, in twenty-four photographs spread over six pages there are pictures of me naked but for my stockings and suspender belt on the first page and pictures of me wearing my knickers on the final page. The only real interrelationship between the shots is the fact that each one is carefully chosen to raise your lust factor to the maximum. To make you want to reach out and touch me. Feel me. Lick me. Sniff me. Fuck me. Beat me, maybe. Subject me forcefully to your most degrading sexual needs. (I wish you were here with me right now.)

Over the page, I'm squatting on the floor on one knee, my legs apart, my other foot beneath my buttock. You can *almost* see my snatch, but not quite, because my pubic hair is long and thick. It needs parting to find that wet, pink gash that you want so badly. In the next shot – it's the first full-length shot of me since the opening picture – I'm shown standing, facing the camera. I'm naked from the waist up. My pretty breasts are thrust forward, and my hands are still bound behind my back, and the shackles and chain between my ankles are prominent in the photograph. I've got my knickers on again. The new thing in this shot is that there is a rope, running from somewhere unseen behind my back – presumably my wrists – down to the chain that is around my ankles. The effect of this rather short rope is that I am forced into a rather bent-over position.

It's all change in the next shot. This is of me from the waist up, and this time my wrists are bound up beside my face, by tight cords, tying me to some kind of crossbar behind me. The studded leather collar around my neck is very much in evidence in this picture, as is a peacock feather, the end of which is brushing against one of my nipples. My eyes are closed, as if in ecstasy. The adjoining picture is a close-up of the same feather. This time it is teasing my pussy.

And then, suddenly, everything comes together. The following shot is a whole-page picture of me sitting on the floor, my arms raised and bound behind my neck, my legs spread. My knicker-crotch has been pulled to one side, fully exposing my naked cunt for the first time. Standing behind me is a beautiful dominatrice, dressed much as I am but without the bondage gear. She is leaning over me, tickling my exposed cunt with the peacock's feather. I'm not certain, from the expression on my face, whether I'm showing pain or pleasure. Perhaps both. There are two smaller prints inset over the main photograph, one of which shows my hands handcuffed rather than bound with ropes, and a second one, which is a close-up of the dominatrice woman standing over my head, which is thrown back. I have my rigid tongue poking out of my mouth, just millimetres away from the woman's knicker-covered pussy. I am obviously about to lick her snatch through her panties. In the next shot, I am kneeling down, my buttocks to the camera and with my face buried between the dominatrice's legs. You can't actually see what I am doing, but I don't think I need to spell it out. You can see the top of my head, over my naked buttocks.

The rest of the shot is cropped tightly around my bottom, the centre of which features my extremely hairy anal cleft and my nakedly exposed anus. My tightly clenched dark-skinned anus is puckered, and shining wetly in the studio lighting. If the camera were a man, it would bugger me forthwith. In the final picture, I have a dog-lead attached to the studded collar around my neck, and I am being led off camera by the dominatrice, who is now fully dressed in an elegant, full-length evening dress. In my fantasy, she leads me off to a luxurious bedroom, next door to the studio, where she assists a handsome young dark-haired stranger to rape me in each orifice, a number of times over. She guides his huge weapon into me, masturbating him back to full erection when he has jetted his hot sperm up one or other of my entrances. She greases my rectum prior to his raping me anally and coats his huge tool for him slowly, with the same lubricant.

She makes up my face carefully, paying much attention to the colour and thickness of the lipstick that she uses on me, before he fucks my mouth, and she holds my head for him as he ejaculates his flood of semen down my throat. When it is finally all over, she performs cunnilingus upon me until I orgasm, and then she forces me to do it to her. I enjoy her sucking my pussy, but initially I resist doing the same to her and she whips me. It is extremely painful. She thrashes me and she goes on whipping me long after I have screamed out that yes, yes, I'll suck her pussy, just stop, please stop hurting me. She seems to enjoy causing me pain. When I finally get to suck her, I actually enjoy it. She tastes delicious. It's difficult to describe, but she tastes so *feminine*. And she smells so nice. A gentle fragrance, reminding me of some exotic tropical fruit.

When I make her come, I come myself, partly from sexual excitement at what I've done to her, partly because I want her to love me as much as I now love her. I wish I could turn these fantasies into reality. Are there any attractive young dominatrices out there who would take a willing, submissive female bondage freak and teach her what S&M is all about? But one thing is vital in any such arrangement: I have to get fucked at the end of it all. Up where, I don't mind. Preferably everywhere. Will somebody help me, please?

K. R. Belgravia, London.

Any offers? Sounds like a willing servant.

AMERICAN PIE

I'm from Miami. I was born and bred there. Florida may be known as the Sunshine State, but we don't really have that good a reputation any more, sadly. The state has been taken over by immigrants in recent years, that's for sure. But it still isn't a bad place to live, if you know your way around. The weather's mostly good. Why else do all you New Yorkers come down here in December/January? Not to mention retiring down here. But it's still a great place to pick up women. Let me tell you about it.

I was in one of the resort bars the other evening, and this archetypal hippy-type girl comes in. I mean, maybe she was a few years out of place, but she looked pretty good to me. I was sitting at a table when she came in and sat down at the bar. I was instantly attracted to her. I think it was her smile. And so I went and asked her if she minded if I sat next to her. 'No, honey,' she said. 'Why should I? Tell me your name.' I told her it was Vince, and she told me hers was Jessie. Lovely old-fashioned name, isn't it? Biblical, almost. At first she told me that she was a dancer. It turned out, in fact, that she was a stripper, on her day off. She had a small apartment near by, and she felt like a little company, she said, So here she was. My good fortune, I told her. She laughed.

To cut a long story short, we ended up back at her place. She got out this sensational grass and we both got pretty ripped. Then, after a while, she asked me if I would like her to strip for me, and of course I said yes. Please. So she disappeared into the bedroom and came back about ten minutes later, wearing this amazing tasselled silver-and-white bikini. It put a whole different aspect on her body, which had looked pretty good to me before. Now it looked sensational. Then she put on a record. You know the kind of thing. The sort of music that strippers strip to. And she did a strip for me. My own show. Fantastic. She did some real dirty bits, too. Like she came up to me, just after she'd taken her panties off, stood right in front of me, stuck her fingers up her pussy, waggled them around – and then stuck her fingers in my mouth. To my intense pleasure, I have to tell you. And then she did that bit that all strippers do, where they turn their backs on you, and bend down, and stick their ass up in the air in your direction, and wriggle it about. Only when Jessie did it, she did it about two feet in front of me, allowing me to peer up (or maybe that should be down) the crack in her ass, including her asshole. I'll swear it winked at me. I sat there with the biggest hard-on I think I've ever had. I had to control myself, not to start jerking off while I was watching her. I only just managed not to.

She was a big girl. Bit tits. Big ass. Big pussy. All in proportion, but *big*. Lovely. When she finished, she was sitting on the floor, her legs spread wide, holding her ankles up above her head. Her hairy beaver was split, and I could see the pink of her cunt. It looked very wet. She held that pose for a few moments, and then she relaxed. 'Well, that's the audition, honey,' she said. 'Do I get the position?' I told her that she could have any position she wanted with me, and which one would she like to start with?

'On my back, baby,' she said. 'I love an old-fashioned fuck. I so rarely get one these days. Everybody wants you to be an acrobat, or a contortionist.' She stood up, stark naked as she was, and came over to where I was sitting on a sofa. She leaned forward and unzipped my fly. She then pulled out my cock. 'Mmmm,' she said. 'I think it's got something on its mind.' It was standing up, fully erect, doing me proud.

'Perhaps this will help it,' she said. She knelt on the floor in front of me and took me into her mouth. She gave sensational head. The best I've ever had. When I came, she kept me in her mouth and swallowed everything I could shoot into her. When I'd finished, she took me out of her mouth and said, 'I always like to start off like that because, first of all, I love to suck cock. And secondly, it guarantees me a better fuck. No one's in any kind of a hurry.' There was no way I could argue with that.

We went into the bedroom, got onto the bed, and I began to suck her vulva. It was really big and fleshy. She started moaning and groaning and came very quickly, after which I simply pushed her down onto her back and fucked her as hard as I knew how. She shouted out loud as she came again, and she kept on coming, more and more strongly, until eventually I came with her and shot my jism into her once more. But this time up her pussy, rather than down her throat. 'Oh, baby,' she said, as I shot my load up her. 'I can feel your hot spunk shooting up me. Oh, God, that's good.' And so on. We spent the night fucking and sucking, interspersed with smoking grass, and by the morning, we were both fucked out. Finished. I mean, *out* of it.

By that time I had fucked her, sucked her, had anal sex with her, and masturbated her. She had fucked me, fellated me, and masturbated me. We'd both had a great time. I left at midday the next day. We exchanged telephone numbers, and since then I've been round to her three times, and she's been to my place twice, in about three weeks. As far as I'm concerned, Florida is the place to be. And Jessie is the lady to be with. Who needs New York?

R. H. L. Fort Lauderdale, Florida.

Who indeed? It sounds as if you've asset-stripped parts of Florida pretty thoroughly. But it's a big state. Enjoy.

HOT TO TROT

I'm single, female, and twenty-three. I love to look at the girl sets in your raunchy magazine, and I get really hot looking at some of them. Since I have no man about the house at the moment, I'm left to handle my own sex these days, if you follow me. I dreamed last night that I was one of the girls in your magazine, and I don't ever remember being so sexually excited. Would you like to hear about it? You would? Good. At the beginning of my dream, I was stopped in the street here in Chichester by an attractive young man, who introduced himself as a photographer (although he didn't, at that stage, say what *kind* of photographer). He asked me if I had ever considered being a model, and, quite frankly, I thought it was all simply down to an attempted pick-up. However, he gave me his card, with your editorial number on it, and – to my surprise – he checked out. I telephoned him back after a few days, and he invited me round to his studio for a glass of wine and a chat. With no commitment on either side. When I got there, I was pleasantly surprised at both the amount of equipment in his studio and the sophistication of some of it, when he explained to me what one or two of the items did. (All this before I'd even *thought* about *his* equipment!) After a pleasant conversation I came away, having agreed to go back a couple of days later to do some test shots. It had been agreed that we would both make up our minds about progressing further – or not – when we saw the results of this photographic shoot. I dreamed that I arrived feeling good on the morning of the day arranged for the shoot. I'd had my hair cut and set, and had a massage, which had made me feel relaxed. At home, first thing, before I left, I'd wallowed in a long, luxurious bath, and after that I had shaved my pubic hair, as I normally do. (This is true in real life, as well as in my dream. I find that men like girls with shaven pudenda. It excites them sexually, although I'm not certain exactly why).

Tony (that was the photographer's name) seemed pleased to see me, and gave me coffee and biscuits when I had taken off my coat. He pointed to a screen over at the far end of the studio. 'Will you go and undress, please, sweetheart?' he said. 'We need to allow the elastic marks on your thighs and bottom to wear off before we can take any photographs. So if you'll strip off now . . . You'll find a robe hanging up behind the screen to put on.' I'd never thought about elastic marks on my flesh, but he was right, of course. I don't wear a bra, so marks on my breasts weren't a problem.

When I got back to where Tony was, he was looking at a selection of underwear. A lot of it was very exotic. Tart's knickers, I'd call them. But he held up a pair of plain grey cotton knickers for me to look at. Made by Benetton, as I remember. They had just a hint of cotton lace around the edges. 'Do you like these, sweetie?' he asked me. 'I think the grey will go nicely with your tan, and this ribbed cotton clings well. Fits around all the interesting places.' He grinned at me, and I laughed with him, thinking about the only place where knickers can cling. 'Yes, they're neat,' I said. 'I like them. I like simple underwear.' Tony next produced a pair of white stockings. 'I think just the knicks and the stockings,' he said. 'That's all we need. Slip the robe off for a moment, sweetie, and let's see if there's anything we need to cover up.' I took off the robe, and Tony walked around me, examining me closely. 'Mmmm,' he said. 'Pretty tits.' 'Thank you, kind sir,' I said, and bobbed a pretend curtsey. 'Oh, don't mind me,' he said. 'I don't mean to be rude. It's just how I react.

It's my job, you see.' He smiled at me again. 'No,' he said, finally. 'Not a blemish in sight.' Just then the doorbell rang, and Tony went and let in a young woman who smiled at me when she saw me. 'This is Angie,' said Tony. We shook hands. 'Angie will do your hair and make-up,' Tony told me. 'After which we should be ready to go.' Angie pointed to a chair in front of a mirror over in a corner of the studio. 'Shall we go over there?' she suggested.

I went and sat myself down, and Angie began to do my make-up. She did my face first, and then surprised me by asking me to take off my robe. It makes sense, of course, if you think about it, that if you're taking pictures of a nude body, then the body needs making-up too. She powdered me thoroughly, all over, and then surprised me again by anointing my nipples and areolae with a brownish-pink lip colour. I was faintly embarrassed to see my nipples stiffen up under her attentions, but neither of us said anything. I guess she was accustomed to it.

Then she did my hair, in a fairly loose, casual style, and just before she finished she picked up my hand and looked at my nails. I stood up while she did that, and she looked at me and smiled. 'They're fine,' she said. 'Is this your first nude modelling session?' I had to admit that it was. 'Good luck, then,' she said. 'I'll be off now. That should last you through the session all right.' 'Thanks,' I said. 'Good to meet you.' Angie called over to Tony: 'She's all yours now, Tony. I'm off. See you Tuesday.' 'Thank you, darling,' he called back. 'See you then.' He looked over at me. 'OK, sweetie,' he said, 'let's go.' I walked over to him. He had constructed a fairly simple set, consisting of a rather pretty Victorian *chaise longue* covered in a pale-yellow, patterned, heavy silk material, standing in front of a plain, dark red velvet wall hanging.

'We'll do the nude shots first, now that your knicker lines have disappeared,' he said. 'And then we'll do the knicker-

and-stocking shots after that. OK?' 'Fine,' I said. 'Just tell me what you want me to do.' 'Sure,' he said. 'First of all, just sit on the *chaise longue* and think pretty thoughts.' I did as he asked and he moved about me, using a hand-held Pentax camera. After a while he said, 'Now, sweetie, if you'll just move around a bit. You know, change your position. Just keep moving. I'll tell you when to hold it.' Again I did as I was asked, and as the time passed, I began to relax, and then, eventually, to actually enjoy it.

Tony kept saying things like 'That's good, sweetie', 'Hold it right there,' 'Just move your head a tiny bit to the right', 'Smile now, darling', 'Open your legs a bit more', 'Can you take a deep breath, and hold it?' and so on. From time to time he would rearrange me completely, like having me kneel over the *chaise longue* rather than sit on it, and when that happened, I was conscious that he was taking close-ups of my anus. 'Just put your hands behind you, and hold onto your buttocks,' he said, at one stage. And then, 'Now pull your cheeks apart. Yes, that's it. Lovely. Oh, yes. Terrific.' I was embarrassed because, although I shave my pubes, I've got a very hairy anal area. It's simply that I can't get at it myself. Not with a razor, anyway. And because my pussy is so smooth, it makes my entire anal area look even more coarsely hirsute. But Tony didn't say anything, so I guess that was OK with him.

And speaking of being embarrassed, I spent most of the shoot being embarrassed, one way or another. For example, after Tony had told me to take a deep breath, and hold it, he said, 'Hang on there a second, will you?' and went away into the kitchen, off the far end of the studio. When he came back, he had some ice cubes on a saucer. 'Just rub your nipples with these, darling,' he said. 'The ice will make them nice and erect.'

I remembered how erect they had been when Angie had

been putting lip colour on them, and I had to admit that they certainly weren't erect now. I felt a real failure. But the ice cubes did the trick. Instantly. And from then on, Tony just handed me the saucer of ice cubes whenever he wanted my nipples to stand out. But my main embarrassment was that when Tony started doing close-ups of my pussy, he used a different camera from the Pentax. He used a rather bigger camera, on a tripod. I could see the name Hasselblad across the top of it. It wasn't the camera that embarrassed me, it was the fact that the more he focused on my pussy, the wetter I could feel myself getting. Eventually I could feel my sexual lubrication beginning to trickle down my thighs and, blushing madly, I said to Tony, 'Can you hang on a second, while I just go to the bathroom and wipe myself? I don't know why, but I'm getting rather wet.' 'Wipe yourself, darling?' he said. 'Don't be silly. It's gorgeous. The punters'll love it. They'll all be wanking themselves silly at the sight of it. Get as wet as you like. It's good for business.' So I stayed where I was. Eventually, Tony decided that he had run the gamut of nude shots, and he asked me to put on the gray cotton knickers and the white cotton stockings with the lacy tops.

This time, I *did* go off and mop myself up. I wasn't just wet. I was horny. Seriously horny. Well, think about it. I'd been lying around stark naked in front of an attractive young man who had spent the entire time we'd been together focusing his cameras on my tits, my arse and my cunt. Now what would *you* think about, whilst you were doing that? That's right. And so did I. When I'd dried myself off and put on the knickers and stockings – which were of the self-supporting kind – I made my way back to the set and we started off again.

We repeated pretty much what we had been doing up until now, with the difference that, this time, in each picture I was either putting on or taking off the knickers and stockings.

There were what I now began to realize were the inevitable open-leg shots, with Tony homing in on my crotch, now covered with grey ribbed cotton. As he had quite correctly put it at the start of the day, the ribbed cotton clung beautifully. To my pussy. I couldn't see myself down there, of course, but putting my fingers down to feel the material stretched so tautly across my pussy, I could feel the lips of my outer labia clearly outlined in the thin fabric. And to continue my almost non-stop embarrassment, I could also feel how wet the material had become. 'Oh, great,' said Tony, cutting across my reverie. Startled, I pulled my hand away from my crotch. 'Oh, no,' said Tony. 'That's what I was appreciating. Your hand on your twat. Put it back. Please.' *Twat*, I thought. *How delicate. How feminine. How intensely romantic.* But I did as I was told, and put my fingers back down there. 'Oh, yes,' said Tony. 'Put your forefinger down, as if you were playing with yourself.'

I wasn't at all sure that I wanted to have pictures of me taken looking as if I was playing with myself, but who was I to argue? And as far as I knew, I had the right of veto if I didn't like what I saw when the pictures were developed. I put my forefinger down, found my outer lips, and pressed my finger firmly between them so that the outline of what I was doing would show clearly through the ribbed cotton. 'Oh, yes,' said Tony. 'I like it. Keep still. Don't move. Oh, yes.' As he was speaking, he was moving around me, once more with the hand-held camera. He was using the motor, and the camera was going *click, buzz, click, buzz, click, buzz* as he worked. At one stage he got me into quite a complicated position. I was sitting down on the *chaise longue*, with stockings on but no knickers. My legs were together and I had my arms around my knees as if I was hugging them, and my thighs were raised off the seat.

If you can imagine that position, then you will instantly

see that my naked pussy was completely exposed and, as you will have realized before I spell it out to you, that was where Tony's camera was duly focused. After a while, I began to look at his crotch, to see if any of my more raunchy poses – the ones where he was shooting close-ups of my pussy, or my anus – were having any effect at all upon his cock. But no. There wasn't – as far as I could see – the slightest suggestion of an erection.

I began to worry about whether or not I was going to get laid before I went home. It was becoming a matter of some urgency. I didn't fancy going home and getting out my bloody vibrator yet again. Here I was with a real live male only inches away. He could see absolutely everything that was on offer. Didn't he find me attractive? He must have done, or he wouldn't have asked me to model for him in the first place. He didn't *look* gay. But you never can tell. But even that was all right. If he wanted to bugger me, I was more than happy to offer him my bottom. I looked at him, trying hard to read what was going on in his mind.

Right at that moment, he stood back from both me and his cameras. 'I guess that's about it, baby,' he said. 'Thank you. I reckon we've got some pretty good stuff here. I find it difficult to believe that you've never been photographed before. You're a natural. An absolute natural. I think you'll love these shots when you see them. Do you want to come around about the same time tomorrow? They should be back from the lab overnight. I would expect to see them delivered here by about ten o'clock tomorrow morning.' At least it would appear that I had *something* going for me. 'Thank you,' I said. 'And yes, I'd love to come and look at the pictures. Thank you again. I'll be here.' I got up and stood beside him. 'Is that it?' I asked him. He looked at me. 'Yes, darling,' he said. 'Unless you'd like some tea or coffee. Or a drink. What do you feel like?' 'I feel like a fuck,' I told him. 'What do *you* feel like?' He looked somewhat surprised. 'Jesus,' he said. 'Thank God for that. Normally, I'd have been trying my luck hours ago. I haven't seen a body like yours in years. Literally. Years. But, this being your first photographic session, I didn't want to risk putting you off for life. Frankly, I can't think of anything I'd enjoy more.' I reached out a hand and carefully unzipped his fly, and then I reached inside and pulled out his dick. It swelled in my hand as I stood there. It was big, and getting bigger. I knelt down in front of him, and took it into my mouth.

As I sucked him, he put out his hands, one on each side of my head, and held it while he started to fuck my mouth. I began to wank him as well as suck him, and seconds later he came in my mouth, a great *swoosh* of creamy, warm come. 'Mmmm,' I said, it being about all I could manage, what with my mouth being full of cock and come. I swallowed rapidly. He kept coming for a little while, and I kept sucking, until everything was finished. Then I took his flaccid cock out of my mouth and stood up. 'How would you like to suck my wet pussy now?' I asked him. 'One good turn deserves another. And which way is the bedroom?'

'Love to,' he said. 'And through the kitchen, and up the spiral staircase.' I walked through the kitchen and went first up the iron staircase, enjoying the feel of the finger he was sticking up my arse as we climbed the stairs. I looked down at him over my shoulder. 'That's *naughty*,' I told him. 'Isn't it?' he said. 'But if you were me, this is exactly what you would be doing in my position.' The spiral staircase led directly into the huge bedroom. It was almost the size of the studio beneath. He had the largest bed I think I've ever seen. We had ended the photographic session with me wearing the grey cotton panties and the white stockings. I now divested myself of the panties. Suddenly they seemed superfluous. Their white cotton gusset was indeed very wet. I dropped them on the floor. But I kept the stockings on. They made a nice frame for my pussy. I lay back on the huge bed and opened my legs. 'At your service, kind sir,' I said.

Tony had by this time taken off the trousers, sweatshirt and underpants that he was wearing, kicked off his shoes, pulled off his socks, and, as I spoke, he buried his head between my legs, and began to return my oral compliment to him of earlier. He was both an enthusiast and an expert, and I came very quickly. I continued to come, almost non-stop, as he worked away at me. I didn't even stop coming for very long when he pulled away from my pussy, turned me over onto my tunny, pulled me up into a kneeling position, and started to fuck me doggy fashion. It was months since I had been properly fucked, but Tony certainly made up for the absence. By the time he had finished with me, I was all fucked out. He was almost literally unstoppable. He fucked me in every possible position. When he finally practically fell off me, after the umpteenth copulatory act, I was about to call *pax*. I put my arms around him, and we fell asleep in moments.

The photographs were, of course, perfect. They made me look terrific, and the fee that Tony paid me for my modelling was only exceeded by my excitement at eventually seeing them published in the pages of your wonderful magazine. All good things, they say, come to an end, and, sadly, so did my fantasy. I woke up! But I can dream, can't I?

G. H. L. Chichester, Hants.

Yes, of course you can. If you would like to send us some nude photographs of yourself, we'll tell you, honestly, by return, what we think the chances are of turning your dream into reality. At least as far as the photography goes. (Editor's note: Ms G. H. L. did *send us some photographs. Three months later, we featured her in a six-page girl set in the magazine. Since then, she has become an internationally famous nude model. She tells us that she no longer has any complaints about her sex life).*

SUBMISSIVE MISS

I have been a submissive ever since I can remember. I try and explain this to my girlfriends sometimes, but they simply don't understand. I wonder if I might describe a recent day that I spent with my husband during one weekend recently, and then enquire of your female readers whether they can see how this could bring me such sexual pleasure? I'm curious to know if others are like me.

My husband and I both work and I'd had a particularly bad week at the office, which made for a pretty short temper by the time the weekend came around. On Saturday morning I went out and did the weekend food shopping at the supermarket, and so on, and when I came back my husband was cutting the grass in our largish back garden. Shopping hadn't improved my temper any, and I guess that when I criticized the fact that he had missed a couple of places on the lawn with the mower it was probably the proverbial last straw. He stopped the mower, got off it, and attacked me, in the sense that he began tearing my clothes off. I got very excited.

This was something entirely new. He was obviously really angry with me, and at first I fought back as hard as I knew how. However, Hugh is a big man, and my resistance was useless. He very quickly had me completely naked, and to my amazement he produced a length of cord from his jacket pocket and bound my hands behind my back with it. I couldn't believe it when, as I was lying there, he kicked my ankles apart, effectively spreading my legs. Then, as he stood there, his feet keeping my legs open in that position, he undid his flies, pulled out his cock, and wanked all over me. He deliberately aimed at my cunt.

He then left me there, his spunk running down all over my body, and went into the house. When he came back, I saw that he had brought a couple of the nipple clamps that we normally keep in a bedside drawer in our bedroom. This particular pair is joined by a chain. He bent down and fixed first one, then the other, to my nipples. The difference between his usual use of these clamps and now was that this time he screwed them up so tightly that I was screaming with pain and pleading with him to loosen them off, at least a little. He ignored both my screams and my pleading. He next knelt over my face, and started to fuck my mouth. There was no question of my fellating him. He was simply fucking my mouth and throat. When he came, flooding my throat with his come, I nearly choked. He took very little notice of my problem, other than to make sure that I *didn't* actually choke. He then left me where I was.

During the whole of the rest of the day, he left me where I was. Naked, bound, lying on my back on the back lawn. Thank God that it was summer, or I could have frozen. And thank God, too, that our back garden isn't overlooked by anybody. From time to time, during the day, Hugh would come and perform some sexual act or other upon me. At different times, he fucked me, he frigged my clit with his fingers until I came, he had anal sex with me – something normally reserved as punishment for some really serious marital infringement, since I am not greatly fond of being fucked up my arse – and he fucked my mouth again. He didn't piss on me, though, for which I was grateful.

Throughout the day, he repeated all the sexual acts, whilst totally ignoring my attempts to talk to him, to reason with him, to plead with him to release me. But here is the extraordinary thing. Despite the pain and the discomfort, despite the humiliation and the degradation of what he was doing to me, every time he sexually assaulted me – for that was what he was doing: making love he wasn't – my orgasms were the greatest that I have ever experienced in my entire life. They were fantastic. Can anyone explain that to me? At the end of what became a very long day – it must have been early evening – Hugh came out and stood and looked down at me. He then told me that his actions of the day had been intentionally and deliberately to punish me for being a real bitch for the entire week. He'd had enough, he said. If I either wanted, or needed to be released, it would only be on my sincere promise never to behave like a bitch again. *Ever*. If I didn't promise, then I would stay where I was until I did.

I couldn't get my promise out quickly enough. I promised, tearfully, to be a better wife and partner. And I meant every word that I said. Hugh unbound me, and helped me up. I spent some hours in the bathroom, soaking off the despair and humiliation – and the stink – of the day. That night, we neither of us referred to the day's events. Nor at any time since. But we had the best sex since our marriage.

P. B. Tonbridge, Kent.

What can I say? It has always been a firm rule with me that whatever two (or more) people do together sexually is fine, provided that (i) everyone is in agreement about what is being done and (ii) no one is injured.

HER SUIT

I read many letters in your columns saluting the joys of shaven pussy, and to a certain extent I can understand the appeal of a well-trimmed pudenda. The sheer smoothness against one's face when performing cunnilingus, for one thing. The clarity with which the female sex organs are exposed when clean-shaven, for another. But when I get down to it (and I do, as often as possible!) for my money you can't beat a really hairy snatch. A totally untrimmed, thick, coarse-haired, black, curly snatch. Not for me the inconsequential frivolity of dyed blonde pubes. Give me a girl who lets it grow long. A real bush. A feminine bird's nest, within which nestles that lovely pink gash that we males so ardently favour with our full attention. My ideal woman wears a black wool short-skirted suit, to meet me for a drink before dinner. She will probably wear a plain white or cream silk shirt beneath her suit, and her short skirt will reveal the fact (when she sits down and her skirt rides up) that she is wearing old-fashioned black silk stockings, with (unseen, but absolutely essential) black silk knickers and a matching black silk suspender belt. If her skirt is *really* short, it will reveal, as she sits down, the beginning of that wondrous gap of naked thigh exposed between stocking top and knicker leg.

Not to be seen until later is the fact that her delightfully hirsute cuntal tresses extend from where they begin just below her navel, all the way down, through between her legs and back up through her anal cleft – surrounding her rectal opening with a particularly spectacular growth – until they fade away just beneath the small of her back. Hidden by the neat black suit, as we enjoy our meal, is the black silk underwear I have already described. Other parts of the same essential woman are the full lips, painted a deep crimson, and the dark brown, almost black nipples, areolae, and pussy lips. She will have full, fleshy, oversize outer labia, hanging down when at rest, swollen when sexually aroused. Lips that you can take between your lips as you suck at her altar of desire. She will exude her love juices copiously before, during, and after the varying acts of sex, and she will accept you into all and every orifice her body offers, with welcoming warmth. She will have no inhibitions whatsoever, and will expect you to be as completely devoid of them as is she. She will not want protected sex. She will want to trust you. Completely. Her underarms will be unshaven.

Almost the sexiest view of her shock of pubic hair will be as she drops her short skirt and steps out of it, exposing herself to you in only the briefest of black silk bikini knickers. They will be so thin as to be totally transparent and will permit you to ogle her tumescent labia, glistening wetly at you through the silk from within the centre of her pubic bush. This sight is only slightly exceeded in its carnality, its sheer, prurient sensuality, by the same view of her naked, as she pulls those tiny knickers down her legs, steps out of them, lies down and spreads her legs, waiting for you to do that which she has been wanting all evening. She will probably reach down with her long, slim fingers, with their manicured talons – painted the same crimson as her lips – and pull her vaginal lips apart for you, that you may see, feel, taste, scent her wanton sex.

Similarly, as you enfold those luscious, moist labia between your eager lips, she will take your engorged penis and suck it between her own full, lascivious, wet crimson lips. She will do things to your sex with her mouth and tongue and fingers that you never before thought possible, and as you suck and lick and kiss her hirsute cunt, your fingers will stray through her thicket, tantalizing you with the feel of its unexpected silkiness. When you have had your fill of cunnilingus and move to thrust your painfully erect pole between her legs, she will fold her arms behind her neck and allow you to lick and suck at the soft hair in her armpits, relishing the tart, exhilarating scent which emanates from there.

As your manhood pierces her sacred entrance, she will bring into play muscles that you didn't know existed, and she will grasp you and massage you, clenching your rigidity, stroking your maleness, until you succumb to her entrancing mystery, shooting your seed up into her in almost painful spurts, and she will scream and call out your name, and orgasm over and over again herself as you spend yourself in her. Here's to happy, hairy handmaidens. Long may they last.

T. O. Northallerton, North Yorkshire.

She'll obviously always be true to you, in her fashion.

STRINGING ALONG

It's always been my fantasy to be a stripper in a small strip club. Small, so that the strippers have to get out there, in amongst the paying customers. There's no stage as such. The girls do their acts in between the tables – and sometimes *on* the tables. I start off with just a G-string – black, of course, and very small – black self-supporting stockings, black gloves, and a black top hat. I dance about to really raunchy music, and my particular thing – the thing that makes me different from the other girls – is that I'll stand in front of you and let you feel inside my G-string, provided that you tuck a note down it before you start. The value of the note dictates the amount of time you get to feel my pussy (because that's what all the men do, in my fantasy). I'm rather over made-up to perform my act and I move from table to table, bumping and grinding, thrusting my pubis out in front of me, putting my own fingers down inside my G-string and very obviously playing with my pussy. It isn't long before the first punter waves a ten-pound note at me, and I go over, climb up onto his table, and kneel in front of him. I very slowly pull down the front of my G-string, exposing my hairy pussy and my wet slit to him. To cheers from his companions, and from the rest of the audience, the man puts his fingers down into the crotch of my G-string, and his fingers find my – by now – soaking wet pussy. He pushes his fingers inside me, and I thrust hard against them, enjoying the feelings that they deliver. As he touches me up, I have a huge orgasm, and I wriggle about and blow kisses at him to indicate my grateful pleasure.

I forget about the time, and the fact that a tenner isn't supposed to get him all that much, and I just go on kneeling there on the table in front of him, letting him feel me up, until the MC, on the club's microphone, suggests that there are other customers waiting. Embarrassed, I pull the man's hand out of my G-string and, with a great show of enjoyment, he puts his fingers into his mouth and slowly sucks and licks them. I usually dream up this fantasy while I am in bed, and you won't be surprised to hear that it always ends with my frigging myself violently to orgasm as I imagine that member of the audience coming into my little room backstage after the show, unzipping his fly and taking out his huge, swollen member which he then forces me to suck off before he rapes me with it, over and over again. In my fantasy, cocks stay hard for ever.

S. L. Montreal, Canada.

Sweet dreams!

ROUGH STUFF

I'm a male who is into discipline and domination, and while I read avidly the occasional feature that you devote to those topics, in my limited experience the real thing is difficult to come by, if you'll forgive the pun. For that reason, maybe you'll allow me to indulge my favourite B&D fantasy? In it, I'm a famous Hollywood film producer, and as with all Hollywood film producers, I am constantly pestered by amazingly available, incredibly beautiful young women, all of whom are anxious to submit to my every sexual desire, in order to help them, they believe, along the road to certain movie stardom. The names, hair colours and styles vary as the girls come and go, but they all have certain specific qualities in common. They all have long legs with muscular thighs, and heavy breasts with huge, oversize areolae and long, thick, teat-like nipples. They have full, fleshy buttocks, and they have either extravagantly hairy cunts, with thick, coarse, long tangles of pubic hair, or they are completely clean-shaven, with their fleshy cunt-lips thus nakedly, blatantly displayed. There is nothing, in terms of pubic decoration, in between the two extremes.

As I pursue my business week around the various offices of Hollywood agents and those of the film studio executives, I meet hundreds of these big-bosomed aspiring young actresses in the waiting rooms, and I hand out my business cards to them without any thought of expense. When they telephone me, I ask them to come to my offices to audition where, naturally enough, I ask them to strip off. This is, of course, to see if they fulfil my private requirements, but I tell them that there is a nude scene in the movie I am casting and so I need to see them naked.

If they are close – for example, they may be perfect, bar the need to shave their pubic hair – then I will tell them that, provided they shave their pudenda, I will then audition them properly. It never fails. Then I arrange the audition at my home, a typical Hollywood mansion, up in the hills behind Hollywood, looking out over the city, with a pool, and a view of the sea in the distance. When the aspiring young actress arrives – let us call her Olivia – I tell her that the film is about a depraved movie director, and that her audition is a scene from an orgy which takes place as the grand finale of the movie. She may, I warn her, find parts of it quite shocking. She smiles at me, rather nervously, but she doesn't say anything. I take her to my punishment room, which I tell Olivia has been built as a set for the audition, and I tell her to strip.

I watch, lustfully, as she releases pendulous breasts from her straining white lace brassiere. Next she peels down her white lace panties. This particular girl has auburn hair, and a particularly thick mane of auburn growth around and in between her heavy thighs, virtually covering her pudenda. I feel my cock swelling as I look at this intensely erotic display. She next pulls down her tights, and then she is completely naked. She smiles at me, and I smile back. I then give her a pair of leather anklets, joined together by a chain, and I tell her to put them on. I help her to pull the straps tight. I next show her a leather thong, and explain that this is to bind her wrists together, behind her back. She turns away from me, and I bind her wrists for her. I find it difficult to keep my hands off her full, naked buttocks. I can see a fuzz of auburn anal hair rising out of the cleft between them. Then, when her wrists are tied to my satisfaction, I explain that I am going to attach a rope to the chain around her ankles. The rope, I tell her, is attached to a pulley in the ceiling which, when I pull on it, will haul her up, feet first, so that she is hanging head down.

Olivia looks somewhat startled, but she doesn't say anything in reply. I pull her up, and secure the end of the rope to a bracket on the wall that is there for the purpose. Olivia is now hanging upside down, with her head on a level with my groin. Yes, you've guessed. I undo my trousers, take out my now rampant cock, and say to Olivia, 'Here, suck this. And suck it good. If you don't suck it to my complete satisfaction, I will thrash your bare ass until it is raw and bleeding. Oh, and yes,' I say, grinning to myself, 'make it as realistic as you know how.' I feed my cock into Olivia's mouth. She takes me between her full lips, and starts to suck. At the same time, she puts her tongue to work. She has obviously sucked cock before. Haven't they all?

I stand there, being orally serviced rather well. Immediately in front of me, upside down, is Olivia's hairy cunt. I reach out, part her thatch with my fingers, and find her cunt lips. I spread them with my fingers, and discover – to my surprise – that she is very wet inside. I lean forward, and give her sticky gash a long, slow lick, from top to bottom (actually, from bottom to top). She tastes good. Gamey and strong-tasting, as red-heads usually do. I love it. She smells strongly too. Of sex. Of cunt (reasonably enough). I hold her by her bare buttocks, and pull her towards my mouth, and then I begin to suck her cunt. She moans. Or, at least, she moans as well as she can, with her mouth full of my cock. I think she is trying to tell me that she is enjoying what I am doing to her.

I thrust my tongue deeply into her cunt, and she moans again. I start to lick her clitoris, and she begins to move her ass, at least as best as she can in her predicament. She is doing magnificent things to my cock, and I start to feel my ejaculation building. I too begin to move my hips, and I start fucking her mouth. I let go of her buttocks and reach down and hold her head as I fuck her mouth. In moments I am jetting my sperm down her throat in huge, throbbing spurts. She begins to choke, so I withdraw, and she coughs and splutters, my sperm dribbling out of her mouth. I thought this clumsiness of hers unnecessary, so I selected a cane from an assortment hanging along a rail on the wall, and, standing behind her, I thrashed her naked buttocks for ten minutes or so, until her sobs and screams had died away into a kind of bubbling, throaty mumble. Her skin reddened under the cane's assault, and her arse became criss-crossed with raised weals.

This titillating interval quite restored my erection, and I lowered the rope by which she was suspended until her still-wet cunt was on a level with my newly rigid cock. 'Oh, please,' she said, through her tears. 'Please fuck me. Please do what you want with me, but please don't cane me any more. I can't stand that much pain. I don't care if I don't get the part, but please don't cane me any more.' Since she *had* done a pretty good job of fellating me, and I had enjoyed thrashing her bare bottom, I took pity on her and let her down from the hook in the ceiling. This left her lying on the floor, with her hands still bound behind her back, and her legs still bound together by the chain and the ankle shackles. But at least she could now spread her legs, a difficult thing to do when suspended upside down.

I picked her up off the floor and threw her, face down, over the padded top of a whipping block. I then kicked her legs apart and, without any kind of preamble – least of all any kind of lubricant – I forced my aching cock up her arsehole, and began to fuck her. She screamed as I thrust my way up her tightly clenched anus, but very soon the anal mucus in her secret flesh-depths lubricated her rectum, and I began to slide in and out of her asshole rather more comfortably. For me, anyway. Her screams subsided quite quickly, and she began moving with me as I humped her up her fundament. When I spurted my semen into her once more, she cried out. Whether with pain or pleasure I shall never know, but it didn't feel to me as if she had any kind of an orgasm.

I pulled out of her, and left her where she was while I went off to my bathroom to clean myself up. I showered and dressed, and then went back to my punishment room, to find her still bent over the whipping block, sobbing. I lifted her up, undid her various bonds and shackles, picked up her clothes from where she had dropped them earlier, and led her through to my bathroom. I left her there. When she emerged, she was more or less back to normal, at least from what I could see. Whilst she had been freshening up I had taken the tape from the two video cameras that had been running all the while through our 'audition', and I now asked her if she would like me to run through them with her. She looked horrified, made her excuses, and left. Hurriedly.

I never heard from her again. In my fantasy, I put a different girl through this and similar (sometimes rather more painful) kinds of S&M experiences, regularly. I'm into whipping girls' breasts and cunts, the use of clamps on nipples and labia, and the whole gamut of sadomasochistic fun and games. I appreciate that these are not everyone's ideas of amusing sex, but we S&M enthusiasts find them both exciting and satisfying. Does anyone know where I can turn my fantasies into realities? Are there any women out there who would like to explore the pleasures of pain with me? Please write.

W. A. A. Chelsea, London.

You've got me beat there, I'm afraid. But we'll forward any letters. (Editor's note: we actually forwarded over twenty letters to W. A. A. We don't, of course, know what the contents were.)

CAVEMAN

I like to believe that I'm as sophisticated as the next man. I think that I understand most of what women are about, and I have reason to believe that I understand at least the basics of what the average woman desires in bed. They like – not in any particular order of·priority – a good, large, hard cock. This thing about size not being important is codswallop. The bigger the better. Ask your girlfriend! They like cleanliness. It's not so much next to godliness as next to a big, hard cock! They like men who are gentle, and thoughtful. Men who consider their bed partners. Men who spend time on foreplay. Most women – if they're honest – adore oral sex. Having cunnilingus performed upon them, that is. A number cry off oral sex altogether, simply because they don't want to have to fellate their partner. Here again, cleanliness is relevant. And perhaps most importantly of all, women adore men who have good sexual manners. Me? After years of practice, I get by. I don't get too many complaints. (Nobody's perfect!) But by choice, from preference, given the opportunity, I'm a caveman. Give me a club, let me knock them unconscious, and drag them back to my cave by their hair, and I'm happy! Sadly, my preference only happens in my wildest fantasies. Which is why I'm writing this letter to you today . . .

It excites me to think of living in some kind of primitive landscape, where everything in sight – including other human beings (men and women), animals, birds even – are potentially my enemy. And the women, of course, are also potential prizes.

I imagine being out of my home cave, hunting, with my stout bow made of fine yew and my arrows tipped with pointed, sharpened flint. I also have a flint knife, and a flint axe. As I tread warily through the forest looking, essentially, for something to kill to eat, I see in the distance another young tribal warrior, accompanied by his woman. I watch carefully for a while, following them silently, and as far as I can see, they are alone. Both have woad tattoos stencilled upon their faces. The man is black-haired, the woman also. He wears a sort of fur sarong, with a single shoulder strap. She has only a fur skirt. Her breasts are bare, and as I look at them, I realize that this woman is of fuckable age. Certainly under twenty. Her breasts are firm and pointed. Her stomach – as much I can see of it – is flat. Her face is unlined, and she smiles at her companion often. He smiles back. They are obviously lovers.

I try and imagine that other little furry animal between her legs, with its soft, wet centre like raw meat. I wonder if it is still reasonably unused, and therefore fairly tight and pleasant to dip into, or whether the woman has been much used, and has borne many children, and has a slack, loose centre to her furry muff. But there are no children with them, and her breasts do not look as if they have been over-sucked. There is only one way to find out for certain. My penis is stiff as I creep up upon the couple. I do not have a woman, and I do not get to dip my penis in a woman's place very often. Maybe I can capture this one, and keep her for my own. As I gain upon them, they both suddenly stop. It looks as if they are going to rest for a while. Good.

I hope the woman isn't menstruating. The gods strike down any man who fucks a woman who is menstruating. Or so they say. I imagine that I can see her little pink mouth, open at the centre of the fur in her groin, but this may be wishful thinking.

The man starts to collect wood to make a fire, and soon he has collected a small pile of dry twigs. He strikes flints together, and soon his fire is crackling away. He is watching the fire so intently that he is careless, and I creep up on him and fell him with a blow from the blunt end of my axe. The woman attacks me, screaming and clawing, but one carefully aimed blow to her chin renders her unconscious too.

While the man is still out, I bind his arms and legs together, and then I tie him, very carefully, to a tree. I go over to the woman, who is still unconscious. I pull her through the undergrowth out of the sight of the man when he regains consciousness. I lift up her fur skirt and spread her legs, exploring with my fingers. At close sight, her furry muff is thick and black. I part this heavy pussy beard and find her pink lips. I press them apart and put a finger inside her. She is not menstruating. She is gloriously tight: I kneel in between her legs, and feed my rampant tool up her. I hold her arms by the wrists and, while she is still unconscious, I begin to fuck her. Her pointed breasts are quivering as I move her body beneath me with the intensity of my fucking, and as I watch, her nipples stiffen. I lean down, and take one in my mouth. It tastes sweet, and I feel it thicken and grow in my mouth. After a while, I take the other one in my mouth, and do the same to that. Suddenly, after I have sucked both her tits, I am looking at her woad-stained face as I fuck her, and she opens her eyes.

Three moods pass across her face in rapid sequence. At first, the only thing she realizes as she becomes conscious again is that she is being fucked, and she begins to smile. Then she realizes that the face above hers isn't the one that she is accustomed to, and the smile becomes a look of abject fear. And then she realizes that, first of all, I am alone – there isn't a whole tribe queuing up to rape and sodomize her – and that, all things considered, I am fucking her gently, with at least some concern for her physical comfort. I am not actually beating her, for example. So the smile that began as she first became aware of me finally returns, and she begins to move her body with mine, thrusting hard upwards as I thrust down. She says something, but it is not in a dialect that I understand. I speak to her and she shakes her head. But she continues to smile and she humps away happily until I begin to spurt my seed into her, at which she moans and closes her eyes, the smile still firmly in place.

I let go of her arms and collapse across her. As my manhood shrinks, I pull it out of her and roll off her. I expect her to make a run for it. But instead she takes my flaccid tool in her hand, and, putting her other hand on my chest and pressing to indicate that I should lie down on my back, she takes me in her mouth and begins to suck at me, suckling my cock as if she were a baby suckling a woman's teat. I have heard from older tribesmen of the secret activities of women who like to be fucked in the mouth, and have always rejected their stories as being boastful male untruths, just as I do those of men who say that there are women who like a man's weapon up their excretory passage.

Her attentions are indeed delightful, and she uses her hand rather as I used to use my own, when my hand was the only thing available to me to fuck. I am quickly stiff again in her mouth, and very quickly after that I again shoot my seed into her, this time between her eager lips. To my surprise, she swallows as I pump away, and when I am finished, she smiles at me and licks her lips lasciviously, indicating that she enjoyed the experience. Her next action has me confused for a while. She puts a forefinger on my mouth, and then she takes it off and, spreading her legs open wide, she puts her finger onto the mouth of her child-hole. As she looks at my puzzled expression, she once more licks her lips, and again puts her finger on my mouth, then down to that other mouth between her legs.

Eventually I realize that, having sucked that which I use to piss through, she now wants me to suck her piss-hole. Can this be so? Can I possibly have misunderstood her? I put my own fingers on my mouth, and then press them against her piss-hole, and I raise my eyebrows quizzically as I then mime a licking motion with my tongue. She smiles broadly, and nods enthusiastically. Since this has been a day of pleasant surprises, I think to myself, perhaps this is but another secret that all men eventually learn about as they are able to practise the humpbacked monster with willing women. Certainly I enjoyed putting my penis in her mouth. Why should I not enjoy trying to take her in mine?

I indicate to her to lie down and she does so, opening her legs for me as she does. I lie down in a position that allows me oral access to her piss-hole and, tentatively, I lick it. It tastes rather pleasant. Rather like those shellfish that are found down at the mouth of the local river. Oysters, they call them. She tastes meaty, but with a slight overtone of fish. I decide that I like it. If it is an acquired taste, then I realize that I have acquired it and I begin to suck at her with enthusiasm. Quite quickly she begins to writhe her hips about beneath my mouth and, as I continue to suck her, she starts again that strange moaning noise which she made when I was first fucking her.

Then, all of a sudden, she is holding my head in her hands and grinding her piss-hole against my mouth as I lick and suck. Then, with a final, high-pitched moan, she lets go of my head, pulls my mouth up to hers, and kisses me. Passionately. What I have been doing to her has aroused me once more, and I thrust my erect cock in between her legs yet again and fuck her, quickly, excitedly, strongly, as we continue to kiss each other. I can taste her piss-hole juice on my lips as I thrust my tongue into her mouth, and the mental image of that first early glimpse of her is enough to take me rapidly beyond the point of ejaculation once more.

And then our sexual introduction was – at least for the moment – over. I walked back to where this woman's man was still tied to the tree. When he saw us, he struggled in his bonds, and shouted at me in their unintelligible language. I expected her to at least comfort him, if not attempt to release him, but no. She first spoke to him, low-voiced and gutturally. Then she spat on the ground in front of him, after which she picked up her small parcel of belongings and, taking me by the arm, she led me off, away into the trees.

I supposed that some member of his tribe would discover him and release him before some wild animal killed him. I didn't feel too strongly about it. He would have done the same with me, given the opportunity. My cock was rising again as the woman led me away. I wondered what else I was soon to discover.

T. L. H. Winchester, Hants.

Probably that it was time to organize lunch! Seriously, maybe there are still a few women out there who are looking for a real caveman. We'll let you know if we hear from any.

COOL AS A CUCUMBER

I met a girl this summer who has made a profound impression upon me, in that she is the finest example I have ever met of whatever the opposite of sexually repressed is. Free, perhaps? Liberal? You tell me. She has no hang-ups whatsoever. She'll take it any time, any place, anywhere. You want it, you can have it. In her mouth. Up her arse. In her hand. You name it, you've got it. She just loves sex. You will remember that this summer just past is on record as the hottest for many years. Would you believe, this girl taught me how to have a cool fuck? No, I'm not kidding. Really. We were lying there in bed one evening, sweating like the proverbial pigs, having enjoyed a serious session of Hide the Sausage, and I said something about wouldn't it be pleasant, in this kind of weather, to have a cool fuck. 'Haven't you ever had one, darling?' she asked. I had to admit that I hadn't. 'No problem,' she said, looking at her watch.

'It's probably too late to arrange it now, but I promise you that tomorrow I'll provide you with the coolest fuck you've ever had.' I fell asleep wondering just exactly what she had in mind. The following day, around mid-morning, after she had been out food shopping, Marie announced that she was ready – and available – for a cool fuck, any time I felt like one. 'How about now, darling?' I asked, never being one to turn down an opportunity. 'I'll see you upstairs in the bedroom in two minutes,' she replied, smiling. Two minutes later, she arrived upstairs, carrying something in an icebox. She stripped off, lay down naked beside me, and opened her legs.

'Can you open that icebox, darling?' she asked. I reached down and picked it up from off the floor where she had left it and opened it up to discover, inside, a large, peeled cucumber. Just shove that slowly and carefully up my cunt,' she instructed. Doing as she asked guaranteed a humdinger of a hard-on. About ten minutes later, she said, 'OK, sweetheart, you can pull it out now, and fuck me.' I did as she told me, and I certainly had the coolest fuck ever. It was a most unusual, and delightful, sensation. I recommend it to anyone who gets bored with lovemaking in the long, hot summertime. And as you can probably guess, after some cool sex, we had some pretty cool cucumber sandwiches for our tea.

S. B. Shoreham-by-Sea, Sussex.

Did you remember to invite the vicar?

BLACK IS BEAUTIFUL

Living as I do in a small town in the sticks, I've grown up – I'm twenty-three – in rather secluded circumstances. We have neither the facilities, nor the anonymity, of big cities, and for this reason, my main fantasy stays as exactly that. I'm happy to say that, yes, we *have* heard of sex down here, and it's in plentiful supply. Country lasses are something else, and they aren't backward in coming forward. But for ages now, I've wanted to indulge in a relationship with a black girl. Of which there are very few around here. Irma, in your last issue, is exactly what I am looking for. She's gorgeous, isn't she? In my fantasy, I can see myself beside her on that lovely big bed, with her wearing just those tiny white knickers – more of a G-string, really – that (I'm sure unnecessary, but very sexy) white brassiere, and those lovely white stockings. She looks fabulous, with that mane of long black hair spread out on the pillow, and with her hand down inside her panties. I can see her thick bush of black pubic hair peeping through the transparency of her knickers, and I can imagine what she is doing to herself. I've always wanted to see a real live girl playing with herself, but that too, sadly, is still a fantasy. Perhaps Irma would like to help me on both counts? I particularly like that large picture where she has her eyes closed, her mouth open, and this time her fingers are outside her panties, but she is still playing with herself. She has also by now taken her bra off, and her other hand is playing with one of her dark – almost black – nipples, pulling and twirling it until it is standing there erectly upon her large, similarly, almost black areola. Her breasts are full and shapely, and I can imagine the feel of them under my fingers. Over the next few pages someone – in my fantasy it is me – is slowly undressing her. First they pull down her virgin white panties. I can imagine easing them over that gorgeous arse, revealing her bushy black pubic hair, out of which are pouting those surprising bright pink inner labia, surrounded by her almost black outer lips. I touch the gusset of her sodden knickers to my nose as I take them off.

Both sets of lips are glistening wetly in the studio lights, and I can see, in one picture, that a thread of mucus is hanging down from her wet pussy, and I imagine myself catching it on my tongue and sucking it into my mouth. I can smell the scent of her cunt, and the taste of it, as I begin to suck her fleshy lips into my mouth. After a while, she sighs and draws her legs up beneath her, raising her arse in the air so that I can see, then touch and feel, then suck, her black anus, peeping at me out of another hairy mound, higher up now than her pussy, in this new position. Her pussy juice is running out of her in a small stream and has run down into her anal crevice and onto her rectum. I put out a finger, and stroke her black, puckered, forbidden entrance. She moans, slightly, and her whole body quivers as she draws in a deep breath. Her full lips are open again, and she is licking them. She is saying something to me. So very quietly. I lean down, my ear to her mouth. 'Your cock,' she is saying. 'Give me your cock. Please. Put your cock in my mouth, so that I can suck you off.' She is lying on her back now, and I kneel over her face, her full breasts beneath my stomach, and she takes my tool in her hand and guides it into her mouth, where she closes her full lips about it and sucks me, as she uses her tongue to tantalize my knob-end. My tool jerks in her mouth at her first oral contact, then it settles down, and I begin to fuck her mouth, very, very slowly.

As I am doing this, I am looking down, immediately below my face and mouth, to her blue-black labia, which are even wetter now, the juices running down her thighs, the pink inner lips open, and silkily wet too. I thrust my middle finger down into her, all the way in to my knuckle. She is delightfully warm, very wet, and unbelievably tight. It is akin to thrusting my finger into a firm, well-made jelly. The aroma of aroused cunt invades my nostrils. She smells like an overripe tropical melon, with an underlying breath of something slightly fetid. It is exciting, tangy, and I reach down and lick her, slowly, running my tongue from just above the wrinkled entrance to her rectal passage, tentatively, enjoyably, lustfully, joyfully, gratifyingly, all the way back to the apex of her wet black outer vaginal lips.

I thrust my tongue down beneath its hood and find her swollen clitoris within reach. I lick and suck at the same time, and she wriggles beneath me and starts to jack me off into her mouth at the same time as she is fellating me. This is oral sex beyond the dreams of ordinary man. This woman is the Sistine Chapel of fellatio. The female God of oral sex. Her mouth should be a national treasure. I pump away at her hand and mouth, and she masturbates and sucks my swollen prick as I thrust away, bringing me quickly to the point of ejaculation. I can hardly tear myself away from my oral devotions at the altar of her increasingly freely moistened cunt. I'd almost rather not come than stop sucking her gorgeously scented, exquisitely tasting, open, wet pussy. But then, there I am, suddenly, exultantly, happily spurting my warm, creamy seed into her all-encompassing mouth. She sucks and swallows me, thirstily, as I spurt my semen into her. I promise to pump my come into her, now and forever more, world without end. Amen.

I wish I had a hundred cocks, so that she could suck all of them. That I could maintain a permanent erection, for her to fellate. Continuously. I wish I could keep my mouth, tongue, lips, nose, forever buried in her hot, black, fleshy cunt. I believe that I am finished. Fucked out. Sucked out. And then she takes my limp cock in her hand, and she masturbates it for me. Exquisitely. So gently. So erotically. It was as if I had never before tossed myself off in my life. Never been given a quick wank by some girl – any girl – anxious to get rid of me but realizing that I needed to ejaculate before she could reasonably expect me to let her go without raping her. At least in my mind.

As if I had never enjoyed a quick one off the wrist from a young lady, one who wanted to say 'Thank you', but who didn't want – for whatever reasons of her own – to drop her knickers for me. Perhaps she had the rags up, as we used to say all those years ago. It was pretty much the only acceptable excuse, in those days. It was many years before *Hustler* magazine in America had turned menstrual copulation into a pastime for the allegedly sexual erudite few. And, I suppose, any girl still a virgin (and wanting to stay that way) but willing to pull a chap's plonker for him, until his semen spurted all over her hand, was generally thought to be pretty good news. At least by the chaps. Better by far than having to go home and do it on one's own. Sniffing the finger that one had reluctantly been allowed to slip up the forbidden vaginal orifice, whilst wanking off madly with the other hand. Oh, the excitement of youth.

So my fantasy continues, despite my sexual excess so far, with this exotic, desirable woman masturbating me back to erection. In my dream, as soon as I am fully erect, she then turns over onto her stomach, draws her knees up underneath her, and pulls herself up into a kneeling position and with her legs apart, offering me both her pussy and her anus. They are both black and beautiful, running with lubrication, and fully available. She turns her head, looks over her shoulder at me lasciviously, and says, 'I love it up my arse. Why don't you fuck me anally?'

As you all know, there's only one answer to that particular invitation. I spat, hugely, onto my fingers, and – despite her own, obviously welcoming lubrication – I rubbed my spittle thoroughly into her anal orifice, making it even wetter. Greasier is probably a better word. She felt gloriously tight. She squirmed, and said, 'Oh, yes. Oh, baby. Oh, God. I'm ready for you. Fuck my arse. Stick your huge cock up my arsehole. Come in my bottom. Fuck me up there. Now. Please, darling. Do it to me. Bugger me. Now. I'm ready.' Her anal hair was wet with her emanations, and I thrust a finger, gently, up her pinkly glistening arsehole. Very tentatively, I have to admit. It slid in, all the way, without the slightest resistance from her. She really *was* ready. And willing. And able. I pulled my finger out, and then I took my cock in my hand and fed it into her anus. She breathed in, strongly, as the tip of my cock entered her. I continued to press, and my knob-end popped into her. She gasped and said, 'Ooooh.' Nothing else. After that, it was roses all the way. I thrust up into her, up to my hilt, my balls slapping against her taut, firm thighs. 'Oh, yes,' she said. 'Don't stop. Fuck me now. Give it to me. Bugger me. Fuck my arsehole. Fuck me now. Oh, Jesus. Do it to me now.'

I began to move my hips, thrusting my already almost bursting penis up into her, then slowly withdrawing it again, revelling in her tightly clenched anal cavity. She became slightly looser – more slippery, perhaps, is a better description – as I continued to fuck her, presumably from the lubricant that her rectal passage was exuding as my cock massaged her internally. Whatever the cause, the effect was absolutely terrific, and I knew that it was only a matter of time – almost certainly a very little time – before I spent myself, spending my jism in the delightful warm, moist constrictions of her bottom-hole.

Why is it that the naughtiest things, the forbidden things, the things that society most disapproves of, are always the nicest things? Why is it that they are that much more enjoyable than the things that nobody cares about? Buggering ladies' bottoms is high on my list of forbidden treats. And, happily, I know a number of ladies who agree with me. But don't tell anyone, please. Sadly, it's still against the law. As I felt my ejaculation building, the girl reached a hand around behind her, took my right hand away from her waist, and put it down between her legs. 'Play with my clitty, darling,' she said. 'Please. Make me come now.' And then she reached behind her again, and took hold of the base of my cock as it thrust in and out of her lovely blue-black tiny little anal flower and, as I masturbated her clit, she wanked the base of my tool. Then we almost immediately came together, laughing at our pleasure.

'Oh, God,' she said, as I started to spurt my come up her arsehole. 'Oh, Jesus. Oh yes. Oh, darling. I'm coming. You're coming in my arsehole, and I'm coming too. I can feel your hot spunk spurting up me. Oh, God. I like it. I love it. Oh, Jesus. Oh, fuck.' I continued to frig her, for as long as she was having what became a long, almost continuous, series of orgasms, and she kept her busy fingers doing the same for my cock, for as long as I kept spurting my semen into her, until finally, we both collapsed, sexually spent, still giggling slightly at our mutual, breathless, completely out-of-condition – but very happy – physically fulfilled state.

After that, we continued to make lazy, self-indulgent love, on and off, for most of the night. We were happy with each other, relaxed with each other. Turned on by each other. Appreciating the feel, the smell, the taste of each other. Loving the sensations that we were able to stimulate in each other's bodies. Liking the excitement produced by each other's hands, mouths, tongues, fingers, sexual organs, orifices, protrusions.

Making a meal of each other's bodies. Until we fell into a deep, satisfied, completely sexually replete slumber. I hope this fantasy explained to you my love of – and lust for – black women. If there are any black female readers out there who want to become an integral part of my single-minded sexual fantasy, please write to me.

P. G. W. Bridgeport, Connecticut.

Sounds like an invitation to become a personal sex slave!

ELIZABETHAN EULOGY

I've always been tremendously excited by what I imagine to be the Elizabethan way of life, particularly with regard to sexual matters. From what I have read about the period, it was one long orgy, provided, of course, that you were rich. It certainly wasn't a great time in which to be poor. I love the thought of myself, with a group of my men friends, sitting down in a private room in an Elizabethan inn and being served a splendid meal by a selection of attractive serving wenches, their ample bosoms barely concealed, as we eat and drink our way through the feast put before us. Naturally enough, when the table is cleared, our thoughts turn to sex with the young women servants, who are not averse to earning a little extra on the side, and the orgy begins. It starts with the girls lining up in front of us and undoing the bodices of their dresses to reveal their naked breasts in all their mammary glory. Nipples are pinched and tweaked into a state of full arousal, and the bulges in our hose indicate that the men are aroused too. There is much jocular banter as we men inspect the objects of our growing desires closely, and we feel and suck the girl's breasts as we inspect, making comparisons, and probably choices, for later, closer attention. We are, of course, quaffing quantities of good French claret as we carry out our inspections, and the ladies join in with us as we drink. The party consequently soon becomes merrier, and it isn't too long before the girls' long Elizabethan skirts are being voluntarily hoisted, and voluminous pairs of drawers opened at the crotch, or dropped, to display an interesting variety of hairy love-mounds sitting between their open thighs. Serving wenches are not renowned for their shyness, and they happily sit on the now cleared long table, spreading their legs, and offering themselves to the highest bidder.

Bidding begins, with the oldest of the wenches acting as auctioneer, and the bids are accompanied – quite properly – by extremely close inspection of the differently hued muffs on offer. Pubic hair is parted, vaginal lips are spread by willing fingers (both male and female) and the girls encourage fingers to be inserted into orifices in order to verify the degree of tightness, the level of elasticity, and the quantity of wetly indicated anticipation and enthusiasm shown by each individual girl. One girl is cheered loudly when she bends down over the table, raises her plump arse in the air and then, putting her hands behind her, pulls her arse cheeks apart, exposing her tightly clenched anus. She is quickly – and expensively – bought.

All of the girls, naturally, pass the tests, and the bidding begins to take on a more urgent tenor. Heavy purses are extracted from hitherto deep pockets, and golden sovereigns are tipped onto the table in seemingly limitless quantities. The next girl to strike a deal gets a cheer, due to the fact that she has been bought entirely due to the quantity of sticky lubrication that is issuing from her cunt, its flow obvious, since she is holding her cunt open widely with her fingers, and asking who wishes to plug it for her. As the bids get higher, the girl masturbates herself frenziedly, to the delight of her cheering audience, and the highest bid is made as she doubles over in the thrill of reaching orgasm as the auction ends. She has attained the astonishingly high price of two guineas. But it is necessary to remember that we are in an age in which a twelve-year-old common prostitute from the streets of London may be used for fourpence.

I have to admit that I am the one who bought the girl who was offering herself anally. The sight of her generous buttocks, their fleshiness plumply surrounding her dark brown, tightly puckered rectal flower, was all too much. It was simply pleading to have me distend its petals. I couldn't look at it without imagining sinking my swollen penis between its tender lips. As I looked, I could practically feel its hermetic rigidity gripping my member as I thrust into it, dilating it, feeling its inner warmth and moistness. I almost came in my hose in frantic, excited anticipation.

The girl was pretty with it too. She had short black hair that shone with health and much brushing, and a black, coarse pubic growth that was repeated all the way up (or down, if you prefer) her anal cleft. She had a small, elfin face, rather heavily made-up, and long, slim legs. When she stripped off, I noticed immediately that her armpits were unshaven, in the Continental manner. When I later took her in my arms, I licked her armpits and they were damp and heavily scented with her bodily secretions. Their odour went straight to my penis, which grew magnificently as a result. Her breasts were heavy, and her nipples and areolae were also surrounded by a sprinkling of long black hairs. I had taken her up to one of the inn's rooms, not wanting to bugger her publicly, and on the way upstairs she had asked me to excuse her and said that she would be but a few moments before she rejoined me. When she arrived and knocked at the door, as I opened it I could see that she came with a dish of mutton grease in her hand. 'All the better to grease your entry,' she said, blushing slightly. A very sensible precaution, I thought. For both of us.

She undressed, as did I, and without further preamble she knelt on the bed, her delightful haunches facing me as I stood there, and suggested that I grease her anus for her. I took the mutton grease from the side table where she had put it and began to anoint her. I slid a finger deep into her and she shuddered and waggled her bottom. 'Mmmm,' she said. Nothing else. Just 'Mmmm.' I took it as a sign that she was enjoying my attention.

She was exquisitely tight, and I felt her rectal muscles grip my finger as I thrust into her, and then withdrew. I took it that she was no anal virgin. I would guess that she made a practice of what she and I were about to do, and probably made an excellent living at it. I greased her thoroughly, and then gave her the dish of fat, with the suggestion that she now perform the same service on my penis. Why keep a dog and bark yourself, as they say? She smiled at me and then, as she greased my cock, she said 'Oh, my. That *is* a big one, isn't it? I hope you're not going to hurt me, sir.' But she smiled as she spoke, and I don't believe that she really thought anything of the kind. She wasn't worried in the least bit about having her fundament uncomfortably stretched. She simply knew that men like to be complimented on the size of their sexual equipment. She finished her job, to her *and* my satisfaction, and wiped her greasy fingers on one of the crisply laundered linen sheets. 'There, sir,' she said, looking at her handiwork. I was fully erect, and extraordinarily well greased. 'I think we're ready now,' she said.

And so saying, she knelt once more on the bed and again put her hands behind her and pulled her buttocks well apart, thus revealing her anus, now partially dilated, extremely well greased, and showing just a smidgen of her own anal lubrication which was beginning to trickle out and run down her anal crevice. For the first time I could now actually see inside her rectal passage. Down through the dark brown, closely puckered surround, held enticingly open by her fingers, she glistened pinkly inside, very like a vagina, apart from the hole itself.

Below her anus, I could see her vaginal lips, hanging down loosely. They were the same dark brown as the flesh of her anus, and they were perhaps the largest outer pussy lips that I had ever seen. They were about four inches long, as far as I could judge, and they were quite fat. 'Fleshy' is perhaps a better word. They reminded me of bats' wings. I could just make out a pink slit at their centre, and unthinkingly I put both hands down to her, and spread her outer pussy lips, and thrust my forefinger up her cunt. It was warm, and very wet, and she shuddered as I fingered her. She looked over her shoulder. 'Have you changed your mind, sir?' she asked. 'I thought that you had got your heart set on a bit of buggery. You won't be dissatisfied, I promise you. If you want a bit of cunt after that, I'm more than happy to throw that in for nothing. But I'd rather have it up my arse first, if it don't make no difference to you, sir.' 'And so you shall, my darling,' I told her. I took my finger out of her cunt and, taking hold of my rampant erection, I began to feed it up into her anus. She pulled her cheeks apart again with her agile fingers, and at the same time she pushed back against me, enabling my cock to slide all the way into her. As I slid in, she let off a small, squeaky fart. 'Oops,' she said. 'Pardon me, sir.' I found it rather endearing.

As I started to bugger her, she clasped hold of my cock with her anal muscles, as tightly as it had ever been grasped by any woman before, and as I thrust deeply in and out of her greasy back entrance she thrust back towards me, as hard as she knew how, and squeezed me hard with her powerful rectal muscles. I wondered how many of the local gentry, with whom I foregathered at this very public house of a Saturday evening, had been up her delightful tight young arse before me. Quite a few, I would imagine. She was no stranger to what I was doing to her, that was for sure, and it must have taken a great deal of very regular practice for her to get her rectal muscles into the highly developed condition that they were presently in.

So joyful was our congress that in no time at all I was shooting my hot spunk up her back passage, to cries, from her, of 'Oooh', and 'Ohhh', and, finally, 'Ohhhh, Jesuuuusssss, yeessss'. She squeezed and sucked my jism up into her arsehole, with seeming pleasure, until I was completely spent. As my penis shrivelled back to its more normal state, it plopped out of her, and she got up off her knees, turned around, and sat down beside me. She stroked my hair, as I lay there. I was sexually more than replete, at least for the moment.

'I enjoyed that, sir,' she said. 'I think you've probably buggered a few of us young girls, before me.' 'I have that,' I told her. 'But never one that I have enjoyed as much as you. You've got a regular customer, if you are looking for one.' 'That's very kind of you to say that, sir,' she said. 'There's a good few young women in this part of the world would give a lot to hear a gentleman like yourself say that to them. I appreciate it. Thank you.' 'My pleasure, darling,' I told her. She lay down beside me, and we lay together in silence until we were both rested. After a while, she reached out a hand and took hold of my flaccid penis. It began to swell under her touch. She sat up and said, 'I'll just get a flannel, and wash this little man here, before he becomes a big man again. And then we'll find a different place to put him. Is that all right with you, sir?'

'That's very all right with me, darling,' I said. 'Feel free.' She went over to a corner of the room, where there was a washbasin and a jug of water. It must have been hot when we first came upstairs, for it was still warm now. She came back with the basin half full of water, and a flannel, and began to wash my cock, carefully and gently. By the time that she had finished, it was beautifully clean, and wonderfully erect. She put the basin and the flannel down on the floor beside the bed and, leaning down, she took my now fully erect penis in her soft, warm mouth. She held it delicately in her right hand, slowly masturbating it into her mouth, whilst she kissed it, and tongued it, and sucked it. She ran her tongue the full length of it, from its swollen purple tip to its base, down by her fingers, wetting it all over with her saliva. She then held it steady in front of her mouth, and gently blew on it, making it cold, and all the more sensitive to the attentions that she was giving it.

She saw me watching her, and she took me out of her mouth and smiled at me. 'It's all right, sir,' she said. 'You can fuck me with this any time you like. I just thought that I'd give it a little treat before you started. I don't know if you're married or not – and I don't want to know—' she said, hurriedly. 'But a lot of the married gentlemen I service tell me that their wives won't take their cocks in their mouths. They say they don't like the taste of them. Me,' she said, positively grinning at me now, 'I *love* the taste of them. And the feel of them in my mouth. And the taste of come. If you want to spunk in my mouth, then that's fine with me, sir,' she said. 'I'll swallow every drop. You just try me.'

'I'm not actually married, darling,' I told her. 'But I'd love to come in your mouth. It's the final pleasure.' Then I thought for a moment of the gorgeous sensations that I had enjoyed recently, shooting my semen up this young girl's anus, and so I slightly changed my statement. 'Well,' I said, '*One* of the final pleasures. And I still haven't fucked you . . .' She grinned at me again. 'Don't worry, sir,' she said. 'I don't know about you, but I've got all the time in the world. For what you're paying me, you can fuck me, suck me, bugger me, frig me, and then play noughts and crosses with me, all day and all night, for a week.' And so, in my fantasy, I do all the things that she suggested. Well, except the noughts and crosses. And in slightly less than a week. My own, private, Elizabethan orgy.

P. C. Newton Abbot, Devon.

Cakes and ale and *crumpet. What fun!*

MALE MENAGERIE

My boyfriend and I love to read your excellent magazine together. We delight in the girl sets. They turn us *both* on (no, I'm not a lesbian). And the features and stories give us lots of lovely ideas for ways to bring both fun and variety into our sex lives, for which I, for one, thank you. But may I make one small complaint, please? We enjoy your letters columns too, and my own favourite topic is that of reading about other people's fantasies. But you seem to concentrate on publishing letters from men. Reader's letters from women, describing *their* fantasies, are few and far between. So how about publishing mine?

My fantasy is like a favourite film. I can run it any time I like. At home. In the office. In a restaurant. I like it best when I'm in a situation where I can slip my fingers down between my legs, and masturbate while I run it through. Without anyone seeing me, of course. Sometimes – particularly in the office – that means that I have to go and lock myself in a cubicle in the ladies' loo, drop my panties, and finger myself off in there, which means I often go back to my desk looking rather flushed. In my fantasy, I am rich. Very rich. I live in an enormous penthouse apartment, on the top floor of a very high building. I have an enormous bedroom with – what else? – an enormous bed. I have my own private, fully equipped gymnasium, and a terrace which runs all the way around the apartment. I have a retinue of servants. All men. All handsome, physically fit, attractive men. All men who like to fuck. Me.

Some of them do other things, like cook and look after the apartment, take care of my clothes, and so on. But they are *all* capable of taking care of me. Fantasies being what they are, there are no jealousies, no squabbles, no problems. Life is tranquil. There is, essentially, much variety. I have in my collection black men, white men, brown men. Some are employed full-time, some have fixed-term contracts, some are rented by the day or week. If I get bored with any one of them, they are immediately discharged. Paid off. All are totally obedient.

If one of them passes through a room when I am in it, and I snap my fingers, he comes and stands in front of me. If I want to unzip his trousers, put my hand inside, and play with his cock until he has a raging erection, then that is what I do. If I say to one of them, 'Get your cock out and toss yourself off', then that is exactly what he will do. If I am watching television and I feel like having someone suck my pussy as I watch (and that's whenever Richard Burton is on, for a start) then I simply summon whichever one sucks pussy best at that particular time and tell him to get on with it. All I have to do is spread my legs. I let *them* pull my panties down. If I want to get fucked all night, I have them stand in line outside my bedroom door and as one ejaculates and pulls out of me I press a bell to summon the next one in. In order not to waste time, I have a pretty girl standing inside the bedroom door to jack them off, or suck them off, until they are fully erect, and then I just plug them in and let them fuck me until they come. I never, ever, *ever*, suck their cocks myself. As a matter of principle (sorry, chaps). But I have girlfriends who love to come and suck cock at my place (amongst other things!) and it amuses me to watch my fellas ejaculating down their throats, if that is what one or other of the girls happens to feel like on a particular day. Some of us girls obviously *do* enjoy it. I have done it – and will do it – for men I love. But not for my fantasy team. With just one exception (tell you later).

The nicest thing about my fantasy is that it is almost infinitely variable. It allows for endless new recruits, or the permanent retention of an old favourite. I can be fucked endlessly, even mindlessly, if that seems appropriate. I can enjoy continuous orgasms. I can choose quality or quantity, or both. I never, *ever*, have to say to myself (or to anyone else) gosh, I really feel like a fuck (or having someone masturbate me, being sucked off, fucked up the arse, *anything*). I just snap my fingers. Literally.

I only take it up my arse in my fantasies. In real life, I'm too nervous. Originally, I intentionally hired a man with rather a small cock (most unusual in most of my fantasies!) to initiate me. Now I can take anyone up there. I love it. In my daydreams. But don't ever believe those stories, girls, about 'It's not how big it is, it's what you do with it.' They're put about by men with small cocks. Big cocks are the greatest. Take it from me. And of course I've tried out all kinds of sexual acts that I don't do in real life. Being fucked, for example, up my arse, up my pussy, and sucking a man off (well, that was the exception I mentioned earlier: just that once!) all at the same time. Just for the novelty of it. It wasn't any great experience, really. In point of fact, I discovered that I didn't know whether I was coming or going. I simply didn't know which one to concentrate on. Each one seemed to detract from the other. It's more fun in succession. One after the other. Of course, it isn't all serious sex. Not really. We have fun too! Particularly when two or three of my girlfriends are with me.

What I like to do is to have dinner in the apartment. You know, lashings of good food, and delicious wine, and plenty of liqueurs with the coffee. That sort of thing. And sometimes I tell the chaps to serve it with them all completely naked. So that, if any of the girls sees something that she particularly fancies, then she asks his name, and he is hers afterwards. Well, usually she's first. It's not an exclusive arrangement. And one evening, one of the girls suggested a competition. She suggested that we have a contest where we would compete to see which one of us could make the most men ejaculate in the shortest possible time. We all thought that was a terrific idea. Well, we were all well pissed at the time! And so we worked out a set of rules.

First of all, it had to be public. In other words, the competition had to take place with us all in the same room. There was no question of going off into a spare bedroom and coming back and saying, ten minutes later, that you'd made ten men ejaculate. Then, we decided, we would have to have an official, a judge, to keep the scores. Scoring would be simple. One man, one ejaculation, one point. Next, we decided that it would be both more practical, and more fun, if each girl entered individually. Meaning that we each made our attempt on our own, with the others watching. (If they wanted to. And, of course, they did!) Which would make it a long night, but most of the evenings thus spent with the girls *were* long nights! We decided that we would draw lots to decide the order of entry. And, naturally, the judge's decision was final. There were no objections to these rules.

I won't bore you by describing every act that every girl performed that evening, but I'll relate, if I may, a couple of the more amusing incidents. First of all one girl – Amanda – was disqualified, after the judge had decided that she wasn't entering into the true spirit of the game. In other words, instead of seeing how many man she could bring to ejaculation in the shortest possible time, she was simply seeing how many times she could get laid. Full stop. Speed wasn't a part of her game at all. She had achieved getting fucked by seven different men by the time the judge stepped in and disqualified her. She then carried on in one of the upstairs bedrooms. 'Whatever turns you on' is the rule of the evenings at my fantasies!

And the winner was the first amongst us (a sexy redhead called Jennifer) to realize that we had omitted to make a rule, which, had we thought about it, would have made it a much more even contest. But Jenny realized right from the start that we hadn't specified how many men an entrant could attempt to bring to orgasm at any one time. Consequently, when her turn came, she had a line of men queuing up to take the places of earlier men as each one with her was brought to orgasm. And she started off with five men. *Five!* One in each hand, being tossed off. One being sucked off in her mouth. One fucking her normally. And finally, one fucking her anally. It was the equivalent of one of those one-man-band buskers that you used to see outside cinema queues in Leicester Square.

As each man with Jenny came to orgasm, and was checked off by the judge, he was immediately replaced by another. After she had wanked off three pairs of men, Jenny stopped using her left hand, and concentrated on her right hand, while she gave up being buggered after the second man had spurted his come up her backside. It was too distracting, she said, in a quick moment of respite between gobbling two men off. Nevertheless, she had brought twenty-three men to orgasm when the rest of us threw our hands in and gave her best, to a rousing cheer from the men she had worked with to achieve this figure. It ought to be in the *Guinness Book of Records*, but we didn't approach them, on the basis that we didn't think that they accepted sexual contests. Maybe they should?

H. K. V. Abingdon, Berks.

I bet you girls would make a sharks' feeding frenzy look like a vicarage tea party. Seriously though, your fantasy sounds like a lot of fun. It's certainly in our *record book.*

ICE MAIDENS

May a mere male confess to a full, red-blooded appreciation of the wonderfully sexy costumes worn by (maybe that should be *almost* worn by) those amazingly attractive young girls entering the international ice-dancing championships so beloved by television companies these days. And for the best possible reasons. All those gals are so eminently fuckable, aren't they? I don't know anything of the technicalities – or the buzzwords – used in ice dancing, but I just adore the way that the girls skate about on one foot, with the other foot raised up behind them, parallel to the ground, exposing their pretty little crotches to all and sundry, glimpsed from underneath their tiny thigh-length skirts. I can watch for hours, fantasizing about what lies beneath those narrow strips of gauzy material, and imagining, as the girls get worked up and excited during their performances, just how wet and sticky the inside of those panties must be. I'd love to be a dresser in the girls' dressing rooms.

P. B. Hastings, Sussex.

We're with you. It's a really heart-warming experience. Would an ice-pack help?

WILD VIBRATIONS

As a single woman presently without a regular male partner, and not being much of a girl for one-night stands, I recently made use of one of the mail-order advertisements in your splendid magazine and ordered myself my first vibrator. This may not sound greatly exciting to those of your female readers accustomed to these delightful additions to every woman's list of essential items to carry around in her handbag. But it was something completely new in my life, and I had a lot of fun that first evening (and most evenings since!) trying out the various heads with which the vibrator came equipped. As a variation on the old UYOF (use-your-own-fingers) technique, learned at boarding school, the vibrator is a distinct improvement. The only disadvantage that I can see (feel?) so far, is the fact that I may never need a man in my life again! Positive advantages noticed so far are (i) the variety of heads, and the variable speeds, giving me what is tantamount to a whole wardrobe of men. I can choose one to suit any mood. (I love the anal probe. It has brought a new kind of love to me.) (ii) The vibrator's erection never fails. It can fuck me all day, and all night, and then some. (iii) It never wants to fuck me when I've got my period.

Disadvantages noticed so far: (i) It *is* a bit noisy. But who cares? (ii) I love to suck cock, but, much as I like the flavour of my own pussy juice, it's not much fun to suck. (iii) It doesn't ejaculate. (My girlfriends tell me that I should buy one of those dildos that *does* ejaculate, and which takes a vibrator as an insert. I'm looking for one.) (iv) I haven't succeeded in wanking it yet. (Although I did tell it one evening that I had a headache). On second thoughts, is there a woman out there who would like to swop her man for one fairly new vibrator? Five heads. Well run in. Still in its original packaging. Low mileage. Four spare batteries.

J. M. C. Glasgow, Scotland.

It does make sex sound somewhat mechanical. Why not use it as an adjunct to, rather than as a substitute for, the real thing?

BATH TIME

I think I'm a fairly normal man as far as most sexual matters are concerned, but with one exception: I love the combination of sex and water. Water as in a bath, or a jacuzzi, a swimming pool, or even the ocean. Bath water is my favourite fantasy. Add together *two* naked girls, one giant size bath-tub, lots of hot, soapy water, and me, and you have the basis of my sexual dreams. I will always remember once, on a business trip to New York, going to a so-called 'leisure spa', in Manhattan, and bringing all my water fantasies to life. It was fantastic! The spa was on Third Avenue, between 50th and 51st Streets. I was taken there by a man from the company that I was doing business with.

We went into what appeared to be a normal bar, with the exception that there were a number of girls there – all very pretty – dressed in a sort of Hawaiian costume. Basically minuscule bras, and very brief hula-hula skirts. We drank exotic, allegedly Hawaiian cocktails, and the girls were all over us. The guy who I was with said, 'Choose any two you like, Mac. It's on the house.' By which I took it that he meant that he would be picking up the tab. I chose a couple of attractive girls and they took me down along a corridor, then down a small staircase, and opened the door into what I can only describe as a sort of fucking parlour.

The floor was upholstered as if it was an enormous mattress, the whole thing covered with silken sheets. The curved walls and the ceiling were entirely of mirror glass, while over in one corner was a huge jacuzzi. The whole place was full of exotic tropical flowers, and it smelt of incense and scented water. The girls turned on the jacuzzi, and poured me yet another rum cocktail from a cabinet at one end of the room. They next undressed themselves, and then me. One of them grabbed my cock and quickly masturbated me to a splendidly huge erection. They then brought out a bottle of sun oil, and suggested that I oil their bodies for them. This I spent a long time doing. Oiling their bodies included oiling anything that I wanted to oil, and I oiled all four breasts, and both their pussies, bringing them both to orgasm as I attended to their quims. They were both doing the same to me, and I came a number of times during this delightful experience. I found the girls gorgeously attractive, and they were really friendly. There was none of the 'Let's get this over as quickly as possible, and get our money and get out' approach that one might have expected. I sucked their lovely breasts, and then their lovely pussies, and then they took it in turns to suck my dick. We were in the bath, out of the bath, and back in the bath again. We were fucking, sucking, and playing with each other, taking everything in turns. I fucked both girls. Both girls sucked me off. I sucked both girls off. They sucked each other off, whilst I tossed myself off. There was nothing that we didn't do, a number of times over, until I was completely sexually replete. Not to put too fine a point on it, I was fucked. So were the girls. I'm pleased to be able to tell you that finally, when I came out of the room relaxed, refreshed, and feeling on top of the world, my business friend had gone. But he had settled my bill. To this day, I have no idea how much that tremendous service cost.

D. H. Montreal, Canada.

An arm and a leg, we would guess. Sometimes it's better not to know these things.

SMALL IS BEAUTIFUL

Why the obsession in your letters columns with the sheer size of everything? Huge boobs. Giant buttocks. Colossal pussy lips. Enormous nipples. If I were a woman, I could understand a preoccupation with mammoth cocks, but that's about as far as I can go. As a man, I just love everything about my women to be small *but perfect*. Small, but elegantly shaped buttocks. Small, but firm, exquisitely shaped breasts. Tiny, fully erect, hard little nipples. Not forgetting small but elastically tight cunts. Doesn't anyone out there realize that small is beautiful?

H. Y. Bridport, Dorset.

Beauty, my friend, is in the eye of the beholder. We don't disagree with you. Nor with anyone to whom big is beautiful.

THROUGH THE LOOKING GLASS

As a woman, I am full of admiration for the lovely girls who pose for the pictures in your excellent magazine. I'm fascinated, too, by their ability to look both beautiful *and* sexy at the same time. That combination, I find, is not the easiest to assume. It's something I've been practising in front of my bedroom mirror for a while now, and I think that at last I'm beginning to get the hang of it. This is how one of my sessions goes.

First of all I have a long, languorous bath. I soak out the day's hassles with hot water, and lots of bath essence. I put silk scarves over all three of my bedroom lamps – to give a soft, sexy light – and I dress myself in some of my sexiest underwear. Tiny, flimsy nothings that reveal everything that they pretend to cover. Then I lie across my bed, beside which I have placed one of those old-fashioned pier mirrors. You know the kind? They are long and narrow, and you can tilt them to any angle that you wish. Then I pour myself a glass of champagne, and I lie there for a while, looking at myself, and thinking sexy thoughts. I think about my fantasy man, sitting beside me on the bed, fully dressed. I see the bulge in his trousers as he looks at me, and I reach out and undo his zip, and then I reach inside his fly and pull out his swollen cock. I examine it closely, pulling down his foreskin and exposing his purple cock-head, with its skin stretched so tightly. I see the blue veins standing out down his rigid length, and the coarse pubic hair below, in which nestle his balls. There is a drop of colourless liquid exuding from the tip of his cock. I make a few masturbatory movements with my hand, pulling his skin up and down his shaft, until he is completely erect, and then I lean forward and take him into my mouth. I suck him off as slowly as I know how, tantalizing him with my tongue, licking him, sliding him between my wet lips, sucking him until my cheeks are hollow with my efforts. Reasonably enough, it is not too long before he spurts his jism down my throat.

I keep sucking, and I swallow his salty, creamy, warm come. Every drop. By the time I have sucked him dry, he is fully erect again. He pulls down my panties and rams himself up into my welcoming wetness. I masturbate him with my vaginal muscles. He feels stiff and hard – like a thick steel rod – and, to my noisy delight, he fucks me practically senseless, until I am lying there, having huge orgasm after huge orgasm. I have to plead with him to stop. He knows me too well, of course, to take any notice of my entreaties, and he goes on fucking me until he explodes into me once more. He jets his spunk into my pussy. I can feel it erupting into my womb. The spasms of my orgasms make my whole body shudder: I climax endlessly.

The reality of course, is somewhat different. Back at the beginning, as I look at myself in the mirror, and think about my fantasy man, my hand slips – inevitably – inside my panties, and I spread my dry, tight, pussy lips. I slide two fingers inside myself. Soon I'm really wet, and I begin to masturbate as I think of that lovely, engorged cock in my mouth, extending my lips to their fullest with its circumference, stretching my mouth almost to its limit. My fingers move faster, and I feel my first orgasm beginning to build. This is when I next look at my face in the mirror and try and look sexy. At first glance, I just look like me masturbating. Slightly frenetic. But then I rearrange my face.

I open my mouth a little, wet my lips, and realign them

into a sexy pout. I pull my fingers out of my pussy long enough to use both hands to slip my knickers down my thighs, until they are stretched tautly between my open legs, a moist, grey spot showing on their – up until then – virginal white gusset. I slip my fingers back inside myself, and start frigging again. Harder this time. I come. I lie back and enjoy it until it is over and that first – essential – orgasm has been and gone. I then look at myself in the mirror again, and – thinking of the pages of photographs of your models in the magazine – I realize that I have forgotten a number of essential positions.

So I start again. I've done the hands-inside-my-knickers-playing-with-myself shot, so I don't need to do that again. But I haven't done the no-knickers-on, is-my-middle-finger-really-*just*-inside-my-slit? picture. I get a comb, and comb my long, curly pubes, until they are in a more suitable state to be photographed. Then I try a number of I've-got-my-finger-in-my-pussy poses, until I find the one that pleases me. I hear the click of an imaginary camera. Next I do the one where my black, silk-stockinged thighs are spread widely, with my knees drawn up – no knickers, of course – for the would-you-like-a-really-close-look-at-my-wet-pussy? pose.

I'm just admiring myself in this position, when I realize, God damn it, that my nipples aren't erect. I spend pleasurable minutes pulling and twirling at them, until they stand up proudly, like a pair of baby cocks. A men's magazine's model's job ain't *all* bad! I decide against the would-you-like-a-close-up-of-my-anus? shot, simply because I'm much too shy. I'm not against anal sex. Absolutely not at all. Given the opportunity, I quite enjoy it. It's just that I have a very hairy anal cleft, and what seems to me to be a rather large arsehole, not to put too fine a point on it. But there is another problem . . .

By this time, I realize that I need to come again. As soon as possible. The hell with being a model. I revert back to being just me, and go and get my vibrator out of the drawer where I keep it. I'm nice and wet, so I don't need any kind of lubricant. (I always think that should be lubri*cunt*!) I lie back down on the bed, on my back, and slide the vibrator up my waiting pussy. I switch it on, turn the handle to the fastest speed, and produce a series of seriously fast orgasms. I enjoy those, and then I turn the speed down and enjoy a lovely, long session of increasingly slow, but also increasingly intense, orgasms. After about half an hour, I'm fully relaxed, sexually replete, and happy. I guess it's time now to go and wash my vibrator. I hope you print my letter. Who needs men?

J. K. Twickenham, Middlesex.

Some do. Some don't. Whatever turns you on. Your letter certainly turned us on.

HAIR OF THE BITCH . . .

What is it about a great mass of female pubic hair that I find so attractive? I don't really understand it myself, but it is a fact that I find girls with big bushes the most sexy. You can keep your pictures of glistening open cunts, and gaping, fleshy labia, so long as you keep on printing the occasional shots of girls with thick growths of pubic hair. Linda, in your January issue, is just too much. Thanks for that tremendous picture of her, side view, squatting down, where you can see her long, thick mane of pubic hair hanging down between her legs. It's gorgeous. It completely hides any sign of her cunt or her arsehole. How I would love to nestle and snuggle my nose and mouth down there. And then there's that fabulous picture of her bending down, with her arse towards the camera, and her huge bush sprouting out of her anal cleavage. It's magic. I fantasize myself lying there and licking those beautiful cuntal tresses all day long. Your Linda is almost as beautifully endowed with her pubes as is my live-in girlfriend Diana. She is the most pubically hirsute woman I have ever come across (and I mean that literally). She loves me to lick and stroke and suck her locks before we fuck. Those of your readers who constantly extol the virtues of shaven pudenda are simply missing out.

F. A. Z. Oldham, Lancs.

We won't split hairs with you about your preference, but for our money, it's shaven lasses, by a hair's breadth.

NOT SO SOLITARY SEX

Many of your letter writers seem to manage eventually to achieve their fantasy ambitions. If one can believe them, of course. My own major fantasy is something that I have – so far – been totally unable to bring to fruition. It's quite a simple one, really: that of watching a woman masturbate, without her knowing that I am watching her. I've watched girlfriends masturbating, but always with their knowledge and agreement. Most of them seem happy to perform this erotic task on request, and for my pleasure. And highly erotic it is, too. But I have never managed to catch a girl wanking herself off, unaware of my presence as an observer. I would love to be able to look in on any girl's bedroom as she lies on her bed, playing with herself. I would like to see her slip her fingers inside her knickers, and begin by stroking herself slowly to wetness, at first just rubbing her outer labia, and then progressing to inserting one or two fingers up into herself. I'd love to see her fingers disappearing up in between her vaginal lips, and then delving deeper and deeper inside her pink cunt, nestling there in amongst her soft brown curly pubic hair.

I'd love to see the sticky, liquid wetness on her fingers as she withdrew them from her moist pussy and then sucked them clean, tasting herself, licking her own pussy juice off her fingers. And then I'd continue watching as she delved deeply inside herself once more and found her clitoris. Then, as she began to manipulate herself to orgasm, she would use her other hand to pull and tease at her nipples, tugging and twisting at them until they stood up erectly, tiny, stiff sentinels, standing guard on the peaks of her firm, pointed breasts.

She would start off wearing transparent pale pink nylon knickers and, at the beginning of her masturbatory session, she would start to rub herself through the thin material. As her wanking became more urgent, she would raise her pretty young bottom up off the bed and hurriedly pull her knickers down. Down around her buttocks, down past her shapely thighs – pulling in her spread knees as her knicks travelled down past them – and finally pulling her feet out of them and discarding the panties upon the floor. She wouldn't bother to take her matching bra off. She would simply pull it up, off her lovely breasts, to allow her fingers free access to her nipples. In my fantasy Peeping Tom capacity, I would be able to stretch out from my hiding place and pick her knickers up off the floor beside the bed. I would press the damp moistness of their sodden gusset against my nostrils and sniff the odour of her wet pussy. The inhalation of the scent of her vulva would instantly produce an excruciatingly stiff erection. And dreams being what they are, as soon as I had watched my lovely lady wanking herself to an all-embracing, highly vocal, shuddering climax, she would look up and – for the first time – see me. She would immediately catch sight of my hard-on, and she would get up and (not questioning my presence there) smiling at me the while, she would slowly and gently – but expertly – masturbate me to *my* climax, finally allowing my sperm to jet in warm, globular spurts onto her soft, quivering breasts as I came.

P. S. K. Blackpool, Lancs.

Wanks for the memory, as the old joke goes . . .

RAKES AND LADDERS

It is only recently that I have realized that I am a stocking fetishist. For a long time, looking at the many magnificent girls in your mag, I believed that I was looking at their crotches. Their tits. Their cunts. Their sexual paraphernalia. You know what I mean. But with your current issue, with those wonderful pictures of Madelene, I realize that what is *really* turning me on is that amazing pair of self-supporting black nylon hose that frames her pussy so elegantly. With her legs drawn up somewhere around her ears, I can see the seams of her stockings running all the way down the back of her beautiful long legs. And those exquisitely decorated lacy stocking tops – it all joins together to make the perfect frame for her pretty little snatch. Tell me, do your photographers sell off the used stockings after they have finished shooting a girl set? I can just imagine myself as the proud owner of numerous pairs of stockings, perhaps still warm from the gorgeous open thighs of the models themselves. Sheer black silk stockings. Pale brown, almost flesh-coloured stockings. White stockings, with extravagantly patterned stocking tops. Black mesh stockings. Soft blue nylon stockings, with slightly darker blue stocking tops. Black stockings with the tops rolled down tightly, looking like the rolled base of a condom. All of the above with, preferably, matching or contrasting suspender belts, and with long thin black elastic suspenders with silver attachments.

A. T. Newark, New Jersey.

David Jones

I'm told that the stockings and the lingerie we use in our photographic sets are normally a perk of the models themselves. What they do with them, I don't know. But we all know what you want in your *stocking next Yuletide.*

CHINESE CRACKERS

I've just come back from my first trip to the Far East. I've been to Hong Kong. I realize, naturally, that one can go a lot farther East then there, but by God! What a revelation, those Hong Kong Chinese girls. I could hardly tear myself away. Living in the country, as I do, I've never been to the Chinese areas of big cities such as Liverpool or London. But I shall certainly make sure that I do now. My life has been completely taken over by daydreams of those small, petite little bodies with their tiny, perfectly-shaped breasts and their slim waists and slender, taut little bottoms. I shacked up for four weeks (I was there on business) with a Chinese girl student, from Hong Kong University. I'd heard, of course, all those schoolboy jokes about Oriental girls' vaginas being horizontal, rather than vertical. But no one told me of their exquisitely soft, long, wispy black pubic hair! Having just spent four weeks running my fingers, my tongue, and my lips over – and down through – this delight, I can't wait to spend the rest of my life doing just that. My girl – Tsai – had beautiful long black tresses to match, and a flat, smooth stomach beneath those charmingly girlish breasts, and she had the longest, softest pubes I've ever seen! She wore black stockings, kept up by garters. (Something else I've never seen before. Not in everyday use, anyway!)

Her always instantly available snatch, nestling permanently wetly amidst that lovely mane of pubic hair, was long – about three inches, I would guess – which *is* long for a small girl – fleshily plump, and with outer labia that were almost black in colour (as were her tiny nipples). She was the deepest shade of pink inside. The lips of her mouth were full, and looked absolutely charming as they surrounded my engorged cock, something of which Tsai seemingly couldn't get enough. Whilst young, Tsai was also obviously sexually experienced. Far more than I, in fact. To my intense, enthusiastic, daily – and nightly – pleasure.

Tsai seemed completely relaxed about sex in a way that I have never come across in English girls, and obviously found sex as normal – and as necessary – as eating and drinking. Her skin was perfect. Her whole body was completely without blemish. Something which was pleasantly demonstrated when she introduced me to anal sex. The sight of her gorgeous, pale, creamy, perfect buttocks surrounding that tiny, almost black, fully dilated, puckered little rectum, was something that I shall always remember with consummate pleasure. All that, and I did some excellent business out there too.

P. S. Y. Llanarmon Dyffryn Ceiriog, Clywd.

Patently your Far Eastern trip was Far Out . . .

HAND TO MOUTH

May I take up a little of your space to disagree with most of the men who write to you about watching girls or women masturbate? I too find watching women jack off extremely stimulating, but I'm of quite the opposing opinion to those readers who say that their fantasies are all about watching women masturbate without the women knowing that they are being observed. My greatest pleasure is to have a woman masturbate in front of me, specifically for the mutual pleasure of watching and being watched. You may be surprised to know that there are many women who get enormous sexual pleasure from masturbating in front of a man.

I love it when a woman will agree to sit or lie down, pull up her skirt, pull down her panties, spread her legs, and finger herself to orgasm while I watch. I particularly enjoy it when the woman frigs busily away at her cunt whilst keeping full eye contact with me as she is doing it. Best of all is when the woman has a big, fleshy wet cunt that has produced enough liquid to make squishy noises as she wanks herself off. It is important to me, too, that the woman has a hairy cunt. There's something so much raunchier to watching a woman with a hairy great cunt tossing herself off than there is looking at someone playing with one of those prissy, tidy, shaven little holes that seem to me to be completely devoid of all sexual character. And the ultimate pleasure, of course, is to pull out my cock and masturbate in front of the woman who is masturbating in front of me. Having both got our rocks off in this delightful way, we can then get down to first some oral sex, and then to some serious fucking!

W. G. Portsmouth, Hants.

I think it's called keeping your hand in.

WHITER THAN WHITE

May I thank you for recently proving something to my friends? I have always known, ever since I've been old enough to get laid, that the most erotic lingerie is not the overly popular black of so many readers' fantasies, but is sheer, unadulterated white. Deanna, the girl on page 23 of your September issue is the ultimate proof of my theory. First of all, of course, Deanna is herself a very pretty girl. She would look good in anything, let's face it. She has a lovely face, an eminently kissable mouth, gorgeous blue eyes, and great tits with delicate areolae and perfect nipples. Add to all that a wonderful body with a fantastic arse, a lovely, blonde, hairy little pussy with neat pink lips, and what have you got? Perfection. I agree. But the white lingerie that she is almost wearing adds about another one hundred per cent plain, straightforward, sexual attraction.

That tiny white completely transparent brassiere, with one side just falling off a perfect breast, is so much more enticing than simple nudity. Isn't it? That minuscule white suspender belt, with its long, narrow, elastic suspenders running down Deanna's thighs, are enough to give the Pope a hard-on. Just look at them! And then those fabulous plain white tiny knickers, with their lace edging, showing everything that Deanna has got down there. I'm lost for words. They just make you want to tear them off and fuck her. Or suck her. Or both! Her pale pink pussy lips are exquisitely accented by the whiteness of her stocking tops framing her spread thighs, while her transparent white knickers, now pulled aside to allow her busy fingers access to her wet pussy, are an immaculate snowy hymn to sexual titillation. You can have my share of girls in sexy black lingerie any day. Give me the lovely Deanna, in her anything-but-virginal, pure white get-up. Now! Please!

P. R. Hounslow, Middlesex.

You're obviously pale with excitement. But we hear what you say. We must admit, as far as coloured lingerie is concerned, to being fans of the Henry Ford persuasion.

PUSSIES GALORE

As I'm only eighteen, you'll appreciate that I am not as sexually experienced as all that, although I'm not in any way complaining. I've got most of my sexual experience ahead of me! But I'm writing to tell you that I'm already fascinated by the different kinds of pussy that there are out there, even within my limited experience. There seems to be an infinite variety. It would be intriguing if you were to get a row of girls, all chosen for their original pussy shapes, and photographed them in a row, with their legs apart, so that we readers could see some of the many variations. There are girls with every shape of labia, from tight, neat, almost non-existent lips, through small, tidy lips, to larger lips, fleshier lips, fatter lips. There are longer thin lips, and shorter fat lips, and medium long/medium size lips. Pubic hair comes not only in colours ranging from pale dyed blonde through darker natural blonde to light brown, medium brown, and dark brown, to black, to blue-black, but there is also a tremendous range of auburn pubic hair, from carroty ginger to dark, almost claret-coloured red hair. The hair itself comes straight, curled, wispy, thick, grossly thick – and shaved. It's heavy, it's sparse. I haven't really got any special preferences as to pussy size or shape as yet. I love them all. Not to mention that smaller hole, situated lower down, but only a few inches away. But that's another story. One thing at a time!

S. K. R. Croydon, Surrey.

We wish you well with your first hole in one.

SMACK ON TARGET

I've fantasized for years about being caned, but I've never dared to tell any man in my life about this fantasy, in case he might insist that I try to turn my fantasy into reality. May I confess all in your pages? I'm twenty-four and 32-22-34, which will tell you that I have a nicely rounded arse. I love to flaunt it at men, in tight, short skirts, hot pants, swimsuits – anything that will let them see the shape of my buttocks against my deliberately, provocatively tight clothes. I love men feeling me up back there. Squeezing my buttocks, and fingering my anal cleavage. And my anus. And, yes, I *do* take it up my arse. That's a reality. And the final reward. But first – strictly in my fantasies – I like to be caned, or spanked. I like to be roughly handled.

I imagine being tricked into visiting an ex-boyfriend's house where I am overpowered by mystery masked assailants. I am tied, roughly – my legs spread-eagled – to some kind of frame. My back is to my audience. I am in a large room. I can see a neglected garden through a window at the far end of the room. There is virtually no furniture, and I am bound tightly with cord to a timbered cross-frame, set against the wall. I can hear three men behind me, talking in low voices, but I can't see them.

The next thing that I know, rough hands are stripping off my clothes. My jacket is torn off my back, followed by my skirt. Then my knickers are torn off. Fingers feel between my legs. They are calloused, hard working fingers. They feel me, intimately but surprisingly gently. And then I hear a sudden *swish*, the noise of someone trying out a cane for size, through the air. The fingers are still between my legs. 'Yer wet, yer dirty cow,' says a flat East London accent. 'Yer cunt's all wet. Ready for a fuck, ar' yer?' He takes his hand away. I don't reply, and then I hear the *swish* again, but this time a stinging pain cracks across my buttocks as the cane lands upon me. I wince at the agony of it, and draw in a deep breath, quite involuntarily. 'Jesus,' I say, through teeth clenched with pain. Whoever is caning me takes no notice, and the thin switch stings my flesh, again and again. Soon, I can feel a harsh glow as my bum skin reddens. To my surprise, I can also feel a copious lubrication erupting from my pussy. The caning is non-stop. Relentless.

I begin to sob, and I hear someone step nearer to me. Then, a moment later, something is thrust into my mouth from behind, effectively putting an end to my making a sound of any kind, unless I want to risk choking. I realise, after a moment, that it is my bunched-up knickers that have been pushed brutally into my mouth. I can taste myself – my intimate juices – upon them. I suffer the continuing thrashing with nothing more than the occasional groan, and I wonder about the damage that is being done to the skin of my behind. I am still exuding pussy juice. Suddenly the caning stops. I hear the cane being dropped on the floor, and then I hear the small – but quite unmistakable – sounds of a belt buckle being undone and a zip pulled down. I brace myself for what I know is coming.

I am right about that which I am anticipating, for seconds later hands grip my shoulders and a huge rock-hard tool is thrust up my cunt from behind. The rapist fucks me, without thought for me. But what rapist cares about his victim? I smell his bad breath, and feel it upon my neck. He grunts as he thrusts, and in no time he is spurting into me. I come with him. Violently. But I try not to let him know that. On reflection,

I doubt that he ever *would* know. He pulls out of me seconds later, says, sarcastically, 'Thank you, darlin'' and another man takes his place. This one is altogether gentler. His breath doesn't smell. His tool is huge, but he slips it up me as would a lover rather than a rapist, and he fucks me gently, almost lovingly. The contrast with the previous lout is so great that, after a while, I begin to respond to his thrusts, clenching my cunt muscles, pushing back against him as far as I can which, because of my bonds, isn't very far. When he comes, I come with him too, and I wriggle my sore arse as he squirts his load up me. His come feels hot as it hits the neck of my womb. I wonder why this man, who has at least some of the attributes of a man who knows what love is, needs to rape. Perhaps it's as simple as just liking the excitement. Perhaps the brutality of it turns him on. Suddenly he's finished ejaculating up me, and he pulls out.

His place is taken by what I hope is the last of the three men who have tethered me. He puts one hand on my shoulder and starts rubbing something greasy up my bottom with the other. *Oh, Christ*, I think. Rape is bad enough. Now it's going to be anal rape. I can smell alcohol on this man's breath. He's breathing hard, and his finger is invading my most private of places. Very few men have done what this stranger is doing to me forcibly. The others have been there by invitation only. 'Do you like it up your arse?' a voice says, thick with lust. It's not the flat accent of earlier in the day. It's difficult to place. More South than East London, I would guess.

I don't reply. I can't. 'Well, like it or not, up your arse is where you're going to get it, darling,' he says. ''Ere it is, then,' he says next, and I feel a sharp stab of acute, horrendous pain as he thrusts an enormous, ramrod-stiff dick deep into my anus. Thank God for the grease that he's rubbed into me, but the pain is still awful. 'Oh, she's lovely and tight. Really tight, Harry,' he says to one of this companions. *Terrific*, I think. He's fucking me like a rutting animal, thrusting savagely up me. I can feel my rectum dilating, stretching to accommodate this abhorrent, agonizing invasion.

I try to relax my rectal passage, attempting to accommodate him, as if he were a lover I was welcoming up my bottom. This is simply to try to lessen the pain, but it doesn't work. I can't relax while I'm being anally raped. He's breathing hard now, in my right ear. 'I'd rather have it in your mouth, you dirty cunt,' he says. 'But seeing as this is the way you're tied, and you're offering me your arsehole, that's what I'm taking. I love it. There's nothing like a bit of enforced buggery, is there? I bet you're loving every moment of it, you dirty whore.'

He reaches around me with both hands, takes hold of my breasts and squeezes them, brutally hard. If I had any way of being able to do it, right now I would kill him. I'm seeing red. Literally. Blood red. I try to calm myself. All I'm going to do, getting angry like this, is choke myself to death with my knickers. I can feel that my tormentor is approaching ejaculation. His cock is throbbing as he thrusts it up me. I tense myself, anticipating the final act of this, the most insulting of all sexual assaults. He comes with a rush, his filthy semen jetting into me. The final bloody insult, I think. He groans as he pumps into me, and then it's over. He pulls out. 'Very nice, darling,' he says. 'Very nice indeed. Thank you. We must do it again some time.' He laughs to himself. He reaches around me, puts a stinking finger and thumb between my lips, and pulls my knickers out of my mouth. 'I may as well use these to wipe my cock clean with,' he says. I don't reply to that either. Although I am now physically able so to do, I'm in too much pain. All I want is to be untied and set free. I'm terrified that they might start on me all over again.

Well, there you go. I can end my caning and bottom-fixation

sexual fantasies in a variety of different ways. All of which make me as horny as hell. And all of them accompanied by, at worst, my fingers. At best, my vibrator. Do you think I'm wise to keep these fantasies as fantasies? Or should I try to act them out, turn them into realities, with a sympathetic boyfriend?

K.O'D. Kilburn, London.

You seem to have got pretty much to the bottom of the problem. But the fact of the matter is, you're *the only person who can answer those two questions satisfactorily. Sorry.*

VALUE FOR MONEY

Do you remember the old song which starts, 'She was poor, but she was honest . . .' and which includes the chorus, 'It's the rich wot gets the pleasure, and the poor wot gets the blame. It's the same the whole world over. Ain't it all a bleedin' shame?' It has always seemed to me that the rich don't get half as much pleasure as they could do, if they really tried. But maybe I do them an injustice. Because I know exactly what I would do if I were seriously rich. And I have never – ever – come across a reference anywhere, in books, magazines, on television, or even in a movie, where there is any kind of mention of them doing what I would do. Which is simply fill the place with women. Every imaginable kind of woman. Blondes. Redheads. Black-haired women. Women with brown hair. Long hair. Short hair. Bald women. Fat women. Thin women. In-between women.

Tall ones. Short ones. Women with huge breasts. Women with tiny breasts. The same with bottoms. Huge, fat bottoms. Lovely slim, tight bottoms. Hairy bottoms. Shaven bottoms. Shaven quims. Hairy quims. Legs. Long legs. Short legs. But always open legs, when wanted. And I'd fuck myself silly. Morning, noon, and night. Some would be elegantly, fully dressed. Others would be completely naked. Some wearing the most expensive, sexy underwear that money can buy. They would all be there voluntarily, and they would all be well paid. No one would need to stay, if they didn't like it. They would all be ready to do anything that I wanted. At any time. If I pointed at one, and said, 'Come over here, darling, and suck my cock', that is exactly what darling would do. If I fancied sticking my hand up the skirt of a beautiful girl who was passing, and having a good feel, that's what I would do. And she would smile at me, and wait for me to finish what I was doing. If I then said, 'Get your knickers off', she would get her knickers off. What fun!

If I called over three of them at a time and said, 'Take it in turns to toss me off', then they would take it in turns to toss me off. All it would cost would be money. But I've never heard of anyone doing it. Can any of your male readers think of a better fantasy? Or, assuming winning the National Lottery, a better reality? But there must be dozens of men out there rich enough to afford to put my fantasy into practice right now. Why aren't they doing it? They must be out of their tiny minds.

P. H. T. Dungarvan, Waterford, Republic of Ireland.

It's almost impossible to disagree with anything that you say. We wish you good luck with the Lottery.

THE PLAIN TRUTH

I have always been fascinated by the letters in your correspondence columns. Particularly those concerned with what I would call fetishes. Men who infer that they can't get it up unless their beloved (or the immediate object of their desires) is wearing (a) black silk knickers, (b) rubber knickers or (c) crotchless knickers. This because I have always found the completely naked female body far more attractive, far more sexually tantalizing, than when adorned with whatever item of lingerie it is that turns others on. If I have a fetish at all – and I would be unusual if I did not, would I not? – it is that I am enormously aroused by a sweating naked woman's body. For this reason (and this reason only) I have had a sauna built into my flat here in Rotherhithe. Thus, under the pretence of enjoying the health-giving properties of saunas, I am able to indulge my own particular fetish. I have yet to meet a woman who can be persuaded into bed who would not, first, be persuaded into a sauna. There I lie back sweatily myself as I watch my loved one's body becoming hot and wet. Her nipples will become erect as the sweat breaks out upon her full bosom. Her pubic hair will become full of drops of her bodily secretions, like moss after a spring shower of rain. The petals of her vaginal flower will slowly open as her cunt begins to sweat, along with the rest of her, and I will inevitably get an erection – albeit entirely involuntarily – as I feast my eyes upon these delightful happenings. Seeing my erection will usually bring my fetish to a happy conclusion, for the woman will normally reach out and take it in her hand, leading to a sexual act which is often of my choosing. Perhaps oral. Maybe vaginal. Even, on occasions, anal. But whatever the sexual act, the major enjoyment for me, at this stage, is to conjoin in whatever way with a body that is wet all over with perspiration. And then, after the sauna and the sex, we will have a shower and depart off to bed, to further consummate our sexual relationship in rather more usual ways.

H. D. O. Rotherhithe, Kent.

That got us all quite hot under the collar.

LESBIAN CURIOSITY

As a 'normal' heterosexual woman, may I be allowed to tell you of my wildest, deepest fantasies? Are you sitting comfortably? Then I'll begin. I love to fuck. I enjoy it, and I enjoy giving and receiving sexual pleasure in any way that my man of the moment likes it. I have no hang-ups (that I'm aware of) and there is nothing that I won't do for you, if I love you. Or even if I only think that I love you. I'll happily suck your cock all day and all night, if that's what you want. And you can come in my mouth. Or I'll deep-throat you properly, if you feel like that. Not too many girls can, you know? I'll wank you like you've never been wanked before, if that's really what you fancy. I'll wank myself off in front of you too, very slowly, while you watch me, if that turns you on. You can fuck me in any position that you can think of, and when you've run out of ideas, I'll show you one or two positions that you probably haven't come across before. And yes, of course you can bugger me, if you're into anal sex. I love it up my arse. All of which *should* tell you that there isn't too much about male/female sex that I'm not rather more than familiar with. So what, then, do you think my biggest fantasy is? Shall I tell you? I spend many a night playing with myself until I fall asleep, just thinking about it.

I want to be made love to by a woman. Women. Girls. Lots of them. I want slim, feminine fingers playing with my pussy. I want a head with long, blonde tresses sunk between my open thighs, with a female tongue and lips playing beautiful music upon my wet cunt. I want to be frigged by a young girl. Sucked off by a mature woman. I want to *soixante-neuf* with another female sex, instead of with a cock. I want to slip my hand up beneath skirts, pull down pretty panties, slip my fingers into eager, waiting, wet little pussies. I want to be kissed by soft feminine lips, to taste tongues that are as agile and as gentle as mine is. I want a really pretty girl to use her vibrator on me, until I'm screaming for her to finish me off with her mouth.

It doesn't seem a lot to ask. I've been to any number of lesbian clubs, to suss out the situation, and I've had them queuing up to get my knickers down. But somehow, so far, I've always resisted. And then, when I get home, I cry myself to sleep again from sheer frustration at not having had the nerve to ask any of them back with me, and let them do their worst (best?). It's not that it's just a one-way thing, either. I want to do all those lovely, dirty things to them too. I don't just want to lean back and enjoy it. I want to give as good as I get. But when the opportunity presents itself, or whenever I've engineered myself into a situation where my fantasy is about to be turned into reality, I back off. Can anyone explain to me why I do that?

B. S. Bristol, Avon.

Beats us. But if you'd rather keep it all as a fantasy, there's nothing wrong with that either.

GOOD VIBRATIONS

Let me ask your readers a question. How would they feel if they had been pursuing a new girlfriend for three weeks, had finally got her into bed, and then, the second time that she lay back with her legs spread, and they were just about to gain entry for their once more rigid penis, the girl said, 'Hang on a moment, darling. If you feel under the mattress at the side of the bed, just about here' (pointing) 'you'll find a vibrator.' Taken more by surprise than by anything else, you feel down there, underneath the mattress, exactly where she had indicated, and you find the said vibrator. When you pull it out, it's off-white, slightly sticky, and *very* BIG. 'That's the one, darling,' she says. 'Now, how would you like to vibrate me, before you fuck me?' What exactly are you supposed to think? Is she telling you that you're a lousy fuck? First indications are that yes, she is. You look at the vibrator again. It's about twice the size of any cock you ever saw in the changing room at the rugger club. You're no expert on cock size (unlike most girls) but you've never had any complaints before. Quite the reverse, in fact. You've been told, on occasions, that your cock is 'a lovely big one, darling.' But it pales into insignificance, in terms of size, beside this intimidating plastic sexual weapon. Or do you simply take the view that this is a lady who likes to get her rocks off, and prefers a vibrator to plain fingers when she's on her own? If that's so, then why does she need it now, when the real thing is ready, willing, and totally available? On the occasion to which I refer, I simply took the course of least resistance and did as I was asked.

I must admit that I found it sexually extremely stimulating. The actuality of leaning over this woman's – up until this moment – largely unexplored vagina, prying it open with my fingers, finding the lady's clitoris, and then finally switching on the dreaded machine and stroking her to almost instant orgasm, got me harder than I ever remember being. Her vocal, highly sexual accompaniment to my shagging her with the vibrator was also highly enjoyable (I love women who talk dirty) whilst the physical result of my efforts was to produce a soaking wet cunt that fucked like a dream when I finally got around to it. Maybe I've answered my own question by relating this experience to you?

Since the first occasion, I have become accustomed to using the vibrator on my new girlfriend in this manner, before fucking her myself. It certainly gets her in the mood, and I have recently added a variation of my own which, whilst she was initially slightly resistant to my innovation, she now tells me that she thoroughly enjoys. It is simply that, having first 'vibrated' her to orgasm in the normal way, I then turn her over onto her stomach, and pull her up into a kneeling position. This is so that I can fuck her doggy fashion. Whilst I am fucking away, I slowly insert the vibrator up into her bottom (which, naturally enough, I have greased well beforehand). I love to watch the diameter of the vibrator dilating her secret entrance, and then disappearing up into her anus. When the plastic cock has all but disappeared, I switch it on, having previously set it at the right speed. The right speed, for this girl, is as fast as it will go. The vibrations quickly bring the two of us to the finest mutual climax that you can possibly imagine. Maybe these vibrators aren't quite so intimidating as I originally thought!

J. F., Wellingborough, Northants.

She sounds as if she likes it shaken, not stirred!

MOUTHWATERING

All my sexual fantasies are about oral sex. I dream that I have been commissioned by your magazine to investigate the world's best brothels, and I am currently in the Far East – Bangkok, in fact – looking for the finest blow-job that money can buy. I am sitting in a comfortably furnished room. I have a long, cool, iced drink in my hand. A fan is turning slowly in the ceiling. Through the open window, the usually strident noises of the street seem pleasantly far away. I look down at the long, soft, shining black hair on the head of the girl that is bobbing up and down between my knees. She looks fifteen, but the madame swears that she is eighteen. She is very beautiful. Who am I to argue? 'Does she suck cock?' I asked, as I ordered my drink. 'Like angel,' says the madame. 'Best blow-job in all Thailand.' 'How much?' I ask. 'You fuck her after?' she asks. 'She almost virgin. Maybe anal sex? She like it up small arsehole. Very tight.' 'We'll see,' I say, putting my hand in my pocket, and trying to hold my rampantly erect prick down. We haggle for a while, and finally the woman agrees an amount of *bhats*, the local currency, which totals approximately fifty pence in English money. As a *farang* – a foreigner – I am probably getting ripped off. Who cares? It's all legitimately on my expenses. And it's tax deductible, too.

I don't know whether anyone else would call what I am getting the best blow-job in all Thailand, but it is most certainly extremely expert. The girl is really working hard at it. She began by taking my cock in her small, long-fingered, shapely little hand, and pulling down my foreskin. After a couple of semi-wanking style movements – ensuring, I think, my full erection – she examined my swollen prepuce expertly, and then she slowly licked it, all over. She next looked up at me and, maintaining her eye contact, she took it slowly, deeply, into her mouth. Her mouth feels warm, and her tongue is soft. She uses it to stroke and lick my length, lovingly, carefully. And then she starts to suck me. The trouble with my fantasies about oral sex is that I am never given a bad blow-job. All these little Thai girls are experts. They suck cock like Scots girls used to bone herrings. Cleanly, quickly, and expertly. Although I must admit that this girl is in no hurry. I wonder idly what percentage of the fifty pence is hers, and whether it is more, or less, than half.

She is producing exquisite sensations in my prick, and I can feel my ejaculation gathering. I consider marrying her, and taking her back to Maida Vale, which is where I live. She could suck my cock all day, every day. With time off, of course, to explore her pretty little cunt, covered as it is with long, soft pubic hair. And not forgetting her nether entrance, enthusiastically described by the brothel keeper as 'very tight'. Right then my orgasm peaks, and I begin to ejaculate into the girl's mouth. I reach down and hold her head in my hands, as I pump my spunk between her full, sexy lips. I fuck her mouth for the time it takes me to ejaculate. She looks up at me as she swallows and sucks, in a long, sensual, continuous motion until, finally, my spasms fade slowly away, and I pull out of her wet mouth. She smiles at me, and some of my come dribbles out of the corner of her mouth. She puts up a finger, pushes it back between her lips and then swallows again. She grins at me. 'You like?' she asks. 'Feel good? Tina suck well?' I didn't know her name was Tina. 'Yes, darling,' I say. 'I like. Tina suck very well. Very well indeed. Thank you.'

She gets up off her knees and stands in front of me. She is completely naked. I love her on her knees. I like the natural subservience of Oriental girls. They are bred to perform sexual acts. They are born to it. And they love doing it. She will probably suck off her boyfriend at lunch time. My cock is getting erect again as I look at her. She can't be more than five foot tall, at the very most. Her small breasts are exquisitely shaped, with almost black nipples and areolae. She reaches out and takes hold of my cock.

'What you like now?' she asks. 'I do anything you like. You fuck me. Bugger me. You spank me. I spank you. Toss you off. I get other girl, we suck each other, then you fuck both of us. What you like? You tell me? You like something very special? All you need do is tell me?' I was literally speechless at the list of acts offered. What on earth could be 'special' after that menu? Tina looked downcast. Patently she felt that somehow she was failing in her duties.

She let go of my now rigid cock and, putting both her hands down between her legs, she took her minuscule outer labia in her fingers and pulled them apart, revealing for me a shiny, wet, bright pink, tiny little cunt beneath those almost black lips. 'Nice cunt,' she said. 'Look. Very tight. Feel with finger.' I put out a hand and she took it, guiding my extended forefinger deeply into her pussy. It really was tight, and very wet, and she began to fuck my finger as it slid into her, right up to the knuckle. Her vaginal muscles were doing things to my finger that I wouldn't have believed that a woman could do with her cunt. I almost came as I sat there, my finger up this delightful girl's vagina. She smiled at me. 'Feel good?' she asked. 'Feel much better on cock.' She suddenly looked at me, and pulled my finger out of her pussy. Then she put my finger in her mouth, and sucked it clean. She smiled at me. 'Don't want finger to smell of pussy,' she said. *You speak for yourself*, I thought. Frankly, I would rather have sucked it myself.

As I was contemplating the varied sexual delights on offer, Tina turned around and, with her back to me, she spread her legs, bent down and putting her hands behind her onto the cheeks of her buttocks, she pulled them apart, revealing the 'very tight' arsehole discussed earlier. I could see her peering up at me between her legs. 'Very tight,' she said. 'Feel with finger. Tight. Like Tina's cunt.' I reached out a tentative finger, and thrust into her tightly closed anal sphincter with it. 'Push in,' she commanded. 'You not feel properly unless you push right in.' I did as I was told, and then, wonder of wonders, she started to massage my finger with her rectal muscles. In exactly the same way as her vaginal muscles had done only a few minutes earlier. That decided me. 'How much for up your arse?' I asked. 'Nothing extra,' said Tina. 'All paid for up front. Tina yours all day. All night. No extras. Just tip at end, if you happy.'

She was telling me that the approximately fifty pence that I had handed her mistress earlier had bought her for twenty-four hours. To do anything I wanted. 'Arsehole it is, then, darling,' I told her. Tina went over to the bed that was up against the far wall and turned it down. She then went to a cupboard and brought back a small round wooden box, of the kind old-fashioned apothecaries used to use in Britain before World War II. 'You like to grease Tina's arsehole?' she asked. 'Most men like.' She took the lid off the box and held it out to me. I looked at it. It contained some pale, yellow-coloured kind of unguent. It looked a bit like axle grease. I sniffed it. It smelt faintly herbal. Quite pleasant, in fact. Tina got up onto the bed and, kneeling, looked over her shoulder at me.

I looked at her perfectly formed plump little buttocks, now some six or eight inches away from my face, and at the long black hair covering her anal cleft and surrounding her puckered little anal rosebud. I leant forward and kissed it. Dead centre. It tasted of slightly over-ripe mango, and smelt quite strongly of rotting, exotic fruit. I felt it dilate beneath my lips, and I stuck my tongue down deeply into its centre. This time, it tasted like some unfamiliar, slightly alien truffle. Earthy almost. My cock almost exploded. It was so stiff that it hurt. 'Hmmmm,' said Tina. 'I think you bugger many girls. You like to fuck arseholes. Yes?' 'Yes, sweetheart,' I said. 'Emphatically, yes. I adore them. Especially tiny ones, like yours.' 'What you mean, em . . . emfat . . . what you said?' she asked. 'You like little boys too?' I sighed.

'No, darling,' I said. 'Girls yes. All orifices. Anywhere. All the time. Boys, no. At any time.' She looked at me again, over her shoulder. 'Englishmen strange,' she said. 'Don't worry about it,' I told her. 'It's just the habit of a lifetime. I'm too old to change now.'

I began to anoint her anus with the grease that she had supplied, and I enjoyed the sexually exciting sensations of pushing my finger in and out of her bottom, knowing that almost any minute now I would be doing exactly that with my cock. She gripped my finger as it entered her, and as I drew it out, she held it so tightly with her rectal muscles that it made a long, slow sucking noise. Tina laughed. 'Rude,' she said. 'Very rude noise.' I had to laugh, too. Here I was, greasing her arsehole, immediately prior to buggering her, and she was seemingly embarrassed by a slow fart. Oh, well. It takes all sorts. After I had rubbed as much of the lubricant in and around her anus as possible, I carefully rubbed my John Thomas all over with it, after which I wiped my greasy hands on my handkerchief, climbed up onto the bed immediately behind Tina, grabbed her by her waist, and thrust myself into her. I watched as my cock distended her sphincter as it entered her, and as soon as she felt it inside her, she began working her rectal muscles energetically. It was sensational. I considered marrying her. Well, think about it.

I'd not fucked that many girls up the arse, despite my boastful conversation with Tina. English girls (other, I'm told, than those from aristocratic families, whose male line go to Eton, Harrow, Winchester, Belmont, and the like) tend not to be greatly enthusiastic about anal sex. I've never fucked a woman with a title, so I can't tell you if the rumour that they are expected to submit, once married, to what their husbands get a taste for whilst at boarding school is true or not. It's a lovely thought. A topic for dinner conversation. 'Do you take it up the arse, ma'am?' Much better than 'Did you see so and so on the box last night?' I'm having the best anal fuck that I've ever had in my life. It is thrilling. Truly, voluptuously, breathtakingly sensational. But I'm not going to last more than a few seconds.

Never mind. We can do it again. And then again. I look closely at my swollen cock as it travels lustfully in and out of that dear hole. The unguent is creating a small, glutinous ridge around her anus, as its tightness strips it off my cock. I can smell the sharp scent of her rectal odour acridly upon my nostrils as I lean over her buttocks, the better to bury my prick as deeply as possible into her. I treasure the sight of her dark brown buttocks, her blue-black rectal flesh, her black anal hair, and I pull her towards me, trying to get even further up her, as I suddenly explode into her, spurting my semen like a demented rapist up her rectal passage. I shout out, 'I'm coming. I'm coming. I'm coming up your arsehole. I'm coming as I bugger you.' She manages a moan, reaches around behind her, and energetically wanks my tool into her, as I spend my jism in hot, spasmodic jets. And then, suddenly, it is all over. I decide that I'm going to stop trying to find the East's finest blow-job for you, and start looking for the best anal sex available. You don't want to commission me to undertake that particular search? Then the hell with you. I'll do it for myself. Freelance.

A. H. Maida Vale, London.

Do you have to be such a pain in the backside?

TONGUE-TIED

I love my new boyfriend, and we have terrific sex, but recently he has started to insist on tying me up during our sexual encounters. He doesn't want to beat, or cane, or whip me, thank goodness. He says that he just loves to fuck me while I'm tied up. Or down, as the case may be. He's obviously into submissive sex. He strips me down to my knickers, and then he spreadeagles me on the bed and ties my wrists and ankles to the four corners of it. He'll suck my breasts for what seems like hours, until my nipples are sore. And then he loves to suck my pussy through my knickers, before he finally tears them off. (If you think about it, that's the only way that they can come off, with my legs tied to the bed.) Then he'll suck me some more, before he finally fucks me. I don't mind all that pussy-lapping. I get lots of lovely orgasms, and my previous boyfriend wouldn't suck me down there. He said he didn't like the taste of cunt. So it's still something of a treat. But after a while, not being able to touch him, or stroke him, or play with his cock – masturbate him, even – while he is sucking me is extremely frustrating. It's not that I want to control him. I just want to be able to react with him, sexually. Do you think I'm being silly? Should I just let him get on with it?

P. T. Ipswich, Norfolk.

Tell him what you're telling us. Sex is for both parties to agree about. If you're not entirely happy, tell him why not.

RUBBER SOUL

I've recently been experimenting with rubberwear, which I find sexually very stimulating. So far, I've acquired rubber stockings, which are black and which come halfway up my thighs, and long red elbow-length rubber gloves. I've tried rubber knickers, but they don't affect me in the same way as the gloves and stockings do, so now, when I've got the stockings on, held up by a sexy black satin suspender belt, and I'm wearing tiny black satin knickers, I'm ready for anything. The problem is that I don't dare tell my husband about this obsession with rubberwear. He's pretty straight as far as sex is concerned, and I think he would find my growing fetish bizarre, if not just plain perverted. This leaves me with my old and trusted friend, my vibrator, which services me whilst my husband is out at work. How can I get to meet like-minded people, or meet men who find women wearing rubber sexy? I'd love to wear it for someone who got as much of a kick out of it as I do, and who would enjoy fucking me while I have it on. Do any of your readers live in Norwich? If so, and they are into rubber, perhaps they would like to write to me? I'm thirty, blonde, blue-eyed, and I'm told I'm pretty.

S. K. Norwich, Norfolk.

You could look for discreetly-worded advertisements in the personal columns of your local newspaper, or check the personal ads in some of the more downmarket men's magazines.

But why don't you start off by finding out if your husband gets turned on by rubber? All you have to do is ask him. You don't have to let him see you wearing it until you know it's the right answer. He might find it the most sexually exciting thing that's ever happened to him. We'll happily forward any mail.

SHARE AND SHARE ALIKE

My wife is bisexual, and always has been. It is something that I knew before we got married, and it has never been a problem since she shares her lesbian sex with me, in that I have always been welcome to watch her at play with her friends, provided that I don't interfere in any way. Up until now, I have always believed that our own sex has been stimulated, even improved, by this situation. It certainly adds spice to my life to watch another woman sucking my wife's cunt, and to watch my wife sucking another girl's cunt. I enjoy seeing them fuck each other with strap-on dildoes, and wank each other with vibrators or their fingers. I love it when they suck each other's nipples, and play with each other's pussies, and I have had many a happy wank watching my wife at sex-play with other women. Now, for the first time ever, we have a disagreement over one of these women. Put at its simplest, I want to fuck my wife's latest girlfriend. My wife says that she doesn't object in principle, but she refuses either to suggest it, or to let me suggest it, to this adorable girl. I think she is being unfair. What do you think?

A. B. Gosport, Hants.

I think you're moving the goalposts. If your original – and seemingly long-lasting – arrangement was that you didn't interfere in any *way, I believe that you should stick with that. If you don't like the heat, stay out of the kitchen.*

KEEPING ABREAST OF IT ALL

Fantasies are made of what the lovely Bernadette reveals in your December issue. Or they are for me! She's everything I have ever fantasized about since I was old enough to get a hard-on. She's got a mouth that was made for sucking cock. Just *look* at those lips . . . All I've got to do is shut my eyes, and I can feel those luscious, full, wet lips softly sucking around my throbbing cock. She must have been invented to illustrate the word 'cocksucker'. Her face is that of an angel's. A sexy, gorgeous, dirty-minded angel. It is surrounded, halo-like, by her beautiful, auburn hair. Then her breasts. Her perfect breasts, surmounted by those long, erect nipples, sitting there like tiny sentries, guarding her areolae, waiting for me to suck them. I can feel them hardening in my mouth, whilst I fuck my erect dick in between Bernadette's lovely cunt lips. Following the natural line of her body, downwards, we come to her exquisite thighs, spread wide just for me. Her white panties are pulled tightly over her hairy cunt. Happily, her panties are transparent enough for me to be able to see the lovely lips of her cunt, peeping wetly at me through the translucent material. It's translucent because it's wet. Wet with her cunt-juice, trickling, exuding freely from between her dark pink, fleshy cunt lips and staining the cotton crotch of her silky panties, shading the white a slightly darker, rather greyish off-white. Stray hairs from her thick pubic bush peep out at me from the sides of her lacy-edged silken gusset. I can smell the heady, matchless aroma of wet pussy, as I peer closely at her crotch. This girl is made to fuck. I fantasize about pulling those lovely white knickers down, revealing her plump pudenda, thatched thickly with her dark brown, three-inch-long pubic hair. I want to pull it, tease it, play with it, part it to show her outer labia. I want to pull her moist lips apart and lick her inner, secret places. I want to taste her, smell her. Sniff her.

In her next picture she has turned over and taken her knickers off. I leer at the plump cheeks of her ass. They expose a completely white-skinned bikini shape, apart from which her buttocks are deeply tanned, a dark, mahogany brown. I want to run my hand over those firm ass-cheeks, squeezing, feeling, playing. I want to run my tongue deeply down and into her anal crevice, tonguing her long anal hair, sucking her cleavage, smelling her intimate smells, licking her forbidden entrance, watching closely as it clenches against my would-be forced lingual entrance. My cock stirs and raises its head as I tongue her backside. I think about greasing her rectum with oil. Pungently scented, syrupy, viscous, glutinous, cock-sliding oil. My erection thrusts itself fully upwards. I want to fuck this delightful girl's pretty bottom. Dilate her arsehole with my huge, throbbing cock. Bugger her. Down, boy. There's no hurry.

I can't believe it. On the next page she's playing with herself. Oh, Bernadette, darling. Why wank, when I can fuck you? Why play with your pussy when I can ravish you, forever and a day? Why waste all that finger energy, when I can fuck you stupid, morning, noon and night, with my massive, eager cock? When I can make you cry, make you plead with me to stop? Make you beg for mercy? To think that you are actually *real*. That, whilst you're a fantasy to me, you're a reality to someone, somewhere. That someone actually fucks you. That you really do take someone's cock between your luscious lips. That you suck him off. Swallow his semen. Wank him, slowly, whilst he sucks your cunt. Jesus.

F. L. Harrisburg, Pennsylvania.

Are you practising your breast-stroke, F. L., along with all those other manual strokes?

WANKS FOR THE MEMORY

I was lucky enough, the other evening, to pick up a new girlfriend in a local pub. Well, actually, to be honest, she picked *me* up. Quite unwittingly, later on that evening, she fulfilled one of my earliest teenage fantasies. I'm only twenty now, and I don't mind admitting that my sexual experience is not all that amazing. But I keep trying. Like everyone says, my life is all before me. It can only get better. But I was going to tell you about Susie. I was sitting there up at the bar in my local, minding my own business, daydreaming about spare cunt, when this gorgeous blonde comes up to the bar, and orders herself a glass of cider. She looks at me and smiles. 'Do you live around here?' she asks me. It's not the most subtle of lines, but why should I give a shit? The lady wants to talk to me. Who am I to complain? Moments later, we're sitting at a table, well away from the bar (and the competition) and we're getting on like a house on fire. Later that evening, after a few more drinks, a lot more conversation, and a curry at the local Indian, we're back at my place, and she's stripping off before I've even said, 'Would you like a glass of red?' I can't believe my luck. She's really gorgeous. I keep humming 'If you knew Susie' to myself.

She's tall, (I'm six foot, and she's well over my shoulder), blonde, with what look like terrific tits beneath the tight sweater that I've been lusting over all evening. I live in a bedsitter, so there's not a lot of privacy. She's stripping off while I'm looking for a bottle of plonk that I know I've got stashed away somewhere, and then I'm trying to find the corkscrew. She drops her skirt, and pulls the sweater up over her shoulders, showing me that they really *are* fantastic tits, and that she neither needs, nor wears, a bra. Which leaves her in baby-pink panties (the kind with just a thin ribbon around her waist and a tiny triangle of transparent material over her pudenda), pale-beige self-supporting stockings, and a pair of beige, high-heeled patent leather shoes. Fuck-me shoes, I think they're called. I'm having trouble finding the corkscrew.

Frankly, I've got such a hard-on, I'm having trouble doing anything. And then she starts doing it. My teenage fantasy. She's lying on my bed, with just her knicks on. Like I said. And she's looking at me, and whilst she's looking at me, she slips a hand down inside her knickers, and she starts playing with herself. Or whatever girls call it. Frigging? 'Just keeping it warm for you, darling,' she says. 'And wet, of course.' I nearly come in my trousers. I mean, there's a beautiful girl – what would she be? – Nineteen? Twenty? At the most. She's lying, almost naked, on my bed, tossing herself off, and looking at me while she does it. I mean, you know. Christ. Her hand, down inside her knickers, is just a blur of movement. Right now, she isn't looking at me any more. She's let her head drop back upon the pillows and she's wanking herself silly. She's making little moaning noises, and she's obviously – even to my inexperienced eyes – about to come. Her legs are spread wide, and her arse is moving up and down on the bed, in what I can only describe as fucking movements. Like a fiddler's elbow, as they used to say. Suddenly she starts shouting. I pray that my fellow bedsitter neighbours have all got their televisions well turned up. 'Oh, Jesus,' she shouts. 'I'm coming. Oh, fuck. Oh, God. Oh yes. Ohhhhh.' She would have collapsed, all of a heap, were she not already collapsed all of a heap, as it were.

I don't say anything. Eventually, she opens her eyes. She

looks up at me and grins. 'There's nothing like a quick wank, if that's what you feel like, is there?' she asks me. I'm speechless. My hard-on is so hard on, it hurts. 'Don't just stand there,' she says. 'Why don't you come and fuck me? Don't you like girls?' I look down at her. Her legs are still wide apart and I reach down and pull her knickers slowly down her legs. She has to squeeze them together so that I can get them off. Once they're off, she opens them wide again.

'Do you like what you see?' she asks, seeing me looking at her wet cunt. It's a beautiful cunt. All open and pink and wet and hairy. I can smell it from where I'm standing. 'You seem to have a problem, darling,' she says. 'Sort of a stiff prick. I think I can help you make it feel better. Much better. Come over here.' I do as I'm told, and she takes hold of my rampant cock and pulls me towards her. She's lying on the bed, and I'm standing beside her, and she takes my cock deeply into her mouth. 'Mmmmm,' she says, not greatly intelligibly, bearing in mind that she's got her mouth full. Of my dick. I'm practically coming already, and it's only been a matter of seconds.

I look down at her splendidly, moistly open pussy. It's surrounded by lovely long blonde pubic hair, and her brownish pink outer lips are pouting loosely up at me, after her manual attentions to them of a few moments back. I can see the ribbed walls of her inner, paler pink, fleshy cunt. I can see it shining wetly up at me, and I want to touch it. So I do. I reach out and push one of my fingers into it. It closes around my finger like those pictures you see on telly of insect-eating plants. Her pussy goes *splat*, around my fingers, and begins to throb and pulsate around my enthralled digit. *Jesus*, I think. *The sooner I get my dick in there, the better.* Meanwhile she's doing unspeakable things to my cock, with her lips and tongue, and all I want to do is keep it there forever, and fuck her mouth, and come down her throat.

What a delightful sexual dilemma! To fuck, or not to fuck? To come in her mouth, or not? After seconds of indecision, she makes up my mind for me, because she puts her hand around my swollen shaft and starts to wank me into her mouth. At the same time I begin to frig her cunt with my finger, and mere seconds later, I'm spurting millions of frantic sperm into her mouth. She slurps, and swallows, and grins up at me around my swollen member. At one stage I've pumped so much of my involuntary stockpile of semen into her that it's dribbling out of the corner of her mouth and down her chin. 'Thank you for coming,' she says. It's an old joke, but, in the circumstances, a pleasant one. I remember my line. 'My pleasure, my darling,' I tell her. 'Thank you for having me.' She laughs, and pats the bed beside her.

I lie down with her, my arm about her shoulders, and she takes hold of my cock again, working it competently, and fairly rapidly, back to full erection. At which point she says, 'I think you're ready again, sweetheart. If you fancy a quick fuck – or even a slow fuck – I know someone not a million miles away from here who'd be happy to entertain you.' She lets go of my stiff tool and I climb on top of her. She spreads her legs wide, and uses her fingers to part her outer vaginal lips. I can see the pinky-brown of her puckered anus an inch or so below her now open pussy. I take my dick in my right hand, and, with the other, I feel how wet she is inside. There's no need for foreplay, or lubrication, or anything, other than a rampant prick. This I have to hand, so I insert it into her and thrust. It slips in like a well-oiled piston into a cylinder. 'Ooooh,' she says. 'That's nice. That feels really good. Now fuck me senseless. Please.' I look down at her again. The lips of her cunt have closed around my cock, and I can feel her muscles working at me.

I begin to move my hips, and I slip my hand underneath her buttocks and pull her up towards me. Her buttocks are firm and sexily plump and I squeeze them as I fuck her. 'Touch me,' she says, and for a moment I'm not sure what she means. 'Touch me,' she says again. 'You know. Down there.' And then I realize that, in holding her buttocks, the fingers of my right hand are only centimetres away from her tightly clenched anus. I move my fingers just the tiniest bit, and they are in her anal cleavage. I move my forefinger around, feeling her anal hair carefully until, quite quickly, I find that forbidden entrance. 'Yes,' she breathes, as I slide my finger into it. 'Oh, yes. Nice. Yes.' I finger-fuck her anally as I continue to fuck her normally, and then suddenly I'm shooting my load into her in the most exciting way. She comes with me. I can feel her orgasming as I shoot my sperm into her, and finally we both relax, our breathing heavy, our efforts leaving us both breathless. 'Wow,' she says. 'That was terrific. Nice. Really good. Thank you.' I say pretty things back to her. But at the back of my mind remains that magic, delightful picture of her with her fingers down inside her sexy pink panties, masturbating herself whilst I watched. It was a one-off for me. I shall always remember it, and I hope it's something that I shall see many times again. But often, the first time stays forever as the best.

P. F. Stoke-on-Trent, Staffs.

Well, you'll never be able to say that you don't give a toss any more, now will you?

LINGERIE TO LINGER OVER

I've always been into two things, from way back. Farther back than I care to remember. One, girls. Two, naughty knickers. The combination of the two together has kept me self-indulgently happy ever since. Add to that the fact that a woman only has to wear three things, actually, to get into my record book. Naughty knicks, as already mentioned. Almost any kind of stockings. And high-heeled patent leather 'fuck-me' shoes. My favourite fantasy begins with my selecting a woman from a long line of women. They are all naked, and they all want me to fuck them.

As I walk along the line, they do and say things which each one believes individually will cause me to choose them over and above any of the others. This may be anything from a shy, reserved smile – presumably indicating unknown pleasures in store – to vulgarly (and delightfully) obvious things like pulling their vulvas open, or bending down, their slim fingers opening up their plump buttocks to my eager sight. Some of them masturbate themselves, their fingers playing with their pussies frenetically, showing – I assume – their enthusiasm for fucking. Some of them talk dirty. This has always been a big turn-on for me. You've only got to get a woman to whisper in my ear, 'How would you like to play with my wet cunt?' or, 'Would you like me to toss you off while you suck my pussy?' and I'm theirs. Instantly.

So, walking along this line of immediately debauchable women, all of them, of course, with perfect bodies, I select a chosen few. I take some with shaven pussies, because I love the sight (and taste, and feel) of baldly available cunt lips. I take some with over-sized nipples, for I adore to suck big teats. I take some with hairy pussies, for the opposite of shaven turns me on just as much. The hairier the better. I take some with big, fat, fleshy, cunt lips, for I love to suck them, and then watch my cock disappear between them. I take some with tiny, prettily puckered anuses, for I love to watch my cock dilate them. I choose some Japanese girls for they are, to me, the most beautiful women in the whole wide world. And I take some simply because I like the idea of fucking them. And then the fun begins.

I let them loose in the world's most expensive lingerie shops, having given each one of them a blank cheque. Then they come home and change into their choice of sexy underwear, and when they're ready, I take them, one by one, and play with them. They are all wearing stockings of some kind. The stockings may be self-supporting, as with modern stockings, or they may be hooked to suspenders, or they might even be held up with garters. Tights are out. It's that magic expanse of thigh, that few inches of naked flesh between stocking-top and knicker-bottom, that is one of the sexiest sights in the world. The girls' feet will be shod in high-heeled, strappy sandals or court shoes, and all of the girls will wear knickers of some sort. Bikini knickers, camiknickers, teddys, G-strings. French knickers, navy blue schoolgirls' knickers, crotchless knickers, suspender knickers. You name it, they'll be wearing it! And in every imaginable colour and kind of material. Plain white cotton. Black satin. Silk in every shade of the rainbow. Rubber knickers. Nylon. Wool. Lace. Striped knickers. Patterned knickers. Flowered knickers. Totally transparent knickers.

Sometimes I'll peel them off myself. At other times, I get the girls to do a slow striptease for me. I love getting them to pose as if for your magazine, pulling the crotch of their knickers aside to expose their vulvas to me. I adore sucking pussy through silky knickers. It's all spelt F.E.T.I.S.H., with a capital F!

P. G. Basingstoke, Hants.

We're with you, P. G. Enjoy.

SPELLBOUND

I often have this terrific fantasy where I'm able to hypnotize women. Think about it! It means that I can fuck any woman that I want to. Let's say I'm in a restaurant, and I fancy the pretty young waitress who is serving me. I simply look her straight in the eyes and hypnotize her. Then I say to her, quietly, 'Go out the back to the men's room and go into the first cubicle on the left. Pull your knickers down, and wait for me.' Off she goes, in a trance. Two minutes later I follow her out, and there she is, her knickers down around her ankles. I have a quick feel, and she's a bit dry, so I say to her, 'Play with your pussy until it's nice and wet.' She reaches down an obedient hand and frigs herself until I can see the juices running out of her pussy, at which point I say, 'OK. You can stop that now, and I'll shag you.' So she opens her legs, and I stuff her silly, until I've spurted all my come into her. I get myself together and then I say to her, 'Pull your knickers back up, go into the ladies and tidy yourself up, and then come back to me at my table in the restaurant.' I leave her there, go back to my table, and a few minutes later, she follows me. I snap my fingers, she comes out of her trance, and I say, 'Just the bill, thank you.' And that's it. Great, isn't it? I do similar things with girls in big stores, and in supermarkets. I have even stopped girls in the street, hypnotized them, and taken them home for the night. They tend to look a little puzzled the following morning, when I take them back out onto the street where I picked them up, and unhypnotize them, but that's not my problem. I don't always fuck them, either. Sometimes, depending upon there being a suitable place to do it, I'll have them give me a blow job, or maybe just a quick wank, if I'm in a hurry and I simply feel like getting my rocks off. I don't even have to pretend that I love them.

Sometimes, of course, it's much more subtle than that. For example, I might meet a girl at a party and fancy her. Well, I can always try my luck, of course, like anyone else. But why should I risk a failure, when all I've got to do is look the girl straight in the eyes, put her into a trance, and say to her, 'When you come out of this trance, you'll want to fuck me more than you have ever wanted to fuck any man in your life before. You'll ask me to take you home, and you'll get me to fuck you all night long, for as long as I can and as often as I can. You'll perform every possible sexual act upon me. You'll suck my cock, masturbate me, have me fuck you up the arse. You'll do anything that I want you to, and you'll love every moment of it.'

Then I just snap my fingers, and she's all over me. She can't get me out of there and back to her place quickly enough. She practically rapes me in the taxi. So much so that the cab driver says, 'You've got a right little goer there, mate', when I pay him off. By the following morning, I can hardly walk, I'm so well fucked. She's done all the naughty, lovely things to me that I've told her to do, and she's pleaded with me to do the naughty things to her that I asked her to. And she's asked me back again for another session this evening. I'm not sure if I'm up to it. But I'll try!

E. H. L. Maidenhead, Berks.

It sounds entrancing.

BOTTOM LINE

I just adore the female ass on display in your magazine. It's seriously high quality. But where I guess a lot of your readers get off on thoughts of fucking those lovely ladies, I get my sexual highs imagining *spanking* them. If you've never tried it, you should. That moment when a girl first exposes her naked ass to you, by dropping her panties. Or maybe you're in luck, and she's let you peel her panties down her thighs yourself. Those wonderful, white, plump buttocks, with her anal hair curling away out of sight, down her anal cleft. The magic of her ass, framed by her skirt – pulled up, of course – her black stocking tops, and her panties, pulled saucily half way down her legs. You reach out and touch that smooth white flesh. It's cool and firm. You squeeze it, and pinch it. Maybe hurt her a little. Run a finger up her cunt, if that's what you want to do. Or up her ass, if – like me – you're into anal sex. But first the spanking. It's better if you can tie her down. That means she can't get up and run away in the middle of the proceedings. It also tells her who's boss. So, tie her down. Strap her wrists and ankles to something solid. I've got a whipping block in my basement. If you haven't got a block, use a broom handle to stretch her legs apart, with an ankle tied to each end, so that when you've spanked her enough to make her cry, you can fuck her whilst she's still tied down. In her mouth. Up her ass. Wherever you want. But the sound of the smack on her naked flesh as your bare hand comes down is the ultimate cock-hardener. You increase the frequency of strokes. And the momentum. I love it!

B. D. Denver, Colorado.

I hope your ladies like it too.

KEEPING YOUR HAND IN

May I suggest that those of your readers who so vociferously extol the virtues of traditional heterosexual sex – i.e. plain, old-fashioned fucking – are possibly ignoring what is for me one of the most exciting and stimulating of sexual activities possible between man and woman? I refer to mutual masturbation. If they have never experienced the joy of watching a woman slowly undress, knowing that she is going to sit or stand immediately in front of them, only inches away, and masturbate herself to orgasm, then they have truly missed out. First the blouse is slowly unbuttoned and allowed to hang half open, revealing firm, braless, naked breasts for just a moment. They are then allowed to disappear again. As the woman bends down and lifts her skirt, she exposes to your lascivious gaze the stocking tops that are covering her plump white thighs, themselves a darker brown than the nylon gauze of the stocking itself, attached to suspenders. She hoists her skirt even higher, and reaches to unclip the suspenders, and then lets her skirt fall back into place, as she rolls down first one, then the other stocking. The almost obscenely rolled nylon reminds you of an unfurled French letter, and your cock starts to harden. You wriggle on your seat, finding a more comfortable position. One that will allow you to adjust yourself, when necessary. It won't be long now. As she bends down to pull the stockings off her feet, her blouse gapes open wide, and you get your first real glimpse of her erect, dark brown nipples. Now she stands up, and discards the blouse altogether. Her areolae are large, and her erectile nipples are swollen with passion. You need your hand, this time, to adjust your own erection. Your lady unzips her skirt now, and bends down to step out of it, exposing her completely see-through white nylon knickers for the first time. You can see the dark brown of her pubic hair through the transparent material, and is that a . . . ? Yes. It is. You lean forward, and you can see a tear-drop of moisture that has just oozed from her aroused vulva, staining the crotch of her knickers, and as you lean forward, you inhale the aroma of her freshly awakened sex. She looks down at you, and smiles as she begins to peel off the knickers. You can feel your heartbeat increase as you watch her. Soon you will need to let your cock free of its restraint.

She rolls down the waistband of her knickers, knowing how this excites you, and you watch as the top of her pubic hair is exposed. It is dark brown, long, soft and straight. Wispy. As she pulls her knickers slowly down her thighs, you can see that the cotton lining of the crotch is adhering to her moist inner lips, and as she continues slowly to pull them further down, the crotch is pulled out of her quim, and she reveals the inner pinkness of her vagina, shining wetly at you. The scent of aroused woman is much stronger now. You run your tongue over your dry lips and watch intently as your woman pulls the white nylon knickers all the way down her long legs, and off, over her shapely ankles, and finally her feet. She doesn't drop them on the floor, as you anticipate, but she reaches out with them in her hand and presses them to your nostrils. You breathe in, and as you once more inhale that divine scent, and feel the dampness of the material against your nose, you hastily unzip your fly and pull your now fully erect cock out of its prison. She laughs with you as you stand up and struggle out of your clothes, and then you sit down again, now as naked as she is, your erection proudly at attention. She spreads her legs, the better to offer you the full, erotic intimacy of her actions, and thrusts two fingers slowly, and deeply, up herself. She draws them out, carefully, and holds them out to you. Her fingers glisten with the wetness of her sexuality. You reach out a hand, and pull her fingers up to your mouth and suck them, savouring the taste of her wetness. Her tangy, strong, female flavour and odour does things to your taste-buds and nose, and via those, to the rigidity of your cock.

Having sucked her fingers thoroughly, you release them. Next she teases you, first using the febrile fingers of both hands to pull her labia wide apart, showing you the depth of her pale-pink love slot, and then she begins, oh so slowly, to massage her outer lips. As her fingers move over her labia, now fat with desire, so do her hips begin to move, keeping erotic time with her sensual fingers, a masturbatory hymn to her femininity. Your hand picks up her rhythm, and you start to masturbate in time with her, sharing the sexual intimacy, the voluptuous carnality, of that which lesser beings only indulge in isolation.

Her expression is dreamy now. Her body language speaks of languorous sensuality, of lazy, pleasurable, sexual warmth. As you watch, her forefinger strays, almost as if by accident, into her vulva, until her expression tells you that she has found her clitoris. Her sexual parts are so wet now, with her lubricious emanations, that her fingers are making tiny squelching noises as she massages her swollen cunt-flesh. Her movements increase just slightly, and she is beginning to make small noises somewhere deep in her throat. Almost a purr. Her knees are now slightly bent, and she is patently nearing her first orgasm.

You are sufficiently familiar with her masturbatory habits to know that when it arrives, this first orgasm will be but the harbinger of further, numerous, and increasingly intense successors, until she builds up to a final, earth-shattering, body-racking crescendo, accompanied by heavy breathing, then screams, and then shouts, a mixture of expressions of love, oaths, dirty language and the strident taking of God's name in vain. There is no need to try and keep up with this progression, nor is there any urgency on your part, since your lady will continue to masturbate indefinitely, should that be your wish. She will also, once she has reached her first serious orgasm, masturbate you if you so wish, something that experience tells you is infinitely more pleasurable than continuing to do it for yourself. She is beginning to sweat a little now. You can see a trickle or two of perspiration running down from her hair line, and her fingers – the two now firmly inside her cunt – are stiffer than they were initially, and her rhythm is faster. Her sexual lubrication is running freely down her thighs. You reduce your own rhythm, now simply pleasuring yourself with the occasional idle pull of your foreskin. Just enough to keep you erect and send small, erotically pleasant messages to your brain, whilst awaiting the culmination of your lady's first real orgasm, and her subsequent manual devotion to your sexual interests. Her mouth is open now, and there is a tiny dribble of saliva in both corners. Her fingers are moving faster now, and her hips are bucking wildly. She's fucking her fingers. There's no other way to describe what she's doing. 'Oh, yes,' she says, suddenly. Loudly. 'Oh, Jesus. Yes.' *This is it*, you say to yourself. Here we go for the jackpot. It won't be too long now, and those lovely long slim fingers, with their immaculately painted finger-nails, will be wrapped lovingly around your cock. You hope she won't be long.

'Oh, yes,' she says again. 'Oh, fuck. Oh, God.' Her fingers are a blur now. 'I'm coming,' she shouts. Bored with her announcements, in that they're not doing a lot for you sexually, you pick her knickers up off the floor and press them up to your nose again. And there it is. The unmistakable scent of cunt. Wet cunt. If only you could bottle it, you'd make a fortune. 'I'm coming,' she shouts. You wonder if the neighbours are listening. 'I'm coming. Oh, Jesus. Yes. Yes. Now. Now. Oh, dear God.' Suddenly she drops down onto her knees, her fingers working overtime, as she wanks herself silly. She's obviously coming in large, regular, enjoyable instalments. *This is it, baby*, you think to yourself. *Enjoy. And hurry*.

And then she's finished. She's exhausted. She's half crying, half laughing. 'Christ,' she says. 'That was a good one. Terrific. Now let me finish you off.' *Please God*, you say to yourself. She takes your cock in her hand and begins to do wonderful things to it. She squeezes, pulls, wanks, rubs, caresses it. She's making love to you with her fingers. You reach out and begin to finger her cunt. It's soaking wet. She wriggles. 'Hmmmm,' she says. 'That's nice. I love it when I'm tossing you off, and you play with my pussy.' You can feel your ultimate ejaculation building, somewhere way down in your prostate. She's kneeling on the floor between your knees now, masturbating you with malice aforethought. She leans forward, and says – quietly, in your ear – 'Do you like it when I jack you off? Do you like me giving you one off the wrist? Are you going to fuck me, after I've made you come all over my fingers?' 'Yes, darling,' you say. You're breathing hard now. You can feel your ejaculation coming up out of your boots.

'Oh, yes,' you say, panting. 'Now. Please. Make me come now. Right now.' She moves her supple fingers just that little bit faster, and then yes, Jesus, you're spurting your come like a hot little geyser. She takes your cock and aims it towards her lovely breasts, so that your ejaculate is spurting all over them. She uses her other hand to rub your sticky come into them. Her nipples stand up again beneath this close attention. 'Oooh, nice,' she says. 'I love your come on my tits.' She keeps up her expert manipulation of your dick, until every last drop of jism has been extracted. 'I think that's it for now, darling,' she says. 'But we'll start up again in a little while.

Would you like me to toss you off again? Or would you rather fuck me? Or shall I suck you off, this time? I quite fancy you sucking me off, so we could start with a little *soixante-neuf*, and see how we go on from there. What do you think?'

My cock is half way hard again already. I'm too far gone to make any kind of a decision. 'You tell me, sweetheart,' I say. 'Whatever you fancy.' She smiles at me, and leans up and gives me a sexy wet kiss. 'I think I'll suck you off for a little while,' she says. 'And then I'll ask you again. OK?' 'OK,' I agree. That's the lovely thing about mutual masturbation. It leaves you absolutely relaxed, and ready for anything.

R. P. Lee-on-Solent, Hampshire.

We like a woman who will enter into the spirit of things and give us a helping hand.

BEST FOOT FORWARD

I think I must have a foot fetish. Or a shoe fetish, thinking about it. Yes. That's more like it. A shoe fetish. I'm fixated on girls who are naked, apart from their shoes. They have to be high heels. That's absolutely vital. I love it when they're naked, and they're sitting down, and lying back, with their legs crossed in front of them, showing their shoes, just in front of their beautiful love-holes. The strappier the shoes, the happier I am. Lydia, in your November issue, had me jacking off for days. I've got her picture beside my bed, and I jack off to it every night, before I go to sleep. She's perfect. Her lovely blonde hair, framing her innocent-looking little face. (I'm sure she's not innocent at all. That's half the attraction.) Her fabulous breasts. They're not too big, but they're nicely plump and in wonderful shape. I can imagine sucking those teats between my hot lips. And that lovely, hairy cunt, with its gorgeous, fleshy cunt lips. They're wide open in your photographs, and that's the way I'd like to see them. I'd like to thrust my tongue up between them first of all, and suck Lydia to a wild orgasm, before I rammed her with my massively erect tool and fucked her brains out. But it would be an essential part of the deal that she kept those fantastic red sandals on while I do all those things to her. As to that tiny little peep-hole, an inch or two below her cunt, well, what can I tell you? Not a lot.

S. L. K. Hull, Humberside.

It's largely a question of keeping body and sole together.

KISS OF LIFE

My fantasies all revolve around girls' lips. Ever since I was sucked off by my secretary at my firm's annual Christmas party last year, I haven't wanted to know about fucking as such. Why waste time pushing your dick up something a woman pisses through when you can have her put it between her elegant lips and mouth you off? I read, all the time, of women whose cunts 'caress like fingers', 'suck like mouths', 'massage like experts', but I've never met one. The only girls who suck *me* off, suck me in their mouths. And that's where I like to be. Now, at parties, or when I meet new women, I don't look at their tits, or at their legs, or up their skirts, or wonder about their cunts. I look at their luscious lips, and imagine thrusting my cock into their hungry mouths and spurting my come down their welcoming throats.

Angela (my secretary) says she loves me to come in her mouth. She also lets me come on her tits, in her hand, over her stomach, and anywhere else I want, after she has sucked me to the point of ejaculation. She doesn't particularly want to be fucked afterwards either. She's happy for me to wank her off, or watch her while she wanks herself. Sometimes she sits beside me in my office, apparently taking dictation (just in case anyone else should come into my office) but in fact she's tossing me off, her hand down my flies. Then she'll toss herself off, and I'll lick her fingers clean for her afterwards. Oh, happy days.

W. T. New York, N. Y.

She's obviously taking you for a sucker.

BLACK LOOKS

As an admirer of the female form, may I relate my favourite fantasy for the benefit of your other readers, who may share my tastes? I'm the only man on board a sailing clipper, sailing the Caribbean. The rest of the crew are all women. They're professional sailors, and completely capable of handling the ship in any kind of weather, but they're also chosen for their looks and their enjoyment of things sexual. They come in all shapes and sizes. There are American girls, European girls, Asian girls, African girls, Chinese and Japanese girls and, naturally enough, girls from the various Caribbean islands. There are very few rules, but there are two upon which I insist before the girls sign on. One, all girls are totally naked, at all times. Two, all girls are available for any sexual act, at all times. The girls are, of course, well paid, and the crew lives in considerable luxury. Domestic requirements, like cooking and cleaning ship, are shared equally amongst all the crew. There are no ranks. I am nominally the captain, but, like the crew, I don't wear a uniform. Certain members of the crew have certain responsibilities, in line with their nautical training, otherwise everyone is equal. When we go ashore, to collect provisions or for medical needs, for example, or simply to enjoy a meal in a restaurant, we all dress, (for want of a better word) in civilian clothes, so as not to embarrass anyone. In my fantasy, the weather is always perfect, and the long, Caribbean days are full of beautiful bodies on deck, some managing the ship, others simply improving their tans. I have my eye on a lithe, long-limbed Caribbean lady called

Joan. She is black, with long black hair in corn rows, which are then tied back. Her breasts are full, and crowned by dark-skinned, almost black, silver dollar-sized areolae, mounted by hugely erect nipples, the size of my thumbs. I can see her generous growth of black, tightly curled pubic hair, and I can also see, down the centre of her pubis, a dark pink, almost black gash, shining wetly in the sunshine.

As I watch, Joan is aware of my interest. It is that, I believe, which is causing her nipples to become so stiffly erect, and it is also the reason for the moistness at her crotch. She is standing facing me, about four foot away from me, leaning against the rigging. As I watch, she turns and leans against the ship's rail, her legs almost up to her waist, her perfectly shaped taut buttocks facing me roundly and revealing the growth of anal hair that is presently hiding her anus. Joan and I haven't fucked yet. She looks over her shoulder at me and smiles. 'Pussy all wet, man,' she says, in that lovely, husky voice that the girls from the Islands all seem to have. 'Pity to waste it,' she continues. 'What you say?' She turns back to face me and spreads her legs wide apart. I can see the glistening, clear liquid which is now trickling down her pubic hair and making its slow journey down towards her strong thighs. She puts a finger between her legs and strokes her pussy lips.

'You like to fuck Caribbean girls?' she asks. 'This girl ready to fuck.' What can I tell you? I stand up, my rampant erection an answer in itself. I grin at Joan. 'Just follow me, darling,' I say. 'Today's your lucky day.' Well, I *am* the captain, when all's said and done. As I stand up and my erection makes my objective obvious to the entire crew, Joan and I get a round of applause from the others. That's nice, isn't it? The stuff of dreams. I lead the way down to my master cabin and through my lounge to the bedroom. It is air conditioned and pleasantly cool. My king-sized bed has been made up with fresh linen and is turned back, ready for the day's activities. Joan looks around her. She obviously likes what she sees.

'Hmmm,' she says. 'Nice.' 'Thank you,' I say. There is a light sheen of sweat all over her perfect body, but it is quickly disappearing in the coolness of the cabin. 'How do you want me?' asks Joan. 'Do you want me to suck your cock a little first? Do you want to suck my pussy? Do you just want to lie there and let me fuck you?' She smiles at me and she's fingering her pussy again. 'I think that, maybe to start off with, I'll just watch you playing with your pussy, darling,' I tell her. 'Then we'll think again.' 'Sure, baby,' she says. She goes over to the bed and sits on the edge, and then she spreads her thighs and begins to masturbate herself. I go and kneel down in front of her, so that I can fully appreciate the sight, sounds, and scents of what she is doing. My cock is standing fully to attention. I take hold of it and begin to stroke it, gently.

Joan's cunt is a deep purple colour, down inside her pinky black labia, and I can see how wet it is. She is fingering herself deeply, but I don't think she has started manipulating her clitoris. She is simply thrusting her fingers in and out of herself. She looks at me, lazily. 'You like what you see?' she asks. She licks her full lips and I wonder, for a moment, what it is going to feel like when she sucks my cock. 'Yes,' I tell her. 'I like. I think I'll suck you now.' So saying, I pull her hand away from between her legs, press her thighs farther apart, and lean forward to take her swollen labia between my lips. She tastes strongly of her feminine juices, mixed with tropical fruits, and with an unusual, overriding sweetness that I don't recognize. It's probably called Jamaican cunt.

Whatever it is, I like it. I find her clitoris and concentrate on it, and she begins to wriggle. I stop what I'm doing for a moment, just long enough to push her flat down upon the bed on her back, straddle her face, and bury my mouth between her legs again. She obediently takes my cock in her mouth (in that position, she can hardly avoid it) and I start to feel what it's like to be sucked by those delightful lips, aided by that busy, experienced tongue. It feels good. So good, in fact, that I quickly shoot my load down her throat. She doesn't show any signs of being irritated by this event and sucks and swallows until all my ejaculate has disappeared.

I continue sucking her pussy, and soon she too achieves a series of orgasms so I feel that I've at least given as good as I've received. I get up off her and go through to the lounge cabin where I open my concealed fridge and extract a bottle of champagne. It's the real stuff. Vintage Mumm. As I open it, I call through to Joan and ask her if she wants to join me. She does, she says. I pour two glasses, and carry them through to the other cabin. 'Cheers, darling,' I say. 'Cheers,' she says. She puts her glass down and takes hold of my cock, which she begins to play with. She rapidly teases it back into a full erection as I watch. I enjoy the sensations which she is so expertly producing. 'You've done that before,' I say. She grins at me. 'If a girl wants to get well fucked, that's something she has to learn how to do,' she tells me. I grin back at her. 'Since you're so expert,' I said, 'keep on doing it. Jerk me off. I'd like that. Then you can make me hard again, and then we'll fuck. OK?' She began jerking me off, energetically. 'You're the boss,' she said. 'Whatever turns you on, baby.'

I began playing with her pussy while she masturbated me. It was very wet, and accommodated my fingers easily. 'You're not doing too badly yourself,' she said. 'Have you frigged a lot of girls?' 'That's almost a "When did you stop beating your wife?" question,' I said. 'But yes. I've frigged a few girls in my time. But I'd far rather watch them doing it themselves, as you already know. This is just so's not as to completely waste the time, since you're so busy jerking me off. I just love the feel of wet pussy.' I dipped my forefinger farther in and began to frig her clitoris. She came very quickly, gasping and muttering under her breath and jerking her hips about on the bed, but she didn't falter in her five-finger exercise with my cock.

'I'm going to make you come now, honey,' she said. And she did. She pressed a knowing finger deeply into me, somewhere just at the base of my cock, underneath it, where my scrotum joins it. The result was instant. It was as if she had massaged my prostate. I shot my ejaculate all over her busy fingers. 'Hmmm,' she said, not for the first time that day. 'That's nice. Was it nice for you, baby?' She wiped her hand clean on the immaculate sheet beneath her and then she leaned forward and, taking my cock in her mouth, she sucked and licked it scrupulously clean. 'Now we can start afresh,' she said. 'Pussy wants you now. Joan wants to be fucked. But tell me,' she said, 'which of the other girls are you going to fuck next?'

'Why do you ask?' I said. 'Because that's how I'm going to get you going again,' she said. 'Tell me.' 'Well, I don't really know,' I told her. 'I hadn't given it a lot of thought. The nice thing about this boat of mine is that all the lovely girls are fuckable. Anythingable. I don't have to work at getting my rocks off. But since you ask, I've been looking at that little Chinese girl. You know the one. Five foot nothing, tiny tits, slim little legs, and great big thick bushy pubes. I'll stake my reputation that she's got a lovely, tiny, tight little cunt hidden away in that bird's nest between her legs.' 'That's Tsai,' said Joan, laughing gently. 'She's lovely. Shall I tell you what she really likes? We girls talk about these things, you know.' 'I guess you do,' I said. 'Yeah, go on, then. Tell me.' Joan took hold of my semi-erect cock once more. Thinking about the Chinese girl had already got me going in the right direction.

'She likes to dress up in sexy lingerie,' Joan told me.

'Black silk or satin. Lots of lace. Black silk stockings. Suspender belts. That sort of thing. And then she likes someone to rip it all off her. Spank her a little. Nothing too serious, mind. Rape-fantasy stuff. You must have come across it?' She looked at me, expectantly, as if she expected me at least to nod my head. 'No, honey,' I told her. 'I've never come across a girl who liked to be roughed up.' All the time we were talking, Joan was slowly kneading my dick. Pulling on it. Peeling back the foreskin. It jumped to almost fully erect, listening to what little Chinese Tsai liked to have done to her. 'But the best is yet to come,' said Joan. 'She likes it up her ass. Do you like to fuck girls in the ass?' 'Some,' I said, lying in my teeth. A lot of girls don't like you even to suggest anal sex, never mind actually doing it. 'Yes,' Joan went on. 'She likes to have someone pretend to rape her anally. Apparently she likes to scream, and shout, "No. Please, God, no. Not up there. Not in my asshole. Please. Please." '

Joan's imitation of Tsai pleading for the virginity of her asshole was almost too much for me. I quickly pulled my cock away from her naughty fingers. 'If you seriously want to get fucked, darling,' I said to her, 'now's the time.' 'OK, baby,' she said. 'No problem. You just lie back there and relax, and I'll fuck you like you've never been fucked before.' I lay back as directed. She stood up over me, on the bed, and put one foot each side of me. I looked up into her hairy snatch. It was literally dripping with her mucus-like lubrication. She put her fingers down and pulled her pussy-lips wide open. 'Here it comes, baby,' she said. 'Genuine one hundred per cent, dyed-in-the-wool real Jamaican nooky. You'll never have better.' She grinned, bent her legs, and ended up kneeling over my thighs, a long leg each side of me, impaling my cock with what felt like her almost liquified cunt as she so did.

She was tight, and she was hot. Literally. Really hot. It was like sticking my dick into a private, miniature, cock-encompassing, slippery steam bath. 'How does that feel, honey?' she asked me. Her cunt-muscles gripped me as she spoke and she began to ride me, working away at me as she rose up and down, gleefully, vociferously, on my joystick. 'Oh, yes, baby,' she intoned. 'This's what Joan's been waiting for. Lovely, big, stiff cock. Every girl's best friend. Oh, yes. I love it.' She threw her head back, and laughed out loud as she rode me.

I soon took hold of her gorgeous buttocks, and gripped them as she rode me. Tempted by her earlier conversation about Tsai, I slowly moved my hands down and then, when they were in the right position, I slipped a finger into her anal cleavage, and felt around for her anus. She was as hirsute there as was her snatch, and I couldn't feel her actual asshole for the quantity of her thick anal tresses. As soon as she felt me fingering her ass, she sat up straight, took hold of my searching finger, and moved it onto her dimpled little anal rosebud. 'If that's what you're looking for,' she said, 'there it is. Don't fuck about. You want to finger-fuck my asshole while I fuck you? I'd like that.'

I slipped my finger into her and felt her tight little hole dilate as my finger entered into it. I had to time the insertion and withdrawal of my finger from up her asshole quite carefully, to coincide with her movements as she rose and fell the length of my cock. If it hadn't been for the number of times that she had already brought me to ejaculation, I would have already come by now, so erotic were the things that she was doing to me as she fucked me. She brought the expression 'I'm going to fuck your brains out' to reality for me. Looking back, I think she probably knew that right from the beginning, and had almost certainly engineered my earlier ejaculations, in order to ensure that she eventually got herself well fucked, once she finally got me around to it. Either way, I was very happy. I was overjoyed.

D. O'M. St Petersburg, Florida.

Some trip. It seems you were fucking up a storm. We'll keep our fingers crossed that you didn't have a mutiny on your hands!

APHRODITE DIET

My girlfriend and I were discussing the theory of aphrodisiacs the other day, and we went through all the old theories that we had read about, from Spanish Fly (which I'm told is the ground-up powder from a dried insect) through oysters – and yes, I've heard the joke about the guy who ate a dozen oysters and his wife complained that one of them didn't work – to raw meat. I've eaten oysters, of course, but never with the intention (or hope!) of improving my sexual performance, and I have to say that there was no noticeable difference, either way. Nor with Steak Tartare – probably not a very popular dish in these days of BSE. But I have always maintained that there is no aphrodisiac in the world that works as efficiently as a new woman. Discovering all her secret places for the first time. Touching them, feeling them. Sucking them, licking them. Inhaling her intimate scents, tasting her forbidden fruit. The first time you insert your penis into her wet vagina. Finding out what turns her on, what makes her scream with pleasure. Learning how best to bring her to orgasm. My girlfriend agrees, and says that the same applies for her with a new man! Thus, whilst I stay faithful to my girlfriend, my fantasies encompass an endless supply of beautiful women, kept in a large house, to which I am the only male who is permitted access. The house is in the country and includes stables, with horses, indoor and outdoor pools, professional cooks (female!) and servants for cleaning, looking after laundry, and the rest. In my fantasy, when I visit the house the girls are instructed to assemble in the main sitting-room (where there is a bar) and I mingle with them, going from group to group, chatting, enjoying a glass or two of champagne, until I see one who appeals to me.

I will then take her up to her room, and the detailed introduction takes place. I undress her, or watch her undress, depending upon my mood. When she has taken off her outer clothes and is standing there in her undies, I will probably tell her to hold everything for a moment, and I'll go over to her and caress her breasts (preferably, at this stage, through a sexy brassiere). I'm not a stockings and suspenders man, so I don't mind whether the woman is wearing those or tights. Whichever she has on, I'll feel between her legs while she is still wearing them and, of course, her panties. This feeling and stroking of flesh and private parts through layers of material is an essential (and exciting) part of my fantasy ritual. The girl responds to my touching her up, pressing herself and her thighs and everything that they conceal up against me.

Next I take off her brassiere, and suck and squeeze the newly revealed breasts. If I'm lucky, the girl will have quite small breasts. From choice, I am not overly attracted to large breasts, but to small, firm, well-shaped ones. I like pretty nipples, which swell beneath my ministrations. After some time playing with the girl's breasts, I will move down and, depending upon whether she is wearing stockings or tights will remove her knickers and then her leg apparel, or vice versa, exposing her pubic bush, and her pudenda, to my delighted eye. You may be wondering about girls who shave between their legs. I find the sight of labia pouting baldly at me most unattractive, and any girls thus shaven are either eliminated (by a written examination) early on, or they are instructed to grow their pubic hair back. All the women are asked to let their pubic hair grow as thickly as it will. Trimming is absolutely not permitted. Once the girls are naked, I take them over to the bed for the next part of my 'getting-to-know-you' introduction. What happens then depends entirely upon mood. I may play with their pussies for a while. I may suck them. I may have them suck me. We may do both those things together. I will, of course, eventually fuck them, but it is this discovering their sexual secrets, slowly, over a period of time, as I said at the beginning of my letter, which gives me so much intense erotic enjoyment.

R. C. Y. Harrogte, Yorkshire.

We certainly agree with the main point of your philosophy, as far as a woman being the only real aphrodisiac is concerned. But aren't you making rather a meal of it?

HOT LIPS

As a woman who is seriously into sex, I love looking at the photographs of the sexy ladies that you publish. But I am embarrassed to see – over a period of time – that the lips of my sex can (by comparison with those of the pretty girls in your pages) only be described as gross. I enclose a photograph taken recently by my boyfriend. You see, I never went to boarding school or played team sports, served in the armed forces, or did any of those things where a woman lives with other women and has an opportunity to compare her body with other women's bodies. Your magazine has given me that opportunity, and, frankly, I'm horrified. My current boyfriend is my first really sexual relationship, and because he says he loves my fleshy labia, I have always assumed that they look like any other girl's vulval appendages. Wrong! Since looking at some recent issues of your magazine, I see that my outer labia look more like swollen bats' wings than the attributes displayed by your models. Can anything be done to make them more normal? Plastic surgery, for example?

K. R. Cardiff, Glamorgan.

To take your last question first, yes, specialist plastic surgeons can *reduce the size, and alter the shape, of women's labia, should that be necessary. But before you rush off to make an appointment, think on this. One: pussy lips come in all shapes and sizes. Every variety has its enthusiasts. Two: we all love yours. Three: a quick straw poll of our male editorial and design staff produced over fifty per cent who prefer larger, rather than smaller, labia on their ladies. And research through our files reveals that of all the models photographed over the past ten years (well over 700 girls) 460 of them have large labial lips. Now read on:-*

LUSCIOUS LIPS

Diana, on page 72 of your last issue, has my blood racing. Into my cock. It's swollen with desire. She fulfills my ultimate fantasy. I have *never*, EVER seen such gorgeously shaped, full, elongated, tumescent, wonderful cunt lips. Please, PLEASE pass my name and telephone number to Diana. *Please*. I have to have those rare, enormous, immense, suckable labia in between my own lips. I have to suck them. I have to lick their length and breadth, and thrust my tongue (and, later, my cock) between them. They look like pinkish segments of ripe orange, peeping wetly from within Diana's glorious thatch of pubic hair. Diana is a cunt-lapper's delight. Imagine easing down a girl's knickers, the first time that you took her to bed, and exposing fabulous lips like those beneath them! Imagine running your tongue down their centre, and parting them, to delve between them! I'm in love. I can't eat or sleep, for thinking about how they would feel in my mouth. Imagine *fucking* them, watching them open to absorb your swollen cock, dilating as you entered them, closing tightly around your tool as it sank deeply in! Imagine watching Diana's fingers idly playing with those lips, as she waited for you to tear off your trousers! In anticipation.

H. A. Highgate, London.

We passed H. A's letter on to Diana, who sent him an autographed colour photograph of herself, emphasizing her special attributes.

WHITER THAN WHITE

I've always had a thing about white panties, and I see from your current issue that at least one of your team of photographers and/or your picture editor are white-pantie freaks too. Those fabulous photographs of Prudence, the tiny Oriental girl, with her legs spread and the crotch of her white knickers stretched tightly over her plump little pudenda, are too much. They tell me precisely the size and shape of her glorious sex mound, and clearly show the outline of her labia through the thin material. What a pity the photographer didn't talk about sex to Prudence, in order to induce her to wet her knickers, as it were, whilst he was taking his photographs. You know what I mean. Get her juices running, so that they stained the perfect white of her knicker crotch and turned the material from transparent to translucent. I love the shot of Prudence with her hand down inside her white panties. We all know what she's doing. In fact, we can more or less *see* what she's doing, and the expression on her face says she's enjoying herself. Later on in the set, she turns around for us and shows us her arse through those skimpy white knickers. I get real horny seeing her plump arse cheeks and the dark shadow of her anal hair, of which wisps peep out from beneath her knicker-leg. Fantasies are fantasies, of course, and fucking is fucking, and for me the first is but the prelude to the second. I love the final picture, where Prudence has taken those lovely knickers off and is holding her pussy open with her delicate fingers, showing us the deep pink hole down which, no doubt, some lucky guy regularly thrusts his prong.

I'd love to eat it out and then fuck it, very, very slowly. I'd make a real Chinese meal of it.

G. E. D. Salisbury, Wilts.

One large helping of number sixty-nine, please, waiter!

DIGGING THE DIRT

I had a new experience recently, which I would like to share with your readers. I'm nineteen and am still learning (albeit enthusiastically and energetically) about sex. I picked up a girl in my local pub the other day, who seemed to take an immediate shine to me. So far, this is a pretty rare occurrence in my life and one not to be taken lightly. Usually, I have to work very much harder to get anywhere near getting a girl to drop her knickers for me. So when she said, 'Why don't we go back to my place and get to know each other better?' I didn't waste any time, other than to stop off at an off-licence on the way to get a bottle of wine. Mary, her name was. She only lived around the corner from the pub, and when we got there I learned that she lived in a well-furnished one-bedroom flat that she was buying on a mortgage. She worked as a legal secretary, and made quite good money. Once inside, she grabbed hold of me and kissed me, at the same time unzipping my trousers and reaching inside to play with my dick. I won't bore you with a blow by blow account, but I will simply tell you about the bit that I found so exciting. Well, I found it *all* exciting, really, but the difference was that, as she got close to her first orgasm, she started talking dirty to me. Very dirty. I'd always been under the impression that girls thought sex and love were interchangeable, and that love-making went on in a gentle atmosphere of sweetness and light. Not with this girl. No way.

She had her clothes off quick as blinking and was lying on her bed naked, her legs apart, playing with her pussy while she waited for me to undress and join her. My hard-on slowed me down a bit, but I didn't waste *too* much time. We were, I guess, about halfway along the road to mutual orgasm when she started talking dirty to me. 'Oh fuck,' she said, breathing hard in my ear. 'Oh, Jesus. I love your cock. Your cock is fucking my cunt. You're going to make me come. Oh, God. Fuck me harder. Fuck me with your great big cock. Fuck me like there's no tomorrow. Oh, yes. You're fucking me. I'm coming now. *Now*. NOW. I'm coming.' I can't tell you how exciting I found it, listening to this delightful young girl using words I'd never heard any woman use, ever before. She was *saying* what I was *thinking*. I'd never heard a girl say 'fuck' before. I nearly came, instantly. I loved it. And this wasn't some downmarket, uneducated little tramp. She'd been to Cheltenham Ladies' College, she'd told me earlier in the pub, and then on to Cambridge, where she'd studied English Literature. To cut a long story short, I *did* come, very quickly. But it was only the first of many times, that memorable night. If you haven't tried it, I recommend it. Get a pretty girl to talk dirty to you while you fuck her. You'll love it.

E. Z. Edgeware, London.

Sounds like you cleaned up, sexually. Congratulations.

The World's Best Sexual Fantasy Letters: Volume Two

INTRODUCTION

Sexual fantasies are a vital ingredient in everyone's sex lives. They are the fuel that motivates our sexual drive. The inspiration, the incentive, the stimulus for life's most vital activity, without which life itself would quickly disappear. Yes, of course, the attraction of women for men, and men for women, is all-important too. The shape of a leg, the curve of a breast, the sheer physical appeal of a specific part of a lover's body will always have their very personal, individual attractions. But often it is what we *think* about our sexual partners, what we *imagine* as we make love to them, that converts the humdrum into the arousing. The everyday into the fresh, the new, the exciting. The unimaginative into the unusual.

The success of Volume One of *The World's Best Sexual Fantasy Letters* has encouraged the New English Library to publish this second volume. As with the first, it is a personal selection, taken from the readers' letters columns of the magazines with which I have been involved during my time as a journalist, editor and publisher of men's magazines, in a career spanning over thirty years, both here in Britain and in the United States. It is also a comprehensive selection. The only difference between the letters which you read here and the originally published versions, as with Volume One, is that the letters published here have largely been left at their original, uncut length, rather than being edited down to the much briefer extent made necessary by the limitations of the fewer pages of a monthly magazine. With fantasy letters, this is often to the detriment of the letter. And the reader.

Whether you keep your fantasies as exactly that – fantasies – or whether you choose to turn them, where appropriate, into realities, is a matter of personal choice. And, as you may discover from this book, there are probably some fantasies that you personally find anything but erotic. One man's fantasy may well be another man's total turn-off. It takes all sorts. The secret is to find a partner who shares your sexual dreams. Your erotic flights of fancy. It's not always easy. I hope that this selection of fantasies from around the world will perhaps give you some new ideas!

David Jones. Hampstead, London. July, 1997.

SLAVE TO THE THOUGHT

One of my favourite fantasies is to close my eyes and fantasize that I live in the Deep South of the United States, at the time when slavery was a part of normal everyday life, and when female slaves were the property of their owners. In every possible way. I wouldn't, of course, ill-treat my slaves. It is simply the thought of all those gorgeous black women – bought by me at auction purely for their looks – as my sexual slaves.

Most fantasies being, in fact, pretty far removed from the reality of life, my women slaves live in great luxury, pampered and looked after by their own servants, dressed in expensive clothes (and underclothes!) and happy to perform for me the services that I require, in return for a better life than most slaves ever actually achieved in those days.

My evening starts with a parade of the available women, along the veranda of my *Gone With the Wind*-style mansion, as I sit comfortably in my rocking chair, a mint julep in my hand, and smile and nod at the girls as they walk by. Those who indulged my pleasures the previous evening are excused 'duty' the next evening, as are any girls who are unwell, for whatever reason, including any who are menstruating. The girls may wear whatever they wish, and it always pleases me to see that they vie with each other in their endeavours to catch my attention. The dresses of the period are renowned for the amount of bosom that they reveal, and the boned and laced corsets of the day are remarkable for the manner in which they present the mammary splendour of a well-endowed woman.

Skirts were long in those days, but were often split high at the front, the back or the side, revealing many a long, slim leg and firm thigh as the wearer walked. Occasionally a girl joins the parade in her underwear, and I have known one or two who join it stark naked, something that always gives me great pleasure. You may wonder why I don't insist on them *all* being naked, if I enjoy it so much, but then it probably hasn't yet occurred to you that what I actually do is to select six 'finalists' from the parade whom I then move into the house where I then get them to strip off, one at a time. Those who start off naked are attempting to obtain an early advantage in the selection process. It often works.

The girls' ages run from around eighteen or so up to their late twenties. After that they are beginning to lose their figures, and I retire them to the job of looking after their successors. It's not a hard life, and they then – with my full agreement – obtain their sexual gratification from the male slaves. I never sell them on, although I get many such requests from other slave-owners. Few owners treat the women as well as I do, and I value their long service.

Watching the six 'finalists' disrobe is most enjoyable, as the girls then take every opportunity to display their private parts to me, spreading their legs, licking their lips lasciviously, fingering their labia, bending over and pulling their arse cheeks apart, pulling on their nipples to make them erect, and even inserting various objects, like small bottles or pieces of wood that they have carved into the shape of penises, obscenely into themselves. This particular evening, I have so far selected a new young girl, mainly because this is the first time that I have seen her on the parade since I bought her at auction fairly recently. I feed them up, and give them time to understand what life with me is all about, before I start to use them sexually. This one is looking nervously at me, but when I smile at her, she manages to smile back. The other girls will have told her that, provided she offers herself freely to me, life will indeed be pleasant. I remember noting, when I bid for her, that she had pert, pointed little breasts, a tautly flat stomach, and a splendidly hirsute pussy, all of which I am reminded of as I now watch her undress.

At the auction, she was on offer, allegedly, as a virgin. But that is something that I never believe, despite the effect this supposition has on the sale price. If she was intact when she came to the auction rooms, she wouldn't be by the end of the first viewing day. Either the auctioneers themselves or – for a price – one of their favoured customers would have sampled the goods on offer. Perhaps as many as a dozen times. In every orifice.

In addition to the new girl, I have selected one that I have sampled many times before, always with maximum enjoyment. She is tall for an African, with full breasts, a large bottom, and lips that were made for cocksucking, an activity that she seemed to enjoy. I indicated to the other four that these two were to be my selection for the evening, and they departed back to their quarters, leaving the three of us to our own devices. Or perhaps to my own *vices* would be a more honest description. Both girls were naked, since the undressing of the six 'finalists,' and they stood there, the newer one still looking slightly apprehensive.

'Come over here, darling,' I said to her. She came and stood in front of me. 'Do you like sex?' I asked her.

She looked down at her feet. 'Some, master,' she said. 'What do you mean, some?' I asked. She looked embarrassed and shuffled her feet, but she didn't answer.

The other girl came over, took her by the arm and said to her, 'You can tell the master. He is a kind man. You do not need to be afraid of him. He will not hurt you.' The first girl flashed her a quick look, then looked back at me and said, 'I no like being raped. I have been raped often. I like sex without rape.'

'I understand that, darling,' I told her. 'No one's going to rape you here. Come a little closer.' She took a step forward. I reached out and stroked her nipples, on the end of her pert breasts. They reacted immediately, standing up like baby acorns.

The girl looked at me, and smiled. She wriggled her hips. 'Mmmm,' she said. I pulled her towards me, took a nipple in my mouth, and suckled on it. While I suckled, I ran my hands down her body, stroking her waist, feeling her firm buttocks, and finally slipping a hand between her legs. She stood stock still. I found her slit and tried to insert a finger up it, but it was painfully dry. I let go of her and said to the other girl, 'Bring our new friend up to my bedroom.' I preceded them out into the hall and up the stairs.

My bedroom was lit softly with candles, and the bed was turned down. I began to strip off and looked at the new girl and told her to lie down on the bed. She did as she was told. I was naked now, and I turned to the taller girl. 'She's very dry,' I said. 'Understandably, since she's so nervous. Suck her off for me, until she's good and wet.'

The taller girl immediately knelt between the first girl's legs and began to kiss and suck at the smaller girl's pussy, licking and slurping loudly, running her tongue up and down the length of it, spreading her saliva all over the smaller girl's cunt, until it was so wet that it opened like the petals opening on a flower, showing the pink interior of her cunt. The smaller girl began to move her hips slowly beneath the other girl's mouth, patently enjoying what was being done to her. I watched intently, my cock stiffening by the second. Women sucking other women have always turned me on.

'I reckon that's probably enough,' I said to the older girl. 'What do you think? Do you think she's ready now?' The girl lifted her head up, away from the other girl's now well-lubricated cunt and, as I watched, she eased a finger deeply into it. She looked up at me. 'Yes, master,' she said, pushing her finger in and out to demonstrate. 'Girl ready to fuck now. Very wet.'

'Splendid,' I said. I stood up. My rampant cock stood out like the yardarm on a sailing boat. I knew that if I began to fuck the new girl in this state I wouldn't last more than a few moments, what with the excitement of a new body and my keen anticipation. I looked back at the woman who had been sucking her colleague. 'You can suck me off before I fuck her,' I told her. 'That way, I'll last a lot longer, and both of us will have a better fuck.' The older girl smiled as she stood up, and the younger one actually giggled. It was a good sign.

I stayed standing up where I was, and the tall woman came over and knelt on the floor in front of me, taking my rigid cock in her hand. She pulled my foreskin gently up and down a couple of times, and looked at my prick admiringly. 'Master have cock like black man,' she said. I assume she meant it as a compliment. She took me into her mouth. She was warm, and wet, and she began tonguing my cock expertly. Her lips were soft, and her ministrations brought me rapidly to orgasm. I took her head between my hands and thrust my cock down her throat. It was something that she had become accustomed to, and she didn't balk at what I was doing, or retch, as I continued to fuck her throat until my semen jetted down it in long, hot, delightful spurts.

I kept my cock in her throat until the last throes of my ejaculation had finished, and then withdrew. 'Great,' I said. 'Thank you. You can leave us now.' She looked positively disappointed. 'Master no fuck me?' she asked. 'After other girl?'

'Not tonight, darling,' I told her. 'You've done well. That was the best head I've had for ages.' She took herself off, muttering something quietly under her breath. I let it go. She *had* done well, actually. I turned back to the new girl, still lying on the bed. Her thighs were spread, and she was playing with herself. 'Master like sex,' she said, smiling. 'I like sex too. What you like to do to me?'

I smiled back at her. 'I think I'll begin where your friend left off,' I told her. I knelt between her legs, as the other girl had, and I began to examine her pretty little snatch from a distance of about three inches. Its wrinkled skin was black, and it nestled in the midst of a thick bush of black, tightly curled pubic hair. It was glistening wetly, both from the other girl's saliva and now, I could see, from this girl's own generously flowing sexual effluent. I could smell the strong odour of her aroused sexuality. Her outer lips were small and neat. Not the elongated butterfly wings of her predecessor. I used the fingers of both hands to part her cunt lips, and looked down into the inside of her sex. It was a bright, scintillating, wet pink. I could see the ridges down the walls of it, and the small nub that was her clitoris, wetly erect. I let go of her lips, and ran my tongue down the full length of her, rather as if licking the jam out of a doughnut. She tasted delicious. Clean, but strong. Gamy, almost. Jungly. Exotic.

I began to suck her, revelling in the feel, the smell, the taste of her. She began to moan and move her hips again, as she had with the other girl, and she put her hands down and held my head, much as I had when being fellated earlier on. She began to hump my mouth, and I sucked and licked even harder, wanting to bring her to the orgasm which she so patently wanted too.

It didn't take long. She raised her buttocks right off the bed as I sucked her to orgasm, shouting out in some language that I took to be an African tribal dialect. It certainly wasn't from this side of the Atlantic. She subsided after a little while and lay there, panting. I stopped sucking her and pulled myself up until I was level with her. I climbed onto her and, as I straddled her, she took my erect prick in her warm hand and fed it into herself. I thrust, and she guided me. I slid in deeply, and I felt her cunt muscles gripping me as I entered her. She groaned, and shut her eyes, and, clasping my buttocks, she began to grind away at me, fucking me as if her life depended upon it.

I leant down and kissed her as we fucked, knowing that she would taste her juices on my mouth as we kissed. She opened her mouth and thrust her tongue deeply into mine, thrusting at me even more feverishly as she worked her muscles on my tool, squeezing and pulling, until I erupted once again. As I jetted my ejaculate into her, I felt the spasms of her own orgasm joining with mine, and she moaned out loud as she came, grinding her crotch against mine and using her vaginal muscles at the same time. We more or less collapsed after that, and I pulled myself off her. I knew that I would never again have to ask her if she liked sex. I knew she did.

You can see how I get carried away with my fantasies of the Deep South. But I hope you also notice that there is nothing nasty in my fantasy. No floggings, no sexual cruelty. The real thing, the history books tell me, was pretty unpleasant. But a dream is a dream. I'm currently saving for my air fare to Atlanta!

P.H.H. Basildon, Essex.

It sounds as if you're training for the Sexual Olympics!

BARE CHEEK . . .

As a reasonably normal male, it always surprises me that my men friends, almost without exception, seem to spend their time eulogizing about women's breasts, or women's legs. Very few, apart from me, seem to exercise their libidos lusting after women's bottoms. Yet, in my opinion, there cannot be a more sexually attractive, more entrancing sight, than a well-shaped bottom, half-hidden by sexily tight, minimally covering silky knickers.

Cleavage is always deemed to apply just to women's bosoms. But is there no one else out there who has the ability to recognize that some of the most attractive cleavage in the world is to be seen *behind* the lady in question? Arse cleavage is an unattractive description, but the actuality is sheer delight. It can be seen, happily, on beaches, in gymnasiums, and – with the recent resurrection of hot pants as a fashion item – once more in discos. Forget the jokes about navvies on building sites, and start looking at the exquisite feminine bottom cleavage that is all around you.

My particular fantasy is to have a whole row of pretty young women, wearing only minimal silk bikini panties, all bending over to expose their behinds and the cleavage thereof, with their silky panties pulled tautly across perfectly formed, generous buttocks. As I walk along the line, each girl pulls down her panties to expose her naked behind to me. I am permitted to feel each girl's bottom, squeeze her buttocks, stroke her anal ring, feel her pussy, finger her sex, all of this in any way that I wish, but I may not have sex – as such – with any of them, until I have made my final selection. This, naturally enough, takes time. Sometimes I have to go back again and check an earlier girl out against one that I have just finished examining. The girls all love what I am doing to them, and they vie with each other to draw attention to their – what shall I call them – divided attractions?

I like to fuck, of course, as much as the next man. My anal fantasies do not often involve anal sex. But my most favourite view of a woman's sex is when she is wearing knickers and is bent over, facing away from me, so that I can see the crotch of her knickers pulled tightly over her pudendum. If there are pubic hairs spilling out along the sides of her knicker-crotch, so much the better. A damp spot, denoting that the girl's sex is already wet, is a bonus. Having, in my fantasy, made my final selection, this is the position that I like the girl of my final choice to adopt, initially. I then like to bury my mouth and nose between her legs, from the rear, sucking and licking at her silk-covered sex, until the material is wet enough for me to feel – and taste and smell – the shape of her vaginal lips beneath.

From there on in, it's pretty much the same kind of fucking that everyone else enjoys. But the fantastic pleasure, to me, of leading up to fucking the way that I do, is unbeatable. My own personal hymn to the glories of the female posterior. Try it sometime. I know you'll love it.

R.D. Northallerton, North Yorkshire.

I'm glad to see that you've finally got to the bottom of your problem.

A RAPE, BY ANY OTHER NAME . . .

I read in your columns occasional stories (and fantasies) about rape. Sometimes from men, sometimes from women. If they are to be believed, many women apparently enjoy rape fantasies, although most of them emphasize that this does *not* mean that they actually want to be raped. But all of these letters have one thing in common. They are all about *women* being raped. As a man, my fantasy is not to rape a woman, or women, but to *be* raped *by* women.

I can't think of anything nicer than being gang-banged by a posse of sex-hungry women. I imagine walking along a street, late at night, when a car with four young women in it draws up alongside me. The front-seat passenger winds down her window and asks for directions to somewhere close by. As I am telling her how to get to this address, I am set upon by the two women from the back of the car, who snap a pair of handcuffs on my wrists, and man(?)handle me into the back of the car. I'm thrown onto the floor, and a blanket is thrown over my head. I have no idea where I am being taken. We eventually arrive somewhere and, with the blanket still over my head, I'm half led, half pushed out of the car, along a path and through a door. I'm taken along what I take to be a passage, and then the blanket is removed. I am standing in a large, expensively furnished living room. My hands are still handcuffed behind my back. I can now see my captors properly for the first time. They are four young women – two blondes, a medium brunette, and one with black hair – and they look to be between the ages of around twenty-five to thirty. I can smell alcohol on their breath. They are all smiling at each other.

'Well, he doesn't look too bad,' says the black-haired one. 'He looks clean, and he seems reasonably fit.'

'He'll need to be, by the time we've finished with him,' says one of the blondes. This sets them all off giggling. 'Let's get on with it,' says the second blonde. 'OK,' says the black-haired one. 'You tell him what it's all about.'

'Right,' says the second blonde, and she comes and stands in front of me. I'm over six feet, and she has to gaze up at me to look me in the eye. I guess that she's about five eight. She's a corker. She's wearing a tight wool sweater over well-shaped tits – one of those sweaters that exposes her midriff – and a black leather miniskirt. She smells of some heady perfume. She's really extremely attractive.

'We're going to fuck you,' she says, grinning at me. 'All four of us. We're not getting enough, and we're pretty pissed off with what sex we are getting from our men, so we're going to take some from you. We're going to rape you. You'll service us in any way that we want, or it will be the worse for you. Behave yourself and we won't hurt you. Be a nuisance, or try to escape, and I for one won't be responsible for what might happen to you. Do you understand?'

Understand? Jesus, I'm delighted. They can fuck me from here to kingdom come. Any time they like. But I try not to show my pleasure. It'll be more fun to let them think they're forcing me. 'Yes,' I say, making a tremendous effort not to smile. 'I understand. And I won't try to escape.' *Escape*, I think to myself? *Try and bloody get rid of me.*

The blonde turns to the other girls and says, 'I guess we'd better take him upstairs.' Two of the girls take an arm each and guide me out of the room, along the passage, up some stairs, and through the first door on the left.

It is a large bedroom, with a huge, king-size bed as its central feature. 'Who's going first?' asked one of the blondes. There was a silence. 'Oh, very well, then,' said the same blonde. 'I'll go first.' She turned and looked at me. 'You,' she said. 'I don't want to know your name. You're going to give me head. Now.' So saying, she took off the jacket of the navy blue suit that she was wearing and dropped it on the floor. She then unzipped the skirt and slipped it down her legs, finally stepping out of it.

She was wearing a pretty pale-blue bra over ample, good-looking breasts, and matching tiny pale-blue knickers. She was wearing tights beneath the knickers, and she now bent down and slipped off the knickers. Then she rolled down the tights, and pulled them off. Still wearing the bra, she went over and sat on the side of the bed. She spread her legs. She had a thick blonde pubic thatch. It was long, straight and wispy. I couldn't actually see her cunt for the hair. She looked at me. 'Right,' she said. 'Come over here, and kneel down in front of me.'

'May I say something?' I asked, as politely as possible. 'What?' she said, looking irritated. I think she was embarrassed about doing what she was going to do in front of the others. They were, all three of them, simply standing there, watching intently. 'If I'm going to give you head,' I told her, 'I can do a much better job, first of all, without these damn handcuffs, and secondly, if I can take my suit off, it will give me more room to manoeuvre. Both those things will make it more fun for you. I give you my word that I shan't try to escape.'

She looked at me, but she didn't answer. Then she looked at the other girls. 'What do you think?' she asked them. 'Do you think we can trust him?' After a moment, the brunette said, 'Well, we've got him heavily outnumbered. If he tries anything, we can nail him to the floor.'

'OK,' said Blondie. 'I guess what he says makes sense.' She got up off the bed, came over and, taking the key to the handcuffs from one of the other girls, she undid them and took them off. I rubbed my wrists. They were sore. Then I stripped off. Altogether. Completely naked. I've got a good body, and I don't mind showing it off.

One of the other girls whistled. I smiled at her. The blonde was back, sitting on the edge of the bed. I knelt down in front of her and pressed her thighs even further apart. I could see her snatch now. It was pale pink, and a trail of colourless effluent was trickling generously down her thighs.

And I could smell her. The heady aroma of wet pussy arose strongly from her open sex. She smelt like the bitch on heat that she was. My cock rose to the occasion. Nobody said anything. This was becoming a great evening. I leaned forward and ran my tongue down the length of her exposed cunt. She gasped, and moved her thighs.

'Oh, yes,' she said. 'Oh, yes, please. Now.' I took her outer cunt lips into my mouth and sucked and tongued them, and then I delved my tongue deeply inside her. She tasted delicious. Wet cunt always tastes delicious to me. I began to concentrate on what I was doing. I found her clitoris. She responded enthusiastically, and within a few minutes I had her orgasming all over the bed. I didn't take my mouth away but stayed with her. I wasn't going to chance starting fucking her until she told me to. I was, after all, being raped. Please God.

I didn't have long to wait. She pulled my head away from between her thighs. 'Now fuck me,' she cried. 'Fuck me like there's no tomorrow. Fuck my tight little cunt.' She lay back on the bed, her legs wide apart, her cunt wetly open. I climbed on top of her: she took my prick in her hand and, masturbating it as she did so, guided it into herself. 'Oh, Jesus,' she said. 'Oh, yes. Oh God. Fuck me. Please fuck me. Fuck my hot cunt.'

I started to fuck her. I thrust up into her and withdrew almost to the very tip of my swollen cock before I thrust deeply into her again. I repeated this time after time, over and over, increasing the speed with which I was fucking her, and very soon she was close to orgasm again. 'Oh, God. I love it,' she said. 'I love your hot cock up my wet cunt. I love you fucking me. Very soon, you'll spurt your come right up my cunt. I'll feel it, jetting up against my womb. Your hot spunk will fill my cunt. You'll make me come even harder. And then these other three girls will fuck you and fuck you, until your cock is so sore you won't be able to fuck any more. That's a promise.'

The very thought of fucking the other three girls brought about my instant ejaculation, and I spurted my jism up her in an ecstasy of enjoyment. Thank goodness, she felt me jetting into her, and it brought on a series of orgasms that built and built until she was screaming out loud with a combination of lust and passion.

I looked down at her as I continued to thrust even harder into her receptive cunt. 'Thank you, baby,' I said. 'I love fucking you. You're the greatest fuck ever.' The hell with the being-raped bit. Sex was what she said she had wanted, and sex was what I was giving her. She was enjoying it, and so was I. There was no need – at least as far as I was concerned – for any more pretence. She subsided, slowly, and I looked at the other three girls. The were all tearing their clothes off.

'I'm next,' shouted the black-haired one. 'Don't worry,

darlings,' I told them. 'There's no hurry. I'll fuck all four of you. And then I'll fuck all of you all over again. There's no need for panic.'

It was the black-haired one that I had really fancied, right from the beginning. Seeing her naked now, I was excited to see that she sported a shaven quim. Much as I love hairy pussies, I also adore bald ones. I love the way those hairless pussy lips pout out from a girl's shaven pudendum. I love to suck their smooth nakedness in the knowledge that their owner has only taken the trouble to shave herself down there because she believes – rightly so, in my book – that it makes her more sexually attractive.

'Come here, sweetness,' I said to her. 'Let me suck that pretty, unadorned, plump little cunt of yours for you. I just love shaved pussy.' She smiled at me and came over and lay on the bed, down beside blonde number one, who hadn't got herself together enough to get up off it yet. I did my best with the girl's delightful shaven pussy, and I have to tell you that my best really is very good. The whole perception of the girls raping me had suddenly – and rather sadly, I thought – gone, and I was now the one in charge. But at least I was giving these ladies what they wanted. And what it seemed they weren't getting from the regular men in their lives. But isn't that the story of all our lives?

I won't bore you with the continuing details of the serious seeing-to that I was happily able to give to all four of these splendid ladies. It becomes somewhat repetitive. But I sucked all four of them, and I fucked all four of them. More than once. You would have been able to do the same. They were so attractive, and so rampantly sexy. So in need of a good fuck. And, of course, I made arrangements to meet all four of them again two days later. To repeat the exercise.

Or so the fantasy goes. And isn't that what fantasies are all about?

P.W.H. Horncastle, Lincolnshire.

What you might call a ravishing evening.

WANKS FOR THE MEMORY

I've recently got together with a new lady who is a lot of fun, both socially and sexually. But, put at its best, all I can honestly say is that she doesn't mind fucking. If you hear what I'm saying, that means that fucking isn't the greatest thing in her life. *Oh ho*, I hear you say.

What, then, *is* the greatest thing in her life? Sexually, of course – that's what I'm talking about. Well, this is where she and I have a problem. The greatest thing in my new girl's sex life is masturbating herself. And yes, that includes when I'm there, and available, and horny. She would rather toss herself off in front of me, than have me fuck her.

Now this, I have to tell you, is becoming a problem. I'm not against masturbation. I love it. We all do it. And it's exciting for me to watch my girl bring herself off. Most men get turned on by the sight of a woman masturbating herself. But I also want to fuck her. And this, she makes it clear, is doing me a favour. Frigging comes first in her life. By the time she's brought herself to orgasm by this method, she's not crazy about getting fucked afterwards.

Many men fantasize in your columns about watching women masturbate. Some of them fantasize about secretly watching women who think that they are unobserved. Others get turned on by watching women who are masturbating for their eyes only. Either way, a fuck usually concludes their fantasy.

I went through a period at the beginning of this relationship where I wanked myself off as I watched my lady busying herself at her self-indulgent performances. This at least had the result of my having an ejaculation. But the long-term effect each time was simply to make me hornier than ever for the 'real' thing. Have you any advice to offer by way of an equable solution to my problem? I'd much appreciate any help that you can offer. I *have* tried to talk to her about this, but my pleas fall upon deaf ears.

H.L. Sleaford, Lincolnshire.

Certainly. No problem. Find yourself a new girlfriend. One who likes the same kind of sex that you like.

HANDLED TO GOOD EFFECT

What amazing pictures of the wondrous Jenny in your December issue. She fulfils every fantasy I've ever had. I think women who are to all intents and purposes fully dressed (i.e. like Jenny, who is wearing a summer dress, a slip, stockings, a suspender belt, even long gloves up to her elbows, but who is revealing, in the first photograph, that she is not wearing any panties) are the sexiest women around. Their sexuality may not be so overt as that of women who can't wait to drop everything and expose their nakedness. But the sexuality of the Jennies of this world is far more subtle, much more concentratedly erotic.

That first picture, with Jenny's knees drawn up, her legs spread widely, the skirts of her dress and slip pulled up, and her legs, clad in black silk stockings, her feet encased in those pretty high-heeled shoes – all this acts as a frame, focusing the eye of the fortunate beholder on that magical vision, exposed between her naked thighs: her cunt. Her beautiful cunt, surrounded as it is by her delightfully thick pubic hair. It is long and coarse, and is a seriously heavy, wonderfully untrimmed growth. Jenny's gloved hand and finger are cleverly caught by the photographer, just inches above her pretty pussy, which glistens wetly in the studio lights. Her cunt lips are thick and long, looking like some exotic pale-pink foxglove, its dew-heavy petals opening at the base of the flower, set in the moist, mossy surroundings of a forest glade. And what, pray, is our delightful Jenny about to do, her fingers poised so charmingly above this voluptuous jungle bloom?

She's about to fondle herself. Stroke her delicate, dewy, erogenous petals. Caress into erection her clitoris, which will then sit so prettily, proudly pistil-like amidst her carnal blossom. She's going to jack herself off.

Oh, how I wish I were there to help her. To kiss her burgeoning, bud-like, sexual flower into full bloom. To lick her into shape, encouraging her gentle vaginal secretions to moisten her sex even further, to incite her to ooze liquid, like teardrops, from her secret well, to slake my constant sexual thirst. I would love to stroke that torrid thicket of her long pubic hair into disorder, and then part her petals fully with my fingers, reaching inside her to rub her clitoris to orgasm, thus preparing her for my final outrageously rampant entry into her well-lubricated orifice.

But before I thrust into her panting pussy, she would take off her silken gloves and insert her fingers into herself, delving deeply, and after a while she would bring out her wet digits, now sodden with her sexual dew, and spread the moisture lasciviously on her upright nipples, moistening them with her scented, strongly-flavoured excrescence, that I might suck it slowly from them. Her breasts, revealed next in your picture, have swollen areolae, on which are mounted her small-but-perfect nipples, sitting pinkly at their tip, awaiting my hot, wet mouth and lips. They swell as I look hungrily at them.

Jenny lies there in your pages, hauntingly waif-like, waiting to be fucked senseless. In your final shot, her naked fingers are *almost* inside her moisture-laden sex. Her cunt lips are swollen with desire. Her breasts are heavy with lustful passion. Beneath her cunt, her half-dilated humid anus glistens damply, just showing the pink beginnings of its interior. Another tunnel of love, offered as willingly, and as mutely, as the rest of Jenny's limpid body. Your last shot simply shows her smile, her mouth a third, poutingly seductive invitation to her sexual favours. I've pinned the whole set to my wall above my bed, so that when I awake each morning and open my eyes, I think I've died and gone to heaven. Jenny is my fantasy angel.

P.U. San Jose, California.

With all that horticultural detail, we think it's more likely to be the Garden of Eden.

MOUTHING AROUND

Do you guys like oral sex? I'm in my early thirties now, and I think I've tried most of the kinds of sex that are about, leave aside a couple things that don't interest me like sex with animals or other men.

I've had girls who are into every kind of sex. Straightforward fucking. Oral sex – both giving and taking. Often at the same time. Masturbatory sex. I quite enjoy being jacked off by a pretty girl, and I'm happy to oblige in return. I've had sex with girls using vibrators, both on me and on themselves, and I'm a pretty dab hand now at giving ladies sex with vibrators. I've enjoyed anal sex with women. I've had a virgin or two (you can have my share of those) and I've paid for sex with hookers. I've had two girls at a time, and group sex once or twice. But, these days, I always come back to the same thing.

In my book, there's absolutely nothing to beat being given head by an experienced woman who enjoys doing it. I accept that there are a few strange girls around who think that to either give or receive oral sex is disgusting, but fortunately I haven't met too many of them. I now have what I would describe to you (but not to them!) as a small stable of women whom I genuinely like, who are attractive, intelligent, and who just love to suck cock. Mine!

Most men, these days, when they meet women, look at the women's tits, their legs, their faces, their crotches. When I meet a new woman, I look mostly at her mouth, and at her lips. I try to evaluate the likelihood of seeing those lips closed around my erect cock, her eyes on mine as she sucks me off. I imagine her tongue tantalizing the purple, swollen head of my penis, and encouraging me to ejaculate my semen into her mouth.

I think of myself taking her head into my hands as she kneels on the floor, between my spread thighs, and fucking her mouth as she sucks me. I think of myself, on a different occasion, kneeling over her face as she lies, spreadeagled, on my bed, her wet cunt beneath my lips, my tongue dipping into her sex, as she takes me in her hand and guides my rigid length into her mouth. I feel her warm, wet lips encircling my tool, her hand gently masturbating me, as she sucks and licks and kisses me off. Her pussy gets wetter and wetter, and suddenly she is bucking her crotch beneath my lips, and thrusting herself up hard against my mouth, her hands pulling my buttocks down onto her, as her orgasm takes over. She tastes divinely of exotic, overripe fruit. A strong, gamy, sexually exciting taste. Her freely-flowing sexual effluent is strongly scented, too. My cock throbs with the combination of my five senses absorbing – and enjoying – what she is doing to me with her mouth. And I to her, with mine.

I hold out as long as I can. The sensations that her mouth, tongue and lips are generating within my cock begin to send me a message that my ejaculation is not far away. I reach down beneath her and take her soft, full buttocks in my hand and squeeze them. For my pleasure, not hers. I love a soft, squeezy, female bum. I stretch my middle finger along her anal cleavage, searching for her forbidden anus, and when I find it, I slide my finger deeply into her. She bucks and groans, raising her hips and buttocks up off the bed as she orgasms. Her mouth works faster at my prick, and then I'm joining her, jetting my spunk into her mouth. She sucks and swallows, milking my ejaculate from me until I am completely spent. I too keep sucking and tonguing her, until the last of her series of orgasms slowly dies away. We are both replete. Satiated. Exhausted. Who needs a fuck?

K.O.C. Atlantic City, New Jersey.

Better fellated than never, as they say. Enjoy.

DIRTY DOZEN

I've never been able to understand the law in the United Kingdom with regard to pornography. I find most pornographic pictures, magazines, films and videos a great turn-on. My various women friends and I get some of our best sex after an initial session with some serious pornography. So let me ask your readers some basic questions, if I may.

What is actually so awful about pornography? Leave aside the extremes, like bestiality, paedophilia, really severe S&M, and the like: what is actually *wrong* with what I would call, for want of a better word, 'normal' pornography? If you look at pornography that shows men and women indulging in the more usual sexual pastimes, you won't see anything that, within reason, you can't see in any suburban bedroom on a Saturday evening. What is so wrong with reproducing still pictures or movies of a man with his tool up a woman's cunt? The act is about as normal as can be. The act itself isn't against the law. Why, then, are pictures of it unacceptable? It looks good to me, and if the people thus shown *in flagrante delicto* are attractive, it can be quite beautiful.

Our European friends, by and large, seem to agree with me. Pornography is both legal and readily available (as photographs, films, videos, books and magazines) in Germany, Holland, and throughout Scandinavia. American pornography laws are far more lenient than are our own. An American presidential review into pornography, a good few years ago – back in the mid 1970s, as I remember – came up with the decision that detailed photographs of male and/or female genitalia were not pornographic so long as the one was not depicted inserted into the other. This despite the fact that hardcore films depicting every possible kind of sex, including any perversion that you can imagine (and one or two that you possibly hadn't thought of), can be seen, perfectly legally, in any large city in almost all of the United States of America.

Pornographic magazines are available, again in large cities, with front covers showing attractive young girls engaged in the act of fellatio. And apparently enjoying what they are doing. Anal sex is similarly freely reproduced. Girls performing cunnilingus on other girls form part of what is available nationwide. In the same way, homosexual pornography is also legally available. These are all things that any adult knows are going on, all day, every day, the length and breadth of Britain. Why, then, are our laws so archaic? The law is an ostrich.

Why may we not enjoy looking at that which we are permitted to enjoy doing? To come to the point, we all know that pornographic films, videos, magazines and photographs featuring every illegal act imaginable are easily if illegally – and expensively – available in every large city in the UK. The establishment and the law in Britain seem to prefer to ignore this highly profitable trade although, without being able to prove it, I suspect that it is probably a trade that, at least in the larger cities, helps to make many an appreciative policeman's pay stretch to a rather better lifestyle than his legal basic income would permit. Why don't we have the sense to legalize it?

F.J. Bounds Green, London.

We regret that there seem to be no sensible answers to those very pertinent questions.

THE BALD FACTS

Back in the late 1970s, whilst on a business trip to New York, I came across a magazine called *The Razor's Edge*, devoted to the glories of shaven-headed ladies. It was basically a fetish magazine, and I bought it originally out of simple curiosity. But I then met a six foot tall, shaven-headed black model in New York in the course of my work there (I'm in the fashion business) and, over a number of successive visits, she and I had a long affair.

She was strongly sexually motivated, and we had a fantastic relationship for that reason. But as I became increasingly familiar with her lack of any kind of crowning glory, the more I became sexually excited by it. Our sex was terrific. And I loved taking her into busy restaurants in New York. A hush would come over most of the places as we entered, and most of the women's faces would take on a kind of 'Oh my God, how could she?' expression, while almost all of the men's faces would indicate that they would pay dearly for the model's telephone number and for the opportunity to fuck the girl.

I mention this now because it seems to me that shaven heads are suddenly popular here in the UK. Mostly with men, I admit. But I have seen a number of girls with shaven heads around the clubs of an evening. Sadly, I do not know any of them. I wonder if, like my American friend, they are *completely* shaven? I'd love to find out. Her genital area was as bald, and as smooth, as her skull. It was always an amazingly sexually stimulating sight for me, to see her fleshy, purple-black labia making their lascivious *moue* at me from her hairless, naked pudendum. And then, of course, came the excitement of satiating myself in cunnilingus with her shaven sex. The only things that she didn't depilate in one way or another were her eyebrows, although I have seen photographs of women who have done even this.

G.J. Croydon, Surrey.

Your model girlfriend was obviously down to the bare essentials.

CANED AND ABLE

I'm half ashamed, half amused, to find myself becoming very hung up these days with the idea of spanking, caning, whipping, and what-have-you. Flagellation of any kind. With the bare hand perhaps. With a slipper, or a suitable trainer. Maybe with a belt. With a whip or a cane. This fantasy has nothing to do with pain, as far as I know (how does one know what *any* fantasy is really about, so long as it remains a fantasy?) but it does have everything to do with women's bottoms.

Take any of the models displaying their attractions in your magazine (I wish I could!). How about Virginia, for example, in last month's issue: she's beautiful all over. But what *about* that arse? Somewhere in the middle of that set, there's a picture of her kneeling on a bed with her knees spread apart and her naked buttocks aimed directly at the camera. First of all, I would love to stroke those beautiful buttocks. They're smooth and firm, and rounded, and strong. There's an adorable white bikini bottom shape from where her skin is unexposed to the sun, and you can see her lovely pussy, surrounded by her pubes, and you can also just see the outline of her anus, hiding away in the depths of her anal cleavage. She's just pleading to be fucked doggy fashion.

I like to fantasize my initial actions of stroking and feeling her bottom, taking my time to caress and explore those cheeks, with little side trips to her naughtier places. But then I would like to tie her down in that position, to some kind of leather-covered wooden framework, so that her arse was fully exposed and her wrists and ankles were restrained. Then I imagine myself beginning by slapping her buttocks for a while. Not too hard, to begin with. Just hard enough to raise a dark pink blush on her skin, and maybe start her snivelling a bit. Nothing serious, you understand. And that would conveniently raise my dick at the same time, of course.

After that, I would spend some time selecting a suitable weapon from my large array of such implements. I would swish the odd cane through the air, make a whip or two whistle as I tested it out, and probably end up by choosing a riding crop. You know, the kind with a piece of leather attached to the end of a cane-like length of thin, pliable wood.

I would stroke Virginia's plump buttocks again, and then I would stand back and place the riding crop across the middle of them in order that my first blow would be accurately aimed. At this stage in my fantasy, Virginia bursts into tears and pleads with me not to beat her. She promises me all and every kind of sexual excess if I will only release her and not hurt her with the riding crop. I leave the crop where it is, held by me and lying across her lovely arse, and I question her about the promised sexual debauchery. Yes, she cries, she *will* suck my cock.

Yes, she *will* allow me to deep-throat her. Yes, she would *love* me to fuck her. Yes, of *course* she will give me the most fabulous, long-lasting, carefully erotic wank. And she will *enjoy* my indulging in a little buggery. What else is a girl's arsehole *for*? Yes, she will be *delighted* to play with herself while I watch. All this through overwhelming sobs and tears.

But then, since I am in control, I know that I can beat her and then *still* do all or any of the things that we are discussing.

So why hold off? I raise the crop, and bring it down sharply across her arse. She screams, and a thin red line appears, then darkens, across both buttocks. I notice with pleasure that it is precisely across the centre of them. I have not drawn blood, but it will soon turn black and blue.

Virginia appeals once more through her tears. 'For pity's sake,' she pleads. 'I'll do anything for you. Anything you want. But please don't beat me. *Please.*'

I take a decision. I put down the riding crop and go into the bathroom to search the cupboard for some kind of emollient. I find a tube of something suitable, and, going back to Virginia, I rub it carefully into her reddened backside. She wriggles her arse as I rub it in, and my hand slips down between her legs. 'Oooh,' she whispers. 'That's nice.' I put down the tube of ointment and undo my slacks, dropping them to the floor and stepping out of them. I shed my jockeys, and I touch Virginia's glorious arse cheeks with my half-erect prick. It leaps to full erection.

I slide my fingers up between her arse cheeks again and feel her pussy. It is open, and very wet. Women, dogs, and walnut trees, the old song says, are all improved by the occasional beating. Not that what I fantasized doing to Virginia was a *real* beating.

I stand close up behind her and, using my hands to part her buttocks, I open her pussy fully with my fingers and thrust my prick up her. It slips in all the way, her wetness aiding its easy entry. She gasps out loud. I take hold of her breasts, one in each hand, and start fucking her. She pushes her bottom back against me, as much as her restraints will permit. 'Oh, yes,' she says. 'Now you're fucking me. I like it. Oh yes. Dear God. Yes. Nice.'

I thrust harder, feeling my ejaculation building. I can feel her nipples, now rock hard under my fingers, and she is so wet between her legs that I have to be careful not to slip out on my downward strokes. Virginia is making happy little noises in her throat. I can feel her sex muscles working on my prick as I fuck her. And then suddenly I'm coming, and I'm spurting my come up her welcoming cunt. This makes her vocal again. 'Oh, yes,' she cries, her voice thick with passion. 'Oh, yes. I can feel your hot spunk. Oh, Jesus. I'm coming now. Oh, yes. Oh, Jeeeesus. Oh, God.'

I keep on thrusting until the last shudder of my ejaculation has died away, and I slowly withdraw. I pull my jockeys and my slacks back on, and then I undo Virginia's restraints and release her. She turns and puts her arms around me, pulls me to her, and kisses me. 'That was beautiful, darling,' she says. 'What can I do for you now?' Of such stuff dreams are made. Spanks – as you would say – for the memory.

P.L.R. Truro, Cornwall.

We only hope that the lovely Virginia fantasizes about being beaten by someone like you. But don't hold your breath.

IT'S JUST A LOT OF COCK . . .

As one of your many female readers, I have to tell you that I get a great deal of pleasure from your crazy magazine. I'm single and modestly promiscuous, in that I don't have a steady man friend. Variety, for me, is the spice of life. And I just love the gorgeous chicks who frequent your pages. I'm not gay, but I like to see a pretty female body. I've got quite a decent one myself. For my money, I like the fact that you don't put women down. You simply adore them. And *then* you ravish them. That's OK by me.

But you do have one shortcoming. You concentrate on female bodies. I know you're essentially heterosexual, with a nod in the direction of being all things to all people. But you seldom offer us girls naked *males* to drool (and masturbate) over, now do you? What I'm talking about is that part of the male body that really turns me on. The penis. You print illustrated, usually photographic, eulogies to female breasts, bottoms, pussies, legs – even faces. But seldom do you show the magical male cock. Having been studying them seriously for a few years now, I would like to pass on a few comments which, if nothing else, will interest my sisters under the skin.

One: for me, the bigger, the better. This is a fact of life. All that cock about it's not how big it is, it's how you use it, is exactly that. Cock. Put about by men with small ones. Two Roundheads or Cavaliers? An ongoing discussion. For me? Anything, rather than nothing. But given a choice, Roundheads get my vote. By and large, they tend to be cleaner. Sad fact of life. (There are exceptions, of course.) And they feel better in girls' mouths. They certainly look prettier when fully erect. Three: long and thin, or short and fat? Going back to the beginning, *long and fat* is what it's all about. But given a straight choice between the last two? It has to be short and fat. Anything which, first of all fills (stretches even? Please God) a girl's pussy, is far more likely to bang against the old clitoris.

Clitoris banging, chaps, if no one has told you yet, is the answer to every young maiden's prayer. A long thin cock is simply going to tickle the entrance to your girl's womb. It's not unpleasant, but it's not basically what fucking is all about.

The nicest thing I can think of to say about uncircumcised cocks is that they're that much easier to masturbate. The old foreskin pulled up and down over the cockhead is a tremendous help, while the protection that it affords all day and every day possibly leaves the penis in a more sensitive state. That's about it, I guess. Here's to seeing a whole selection of (hopefully) erect male penises in a future issue.

J.W. Richmond, Surrey.

The long, and the short, and the tall, you might say. We'll do our best to produce some cock shots for you, but photographs of erect *cocks, sadly, aren't legal in Britain.*

OPEN HOUSE

Those wonderful pictures of Lorna in your current issue are just too much. They are an amazing tribute to the ability of the photographer who took them. He allows us to view Lorna playing with herself in the privacy of her own bedroom. She's lying back on her bed, with her knickers down around her thighs, her slip pulled up, exposing her superb tits, her nipples fully erect, and with her fingers spreading her pussy lips wide open, showing us the shining wet interior of her sex. While Britain's archaic pornography laws won't allow you to publish the next shot – the insertion of Lorna's finger into her cunt – the scene is set so perfectly that it is a simple matter to close one's eyes and imagine it. I'll bet the photographer took the shot anyway.

Lorna's pussy has all the things that I worship in that department of a girl's anatomy. Large outer labia, with thick, protuberant lips. A long entrance, in terms of inches. Lorna's cunt must be, what? Four inches long? Not far off, that's for sure. Her pussy is surrounded by an exquisite thatch of long, wispy, pubic hair that matches the auburn of her crowning glory exactly. It's almost straight, and it looks beautifully soft. The inside of her pussy is really wet, and shows her vaginal mucus trickling down out of the bottom of her pussy and just beginning to run down her thighs. What Lorna is patently thinking about is cock. Stiff, hard, rampant, fuckable cock.

Do you photographers get to shag these sexy models? I can't

imagine spending a day, or a week, or however long it takes, photographing close-ups of girls' sexual parts, without, one, getting a permanent hard-on, and two, slaking one's cock at the fountain of all sexual pleasure about every half-hour.

A.W. Tiptree, Herts.

We've never been so indiscreet as to ask that question of our photographers. You'll have to ask them yourself. But they are *human . . .*

BOUND TO PLEASE

I was fascinated the other day to be shown a collection of bondage magazines by a male friend of mine. He told me that he wasn't into real bondage himself, but that looking at pictures of girls bound in all manner of painful positions – most of them emphasizing one sexual aspect or another of the female body – was a tremendous turn-on for him. While finding the photographs interesting, they did little or nothing for *my* libido.

The European magazines seemed to specialize in showing girls tied up in positions that left their sexual apertures open and available. There was nothing particularly special about the manner in which they were bound. The American magazines mostly concentrated on unbelievably complicated knots in the ropes and cords with which the women were restrained. Any Boy Scout would have been intrigued.

But the Japanese bondage magazines specialized in showing women suffering what looked like considerable pain. Even if only simulated, pain was obviously the purpose of the bondage. Particular attention was paid to photographs of very young women, with their breasts bound in excruciatingly agonizing positions, often stretching or pulling the breasts completely out of shape. They reminded me of some magazines that I saw not so long ago in California, dedicated to the interests of water sports, enemas, and urolagnia. Both these and the bondage mags make me wonder what sex is actually about for some people. Not to put too fine a point on it, do you get any pleasure in tying girls tits up so tightly that it causes them pain? Does it excite you, sexually, to administer an enema to a pretty girl, and then stick a butt plug up her arse? Do you drink piss? (I'll leave the final question to your imagination.)

But really! Am I alone in my reaction to these – to me – obscene sexual ploys? Thank you for your magazine, which always presents sex as it is intended to be seen, in all its delicious variations, while staying well this side of grossness.

J.D. Poole, Dorset.

Thank you for the compliment. But it takes all sorts, as they say. You know our philosophy by now. Whatever takes place sexually, provided that it is with the full consent of all those taking part, and provided that no one gets physically – or emotionally – hurt, is OK by us.

BIGGER IS BETTER

Why do you never show fat women in your magazine? Fat ladies are my idea of what *real* sex is all about. And I do mean *FAT*! Really fat! With huge, soft, pendulous breasts that I can suck on, or be masturbated between. Great big fleshy tits, with enormous dugs hanging off the ends, like fat cocktail sausages on a pair of giant blancmanges. Elephantine women, with gross, gargantuan, oleaginous arses that I can grip in handfuls as I shag them, doggy fashion, from the rear, searching between their folds of fat for that titillatingly masked sex (taking care, of course, not to enter the other similarly concealed entrance). Colossal thighs to lie between, with generously thick, long, hairy growths at their apex.

How can you possibly imagine the libidinous pleasures of sucking and licking at a pussy hidden amongst layers of limpid fat if you have never done it? And finally, these women's voluminous, gorgeously soft, massive stomachs, on which to lie comfortably as I finally fuck into that prodigious pudendum and find my carnally wet welcome in the delightful flabby folds of her labia, looking rather like the lips of a baby dolphin.

Inside every fat girl lies a sexually frustrated woman, more than overly anxious to prove that she is every bit as – if not more so – lustfully inclined as her anorexic sisters. If you should ever be fortunate enough to find yourselves one, I guarantee that she'll fuck your brains out. So what about some pictures of some really BIG girls in your very next issue?

P.E. Lewisham, London.

We weighed your request up very carefully, but I'm afraid that fat girls are not our bag. There are *any number of magazines about that do cater for your interest. But it sounds to us as if this is something that you enjoy more in the flesh.*

OPEN MINDED

I love the chicks in your mag. They are all, without exception, quite extraordinarily beautiful. I guess you people have brought some of that famous British class to skin mags in the United States. But I am amazed that you and/or your photographers are able to get most of these beauties to agree to be photographed spreading their snatches. I mean, seriously, guys, how many girls do you know who, prior to your playing hide the weenie with them, lie back and spread their labia for you with their fingers? I love to see it, but I'd love to see it in real life too, as it were.

My girl has no objection to *my* spreading her lips and giving myself an eyeful of that lovely pink interior before I either suck it or fuck it. But she flatly refuses to spread them for me. 'What are you?' she asks. 'Some kind of pervert?' I don't think I'm any kind of pervert. I just love pussy in all its aspects. If loving pussy makes me a pervert, then OK, yeah, I'm a pervert. But to get back to my original question, what am I doing wrong? If the fellas who take your shots can give me any advice, I'd be real grateful. The only girls I've met who spread their pussies open are either hookers, or girls in pussy bars.

I've been a dedicated pussy bar client since I was in my early teens. I guess I've been in pussy bars all over. From here in New York, down as far as Tijuana, Mexico. All you need to get girls in pussy bars to spread their pussies is cash. Dollar bills. Lots of them. But you know that. In New York, if you know where to go, a fifty-dollar bill gets you a lick or two of pussy. In Tijuana, a fifty-dollar bill used to get you the girl for the whole night, but I haven't been down there for a year or two. Prices have probably gone up. Like I say, what I'd really like is for my current girl to spread for me. I sometimes jack myself off fantasizing about her doing just that.

I'm in a pussy bar, and my girl is one of the six girls 'dancing' (as they call it) around, up on the circular bar. In my fantasy, it doesn't surprise me that my girlfriend is working in a pussy bar. It all seems quite natural. I've just arrived, and I've gotten myself a beer, and I'm watching the girls as they wiggle by. They are all topless, and I spend the first few pleasurable minutes eyeing their tits. They've all got good tits, including my girl. As each one passes by, she stops in front of me (just like she stops in front of each of the punters around the bar) and bends her legs, which are spread wide apart and, squatting down, she gives me a great view of her cunt, barely covered by a tiny, tightly stretched bikini bottom.

This first girl is wearing white bikini panties. She has auburn hair, and I can see curly auburn pubic hairs escaping sexily from the sides of her panties. 'You wanna see more, honey?' she says. Her voice all low and sexy. 'Just tuck a bill down the front of my panties.' I get out my roll, and let her see how thick it is. She doesn't know whether they're hundred or single dollar bills.

I select a five and tuck it down the front of her panties. 'Hey, thanks, mister,' she says. She stays in her squatting position, but she pulls her panties down to just above her knees. I can now see her whole auburn bush, and I can see her pink gash running wetly down the centre of it. She reaches down and slowly spreads her cunt lips, wide. I get a flash of deep pussy hole, gleaming with her wetness. I can smell her cunt. I get a giant hard-on.

'There's plenty more where that comes from, baby,' she says, pulling her panties up and standing. 'Next time I come around, just tell me what you want. OK, baby?'

'OK, darling,' I say. I've heard it all before, you understand. But I still enjoy it. Pussy is pussy. I like to look at it. And that's what I'm doing. I also like to suck it. And fuck it. All you need is money. And in my fantasy, man, I'm loaded.

As the girl moves away, she looks back at me and waggles her tush, saucily. I grin at her, and wave my bunch of bills. She breaks out into a smile. It might even be genuine. Girls who work in pussy bars always smile – usually quite genuinely – when they see dollar bills. The bigger the denomination, the bigger the smile.

The next girl is a dyed platinum blonde. She's my girlfriend. She's cute, and she knows it. In my dream, she comes on real sassy, and as if she doesn't know me. 'Hi, Mac,' she says. She's chewing gum, and she looks a bit younger than her twenty years. She squats, like the first girl. Her panties are pale blue, and to all intents and purposes they are transparent. I can see her cunt lips clearly through the thin material, and there is a damp patch where her pantie crotch is stretched tightly over her wet pussy. 'Do you like snatch, baby?' she asks me. 'Mine's real pretty. You can buy yourself a peep if you like.'

She winks at me, and leans forward. 'Or you can buy all of it, if you want,' she tells me. 'A hundred and fifty bucks buys it for a whole hour, and you can do anything you like with it. Anything.'

Hearing my girl talk dirty like this really excites me because, in reality, she not only won't spread her pussy for me, she never ever talks dirty. It's just not her. So I take advantage of this dream-fantasy-induced change of her philosophy.

'Anything, baby?' I ask her. 'Do you like it up your ass?'

She grins down at me. 'Oh, do I, baby,' she says. 'I *love* it up my ass. Especially if your dick is real big.' I hand her a hundred. She looks at it, tucks it in her garter, and drops her panties. She leans back on her hands and shows me both her orifices.

'There you are, baby,' she says. 'They're both yours.'

'OK, honey,' I say. 'I'll meet you wherever, whenever. You tell me. You get the other fifty then. And a bonus if you're real sexy.' She kneels forward and pulls her panties up. Then she looks at her watch.

'I finish here in just under an hour,' she tells me. 'There's a bar just up the block called Annie's. I'll meet you in there in an hour. My place is just around the corner from there. I'll fuck your socks off,' she promises. 'See you, baby.'

I grin at her, and spend another happy half-hour watching the six girls at work, and keeping my hard-on going. There is so much wet snatch being waved about in there between the girls that I can smell it on the air, even with the cigarette smoke that is fouling the bar. I remember that it's lunch time, and that I haven't eaten.

The smell of pussy makes me yearn for a dozen oysters. I've never been able to decide whether I like oysters because they smell and taste of pussy, or if I like pussy because it smells and tastes of oysters. Either way, the one often reminds me of the other. Although, I must admit, I've never fucked an oyster. Pussy bars don't normally sell food, and this one's no exception. But there's a seafood bar and restaurant across the road. I finish my drink, wave goodbye to the girls, tuck my now diminished hard-on away comfortably, and cross the road. Yes, they do serve oysters. They've got a pretty good selection. I order a dozen plump Chesapeake Bay oysters, and eat them with brown bread and butter, lemon juice, shallot vinegar, and just a touch of tabasco. And I order a half bottle of Californian Chardonnay.

Delicious. I follow the oysters with a three-egg ham and tomato omelette, French fries and a tossed green salad, and accompany that with a half bottle of excellent Australian Shiraz. Great. All I need now is a good fuck. I look at my watch. I've got seven minutes to get there. I pay my bill, tip well for good food and service, and hope that's going to continue at my next appointment.

I get to Annie's with a couple minutes to spare and order a Beefeater martini on the rocks, with a slice. A short while later, in comes my girlfriend, but in the guise of this stripper from the pussy bar. 'Hi,' she says. 'I'm Gloria. What's your name?' Her name isn't Gloria at all, it's Wendy, but a fantasy is a fantasy, I guess. 'I'm Dave,' I tell her. Which *is* my name. 'What'll you drink?'

'I'll have a Cutty Sark on the rocks,' she says. 'Thanks.' Well, we sit there and chat about nothing for a while, and then she finishes her drink and says, 'I guess it's probably time for us to make a move.'

Her pad is, like she said, five minutes, walk away. It's a third-floor walk-up, but once you're inside, it's large, comfortable, and well-furnished. There's a lot of leather furniture, and wall-to-wall rugs, some decent pictures, and it looks good. She takes me straight into the bedroom. There's a good-size double bed. She turns down the duvet and everything is clean and fresh. She strips off and reveals the body that I know so well. Great tits, great buns. Long legs. Pussy hair dyed to match her platinum-blonde head. I get a hard-on just looking at her.

'If you wanna fuck my ass, I'd better get some K-Y jelly,' she says, and takes herself off to the next-door bathroom. She's back a moment later with a tube of K-Y. She puts it in my hand

and climbs up onto the bed, where she kneels down on all fours, her lovely ass facing me. 'It's more fun for you if you do that,' she tells me. I've got a bigger erection than I think I've ever had in my life before. At which point I wake up. My erection is still with me, but my fantasy is ended. I still haven't fucked my girl in the ass. But that, they tell me, is what fantasies are all about. What do you say?

R.F. Rockford, Illinois.

We say that it sounds to us as if you're a very lucky fella. Don't push your luck.

VANITY FAIR

Your girls are all dreamboats, but Susie, in your last issue, is my fantasy girl. She's the personification of everything I've always desired in a woman, and have never found. It's the sheer feminity of her and her surroundings that fires my engine. First of all she's beautiful. Really beautiful. But so are all your girls. Then Susie is petite. At least her overall height and shape is petite. Her long blonde hair is delicately coiffed, and surrounds her lovely face like a soft blonde halo. It is exquisitely dressed, but manages to look casual. The secret of attractive hair. Full marks to your hairdresser. The blonde patently comes out of a bottle (or a sachet) but it is none the worse for that.

Next, Susie's pretty face is fully – and expertly – made up. There is no question of hiding her light behind a bushel. Susie's appearance is gorgeously enhanced by every beauty aid known to woman. And she looks ravishing. Blusher, eye liner, mascara, powder, and lipstick. They're all there, adding to her youthful beauty. And probably a few things that I'm unaware of, too.

She's wearing false lashes. Her long nails are well manicured, and perfectly painted, as I am sure her toes are too, although they cannot be seen beneath those pretty white stockings. She's wearing earrings. Her full breasts are heavy, but prettily shaped. There is no question of crease or sag. Her pink areolae and nipples are small but perfectly shaped, and her nipples are erotically erect. Her magnificent pubic growth has been left, quite properly, untrimmed, but it has obviously been carefully and lovingly shampooed and brushed, leaving her pubes as soft and silky as her hair.

Susie's legs go all the way up to her bottom (of which more later) and are slim and pretty. Her fingers, too, are long and slim. I can fantasize them wrapped around my willing cock. Her mouth is divinely sensual. I would love those carmined lips around my rampant tool, those pale-blue eyes looking into mine as she sucks me off.

Her knickers are daintily, whitely chaste, but sexily trimmed with tiny red bows. Her suspender belt is similarly wickedly lascivious, the long, thin white suspenders emphasizing her firm, tanned thighs. Her slip is palely decorous, but is pulled up over her breasts, in urgent display of her swollen nipples. Her knickers are pulled down below her thighs, exposing the gusset to our gaze, for Susie knows the attraction of virgin-white knicker gussets to horny young men.

Her delicate fingers spread her pale pink pussy lips widely apart for our delectation, and we know that any moment now, she is going to turn and look us in the eye as she slides her middle finger deeply inside herself. And we know with certainty that she is going to turn that innocent face towards us, and smile, and talk really dirty to us. 'Do you like to watch me play with myself?' she'll ask. 'Do you like to see me with my fingers in my cunt?

And then she'll slowly withdraw her fingers, now all wet and shiny with the running juices that her masturbation has prompted, and she'll hold them out towards us. There will be no need for her to ask us if we would like to lick and suck them, for we will already have grasped her wrist, urgently, and pulled her fingers quickly to our mouths, so that we can do exactly that. And she will taste and smell divine, and we'll ask her to play lucky dip again. She'll dip, and we'll be lucky.

And at last she'll open her legs wide, and we'll know that we are being invited to worship at her strongly-scented altar of desire. To begin to consummate our lust, by performing cunnilingus upon our little darling's pretty little pussy. And as we press our lips to hers, and part them, delving in our search for her clitoris – that we may bring her to immediate orgasm – we slide our hands around those gorgeous buttocks and squeeze their firm, warm flesh.

She groans and rolls over, revealing her perfect arse with her deeply carved anal cleavage, filled with lustrous, dyed-blonde anal hair. We part it with our fingers, deftly finding her other tiny secret puckered passage. We touch it, gently, and it half opens, and she turns back quickly, a secret smile on her lips, and simply says 'Naughty' as she parts her legs again for us to continue our oral worship.

We do our pleasurable duty, and suddenly she is pulling at our body and legs, indicating that, while we should keep our mouth and tongue where they are, we should rearrange ourselves so that we are kneeling over her mouth. In our excitement at the thought of what she is about to do to us, we practically shoot our load before any kind of contact is made. But we manage to control ourselves, and we feel those cool fingers take our erection and place it immediately above those painted lips. Which open, and then she puts our cock in her mouth and begins to suck and lick it. Gently. Sensually.

Like an expensive whore. She manipulates us with her hand as she devours us with her mouth and tongue, and then she squeezes hard at the base of our cock and we spurt our semen into her mouth in hot, rapid, exquisite jets. She comes as we come, and for a few moments our two bodies react violently as we shudder and shake in our orgasmic triumph.

'That was great, darling,' she says. 'When you've got your breath back, you can fuck me.' She looks at me, and smiles. 'That's only if you want to, of course.' *Jesus*, I think. I look at her. 'I want to, darling.'

She's lying on her back on the bed, which is rumpled from our activities to date. The sheets and pillows, like everything else about Susie, as I mentioned earlier, are very feminine. They're the palest blue silk, edged with lacy white cotton, and the pillows are pure white silk, edged with lacy pale-blue cotton. They're not the kind of sheet that you buy in John Lewis, or Debenhams. I'd guess that they came from The White House, in London's Bond Street. The bedhead is brass, and very *art deco*. There is gilt and marble and tapestry everywhere, all over the bedroom. But, most of all, there is Susie. And Susie's cunt. It's wet, it's willing, and it's waiting for *me*.

I move over, and lie alongside her. She takes hold of my cock and begins to masturbate me back to full erection. I reach down and slip a finger inside her wetness. Finding her clitoris, I massage it up to its full stiffness. I'm as rigid as a poket.

'You're ready now, darling,' she says. 'Fuck me now. Fuck me with your lovely big cock.' I climb on top of her, and she opens her legs wide and puts down her fingers between us. Then she's spreading her outer lips with the fingers of her right hand as she takes my cock in her left hand and guides it into her. I slide in, up to the hilt. She's wet, and hot, and she feels as if she's got some kind of little suction machine up there. She begins working her vaginal muscles, and I begin to thrust in and out of her – pulling up until I'm almost out of her, then thrusting hard back in again, slamming against her clitoris as I fuck her hard and fast. She begins to move beneath me, thrusting her hips hard up against me. And then she begins to shout.

'Oh, shit,' she says. 'Oh, fuck. Oh, yes. You're making me come. You're fucking my cunt, and I'm coming. Oh, Jesus.' And much more, in similar vein. Singularly unfeminine. And totally out of character, I thought. But coming she is. I join her, and once more spurt my seed happily up her receptive pussy. Fantastic fantasy!

G.F. Mildenhall, Suffolk.

If you knew Susie, like we knew Susie . . . Frankly, it sounds as if you know her rather better *than we do. She's a great gal.*

TELEPHONE SEX

The advertisements for telephone sex that one sees in all men's magazines these days are really quite appalling, although I suppose if that's the only way some guys can get off, it doesn't actually do any harm. But the subject reminds me of my own one-off experience with telephone sex, which was of a rather different nature.

I was living with a girl, whom I realized quite quickly was incapable of remaining faithful to anyone for longer than about five minutes. Sarah, her name was. I lived in London, and one day I had to go up to Birmingham on business and stay overnight. I stayed in one of those big expense account hotels in the Bull Ring. After dinner with my clients I had a couple of drinks in the bar, and at about eleven o'clock I took myself off to my room, and to my lonely bed. Thinking that I would say goodnight to my girlfriend, I telephoned the flat that we shared in London.

This was in the days before direct dialling in hotels, and I had to go through the switchboard to get a long-distance number. The telephone rang in our London flat. And rang. And rang. The operator kept it ringing for a while, and when it became obvious that there was no reply, she said, politely enough, 'I'm afraid there's no reply, sir. Shall I cancel the call?' I asked her to let it ring for a while longer, thinking that Sarah might be in the bath, or on the loo, and I struck up a conversation with the telephonist against the background noise of the telephone continuing to ring unanswered.

It was obvious that Sarah, the dirty cow, was out, getting fucked by somebody else. I said as much to the telephonist, who was very sympathetic. To cut a long story short, I kept calling Sarah, through the telephonist, and there continued to be no reply. By midnight, the telephonist and I had struck up a kind of a friendship, in as much as you can with someone who is only a voice in the night. She had an attractive voice, and when she told me that she was ending her duty at midnight, I said, half jokingly, 'Why don't you come to my room and have a drink with me on your way?' I had a bottle of whisky, and there were two glasses in the bathroom.

To my surprise, the girl said that yes, she would like to do that. I still thought that she was probably having me on, and that she wouldn't turn up, but no. A few minutes after midnight there was a discreet knock on my door. I answered it rather nervously, wondering if I would find a fat, unattractive fifty-year-old outside. To my delight, I would guess that the girl was in her late twenties, and extremely attractive.

Fortunately for me, we took an instant liking to each other, and only minutes after pouring us both a drink, she was in my arms, and kissing me passionately. 'Let me make it up to you, darling,' she whispered in my ear, as her fingers found my fly and slowly unzipped it. 'I'll make it up to you, for your girlfriend being unfaithful to you. By the time that I've finished with you, I promise you that you won't be sorry.' Nor was I. Jesus H.

She spent the entire night with me, during which time she sucked me off, tossed me off, and I sucked her off, and fucked her. Over and over again. She was seemingly tireless, and ceaselessly found naughtier and naughtier ways of getting me hard again after each ejaculation, including sticking her finger up my arse and massaging my prostate. It was as if she was on heat. She loved sex, and patently couldn't get enough of it. It transpired, as I found out during one of our brief breaks, that she was single, had no particular boyfriend at the moment, and wasn't getting as much of it as she liked, which was my good fortune.

She was a live-in member of the hotel's staff, so that it was no problem for her the following morning to take herself off quietly to her own room to get ready for her next shift. It was one of the greatest nights of my life. When I got back to London later that day, I moved out of the flat I shared with Sarah and soon found myself a new girlfriend. One who turned out to be a much better fuck than Sarah was, and who was in addition as faithful to me as I was to her. Sadly, I didn't keep in touch with my lovely Birmingham hotel telephonist. Leave aside some fantastic fucking, I've always been grateful to her for her kindness and sympathy at a time when I was feeling rather down. And in fact she changed my life. Very much for the better. I stayed in the same hotel again some months later, and hoped that I might repeat that unforgettable night, but enquiries revealed the fact that the girl had found herself a new job, and moved on.

P.H.R. Maida Vale, London.

That's your rather nice version of what a travel-writing woman friend of ours refers to as 'Nights that pass in the ship'.

SLAVE LABOUR . . .

You devote a lot of space in your columns to male fantasies, reasonably enough, I suppose. So how about indulging a girl's sexual desires for a change? My favourite fantasies all take place in the African jungle, sadly a place that I have not, so far, actually visited.

I am making my way, alone, through the jungle. It's hot (naturally) and steamy, and I am terrified. Terrified of snakes, of wild animals, and of the savages, whose jungle drums I can hear beating in the distance. Suddenly I realize that they are getting nearer and nearer. I'm wearing a white safari suit, but it's soaking wet with my sweat, and my knickers are wet through, for the same reason, and the crotch is rubbing my pussy lips. It's not painful. In fact, it's rather nice, but it's making me dead horny, and I'm seriously beginning to need a stiff cock. There not being one handy anywhere, I am forced to stop, pull up my skirt, pull down my wet knickers, and start to frig myself to orgasm.

I'm just having my first sneaky little come when I realize that the drums have stopped beating. I'm standing there with my knicks around my ankles and my fingers in my sticky pussy and my pussy juices running down my thighs when all around me the bushes part, and a dozen or more native heads appear. Before I can even scream, I am stripped naked, my hands are tied behind my back, and I'm marched for what seems like hours through the dense jungle until eventually, just when I think I'm going to drop, we reach a native village. I am taken to what I imagine to be the chief's hut, outside which I am stood with my hands still bound. A crowd of men, women and children come and crowd around me.

The chief comes out and says something to me in a language that I don't understand. I tell him, in English, that I don't understand him, and that obviously makes two of us. He takes a knife out of his belt, and cuts my hands free. He then takes me into his hut, and takes off what little he is wearing, revealing a giant tool. I'm mesmerized by its size. It's bigger than any cock I've ever seen, and I have to admit, through my blushes, that I've seen a few. He holds it up, and beckons to me. I stand in front of him, and he indicates that he wants me to suck his cock. It will obviously be something of an experience.

I kneel in front of him and take it in my hand. It grows, alarmingly, as I hold it. I take it in my mouth, which it almost fills, and I begin to suck it. It tastes good. I enjoy sucking cock, and I do my best for the chief, who makes the occasional grunting noise, which I take to mean that he is enjoying what I am doing. After a while, I begin to wank his vast tool with my hand, to help things along, simply because the size of his cock, and the work I am doing on it, is making my jaw ache. This has the desired effect, and he is soon pumping his hot, creamy come down my throat.

Well, I guess you've probably sussed out the scenario by now. Yes, you're right, of course. The next thing is that he fucks me. He does it doggy fashion, and while this is my least favourite position to get fucked in, his cock is so big that, even in that usually non-orgasm-producing position, it generates more orgasms than most girls get in a lifetime. And, yes, you're right again! When the chief has finished, I realize that there's a queue outside his hut of some hundred or so large, virile, native tribesmen, all naked, and all with their erect dicks in their hands, waiting to be serviced by yours truly. As you can probably imagine, I regularly wake up from this favourite fantasy a very, *very* happy lady. *How* much is the fare to Africa?

J.W. Macroom, County Cork, Republic of Ireland.

We're reasonably confident that you've probably kissed the Blarney Stone too, Ms J.W. And why not? Why not, indeed.

TO BE, OR NOT TO BE?

I'm fascinated by the continuing exchange in your columns currently about whether fantasies are best worked out (or maybe that should be worked *through*?) or are best kept as fantasies. You've just printed *my* fantasy, in the shape of that unbelievably beautiful Annabel, in your last month's issue. And if she were to appear in my life, there is absolutely no question about it: I'd fuck her to death. Or die trying.

It might look like a simple recipe to you, but it's my entire life's fantasy. Take one very beautiful girl. About five ten, I'd guess. Pale skinned. With long brunette hair, softly waved and falling over her brow. Make her up expertly, so that she doesn't really look as if she's wearing make-up, apart from a little pale-red lipstick, and maybe just a touch of blusher. Dress her in a white, *broderie anglaise* middy blouse, and matching, very brief, *broderie anglaise* knickers. Paint her long, well-kept nails to match her lipstick. Put her pretty feet into white socks, and black patent leather strappy sandals. Then photograph her.

Start off with her sitting on a white painted cane chair, bending forward as she does up the strap on one of her shoes. Let the photograph show her breasts welling out over the top of her middy blouse, and have her with her knees tightly together, so that all the reader can see is her lovely face. Looking directly at him, with most everything else carefully hidden. All you can really see are her knees.

Behind the cane chair is a bed. The bed-clothes are tousled, and it is left entirely to our imagination to decide whether Annabel is dressing, undressing, has been to bed, or is going to bed. Tantalizing. In the next picture, Annabel is doing that naughty thing that seems to affect all the pretty girls who undress in the pages of your magazine. She's pulling aside the crotch of her white panties, showing us the closed, pouting, fleshy lips of her lovely little pussy.

Her legs are wide open in this shot, and as well as having trouble with her knickers, poor Annabel's middy top seems to have come undone, and one of her delightful young breasts can be seen in all its pristine glory. Whatever next, I wonder? This naked breast reveals the fact that (assuming that the other, still hidden, breast, matches this one) Annabel is blessed with those fantastic tits that seem to have something just behind the areolae, thrusting it up and out, with her nipple perched delightfully, cheekily, on the end. We can tell from the photograph that Annabel is feeling sexy, and this notion is supported by the other patently obvious fact that her nipple is rigidly erect.

The next picture charmingly focuses on just her face. Her lips pout slightly, and her head is just the tiniest bit lowered down, towards the camera. To me, she looks as if she is about to go down on me. I can imagine those soft, full, redly lipsticked lips sucking on my cock. Any time. Dear Annabel.

We next see her kneeling on the floor, her arms propped on the white cane chair, this time with her exquisite arse towards the camera. This particular shot suggests to me things that I couldn't possible write to you about. All I can say is that it's still against the law in Britain. And I want to do it to her. Now. I don't care if I do go to prison.

The next four photographs are similar, but not the same. They all, however, display Annabel's charms, with her seated, and from the front. She is naked from the waist down, and in one of them, she is displaying her fabulous cunt. Full face. It is nestling in her dark brown pubic hair, which is erotically long, and surprisingly straight.

Here one is given a better view of her actual pussy than one saw in the first picture, in which she was pulling the crotch of her knickers over to one side. Her pussy is fully exposed. And I want to suck it. Lick it. Sniff it. Play with it. Wank it. Fuck it. Push my nose up it. From the slightly petulant expression on the lovely Annabel's face, I think she wants me to do all those things to her. She obviously isn't getting enough.

But the final three pictures on your last two pages are the real cock-stiffeners. There, Annabel has decided that she isn't going to get any of that which she so obviously wants, and she is doing the next best thing. She's wanking herself off. She has her fingers in her cunt. It's too much. To think that, even if only as a fantasy, anyone who looks like Annabel can't get a fuck is soul-destroying. Her long legs are wide apart, she's lying back in the chair, her fingers are in her cunt, and she's doing it to herself. My God. What a waste. But what a sight!

Her eyes are closed. Her mouth is open. One can almost hear the soft, squidgy, wet, frigging noises that her fingers are making in her pussy. And in the final two photographs, she is obviously relaxing, having finally reached her much-needed climax. In both shots she is lying on her stomach, her legs again apart, showing her anal cleavage, with her entire sexual apparatus displayed, and with her face seen from the side, her eyes still shut, enjoying that which she has just completed. In both these shots, we can see her tiny, wrinkled, pink little arsehole, revealed in its naked, sensual desirability. I can actually smell it. Magic!

It lies there, unsullied, inches above her hairy pussy, her

swollen pussylips now closed, her arsehole totally available to anyone with a stiff prick and sufficient nerve to kneel between her legs and thrust it up her anus. In the most sexually attractive of the two pictures of her rectum, her forbidden orifice looks wetly lubricated, as if ready and waiting to be pierced. Annabel's eyes, as I said earlier, are still closed, and one can imagine that she is waiting for that desired stab of welcome pain, of delightful, hurtful agony, as a ramrod-stiff penis assaults her arsehole. She's waiting to be buggered. Bless her. That's one ring of which I would like to become the ringmaster. I wish!

P.S.F. Preston, Lancashire.

It sounds as if you would like the lovely Annabel to turn the occasional trick for you!

SEX MACHINE

I love sex, but I'm bored with relationships. Intercourse certainly beats masturbation, but why, oh why do I have to pretend to like a girl before I can fuck her? Hookers aside, sex is supposed to be between two people who are also at least friends. But why? It doesn't make any kind of sense to me.

I have this – to me – magical fantasy, where anyone who feels the way I do (there must be some, surely?) can join a club where the only reason for membership is to fuck without any emotional involvement. This means that a man walks into the bar at the club's premises, knowing that all the women in the bar are there to be fucked, if they like the look of you, without any other kind of involvement whatsoever.

It's a terrific idea, don't you think? One can take it further. Members could wear badges denoting the kind of sex that they preferred, thus both saving time and avoiding the need for unnecessary conversation. Men and women could wear a small golden penis if their wish was for ordinary, straightforward fucking. The addition of a golden mouth badge on a woman would indicate that she liked to fellate men, and on a man, that he enjoyed giving head. Two mouth badges would mean that a person liked both to give and to receive oral sex. A golden hand would tell possible partners that a woman enjoyed giving a hand job, while a single golden finger would show that they enjoyed being masturbated. Worn by a man, the latter would show that he liked to frig women. A golden bosom could indicate a penchant for giving tit-wanks. A small golden fountain or a golden circle surrounded by golden hair would, I believe, also be indicative of certain rather specialized sexual preferences. Homosexuals of both sexes should, I suggest, have their own exclusive club, to avoid confusion. It would be interesting to see how many badges individual men and women chose to wear. A full set ought to guarantee each partner a good time!

To take my fantasy at face value, just imagine yourself and the lovely Pauline, from the current issue. You meet her in the bar, and she's wearing just a small golden cock on the lapel of her jacket. So you know, straight away, that she's looking for a good fucking. Nothing else. So you look at her badge, then at her, and raise a quizzical eyebrow. She checks out your lapel, and sees that you are wearing the same badge. She smiles and nods. Imagine then taking her up to one of the club's bedrooms and watching her undress and strip down to those naughty little pale beige frilly knickers. Imagine yourself kneeling in front of her, and pulling them slowly down those gorgeous long legs, and revealing that wondrous, hairy snatch, and those fabulous buttocks. Think of unfastening those suspenders, and peeling off those pretty seamed stockings.

Think of yourself taking those buttocks in your hands and pulling her towards you as you bury your face in her pussy. Contemplate the scent of her sexually aroused cunt. You have already stripped off yourself, so you quickly stand up, your rampant cock sticking out proudly, and Pauline reaches down and encircles it with her cool, expert fingers as you kiss her wetly.

You feel her tongue in your mouth. You slip a hand between her legs, parting that softly curled hair, and you find her pussy lips, swollen with desire. You part them with you forefinger, and slide it into her. She's so wet, your finger sinks in right up to the knuckle, and she squeezes it with her vaginal muscles as you find her clitoris, and stroke it, oh, so slowly, until she groans and says, 'Please, fuck me now, darling. I want you. I need your cock inside me.' She pulls away from you, and goes and lies on the bed on her back. She opens her legs wide, and pulls her pussy lips apart for you. 'Put it in here, darling,' she tells you. 'Fuck me with your beautiful cock.' You climb onto her, and she takes you, and feeds you up into herself.

She's warm and wet and you slip in quickly, and she closes her pussy on your cock. She's tight. Wonderfully tight. As you begin to fuck her, you can feel her muscles working your cock. She looks up at you, and smiles. 'Suck my breasts,' she pleads. You lean down, obediently, and take one of those erect teats between your lips. As you suck, you feel her putting a hand down between her legs, and you feel her fingers inside her pussy.

She pulls them out. They're wet with her juices, and she pulls and strokes at her other nipple, covering it with her sexual effluent. 'Suck the other one now, darling,' she tells you. 'It will taste delicious.' She puts her lips by your ear, and whispers, 'It will taste of my cunt. Do you like the taste of girls' cunts?'

'Yes, sweetheart,' you tell her, quickly, before you start to suck her nipple. You're still fucking her, of course, and she's giving you a right seeing-to with those pussy muscles. She's right, you discover. Her tit *does* taste of her cunt. You wish now that you'd started off by sucking her down there, but she wasn't wearing a suck-my-cunt badge, and you always play by the rules. Maybe she'll ask you to suck her later.

While you're enjoying sucking her sticky tit clean of her juices, she puts her fingers between her legs again and prepares the other nipple for you, and you change over, sucking at it greedily. 'Do you like it when I talk dirty to you?' she asks. 'Do you like it when I say "cunt"?' You nod your head as best you can with your mouth full of swollen teat, so as not to have to stop sucking it and lose the flavour of her pussy.

'I love to talk dirty,' she tells you. 'It turns me on, too. I love to say fuck. *Fuck.* You're fucking me with your huge cock. Your huge cock is right up my tight little cunt, and you're fucking me with it. I like you fucking me. My cunt's all wet for you, so that you can fuck me easily. But it's still tight around your cock. I want it to feel like a young nun's cunt for you. Tiny and tight, while you're fucking me. I wish I'd asked you to suck it for me, before you started to fuck me. I loved it when you kissed my cunt, after you'd pulled my knickers down. But I wanted you to fuck me then. Will you suck my cunt for me, later on, please, darling?' This is worth letting go of her nipple for, so you release it, and lean down and kiss her.

'Yes, darling,' you say. 'I'd love to suck your cunt for you later.'

'I'm going to come soon,' she suddenly tells you. 'You're fucking me, and making me come. I'm going to come now. NOW.' She starts to buck her hips beneath you, and you feel your own ejaculation beginning, hastened by the dirty words she's been saying with that pretty mouth of hers. As you wonder whether she'll suck your cock later on with that pretty little mouth, you start to pump your come into her.

'Oh, I'm coming, and I can feel your spunk,' she shouts. 'I can feel your hot spunk up my cunt. Oh, yes. *Yes.* YES. I'm coming NOW.' Doesn't that description get your votes for sex without emotional involvement?

J.Y. Bromsgrove, Cheshire.

We can see that it might appeal to certain individuals. But surely, taken to its logical conclusion, you do away with live women and have sex with female robots? The problem, of course, being that robots don't talk dirty. Or flavour their nipples with erotic juices. Our vote goes for the real thing. Sorry.

ON THE GAME

As a businesswoman away from home, sex, up until now, has always been either a hand job or a matter for my trusty vibrator. But on a visit to New York recently on business, my client – herself a woman – introduced me to a new (to me) phenomenon. A brothel for women.

Situated in a smart apartment block in the low Fifties, the brothel was run by a woman called Kathy. I don't know whether that was her real name or not. She had started out in life as a hooker, working in turn at a number of the many ordinary brothels in midtown Manhattan. Ruminating over a drink with a colleague after work one evening, her companion was complaining of the difficulty of getting laid by anyone other than customers of the whorehouse in which they worked. For many different reasons, getting laid at work apparently didn't count to either of the girls as sex. It was simply their work. Her companion said something like, 'What we need is a brothel for women. Somewhere where *we* can go and pay to get well fucked by an attractive man of our choice.' And the idea was born.

The two girls asked around among their menfolk, and finally selected half a dozen men who looked good physically, fucked well, needed the money, and had no qualms about hooking for a living. As far as the six were concerned, they were delighted to be getting paid for something that they enjoyed doing anyway.

At first the two girls ran the male brothel out of their shared apartment. Kathy ran the business, and her companion delicately touted for business. But they were very quickly so popular that they soon moved to a much larger place, where they ran a permanent staff of twelve. For pretty obvious reasons the men worked rather shorter hours than do female hookers. Particularly on busy days. Their clientele was made up mainly of housewives, with a proportion of businesswomen and a smaller proportion of single girls.

Kathy charged a standard $150 an hour, which included everything other than drink. Horny women could get laid, lie back and enjoy oral sex, be masturbated, fucked anally, or anything else that they fancied. If anyone wanted to indulge in flagellation, that was extra. Fellating the men, should anyone so wish, was included in the $150 rate. Surprisingly, I was told that this was a very popular pastime with many of the lady customers. And, reasonably enough, with the men working there.

My first (and so far only) experience of what is known among its clientele as Kathy's came after my business colleague had bought me dinner at Windows on the World, that marvellous Manhattan restaurant at the top of the World Trade Center, where you can look down out of the windows and watch the jumbo jets on their approach paths into Kennedy Airport as they fly some hundreds of feet below you.

I had really enjoyed my meal. The food was fantastic, the wines superb, and the company extremely agreeable. As I sipped a large cognac with my espresso coffee, I tried to tell my hostess how much I had enjoyed it all. At the end, I said, 'All I need now is to get well laid.'

'No problem,' she said, and started to tell me about Kathy's. Naturally enough, I was much intrigued. In the cab on the way uptown, my friend told me how the whole thing had started. She also told me that new customers had to be introduced by existing customers, and that Kathy gave every new arrival a ten-minute private interview before accepting her. At mine, she explained that she relied upon her customers' discretion, in that the services that she was supplying were illegal. Since unprotected sex was available for any woman who wanted it, she also insisted that everyone signed a slip stating categorically that they had no known sexual diseases.

She said that if, for any reason whatsoever, a customer was dissatisfied with the sexual service supplied, then she, Kathy, should be notified immediately and – provided that she agreed that it was a problem posed by the male hooker – then a refund or a substitute – whichever was preferred – would be given. Apparently, the men's libidos were known to fail occasionally. Whether from overwork or from the inability to provide an erection for an unattractive customer, I didn't ask. Some things are better left unsaid. I was then taken into the bar where my friend was sitting waiting for me, chatting to a group of men and women.

The women were other customers, the men were for hire. Kathy had explained that, if one so wished, one could tell her which of the men one had selected, and she would then make the necessary arrangements. This meant that one didn't actually have to say to one of the men, 'Hey, buster, do you wanna fuck?' Unless, of course, that amused anyone so to do.

There were seven men in the bar, all of them aged around the twenty-five to thirty-five age group. There were blonds, medium brunettes, a redhead and one with black hair. Six were white, one black. He was known, rather unsubtly, I thought, as Cocky.

Kathy introduced me all around, and offered me a drink

on the house. I noticed that my business friend (who was extremely attractive) was fondling, through the material of his trousers, the obviously erect cock of the man standing next to her. She had patently made her mind up already. In the cab on the way uptown, she had insisted that this was her treat. Kathy, she told me, gave receipts on headed paper that said Kathy's Restaurant. Restaurant bills, apparently, are still accepted in the United States as a legitimate business expense.

All seven men were good-looking, although two of them were too TV-idol looking in appearance for my particular taste. I took my time, and finally chose Cocky, despite (or perhaps because of?) his name. I'd never fucked a black, and I have always found them, sexually, extremely attractive.

I didn't bother with the pretence of telling Kathy. I simply said to Cocky, 'Come and fuck me, Cocky.' Well, it *was* a brothel, for God's sake. I asked him to suck my pussy for a while first, and it was rapidly apparent that this was something that he was a past-master at. He obviously loved to suck pussy, and he made me come over and over again. I love men who suck pussy well. It's an art form.

I had already decided to insist that he used a condom, since I knew nothing of his personal habits, other than that he worked in a brothel. A good enough reason in itself, I would have thought. This is the world of Aids. Sad, really, since I love the feel of semen spurting up inside me. It's one of the world's great experiences. But a girl can't always have everything.

I deliberately made a joke of it, and insisted on unrolling the condom down his erection myself. Which wasn't the easiest job in the world, with a tool that size. It really was a very large cock, but Cocky didn't seem in any way particularly aware of the effect it was having on me. I was wet from his cunnilingus, but handling that gorgeous weapon was making me even wetter.

When I had stretched the rubber down its entire impressive length, I took it into my mouth, just to excite myself even more. It was, in fact, almost too big for comfort, but I had to do it. I was going to dine out on this experience at dinner parties with my women friends for the rest of my life. So that, when I described it, and someone said – as someone inevitably would – 'Did you take it in your mouth?' I could honestly say yes. The thought of the thick creamy come that would spurt out of it as I sucked him off made me stop what I was doing (reluctantly), lie back on the bed, and say, 'OK, Cocky, baby. Fuck me now please.'

I've never been mounted by a stallion (except in my fantasies) but this was what it had to feel like. His giant tool slid into me easily enough, but it stretched me and totally filled me. It felt terrific. Better than any cock I'd ever had inside me before. He began to thrust up me in long, slow strokes, and I began to come immediately. It was a combination of the fact that his cock was so big that it was in permanent contact with my engorged clitoris all the time, and the excitement of being fucked by a man whom I had only met maybe fifteen or twenty minutes earlier. Plus, of course, the lascivious idea of actually paying someone to fuck me anyway.

Cocky grinned down at me. 'Looks to me like you enjoyin' this,' he said. 'Damn right, Cocky,' I told him. 'Damn right. Fuck me harder.' He did.

My orgasms increased in both intensity and frequency, until they built up into the big one, during which Cocky came too. I actually felt the end of the condom fill with semen as he ejaculated into it and as he pulled out he said, 'Great, ma'am. Really great. Thank you.' I kissed him, and said, 'Not a bit, Cocky love. Thank *you*.'

As we showered and dressed, he told me that the men

were given a half-hour break after servicing a client. If he was anything to go by, they certainly deserved it. Cocky had to go down in my sexual history as my best fuck ever. Now I'm seriously thinking of starting a similar establishment here in London. What do you say, girls?

J.D. Chelsea, London.

Our girls say it sounds like a lot of fun, but that they would probably be tempted to spend more money there than they could really afford. But please let them know if you do *start a male brothel, they ask. They'd be happy to help with any training that the staff might need. Discretion assured!*

THREE'S COMPANY

I'd like to share a recent sexual experience with your readers. It's something that I still can't actually believe happened to me. But let me begin at the beginning.

I was in my local supermarket late one evening. It was just after ten, and there weren't too many people in there at that time. I was looking at the TV dinners and wondering which disgusting apology for a meal I should take home when I became aware that someone was standing quite close to me. I turned my head to find an attractive young woman of about thirty beside me, looking at me rather than at the TV dinners. When she saw me looking at her, she said, 'Hi,' and smiled. 'Hi,' I said, wondering what she wanted. I hoped it was me. 'Do you like to fuck?' she asked. I couldn't believe my ears. 'I'm sorry,' I said. 'What did you say?'

This time she laughed out loud. 'Yes,' she said. 'That *is* what I said. Let me say it again. Do you like to fuck? Or, not to put too fine a point on it, would you like to fuck *me*? And two of my girlfriends, if you're up to it. They're both very pretty. All you have to do is say yes, and then I'll explain what it's all about. If the answer's no, then I'll stop bothering you.'

'The answer is yes, and yes, and yes,' I told her. 'Yes, please. I don't know if I could manage three. I've never tried. But I'd love to have a go.'

'Oh, good,' said the girl, taking my arm. 'And you don't need to worry about food. We'll feed you. OK?'

I put my TV dinner back on the shelf without feeling the slightest regret, and allowed the girl to guide me. She lived about ten minutes' walk away, she said. She and her girlfriends liked sex, but they didn't, any of them, particularly want to become involved with anyone. They were career girls, and preferred to keep their emotions for their work. So the three of them got together in one or other of their homes once a week, and the girl whose place it was, was responsible for going out and picking up an acceptable-looking man to service them. That way, they got fucked regularly, but didn't feel obliged to become involved with anyone.

'What fun.' I said. 'But don't you miss being taken out? You know, to pubs and restaurants, and the cinema, or the theatre? That sort of thing?'

'Absolutely not at all,' said the woman. 'Because we can do all that as a threesome. We like each other's company, and we don't need a man for that. Fucking is all that we really need men for. Playing with ourselves isn't really that much fun.' She looked sideways at me.

'My name's Mary,' she said. 'What's yours?'

'Peter,' I said. 'Peter Harrington.' She laughed again. She had a lovely, musical little laugh. 'We even tried playing with each other,' she said. 'It wasn't *all* bad. But at the end of the day, we decided that we aren't *really* cut out to be lezzies. We always ended up giggling, which rather spoilt the sexy part.'

I laughed with her. I began to get a hard-on. Maybe, if I was in luck, I could get them to do their lezzie act for me, I thought.

'Here we are,' said Mary. She had stopped outside a small block of four flats, built on two storeys. There was a common entrance hall, with two doors, downstairs, and then a flight of stairs leading to the upper floor. Mary led the way up the stairs and into another corridor, which was a reproduction of the ground-floor one. She took a key out of her purse, and opened the right-hand door. 'Come in,' she said. I followed her inside the flat.

There was another corridor with various doors leading off it. The nearest door was open, and I could hear music and conversation, which stopped as Mary slammed the front door. 'Here we are, then, girls,' she called out. 'Come and say hello to Peter.' Two attractive girls came through the door, one after the other. Both blondes. Mary was a brunette.

The two blondes looked at me. 'Oooh, nice,' said the first one, holding out her hand. I shook it. 'I'm Beth,' she said. 'And this is Wendy.'

'Hi,' said Wendy, also holding out a hand to shake. 'Let's go inside,' said Mary, leading the way. I stood back, and allowed Beth and Wendy through first.

'So you're tonight's great fuck,' said Beth, as she passed me. 'Have you got a nice big cock?' *Jesus*, I thought. 'I haven't had too many complaints,' I said.

'Come on, Beth,' said Wendy. 'Stop giving the chap a hard time.'

'It's *him* I want to give *me* a hard time,' Beth said. We all laughed.

'What would you like to drink, Peter?' Mary asked. 'There's most of the usual things.'

'I'd love a Scotch and water, please,' I said. 'No ice, if you don't mind.'

'Surely,' Mary said, and began to do the necessary. She handed me a strong scotch. 'Say when,' she said, pouring water.

'When,' I said. Then, 'Cheers.'

'Cheers,' they all said. Beth and Wendy already had glasses, and Mary had poured herself a sherry. An amontillado, by the look of it. 'The food's all ready,' said Beth. She looked at me. 'It's pasta,' she said. 'Spag bol, with a mixed salad, and some decent cheese. And some quite decent wine. How does that sound?'

'It sounds terrific,' I said. *Let's not fuck about*, I thought to myself. Mary had been as direct as anyone could possibly be in the supermarket. 'Tell me,' I said, not speaking to anyone in particular. 'How do you decide who goes first on these occasions?'

'Oh, don't worry about it,' Beth said. 'We draw lots, before you arrive. If you reckon you can manage all three of us, tonight's order of play is Mary, then me, then Wendy. Wendy's got the short straw this evening.' Wendy looked at me and smiled. 'I'm confident that you'll fuck me tonight, Peter,' she said. 'And fuck me well. I know some very naughty things that I can do to get the most wilted dicky nicely stiff again. Don't worry about a thing.'

I smiled at her, and raised my glass. 'I'll drink to that, Wendy,' I said. 'Cheers.'

Wilted dicky was something I wasn't suffering from right then. We all went through to the kitchen/dining room. Whoever had put the pasta together knew what they were about. It was delicious. As was the salad. And the cheese was from the Isle of Mull. One of my favourites. Not too easy to find in London. They served decent coffee and offered me a brandy which, in the circumstances, I refused.

I looked at my watch. It was half-eleven. Then I looked at Mary. 'I'm ready when you are, Mary,' I said. 'There's no hurry, but whenever you feel like it.'

'Fine,' she said. 'But there's something we need to tell you.' *Oh, no*, I thought. *They're into flagellation. Or enemas. Or worse. They're going to tell me something that I really don't want to hear.*

'So tell me,' I said. 'Spit it out.'

'Well, Mary said. 'When we started this whole thing up, a couple of months back, we decided that it was entirely for our joint and mutual amusement. It was for fun. Sex and fun. Why not? We felt that we were offering any guy who joined us a pretty good time, what with drinks, dinner, and three extremely good, enthusiastic fucks, which should keep him happy. But we wanted to make sure that we enjoyed it too. So we decided that whatever we did, we did together.'

I looked at her, somewhat askance. 'Yes,' she said. 'You've got it. So the bedroom's this way.' She got up from the table, followed by the other two girls. As they walked down the corridor to the bedroom, they were undoing their blouses, stripping them off, dropping their skirts on the floor as they went, and generally disrobing. *Terrific,* I thought. *The more the merrier.*

By the time that we got to the bedroom, I was accompanied by three pretty girls attired in full sexual undress. They'd done the whole bit. Suburban fantasy time. See-through brassieres. Matching, transparent knickers. Sexy little suspender belts holding up one pair of black and two pairs of pale-beige stockings. All seamed. Mary was all in transparent black, Beth's chosen colour was pale beige, and Wendy was in virginal white. I wanted to suck and fuck and feel and lick and sniff all three of them, all at the same time. Talk about pussy galore.

The bedroom was large for the size of the flat. As was the bed. It had been built for serious sexual pleasures. Mary climbed up onto it. I stripped off, exposing my cock, which was sort of half erect. Beth came over and took hold of it.

'Mmmmm,' she said. 'I see what you meant earlier. It *is* a big one. How lovely.' She started to toss me off, unemotionally and expertly, until I was stiffly rigid, which took only a few seconds of her time. She then knelt in front of me and took my circumcised cock into her warm mouth. Her lips were soft, her tongue practised. Her mouth was warm.

'Get off, Beth,' said Mary. 'He's mine. If you suck him off now, you'll be sorry later. Don't be selfish. Just wait your bloody turn.' *Now, now, girls,* I thought to myself. *Temper, temper.*

Beth took me out of her mouth, and looked up at me from beneath modestly lowered eyelashes. 'Sorry, darling,' she said. 'I got carried away. See you later.' She got up and went over to the bed, and put her hand between Mary's legs.

'Let me get you ready for your fuck, darling,' she said to Mary. 'Let me make your pussy nice and wet for young Peter.' She started to rub and massage Mary's pussy through the thin material of her knickers, and Mary lay back, opened her legs, and obviously began to enjoy what was being done to her. Soon she began to moan out loud, saying, 'Yes, oh yes. That's nice.'

Beth withdrew her hand and, putting it inside the elastic waistband of Mary's knickers, she began to ease the knickers down her hips, along her thighs, and finally down around her ankles, and off over her feet. She screwed the knickers up into a handful, and threw them at me. 'There, sweetheart,' she said. 'Get yourself into the mood. Sniff Mary's knickers while I frig her for a little while.'

The knickers fell by my feet in a small black ball. I picked them up and unwrapped them. Beth had started to masturbate Mary, rapidly fingering her clitoris, and Mary was in another world. The knickers were made of black nylon, and the crotch was lined with a soft black cotton material. It was wet through with Mary's sexual effluent. The essence of sex. I held it up to my nostrils, to be enthralled by the acrid scent of her cunt. The immediate effect of my inhalation was to have my cock spring back to instant, full erection. Wendy came over and took hold of it.

'It's a lovely cock,' she said. 'Can I suck it?'

'Sweetheart,' I said, 'as far as I'm concerned, you can do anything you like to it. But don't blame me if either of the other two get uptight about it. OK?'

She smiled at me. 'Come and sit in this chair over here. I'll be able to suck you off better that way.' I did as I was told, and when I had settled myself comfortably into the chair, Wendy came and sat on the floor in front of me and, taking my erect cock between her fingers, began to wank me into her mouth. It was delightful. I was reminded, I don't know why, of that silly joke, a leftover from after the last war. 'No man hath greater love than this; that he lay down his wife for his friend.' I wondered if Wendy was married. I came very quickly.

She swallowed everything, with apparent enjoyment. I held her head in my hands as I came, and I was tempted to deep-throat her, but she might well have found that unacceptable. Lots of girls do, and I didn't want to upset anyone this early in the evening. She had sucked me off very satisfactorily, and there was lots more where that came from.

I looked over at Mary and Beth to see that Beth was now sucking away at Mary's pussy and Mary seemed very happy at what was happening to her. It seemed a pity to interrupt. 'Do you believe that one good turn deserves another, Peter?' Wendy suddenly asked me.

'Surely,' I said. 'What sort of thing did you have in mind?'

'How would you like to suck *my* pussy?' she asked. 'It's nicely wet, and suckable.'

'I'd love to,' I told her. Wendy stood up, prior to peeling off her white knickers. 'No, please don't,' I said. 'Please keep them on. But take the bra off.'

Wendy looked at me. 'So you're another of these dirty old men who like to bury their noses in girls' knickers while the girls are still wearing them, are you?' she said. 'How lovely.' And she did as I asked.

'I don't know about dirty *old* man,' I told her. 'I like to think I'm still a dirty *young* man.'

'Oh, you know what I mean,' she said. 'You're a knicker fetishist, aren't you?'

'I guess I am,' I said. 'Does that bother you?'

'Not so long as you're a pussy fetishist, too,' she answered, laughing.

'That I am,' I told her.

'Great,' she said. 'Let's not hang about, then.' She went and lay on her back on a deep pile rug that was over by the bedroom window, and spread her legs. The white panties were already stained with her juices. I lay down alongside her, and – as she had forecast – buried my nose in her damp knickers. She smelt divinely of cunt.

I began to suck her through the silky wet material, and I could feel the bulge of her outer lips. I felt her with my fingers, and pressed gently, so that her lips opened. Suddenly I needed to get my mouth on the real thing, and I began to pull her white knickers down. She raised her hips obligingly and I slid the knickers down her legs and off. She might have had blonde hair on her head, but her pubic growth was thick and dark brown, and tightly curled.

From as close as I was (about three inches away) I could see the pink wetness of her labia. I closed my mouth over it, and began to suck and lick and tongue her. 'Oooooh, nice,' she said, quietly. 'I like it.'

She reached out a hand and began to masturbate me, very slowly. I would put serious money on the notion that she'd had a lot of practice at jacking men off. She was very expert. I slipped my hands beneath her buttocks to press her upwards, increasing the pressure of my lips and tongue against her sex, and she began to move her hips beneath me.

Her bottom was plump and full, and her buttocks felt enchanting as I held them in my hands. I wondered if any of these girls took it up their bottoms. It's pleasantly surprising how many women *do* like being fucked in the arse. That was something to leave until later, I decided.

Wendy's movements had told me that she had been enjoying a series of orgasms for some time now, and now she started really humping her hips, indicating to me that the big one was on its way. She next increased the speed with which she was wanking me, and I started to move my own hips against the quickening motions of her dextrous fingers. Soon, we coincided nicely, and I spurted my jism over Wendy's hand, and Mary's white wool rug, as Wendy writhed with the pleasures of her big O. I kept sucking, and Wendy kept wanking, until we were both done.

'Mmmmm, nice,' said Wendy. 'I enjoyed that. How about you? I've been told by some that I give a pretty good wank.'

'The best,' I told her. 'Terrific. Thank you.' We lay where we were, on the floor. As we began to relax after our mutual exertions, we could hear Mary start to come, up on the bed across the room. She made a great deal of noise as she eventually came, while Beth sucked her to her final orgasm.

'Did Mary tell you that she and Beth are bisexual?' Mary asked.

'No, not exactly,' I said. 'She said that you all played with each other on occasions, but that fucking was infinitely preferable.'

'Well, that's certainly true for me,' Wendy said. 'But Mary

and Beth do a tremendous act with a double-ended dildo, when they're in the mood. I don't think they mind who's doing what to whom, or with what, as long as they've got something long and stiff up their fannys.'

At that point Wendy and Beth began to take notice of their surroundings again, and I think that they realised – from the fact that Wendy and I were on the floor, and that Wendy had parted company from her knickers – that the chances were that something sexual had been taking place.

'You dirty little cow, Wendy,' said Beth. 'It was Mary's turn for first fuck, and now you've gone and nicked it for yourself.'

'No, I haven't, darling,' Wendy replied, laughing. 'Peter and I have just been indulging in a little of what you and Mary have been doing. No one has fucked anyone. But I think it's probably time that somebody did.'

The other two girls made noises about agreeing, and suddenly they were all looking at me. I've always believed in the statement that a new woman is the finest of all aphrodisiacs, and certainly, in this evening's situation, I was finding myself able to keep coming and then quickly achieve another erection without even thinking about it. Wendy's story about Mary and Beth fucking each other with a dildo had got me going again, so I stood up, proudly displaying my cock-stand to them all. 'Any volunteers?' I asked.

'It's still my turn,' said Mary, slightly petulantly.

'Of course it is, darling,' said Beth. She looked over at me. 'Well, don't just stand there like a spare prick at a wedding,' she said to me. 'Bring that lovely big cock over here.'

I went dutifully over to the bed. I took in the scene as I did so. I reckon any red-blooded man in the entire world would have changed places with me at that particular moment. There I was, bollock naked and fully erect, in a bedroom with three girls, all very pretty.

One blonde, now wearing only a white suspender belt and seamed stockings, had already both sucked me off and tossed me off. And I had sucked her to orgasm. The other blonde, still sitting on the bed, still wearing her full complement of beige-coloured sexy lingerie, had taken my cock in her mouth earlier on, if only for a few moments, and I was promised at least a fuck with her – always provided, of course, that I could manage an erection by the time it was her turn. And the brunette, with her black bra, suspenders and stockings still on, but minus her knickers, had just been sucked off by her friend, and she was now just about to spread her legs for me. I mean, what more could a chap wish for?

'OK, darling,' said Beth, once more taking hold of my cock in her long, cool fingers. 'This way.' Mary spread her legs wide, and I lay between them. Beth put the fingers of her right hand down between Mary's legs and opened up Mary's pussy lips, while with her left hand she guided my rampant tool into Mary's delightfully wet cunt. Her recent activity with Beth had ensured that it was running wet with her juices, but it was still gloriously, sensually tight. And wonderfully warm. This was going to be fun, I could tell. It was going to be a great fuck.

I eased my cock up her, and it slipped all the way into her until my balls were actually touching her arse. She gasped as I entered her. Beth grinned at me, and said, 'You're on your own now, baby.'

'Thank you, darling,' I said.

'My pleasure,' she said. 'But that's not true. My pleasure comes later. When I do.'

It was quite funny, but I didn't laugh. I was too intent on increasing the fantastic sensations that Mary's cunt was stimulating in my penis. She was working away at it with her pussy muscles, rather like a puppy at its mother's teat. It was almost as if her pussy was alive. It was marvellous. I looked down at her as I thrust away manfully, enjoying every moment of what I was doing to her. I noticed that she was still wearing her black transparent bra. I reached down and pulled it up, releasing her full tits, their dark brown nipples fully erect.

Her head was thrown back, her eyes were closed, and saliva was trickling out of the corners of her mouth. She was making soft, moaning noises, and she was using her hips and thighs to work her pudendum and her sex hard up and against me, getting maximum pressure – and maximum pleasure – from what she was doing. I don't know why, but I suddenly remembered her standing beside me in the supermarket, saying, 'Do you like to fuck?' I wondered how many different men she had asked that question of, and whether they had all said yes. I pumped away, feeling my ejaculation building. Mary began to moan, rather more loudly.

'I'm going to come,' she said. 'Any moment now. I'm going to come. Oh, God, I'm coming. I'm coming now.' I let go and jetted my semen into her receptive pussy, and I felt it spasm even harder as I shot my load into her. 'Oh, God,' she said again. 'I can feel your spunk. I can feel your hot spunk. Oh, my God.' I thrust as hard as I was able, endeavouring to keep her orgasms coming, and as I spurted my last, she relaxed, looked up at me, and smiled. 'Oh, Peter, my darling,' she said. 'That was beautiful. Really beautiful. Thank you. Thank you.'

'Thank *you*, Mary,' I said. 'It *was* good, wasn't it?' Just then, Beth's voice interrupted our mutual admiration society. 'Well, Peter,' she said. 'I must say, your record so far is admirable. One down, and two to go.' She obviously saw my slightly puzzled look. 'In serious fucking terms, that is,' she said. 'I mean, you have only actually *fucked* Mary so far. Isn't that so? That leaves me next. And then Wendy. Right?'

I thought for a long moment. And then, 'Right,' I said. 'Absolutely right.'

'Don't worry about a thing,' she said. 'Just tell me when you're ready.'

'I'm as ready now as I'll ever be, darling,' I told her. 'But a quick drink wouldn't go amiss. May I?'

'Of course,' she said. 'What'll it be? Scotch? Water, and no ice?'

'That would be terrific,' I said. 'Thank you.'

Beth got up and went to fetch it. Mary got up off the bed and stood up. 'I think I'll go and have a shower,' she said, to no one in particular, and she too took herself off.

Wendy looked across at me. 'How are you doing, Pete?' she asked. 'Are you still confident?' Actually, I wasn't confident at all. I thought that I might well manage the lovely Beth, with her pale beige transparent lingerie still all in place about her perfect body, and I said as much.

Wendy stood up, came over, and sat down beside me on the bed. She leaned over to me, put an arm around my shoulders, and whispered in my ear. 'I'll tell you something *very* naughty,' she said. 'If you promise to keep it a secret, just between the two of us.'

'I promise,' I said, curiously. 'I think it might help you through your next fuck,' she said. 'And then I think it will possibly help you when it's my turn. OK?'

'OK, darling,' I said. She lowered her voice even further. I leaned towards her.

'I love it up my arse,' she said. 'You can fuck my bottom, if you'd like to. Do you like to fuck girls in their tight little bottoms?' My instant erection was probably all the answer she needed. At that moment Beth came back into the bedroom, carrying a tray with my drink and refills for herself and Wendy. I just looked at Wendy, and said, 'Yes, actually. I do. Very much.'

'Good,' said Wendy. She raised her glass to the both of us. 'Cheers,' she said. 'Cheers,' we both replied. We drank.

Fucking Beth was fun. No doubt about it. She stripped off the pale beige bra and panties, keeping on the suspender belt and the stockings, and I fucked her soundly, loving every minute of it. All the time, though, I was thinking of Wendy's lovely little bum, and what I was going to do to it.

When my fuck with Beth was finished, she announced herself well satisfied, and said that, if we'd excuse her, she too would now go and shower, and then join Mary in the living room, leaving us to our own devices. We both tried not to look overly pleased.

When she'd gone, Wendy said, 'If she hadn't gone, I was going to ask her to leave us alone, anyway.' I grinned at her. My cock was, surprisingly, standing up like a good 'un. 'I'm raring to go,' I said. 'Have you got anything that we can use as a lubricant?'

'Yes, darling,' she said. 'That's very thoughtful of you.' She went over and picked up her handbag from where she'd left it in a corner of the bedroom, and took out a jar of cold cream. 'This should do the job, don't you think?'

'Perfect,' I told her. She handed it to me. She looked down at her white suspender belt and stockings. 'Shall I keep these on?' she asked me. 'Do you think they're sexy?'

'Yes, and yes,' I said. 'Please.' She held out her hand. I took hold of it, and she led me over to the bed.

'You won't hurt me, Peter, will you?' she asked, rather nervously. 'Of course I won't, my darling,' I said. 'All you have to do, at any time – *any* time – is just say "Stop". Just like that. And I'll stop. OK?'

'Thank you,' she said. 'I do love being fucked up my bottom, but I have been hurt, before now.' She got up onto the bed and knelt on all fours, her full, firm bottom facing me. She too had a thatch of pubic hair which didn't match her other, dyed-blonde hair. Her pubic hair was almost black, and short, and curly. Wiry, nearly. She looked over her shoulder. 'Do you think I've got a pretty bum, Peter darling?' she asked me.

I leaned forward and kissed her. Right on her pretty little anus. 'Yes,' I said. 'I think you've got the prettiest little bottom in the whole of the world.'

She laughed. 'That's just because it's right in front of you, and I'm asking you to fuck me there,' she said. 'But as a reward, you can kiss me there again, any time you like.'

I laughed with her. Then I leaned forward again, and kissed her anus once more. I lingered longer this time, and thrust my tongue into her. She tasted richly, lushly, of strong, exotic, jungle fruit.

'Ooooh,' she said. 'That's very naughty. But it's nice. Do it again.' I did. Her bottom was, for the record, fantastically shapely.

I unscrewed the jar of cold cream and, using the fingers of my left hand, I started to rub a dollop of cold cream into her rectal passage. Her crinkled, pale-brown anus dilated as my finger entered it, and her rectal muscles then held onto the circumference of my finger. I rubbed the cream into her as far as my finger would reach. Then I rubbed a couple more dollops of cream into her, partly for good measure, and partly because finger-fucking her elastic arsehole was a highly erotic experience.

'Ooooh,' said Wendy, again. 'I love it. I love it. I can tell you're a bottom man. Oh, keep on doing that. Please. I'm going to come. Oh, God, I'm coming already.'

I kept up my finger-thrusting, and Wendy's whole body shuddered as she came. When she had finished, I gradually slowed down my pace, and then slowly withdrew my finger. My cock was standing up like a steel rod, in anticipation of its replacing my finger up Wendy's anus. She looked back at me over her shoulder. 'Thank you for the *hors d'oeuvre*,' she said. 'I enjoyed that. Shall we start on the main course now, darling?'

'Please,' I said. I looked lustfully at her rear entrance again, the blood pounding in my cock. Her rectum looked like a small mouth. Wendy put a hand behind her and, taking hold of my rigid cock, she pressed it firmly against her well-greased anus. I thrust into her, gently but firmly, and after just a momentary resistance, I slid inside her oily warmth. I thrust again, and Wendy gasped.

I stopped thrusting at once. 'Oh, no, darling,' she said. 'That wasn't pain. That was pleasure. Please don't stop, for God's sake.'

I thrust once more, and then I was all the way in. I always find the sight of a woman's anus, fully stretched by my swollen cock, a lewd and wondrous sight. I began to fuck Wendy, and she picked up my rhythm, and thrust herself back against me. I had known before I started that, even after the many times that I had already ejaculated this long evening, sodomizing this beautiful girl with her enthusiastic participation would have me shooting my load too rapidly, and that was exactly the case.

I could feel my ejaculate gathering, and I reached around in front of Wendy and began to rub at her pussy. She was excessively wet, and I slipped my middle finger inside her and found her erect little clitoris. I concentrated on it, and Wendy began to move her hips and buttocks, until, moments later, we both came together, noisily, shouting out our pleasure.

When we had both finished, I pulled out of her and we lay together, breathlessly, our arms about each other. Wendy turned her head sideways and looked at me. She smiled. 'Whatever you do, don't leave tonight without letting me give you my address and telephone number,' she said. 'At least, that's if you would like me to. I've never met a man who enjoyed fucking girls up their bottoms as much as you obviously do. If you'd like to get together with me again soon, we could do it some more. And you still owe me a straight fuck, by my reckoning.'

Well, that's the end of my adventure, really. You can imagine my reply to Wendy's last statement, and I left that night with all her details, having also given her mine. Neither of us mentioned this exchange of information to either Mary or Beth, both of whom were kind enough to say that they had appreciated my efforts on their behalf.

If any of your readers want to try their luck at my local supermarket any evening, it's a branch of Sainsbury's. You'll need an element of luck, of course, to chance on the right evening, when it's Mary's turn once again to find a willing volunteer for all three girls' sexual entertainment. But worth investing the time in, I would have thought! Good luck.

P.H. Camden Town, London.

Final score, a complete sexual feast, against one lost TV dinner. It sounds as if you're well ahead of the game. We're on our way!

TOYS 'R HER

I met a girl recently in a bar in Covent Garden. I wasn't looking to pick anyone up, and I don't think she was either. I'd just stopped by for a drink after work. Anyway, this girl and I got talking, and we found that we were both in the same business (advertising) which is often a good basis for an interesting conversation. We took a liking to each other, and the drink or three turned into dinner at one of the many restaurants in the area, where we continued the conversation.

During dinner the dialogue turned to sex, and this girl – whose name was Emma – said that she had never met a man who could compete, sexually, with her vibrator. She wasn't aggressive about it. Just very matter-of-fact. Nor did I see it as a challenge. After all, if that was her view, as far as I'm concerned, it's one that she is entitled to. It's her life. And her vibrator. But I was interested to talk about it, and I asked her to go into more detail. To tell me specifically what she found more attractive about mechanical masturbation, in preference to the real thing.

She said that, first of all, she got quicker, more intense, longer-lasting orgasms from her trusty penis substitute than she had ever achieved from getting fucked (her word!) by any man, so far in her life. For the record, she told me that she was twenty-six. Second, she said, was the fact that she wasn't emotionally involved with her vibrator. It didn't have moods, and it could always both produce and maintain an erection. (I think the initial part of this claim is probably arguable, but I let it pass. I was beginning to fancy an opportunity to see if I could get Emma to change her mind, and I wasn't looking for an argument.) Next, she said, was the fact that it is cheap. It doesn't have to be fed, it doesn't drink or smoke, and it is always there. Finally, it is always completely faithful to her. I saw my opportunity immediately.

'Ah,' I said, meaningfully, 'but are *you* always faithful to *it*?'

'Not always,' she said, laughing. 'But why do you ask? Are you wanting me to be unfaithful to it with you?'

'Is that an invitation?' I countered.

She was silent for just a moment, and I thought that perhaps I had blown it somehow. Then, 'It is if you want it to be,' she said.

'I'd love to,' I said. 'Thank you.' I asked the waiter for the bill, which Emma insisted on splitting with me.

'Your place or mine?' she asked, laughing again. 'Mine's literally just around the corner.' It transpired that she had a small flat in Shorts Gardens, just off Monmouth Street, and since I live in Bayswater, we both plumped for her place.

It wasn't that small, and it was beautifully furnished, in contemporary – and expensive – style, with some excellent modern art on the walls. Emma was patently well up in the advertising world. She gave me a drink, and asked if I would like to see her collection before we adjourned to the bedroom.

'Collection of what?' I asked.

'Why, vibrators, of course,' she said. 'What else?' What else indeed? 'If you pull out that top drawer over there,' she said, pointing towards a pine bureau set against the far wall, 'you'll find what you're looking for.'

I did as I was told and pulled out the top drawer. It was deep, and it was literally full of vibrators of every possible size, shape, and kind. And, like Joseph's coat, of many colours. From the basic white plastic jobs in a dozen different sizes to fat rubber vibrators, carefully moulded to simulate large cocks, to replicas that looked so real I wondered if they were mummified trophies.

Many of them were realistically veined and ridged. Carefully reproduced humanoid phalluses. I dipped my hand into the layered collection, and turned them over. Here and there were one or two specialist jobs. One of them, I saw, had two heads, the second one smaller and shorter, the whole obviously designed for simultaneous vaginal and anal penetration. I lifted it out of the drawer, and held it up.

'Well, I certainly couldn't compete with *that* one,' I said, smiling at Emma.

'Who said anything about competing, darling?' she asked. 'And anyway, you're not thinking properly. You've got a middle finger, haven't you?' I swear I very nearly blushed. Silly me.

Some of the vibrators had switches and speed controls on the shafts, others had little control packs, attached with wires. Some were rigid. Others were flexible. Almost all were larger than life. I picked up a particularly gargantuan one.

'By God, that's a whopper,' I said. 'A girl could do herself a serious injury with that.'

'Isn't it?' Emma replied. 'I haven't actually used it myself. I think it's intended for old married ladies. Well, for old ladies, anyway,' she said.

I was glad to hear that she hadn't used it, but I didn't say anything for a while. 'Very impressive,' I said, eventually, referring to the collection as a whole. 'But I'm not sure what it proves, other than a lifetime's devotion to Ann Summers parties.'

She grinned. 'Actually,' she said, 'I've never been to one of those. I'm just into vibrators. Like I said earlier.' She stood up, came over, put her arms around me, and kissed me. Her mouth was open, and her tongue explored mine, wetly and lasciviously. After a while she took her mouth away and put her hand down and found my cock. It wasn't difficult. I wasn't trying to hide it. I'd have been wasting my time. It was almost fully erect.

'Ooooh,' she said. 'That *does* feel nice.'

I put my hand up under her short skirt and between her legs. Her crotch was damp. 'So does that,' I told her.

'So let's fuck,' she suggested, taking my hand and guiding me towards the bedroom, which opened off the sitting room. The bathroom was off the bedroom, I saw, as we went in. It was a good-size bedroom, all in shades of buttery yellow. There was a large double bed, with a pale-lemon eiderdown and white, lacy sheets. Emma started to disrobe.

She dropped her skirt and left it on the floor, followed by her sweater, revealing herself as braless and wearing knickers in the palest yellow. They had to have come from Harvey Nichols, or that other up-market knicker shop in Knightsbridge. I forget the name, but you know the one I mean. They have the raunchiest display of lingerie in London. Emma's yellow knickers were tiny, but you could tell simply by looking at them that the price had to be in an inverse ratio to their size. They certainly didn't come from Marks and Spencer's.

Her breasts were small, pointed, and eminently suckable. I noticed that her nipples were erect. Maybe that 'I'd-rather-my-vibrator-than-any-man' line was just a come-on. But she *did* have that amazing collection. But we all masturbate, don't we?

Well, I do. But Emma certainly seemed anxious to get a real cock inside her, as quickly as possible.

While she had been stripping off, so had I, and I actually beat her to it, which gave me the opportunity to grab her while she still had her knickers on and pull them down myself. There's something terribly sexual about pulling girls' knickers off, don't you think? Particularly expensive, sexy knickers like the ones Emma was wearing that evening.

'My, my,' she said, grinning up at me. 'We are macho today, aren't we?'

I could smell the strong scent of stimulated female sex. Wet female sex. I grinned back at her, picked her up, carried her over to the bed, and placed her carefully down upon it, on her back.

I could see that her auburn pubic hair matched the short helmet of dark copper hair on her head exactly. Her pubes were short, thin and sparse, and I could see the pink gash of her pussy. Without further ceremony, I pushed her legs as wide apart as they would go and buried my nose and mouth between them.

I thrust my tongue deeply into her, and began to suck her as best as I knew how. Vibrators sure as hell can't suck pussy. It was one small area within which I felt I had an advantage, however temporary. Emma reacted enthusiastically to my oral efforts, and began to move herself about under my ministrations. Quite soon, she was virtually humping my mouth. I had to grab hold of her buttocks in order to keep my mouth in place. I sucked and licked and kissed her pussy, giving her everything I had learned from years of dedicated practice. Sucking pussy is my second favourite pastime.

'That's wonderful,' she said, suddenly. 'Oh, sweetheart.

I like it. Please don't stop. I love you sucking my pussy. *Love* it.'

Make no mistake, I was enjoying myself too. Emma, being a redhead, had that deliciously strong, gamy scent and flavour about her sexual parts that girls with her particular colouring seem always to carry. I like my sex strong and gamy. She was fairly wet when I started sucking her, but her juices were really flowing now, and I was able to suck and swallow to my heart's desire, revelling in the flavour of cunt. It's an acquired taste, and one that I acquired many years ago.

I could tell from the way that she was moving beneath my lips that she was soon going to orgasm and, remembering the twin-shafted rubber vibrator from her collection, I moved my right hand from where it was clutching her right buttock and ran my fingers beneath her bottom and along her anal cleft until I found her tight anus.

I ran my finger lightly across it a couple of times, so that what I was about to do wouldn't be a complete surprise. She shuddered as I did so, and moaned quietly to herself, somewhere deep in her throat. It was suddenly obvious to me that she knew what I was going to do, and that she wanted me to do it. I found the exact centre of her anus, and pressed my middle finger hard into it. My finger popped in, and I continued to press. Gently at first, but finding no resistance – her rectal passage seemed to be self-lubricating – I pressed hard until my finger was up her arse, deeply inside her, right up to the second knuckle.

'Oh, yes,' she breathed. 'Oh, Jesus. Yes. Nice.' And then she started to orgasm. It was a whole series of orgasms. A multiple orgasm, as the textbooks say. I kept finger-fucking her arse, and I held my mouth pressed hard down onto her cunt, and my tongue vibrating over her clitoris, and I kept at it until the very last vestige of an orgasm had slowly, luxuriously, fulfillingly died away.

I lifted my mouth up, parting reluctantly from her dripping cunt, and looked up at her, along the flat of her stomach, up over the hillocks that were her breasts – her nipples still starkly erect – up to her face. Her eyes were shut, and she was breathing heavily, her pretty tits rising and falling as she gulped for air. *I bet your vibrators don't do that for you, darling*, I thought, but I was damned if I was going to say it. She regained her equilibrium fairly quickly, and opened her eyes. By that time I had got up from between her legs and was lying alongside her, my fingers stroking her pussy. Nothing serious, mind you. Just a friendly little feel.

She turned towards me and kissed me on the mouth. 'That was heavenly, darling,' she said. And then, 'Oh, I can taste my pussy on your mouth. And you smell of my cunt. Did you like the taste of it? And that was very naughty of you indeed, what you were doing to my bottom. I'm much too shy to use the words, but I liked it. I really liked it. It made me come and come and come. Thank you, darling. And when you're ready, are you going to fuck me? Soon? Please?'

She reached out a hand and took hold of my still reasonably erect cock. Sucking pussy gives me a tremendous hard-on. I was ready and waiting, and I seriously wanted her, but I was determined that she was going to ask me to fuck her. I didn't want her to think of me as some kind of human vibrator. She began to move her fingers up and down my cock, in a delightful wanking motion.

'Please fuck me, darling,' she whispered. 'Please fuck me now.'

I threw a leg across her, and she pressed my rampant cock into her wetness. She was tight and warm, as well as wet. 'Ooooh,' she said, in a little-girl voice. 'Emma likes that.'

Despite the fact that I had suspected that her pussy might well be one large callus inside, from years of using those fearsome vibrators, she was erotically, tightly elastic, clasping my cock with her pussy muscles with both verve and enthusiasm.

I took a nipple in my mouth. It was hard, like a small bullet, and as I sucked it I felt Emma's cunt spasm. I bit it – not hard – and she spasmed again, and groaned. 'Mmmmm,' she said. 'When you bite my tit I can feel it in my cunt. It's nice. Do it again.'

I did it again, and she reacted in the same way once more. I kept at it, and after a while Emma said, 'Now the other one. Please.' So I changed over to the other nipple, and bit that one for a while.

Quite soon, I could tell by her breathing and by her quickening movements that she was soon going to reach her first orgasm, and just as I was thinking that, she told me herself, breathlessly, that she was going to come. Her intense contractions almost brought me off, too, but I managed to hold myself back, and eventually my crisis was over and I was pumping away again.

But for the conversation that had started this whole thing off – the one about Emma preferring a vibrator to a man – I would willingly have come with her. So it wasn't the greatest fuck of my life, for that very reason. I spent most of it thinking about my overdraft in order not to ejaculate until Emma had enjoyed a whole series of orgasms.

But when I did finally let go, and spurted lustfully up inside her, it was good. Really good. I was grateful, once it was all over for us both, when she said, 'That was lovely, darling. Really terrific. Would you like to stay the night?' She didn't make any comparisons, or judgements about my performance, other than to issue that invitation, which I accepted with alacrity. I like to think that it was her way of giving in gracefully, without actually having to say it.

P.D. Bayswater, London.

Obviously you must have managed to set up some good vibrations . . .

DIRTY WORK

I'm cock-a-hoop these days, having recently found a girl who shares with me something which, up to now, has been a long-held but unrealized fantasy. Not only is she all the things any man could ever want – she's young, gorgeous, has a fantastic figure, and loves sex in all its forms – but she does that one thing that no other girl in my previous sex life has ever really enjoyed doing with me: she loves to talk dirty while we fuck. I love to hear those dirty words from an innocent-looking girl, and Janet looks exactly that. I love it when she whispers in my ear, 'You're fucking me. Your big cock is fucking my cunt.' It really turns me on. She will say anything that I want her to.

While we're doing it, I'll say to her, 'Tell me about playing with yourself,' and she'll say, 'I was so horny in the office this afternoon, thinking of your lovely cock, that I had to go into the lavatory, pull my knickers down, and play with my little pussy. It got all wet and sticky, thinking about your cock, and I came all over my fingers, and you weren't there to suck them clean for me. I felt better for a while, but then I wanted to play with my pussy again, and I didn't think I could go off to the lavatory so soon again, so I slipped my fingers up my knicker leg, and played with myself while sitting at my desk. I was sitting there, frigging away, hoping that no one would come into my office and see me sitting there playing with my cunt.'

And then she'll say, 'Do you like it when I say cunt?' And

I'll say, 'Yes.' And she'll say, 'Cunt, cunt, cunt, cunt. Wet cunt. Smelly cunt. Tight, wet, smelly cunt. I love it when you suck my cunt.'

Or I might ask her just to tell me something dirty. I did this the other night, and she thought for a minute, and then she told me a story. It went something like this. While we were fucking, of course.

She said, 'When I was in my late teens, I was at college, and, naturally enough, roughly half the students were men. I don't know about the men, but we girl students used to think and talk about nothing but sex, all the time. One of our favourite conversations was to ask each other what was the dirtiest thing they'd ever done, or what was the dirtiest thing they'd ever had done to them by a boyfriend.

'We were young, of course, and some of the girls told us about sucking their boyfriends off, or wanking them off. That sort of thing. One girl told us that her boyfriend used to fuck her anally. I remember that another girl told us that she'd had a boyfriend who had a knicker fetish, and he used to answer those advertisements in girlie magazines offering soiled knickers for sale. He'd send off for them and then rub his nose in them and sniff them while he was masturbating. And apparently wherever he went, he would ask to use the bathroom, in the hope that there would be a laundry basket in there with dirty knickers in it. If there was, he'd take them out, and sniff them, and wank himself off. And sometimes he'd steal dirty knickers from people's laundry baskets, and take them home to wank into.

'He told her all this, she said, so that he could sniff *her* knickers and wank whenever he wanted to, without having to do it surreptitiously. He liked to do it with her watching him. She said that she got used to it after a bit, and she even got used to sniffing her own knickers, with him watching, or sniffing them together with him, which he liked her to do, because she said that, after all, when you thought about it, it was only like kissing him after he'd been sucking her pussy. A bit of a moot point, that.

'But she gave him up when he started wanting her to do all these peculiar things with dirty knickers that he'd bought mail order. I mean, that's pretty disgusting, isn't it? Apparently some of the knickers that came through the post were quite revoltingly dirty. Stinking. Not just with pussy juice, either. But you can sniff my knickers any time, darling, if that turns you on. Does the thought of that turn you on? Do you like the smell of girls' knickers?'

'Not especially,' I told her. 'I've never tried anything like that. But it turns me on when you say fuck.'

'Oh, all right, darling,' she said. 'You're the original dirty old man, really, aren't you? Fuck. Fuck. Fuck my cunt.

'Another girl told us that the dirtiest thing she'd ever done was once when she got very drunk in this guy's flat, and he had three of his mates with him. She was the only girl. And they were all out of their minds, apparently. And she said that alcohol always made her very randy. Even just a couple of gins. Inevitably, the conversation got around to sex in no time at all. It was all fairly light-hearted, to begin with, but it got more and more explicit as the conversation wore on, and they ended up talking about their fantasies. This girl eventually admitted that she had always wanted to see how many men she could satisfy, sexually, at the same time. Inevitably, of course, she rapidly ended up with four willing volunteers. She took one in her pussy, one in her mouth, one in her bottom, and she tossed the last one off. To be honest, her only regret, she said afterwards, was that there hadn't been five of them. She still had one hand free!

'That particular evening, though, the sex went on and on, apparently, with the four men all wanting to take turns at fucking each of her orifices. She was game for it, evidently, and suffered nothing worse the next day than a hangover and a sore bottom. One or two of the girls thought that anal sex was pretty disgusting, but three of the other girls rose up in its defence. One of them said that she actually preferred it to vaginal or oral sex. When asked why, she said it was because she didn't have to swallow any semen, and she couldn't possibly get pregnant. Some of the girls objected strongly to sex while they were menstruating, on purely hygienic grounds.'

J.M.B. Isleworth, Middlesex.

Agreed! But talking dirty during sex has always been a popular pastime. Hence, perhaps, the expression, 'Isn't it time you cleaned up your act?'

BEHIND THE TIMES

May a mere woman be allowed to put across a point of view in your macho-male stronghold? I love your letters columns. Over the years, you have introduced me to many enjoyable subtleties in the world of sex, which I simply would never have discovered without your splendid magazine. Recently, inspired by one of your fiction pieces, hung, largely, upon the peg of the sexual pleasures of being spanked, I got my man to spank me. I made it a condition of this (to me) adventure, that he would stop the moment that I asked him to, should that become necessary. It was also made clear that this was in the spirit of fun. Not punishment. To be fair to him, he said that this was as important to him as it was to me.

We decided that we would begin our corporal punishment session with me fully dressed, and I wore a short miniskirt – one that could be lifted up off my bottom easily – stockings with a suspender belt (for my partner's visual enjoyment as he chastised me) and my prettiest see-through knickers (ditto!). After much discussion, we agreed that we would begin this experiment with my partner simply using his bare hand. I felt that starting out with a cane, a paddle, or even a slipper, might be too much of a good thing for a beginner.

After all these preparations, we also agreed that we would pretend to have an argument, this being the reason for my chastisement! Having started our 'row', my husband pulled me down onto his knee, pulled up my skirt, and began to spank my bottom. He was quite gentle, really, but it very quickly began to sting, and then burn.

However, after a spell when I thought that I was going to have to ask him to stop, I began to get the most marvellous feelings in my pussy, and I could feel myself getting wetter and wetter down there. When I *did* ask him to stop, it was not from pain, but to ask him – urgently – to fuck me. He pulled my knickers down, almost threw me on the floor, turned me over onto my tummy, and fucked me there and then, doggy fashion. His urgency was just as great as mine. It was the first time that he had ever fucked me fully clothed, apart from my knickers.

When describing his feelings to me, after we had enjoyed our best sex for ages, he said that the sight of what he called 'my tight little arse' through my transparent knickers, plus the suspenders from my suspender belt and the light-brown seamed stockings that I was wearing, added up to the most erotic visual delight he had seen for years. The actual spanking, he said, turned him on no end, and the sound of his hand upon my thinly nylon-covered arse-cheeks and the sight of my pubic hair sprouting up between my legs gave him the finest erection of all time. Certainly he gave me a serious seeing-to when he had me on the floor. Thank you, gentlemen, for bringing such new pleasures into my life.

J.A. Edinburgh, Scotland.

You're more than welcome. Spanks, as they say, for the memory.

SLAVING AWAY . . .

What a fabulous thing it must have been to be a sultan in the days when East was East, and every sultan worth his salt had a harem. While I suppose that any rich man can buy himself as much – and as varied – sex as he can handle, it still can't possibly compare with the sheer sexual excitement of the power of life and death over dozens – hundreds? – of women whom you actually *owned*. Virgins aren't particularly my bag, but imagine collecting women the way some people collect butterflies, or stamps. Imagine the pleasure of having beautiful young women brought to you for your approval – or not – to add to your collection, solely for your future sexual entertainment.

Think of the excitement of going to bed with a different woman every night. One who had been trained by the older women of the harem in a hundred different ways of offering every possible sexual delight. Beautiful girls, with fabulous bodies, subservient to your every desire, there for you to ravage in any way you might wish. Envisage a hundred gorgeous girls waiting to fellate you at a flick of your fingers. A thousand women, with never a headache between them, their under-used, tight little pussies there for your – and only your – delectation.

You could be constantly surrounded by beautiful, completely naked women, if that was what you so desired. You could have pairs of them perform cunnilingus upon each other while you watched, trying to make up your mind which one you would fuck first. You could have one sitting at your feet, fellating you as you read your daily newspaper, if you so wished. Or masturbating you lasciviously in your favourite way while you watched your favourite television programme. (This would only apply if you were a very up-to-date sort of sultan, naturally.) You could fuck them in every orifice, in every position, all day, every day.

Just think of the *actuality* of being a sultan. It meant that you had instant access to as many women as your money could buy. Literally, an endless supply. Blondes, brunettes, redheads. Girls with black hair. Whatever your preference for hair colour. Girls with shaven heads, if that turned you on. Girls with shaven pussies, with the lips of their sex pouting baldly at you all day long. Ready for you every moment of the day. Girls with heavy growths of pubic thatch. Girls with huge tits. Girls with tiny tits.

Girls with fantastic buttocks, who pleaded to be fucked up their pretty little arses. Girls with legs all the way up to their armpits. Girls with lips and mouths made for sucking cock. Girls with fingers trained to wank you into paradise. Girls with enormous, fat, fleshy, succulent labia. Girls with no apparent labia at all. Girls with gorgeously tight pussies. Tall girls. Short girls. Girls in sexy lingerie. Naked girls. Girls with tiny skirts that showed their knickers when they bent down. Braless girls in tight sweaters. Girls in see-through bras.

Girls who, at your command, will play with each other's sexual parts, masturbate themselves, use dildos on themselves and on each other. Girls who will do any unspeakable sexual act for you, with you, to you, at any time. Instantly. The likes of you and I count ourselves lucky if we've got one woman who is sexually amenable. Think of *hundreds* of sexually amenable women! It's too much to assimilate. It boggles the mind, doesn't it? Any contemporary man, given those opportunities, would probably rapidly fuck himself silly. But it would be fun to try.

A.D. Leamington, Warwickshire.

The problem is that, in transferring such delights to contemporary circumstances, you'd almost certainly have to pay each and every one of the ladies an acceptable living wage, provide good working conditions, plus health insurance, holidays, and so on. Just like any other workforce. Not to mention equal rights . . .

COLOUR ME PINK

As a young man, I have to admit that my sexual experience is, in terms of quantity, still fairly limited. (But I'm working at it!) Most of the snatches I have seen, therefore, have been between the pages of your magazine, rather than between girls' legs. Sad, but true. I'm writing to say that I'm amazed at the apparently enormous variation in types of women's pussies. Their colours would seem to vary from the palest pink through darker pink and various shades of reddish brown to actual brown, to almost red, and then, finally, through purply black to black itself. Nipples, areolae and anuses, damn it, arseholes, obviously all match.

But the variation doesn't stop at colour. Breasts, very obviously, vary in shape and size, but I'm still intrigued by the amazing variations in shape and size of the female vagina. First of all, the quantity of pubic hair is diverse. Short pubic hair. Straight pubic hair. Tightly curled hair. Loosely curled hair. Hair in every colour. Thick growths. Sparse growths.

Then there is the almost infinite variation in the shapes and sizes of the outer labia, from comparatively huge, fat, fleshy, swollen, long labia, hanging down between their owner's legs like bats' wings, through slightly lesser but still large labia, comparable, perhaps, to butterfly wings, down through slowly diminishing sizes, until reaching the stage where some women appear to have no discernible outer labia whatsoever. And, of course, I realize that I've omitted from my earlier list of pubic adornment those naughty but nice girls who shave their pudenda, thus fully exposing their labia for all to see, sigh at, and – if we're really in luck – suck.

When adopting those lovely open-leg poses in your magazine, your models charmingly demonstrate just how varied the combination of these various vaginal components is. My personal favourites are the youngish girls who proudly display their thick growths of pubic hair, in the midst of which nestles their well-proportioned (but hopefully still beautifully tight!) large-lipped, wetly shining, fully open pussy. If they can top that off with a pair of small, firm, pointed breasts, blessed with neatly defined areolae on which are mounted small, protuberant and erectly hard nipples and, finally, if they also possess the kind of large, generously-lipped mouth that is made for sucking cock, then my day is made.

Having made, as you can read, something of a close study of my favourite feminine accessory, it is also my intention to become – through further study, and much serious application – a world champion cunt-lapper. I can't believe it when I read, in your columns, the occasional letter from a lady whose man friend won't suck her pussy for her. Cunnilinguists of the world unite! I hereby volunteer to eat the pussy, tongue the clitoris, suck the labia (and/or any other of her bodily parts that she may so wish) of any lady of any age, shape, size, colour, or race, whenever, wherever, or however she so desires, and for as long as she likes. This positively does *not* imply any requirement on my part for any kind of reciprocal sexual involvement whatsoever, although were any to be offered, it would not be refused. If there are any of your female readers who need my services, (gratis, of course) perhaps they would like to write in.

J.N.M. Oxford, Oxon.

You, sir, regrettably, must be the answer to many a maiden's prayer. Regrettably, because we cannot understand any so-called man who refuses to do anything *that his lady might desire.*

BOTTOMED OUT

I read much in your pages of men who describe themselves as breast men, or leg men, but I have yet to see any correspondence from men who, like me, when asked which part of the female anatomy they find the most attractive, would plump – and I use the word advisedly – for women's bottoms. Let me, if I may, just qualify that statement before I go any further. I would like to emphasize *most.* This is because I find all and every part of the female body both exciting and inviting. But of these parts, the bottom – for me – comes out top.

When being shagged doggy fashion, women present their most sexually attractive profile. When on their knees, with their legs wide apart, they present their genitalia proudly and openly, instead of the half-hidden exposure of their sexual equipment that occurs when they are lying on their backs. Viewed from the rear, their cunts are thrust up and out, and are often seen to be gaping open. Ready, willing, and able, as the song says! This position also usually offers far deeper penetration of the penis than any other, and allows – not, not allows, *demands* – the titillation of either the breasts and nipples, or of the clitoris, or of both. Pussies are far more readily stimulated from the rear, and in my respectful opinion, there is no finer position for the performance of mutual cunnilingus and fellatio, than that in which the woman kneels over her partner's face, thus exposing freely her bottom and her entire genitalia to his oral and digital manipulation, while the man, similarly, is offering his erect penis for her attention. A further attraction is the fact that, in this position, women are also implicitly offering that other, forbidden entrance for their partner's delectation and enjoyment, although this is probably not the place to go into that!

To me, female buttocks are in themselves objects of great beauty, with as many carnal opportunities as a man could wish for. The sight of a pair of those sumptuous, firm, malleable globes, divided by cleavage the like of which is never seen between the average bosom, with the occasional bouquet of anal hair peeping suggestively from the crevice, around the object of every man's desire, his woman's sex, is something to be savoured. The feel of those buttocks, of that anal cleavage, beneath one's fingers, as one begins the essential foreplay that leads to the ultimate penetration. Fantastic! Here's to all bottom worshippers. A final request. Will you please do us bottom fetishists a favour, and stop using the words *arse* and *arsehole*? They simply doesn't do justice to two of woman's finest possessions. Bottom. Bum (if you must!) Behind. Butt. Backside. Derriere. Posterior. Seat. Tail. Even tush (as our American cousins so quaintly describe it). And then anus. Rectum. Fundament. Even bottom-hole. Thank you.

H.G. Sutton, Surrey.

I don't think that we can really be of help, in that attempting to stamp out two of the commonest words in the English language just ain't practicable. Sorry! But we soundly endorse your love and appreciation of the female bottom, in all its glory.

LADY LOVE

Tell me, please, and put me out of my misery. Are all those beautiful girls in your two-girl lesbian sets in the magazine *really* lesbians? They turn me on more than any of the other, often much ruder photographs, of single girls in their *dishabille.* Those pretty open mouths, with wet tongues touching each other, are just too much. I'd give my eye teeth to be able to watch the girls at it in real life. I can imagine their tongues slipping into each other's mouths, and then exploring, slowly and lovingly.

I have a penchant for the frilly, lacy, really feminine lingerie that these girls wear when doing their lesbian bit, and I adore it when you photograph one of the girls gently pulling aside the other girl's knickers and exposing her naked, half-open, hairy cunt. The girl doing the pantie-pulling nearly always has her tongue poking out and sited just millimetres away from the first girl's pussy. I can always imagine the shot that you *don't* show, where that naughty tongue has delved into the other girl's sex and is tonguing her swollen little clitoris.

I like it, too, when they're kissing each other's nipples, and taking off each other's brassieres. Their nipples are always erect. I remember particularly one such nipple-sucking photograph, where the photographer had caught the girl just as she had released the other girl's nipple from her mouth, and there is a long, thin string of saliva still connecting the nipple to her lips. Those girls just look so *naughty*! But tell me, please. Are they real lesbians?

G.B. Sutton-in-Ashfield, Notts.

My dear chap, we wouldn't dream of asking them. Surely you understand that our photographic models are employed for their beauty, not for their personal sexual proclivities?

KINGSTON KATHY

In my fantasy, she's standing there in front of me, all five feet ten inches of her. She's wearing nothing but a tiny bikini bottom and a big smile. The bikini bottom barely covers her embarrassment. She's a beautiful dark brown, and she has paler brown triangles over her breasts, with a matching thin, paler brown strap line across her back, from where she normally wears the top half of her bikini. Kathy is Chinese–Jamaican, and we're in Kingston, where all the single girls – without exception – fuck. So, too, do some of the married ones, I hear. But don't get caught at it, unless you want to risk getting your balls cut off with a machete.

We're standing on the deck of this forty-foot yacht, moored in the Royal Jamaican Yacht Club marina, at the far end of Kingston Harbour, and the two-man crew are readying her for the long, slow sail out of the harbour, and then farther out, to one of the string of small, uninhabited keys out there, where we'll drop anchor and then bathe and sunbathe, naked as the day we were born.

Kathy's upper body has a glossy sheen of sweat, and her black nipples stand out upon her areolae like fat June bugs on a leaf. She's feeling randy, and she wants to fuck. Because of the crew – nice enough chaps, but recruited from the Club's employees for the day, rather than being regular crew and thus almost certainly friends – I refuse to fuck her on the deck, within their view. Nor do I want to go down into the cabin, at least until we're under weigh, with the breeze from our speed keeping the cabin cool. Right now, the cabin's a sweatbox.

Kathy's smile is fast disappearing. 'You mean you refusin' to fuck me, man?' she asks.

'No, Kathy, sweetheart,' I tell her. 'I'm not refusing to fuck you. It's just that I don't know these two guys too well, and I would be embarrassed to do it out here on the deck, in front of them. And until we get under weigh, it's far too hot in the cabin. I'm sorry, but you'll have to wait.'

She snorts. 'You a miserable man,' she says, stringing out the word 'miserable' until it sounds like some awful disease. 'Then I'm goin' play with my pussy. Right here. Right now.' She sits down beside me, and slips her slim brown hand, with its long brown fingers and scarlet-painted nails, down the front of her minuscule white bikini bottom. The slip of thin material bulges with the shape of her hand as she begins to stroke her pussy.

I start to get a hard-on from watching what she is doing. Not a great idea when all you're wearing is a small pair of swimming trunks. I'm begining to wish that I'd stayed at home. It doesn't take Kathy long to reach her objective, and suddenly she is given over in her entirety to enjoying the orgasm which she has masturbated herself into.

'Oh, man,' she says, loudly.

'Ssshhh,' I say, a nervous eye on the crew who are unfurling the mainsail, but some five or six feet away from the two of us. They pretend not to notice, but I can see from their smiles, and their whispered conversation, that they are only too well aware of what is going on.

'That'll do me for a while, honey,' says Kathy, smiling again. 'Unless anything better turns up.' She takes her fingers out of her pussy, and from beneath her bikini bottom, and holds them under my nose. 'Smell that, man,' she says. 'Maybe it do what I can't do.'

'What's that?' I ask curiously, sniffing the delightful aroma of Kathy's wet pussy, rising up from off her wet, sticky fingers.

'Give you hard-on for me,' she says, grinning at me.

She put her tongue out at me. 'Honky,' she said. 'No-good, useless honky. Give me a Jamaican man any day.' I laughed with her. She was a delightful girl, but permanently horny. When she couldn't get what she wanted, sexually, she was best kept at a distance.

By now the sail was unfurled, the small inboard motor that we would use to take us out of the moorings and into the main channel and the wind was turning over in neutral, and the crew were ready to cast off. 'OK, boys,' I said. 'Let's go.'

Ten minutes later we were well out in the channel leading to the sea, and I gave the wheel over to one of the crew. I didn't have to say anything to Kathy, for she was right behind me as I led the way down into the yacht's interior, and through the day cabin to the sleeping quarters. All the ports were fully open, and there was a welcome breeze coming through the starboard ones. I wouldn't go so far as to describe it as a cool breeze, but it was the next best thing, until we got out of the harbour and picked up the sea breezes proper.

It took only moments to strip off my bathing trunks and release my erection. Kathy was already out of her bikini bottom and was lying on the bed, her slim brown legs parted, her thick black pubic hair glistening with her sweat, and her black pussy gleaming with her juices from her recent masturbation.

'Pussy ready, darlin',' she said. 'You goin' fuck me now?'

'Yes, please, you old ratbag,' I said. I walked over to the large double bunk, my erection preceding me. As I came within reach, Kathy put out her hand, and took hold of it.

'Mmmmm,' she said, again. 'It's not a bad size for a honky.' Without further ado, she sat up, took my cock in her mouth, and began to suck me off. Despite her recent criticisms, I had actually been aching to fuck her, and it only took a few moments of her delightful, experienced mouth and tongue to have me spurting my semen into her waiting mouth. She swallowed every last jet of it with relish. When my ejaculation was finished, with every drop of my ejaculate swallowed, she gave me a final, loving suck and, taking my tool out of her mouth, she looked up at me and smiled. 'You enjoy that, darlin'?' she asked.

'It was fantastic,' I said. 'Really good. Thank you.'

'You wan' maybe suck my pussy a little, now?' she asked, lying back again and spreading her legs wide. She knew that I loved to suck her black pussy. I was as much in love with her pussy as I was with her. It had a personality all of its own. I knelt down at the edge off the bunk, and looked at the object of my desire. Her pubic growth was lushly thick. Her outer labia were generously full-lipped, the flesh almost blue-black.

I pulled her lips fully apart with my fingers. Inside, she was wetly, lubriciously pink, in total contrast to her outer labia. Her inner labia were small, and when I pulled her open with my fingers, I could see the tip of her clitoris, sitting up and paying attention. I bent down, putting my head between her legs, and licked her open pussy. It tasted, as ever, of exotic, tropical fruit. English girls taste of kippers. Jamaican girls taste of ripe mango, paw paw, and bananas, with a touch of citrus fruit.

'Mmmmm,' said Kathy. 'Pussy likes that.' I began to concentrate on what I was doing, and I worked hard at giving her as pleasant a time as she had provided for me. She started to come quickly, and she continued to come as I sucked and kissed and licked, building up to an orgasmic crescendo, a splendid series of orgasms which got bigger and bigger until she almost exploded as she finally reached her peak. She gets very vocal when she hits her peak, and I could hear the chuckles from up on deck, as the crew heard her shouts and moans and screams. She finally quieted down, and after a while I went through to the day cabin and poured us both a cold beer from the ice box.

By now we were out of the harbour, and the breezes coming in through the open ports really *were* cool. After we had both quenched our thirst, I fucked Kathy slowly, and gently, and lovingly, until she came yet again, but this time the orgasms were gentler. And quieter. By the time we had finished, we were both sexually replete, and after a while we went back up on deck to enjoy the sight of Jamaica's receding southern coastline, as the yacht approached our chosen key.

We spent a long, lazy day in the sun. Totally naked, we swam and sunbathed and gathered shells and picnicked in the shade of a cluster of Royal palms, before once more weighing anchor and sailing back as the sun set, tanned, tired, and happy.

You will have guessed by now that I have never been to Jamaica, that I don't own a yacht, and that there isn't any Kathy. But isn't that what fantasies are all about?

P.A.F. Ruislip, Middlesex.

It certainly is. In the meantime, there are some very pretty Kathys in London, if you know where to look. With a pretty volunteer, a sun lamp, and a bottle of Caribbean rum, who knows what might happen? Or try the next Notting Hill Gate Carnival!

CHINESE TAKE AWAY

I have to write and congratulate you on the photographs of that beautiful Chinese girl – Terry – in your last issue. She is the stuff of my dreams. She's the most sensual woman I have ever been privileged to see, photographed naked. I dream of her as I go to bed at night. She occupies my brain as I awake in the mornings. She's too much. I fantasize about her when I'm working.

I suck those lovely nipples, those two ripe, round, fat, succulent berries perched on the tips of those perfect breasts. I kiss those full, lipsticked, wet, red lips, and I hold her head as she takes my rampant erection between them, her huge brown eyes on mine as she uses her mouth, and lips, and tongue, and her ancient Oriental skills to suck my semen out of me. I pull down those tiny, brief, flowered knickers, and I bury my nose and mouth between those plump thighs and into that soft, wispy, black pubic hair, finding those thick pussy lips, their brownish-pink plumpness open wetly, revealing her pink interior.

I thrust a finger up her wet pussy, and she groans with pleasure and pleads with me to fuck her. I take her hand in mine and guide it down onto my erection, and she takes me between her cool fingers and draws me into that tiny Chinese heaven between her legs. I spurt my ejaculate up into her, and then she turns over when we've finished, kneels up onto those pretty little knees, looks at me over her shoulder, and smiling, says, 'Again, please.' I almost faint with excitement. Terry is one Chinese dish I'd give my right arm to take away. You must know the feeling.

S.H. Lulworth, Dorset.

We most certainly do. We fancy Terry, a portion of 69, and a bottle of good white wine. We'd be happy to make a meal of that.

STREET SEX

I particularly like to read the fantasy letters that you publish, in amongst all the other sexual correspondence in your readers' letters columns. Many of the fantasies are so way out that I wonder if the authors ever get to realize them.

My fantasy is much simpler. I love to fantasize that, when I see an attractive woman in the street, I just go up to her and take her in my arms and kiss her. As I kiss her, and as she returns my kiss, I slip a hand up under her skirt and feel her pussy through her panties. She shows her appreciation of what I am doing by sliding down my zip and putting her hand inside my trousers, pulling out my cock, and wanking me as we continue to kiss. Then she pulls her mouth away from mine, long enough to look up into my face and say, 'Please take me somewhere and fuck me. Do anything you like to me. I feel so sexy, I could rape you. I'll suck you off, toss you off, anything you like. But please, let's do it now.'

As luck will have it, in my fantasy, this is happening a mere five minutes away from where I live. I take her hand, and we almost run back to my place, where she strips off down to the sexiest bra and panties I've seen for a very long time. They're completely transparent, and I can clearly see her erect nipples through the thin nylon of her bra. As I watch, she puts her hands behind her back, unsnaps her bra catch and, removing it, drops it on the floor. Her matching panties show me that she is clean shaven between her legs, and that her vaginal lips are plumply open. From the stain on her knickers, I can see that she is already wet.

She removes the knickers, drops *them* on the floor also, and comes over to me as I discard my underpants. She takes hold of my cock and looks down at it. 'What a lovely big cock,' she says, smiling at me. 'I can't wait to have it inside me, fucking me like there's no tomorrow. But would you like me to suck it for you first?'

'Please,' I say.

'And would you like that to be simply me sucking you, or would you prefer a little *soixante-neuf*?' she asks. 'You choose. I'm happy either way.'

I look at her bald snatch, and I know that there is only one answer. 'A mutual exchange of favours would go down very well, darling,' I tell her. 'If that's OK with you.'

'I hoped you would say that,' she said. 'I love sitting on guys' faces while they eat me. Come on, then, lie on your back on the bed.'

I do as I'm bidden, and she kneels over my face and then lowers herself down, gently, until her wet, shaved pussy is directly over my mouth. As I open my mouth, take her pussy lips in mine, and thrust my tongue up into her cunt, she takes my engorged cock into her warm, soft mouth and begins to suck me.

If there's an international prize for the world's best fellatrice, she must already have won it. If there isn't, there should be. She puts any woman who has ever sucked my dick into the shade. Out of court. I suddenly realize that they were amateurs. This woman is a world-class professional. By which, I do *not* mean that she is on the game. Simply that her abilities within the realms of oral sex are completely unique. Totally professional.

Her shaven cunt looks rather like a slot, and for a wild

moment I wonder whether – when I finally get to put my dick up it – I'll need to pull her right arm down before I can fuck her. I giggle gently to myself, and try to find her clit with my tongue. It doesn't take me long, for her joystick is enormous, and standing erectly to attention. The two of us manage to reach orgasm together, and I pump my spunk into her mouth as she writhes about all over my face and bounces up and down as I suck her into a prolonged orgiastic frenzy.

In what seems like no time at all, she tells me, 'I'm ready, darling. Can you get it up again, or do you need a little help?'

'I never refuse help in these matters,' I tell her. I'm quite sure that I *can* get it up again. No problem. But I'd hate to lose out on any 'help' being offered. When it comes, it is something of a surprise. 'No problem,' she says. She climbs off me, lies down beside me, puts her left arm around my neck, and starts to French kiss me. That in itself would have given the Archbishop of Canterbury an erection, but at the same time, she puts her right hand down between my legs and begins to run her fingers along my anal crack.

When she came to my tightly held anus, she rapidly insinuated a finger inside me and thrust it all the way up. She then began to massage my prostate. Needless to say, I not only achieved an instant erection, I achieved an instant ejaculation.

'Oh,' she said, sounding somewhat surprised. 'That wasn't really my intention.'

'Nor mine, darling,' I said. 'But don't worry about a thing. I'll be with you again in a moment.'

She kept her finger in place – and in action – and seconds later I was erect again. 'I think perhaps it would be wise to stop now, darling,' I said. 'That's if you still want me to fuck you.'

'Sure, baby,' she said. 'And of course I do. But do you mind if *I* fuck *you*? You know. With me on top?'

'Be my guest,' I said. 'I'll just lean back and enjoy it.' She climbed up and, holding her pussy lips open with one hand, she took hold of my cock in the other and lowered herself down onto it. She was warm, tight and wet.

The three things every man hopes for from a new pussy. And willing. God, was she willing! She practically fucked me to a standstill. When I felt my ejaculation beginning to gather yet again, she was showing no signs of achieving orgasm herself whatsoever. *Well,* I thought, *what's sauce for the gander should be sauce for the goose.* I reached around behind her splendid buttocks and ran my middle finger down her anal crack until *I* found *her* anus.

'Ooohh, naughty,' she said, smiling down at me as she felt me easing my finger up inside her anal orifice. She continued to fuck away happily and, since she lacked a prostate gland to massage, I simply began to finger-fuck her rectal passage. 'Mmmm. Oooohh, yeeesss. Nice.' she said, her hips gaining momentum as I thrust my finger in and out of her. 'Oohhh,' she said again. 'Oohhh, yes. Oh. I'm going to come now. Oohhh, I'm coming. Now. Noooowww. NOOOOWWW.' She was shouting aloud as she came, and bouncing about on my cock like a jack-in-the-box.

I decided that it was time for me to come, too, and I jetted my third and last load of semen into her, joyously.

'Oh, yes,' she said again. 'I can feel your hot spunk in my cunt. Oh, God. I'm going to come again. I'M COMING AGAIN.' And indeed she was. Such is the simplicity – but the many and prolonged sexual pleasures – of my personal fantasy.

T.O'H. Dublin, Republic of Ireland.

Your fantasy is streets ahead of many that we read. May you often meet the lady of your dreams.

TOYING WITH SEX

As a woman, I'm fussy about whom I fuck. I'm not a prude, but neither am I into one-night stands. And whilst I love parties and enjoy my fill of alcohol – after which I often I get as randy as all get out – I still don't drop my knickers for any Tom, Dick, or Harry. Dick being the operative word. This possibly means that I miss a certain amount of fun, but it also increases my chances of a lasting relationship when I meet someone whom I feel I *would* like to go to bed with.

Oh, what a dreary cow, I can hear some of you saying. I bet she doesn't even really like sex. Actually, I *do*. And I get plenty of it! How? I've got my own, very personal, vibrating cock, to fuck me whenever I feel like it. It's the kind you can buy by mail order practically anywhere, and the vital way in which it differs from a lot of other vibrating cocks is that its base is a large suction pad. This means two things: you can attach it to any flat surface that you wish, and it leaves both your hands free to do anything else that you might want to do with them at the time.

After trying all kinds of surfaces in my house – my bedroom wall, the edge of my bath, my lavatory – with the lid down – a wooden kitchen chair, and so on, I now plump for attaching my mechanical lover to the wooden floor surrounding my bedroom carpet. This means that, with the help of some soft pillows, I can lie down on top of my lover's cock and fuck myself silly.

And I do! He has a number of advantages that not all real

men possess. For one thing, he has a permanent erection. Other women readers out there will understand the significance of this! He feels entirely realistic, for his plastic, rubber-covered cock is modelled on an extremely well-developed real-life example, complete with veins and contours. He is also circumcised. He is not particularly attractive, but when you're using him for what he is designed for, you can't see him anyway. Think about it!

He not only vibrates, he also thrusts in and out. Just like the real thing. Except, of course, that you can control both his vibrating and his thrusting rates. And he is always the perfect gentleman, in that he *never* comes before you do. And he is always ready to do it again. Immediately, if that is what you want.

As far as fantasies are concerned, he can be anyone you wish. Just shut your eyes and dream. Whether it's that sexy manager of yours at the office – the one who never seems to notice that he's one of the few men that you *would* instantly drop your knickers for – or whether your fantasy is your favourite television star, he'll fuck you, long and hard, for ever. By the time you *do* get the message through to that manager, your pussy will be in very good condition for him. It will be ready, willing, and *very* able! Enjoy!

K.L. Loughton, Essex.

Whatever turns you on, Ms K.L. And however deliciously wet your waiting, anticipatory pussies may be, we advise any other women readers tempted to try out their own mechanical cocks to be sure to use a good-quality sexual lubricant. Cocks this hard can give you a hard time if you don't take the right precautions!

STRICTLY PERSONAL

My fantasies are solely concerned with punishment, domination, bondage, flagellation, and rape (both vaginal and anal rape). This makes the realization of them somewhat difficult, unless I abandon my present girlfriend – whom I love dearly – for the ladies I read about in the ads for bondage and discipline clubs. That is something that I don't really want to do. I don't actually want to really hurt my girl. But I do want to tie her up. To the bed. By her wrists and ankles, with her legs spread wide. Then I want to put my hand up underneath her skirt and feel her, intimately, between her legs. I want to slip my fingers up under her knicker leg, and then into her wet cunt.

And then I want to cut and tear her clothes off her. First her skirt. I want to cut it up the front and tear it off, exposing her black nylon knickers and her seamed, black nylon stockings and her black nylon suspender belt. Then her blouse, exposing her naked breasts, with her nipples fully erect (from the sexual excitement of what she knows I am going to do to her). When she's lying there, in just her knickers, her suspenders and her stockings, I want to feel her and play with her between her legs, but still through the nylon of her knickers, until her knicker crotch is soaking wet with her juices. Then I'll untie her, and she'll think that I'm going to release her.

But I'm not. I'm just going to turn her over onto her stomach and tie her up again. This time I'll simply tie her wrists to the headboard and leave her legs free, so that I can pull her knees up into a kneeling position with them well spread, in that erotic position which offers her entire genital area to me, for my delectation. I'll feel her up a bit more, through the gusset of her soaking wet knickers, and then I'll pull them down, exposing her naked buttocks and her hairy pudendum, with her cunt beneath, all wet and pink and, of course, her arsehole, a couple of inches above. I'll leave her knickers pulled down and sort of bunched around her lower thighs, and then I'll get a long, thin cane, and I'll start to punish her. Not *too* hard. But enough to make her cry.

I'll enjoy hearing the swish of the cane through the air, and the crack as it lands on the taut skin of her shapely buttocks. I'll watch intently as it turns first pink, then red. By now, my erection will be so stiff that I'll have to stop, just long enough to tear my trousers off and let my tool thrust freely upwards, as I go back to caning her. And by now she will be pleading with me to stop thrashing her, and I'll stop for just a moment, and I'll say to her, 'What will you do for me, as a reward, if I stop caning you?'

And she'll say, 'Anything. Anything you want. But please stop hurting me.' And I'll swish the cane through the air a couple of times to let her know that I haven't made my mind up. That I haven't decided to stop yet.

And then I'll say, 'Will you suck my cock and wank me off into your mouth if I stop?'

'Yes,' she'll say. 'Yes. Anything.'

And I'll say, 'Say, "Yes, please, my darling."'

And she'll say, 'Yes, please, my darling,' through her sobs.

And then I'll say, 'And will you ask me to fuck you up your tight little arsehole?'

And she'll reply, 'Yes.' Just that. 'Yes.' Nothing else.

And I'll tell her, 'Ask me. Ask me nicely to fuck your tight little arsehole.' I'll swish the cane a couple more times, and lay it across her red buttocks, and she'll say, as quickly as she can get it out, 'Please, please fuck me in my tight little arsehole.'

Having said that, of course, she'll think that I'm going to stop caning her. So then I'll really lay into her. Just for a moment or two. Just to show her who is in charge.

I kneel up behind her, and thrust my engorged cock into her cunt. When I'm in her, she's very wet inside. I grab her tits, and hang on to them, squeezing and pulling her nipples, as I fuck her from behind. My favourite position. She's moaning now, as I fuck her. It's part relief that I've stopped hurting and humiliating her, and part genuine sexual enjoyment, because, wanting to or not, she has become very sexually excited by what I have been doing to her. You know what they say. A woman, a dog, and a walnut tree. The more you beat them, the better they be. It's true. In my fantasy. In real life, my girlfriend refuses to allow me to tie her up, cane her, or humiliate her in any way. Nor will she let me fuck her in the arse. Can you please suggest anything that might help?

O.G. Taunton, Somerset.

Surely. Talk to your girlfriend, and suggest to her that she finds herself a new boyfriend. One more suited to her lifestyle.

TIT FOR TAT

I've dreamt for years of women tossing me off with their tits. The magical so-called French necklace. But, sadly, it's something that has never happened to me. I've not had *that* many women, but most of the ones that I have had had tits that were far too small to be able to masturbate any man's cock.

But Sheila, in your photo-set this month, has breasts that were surely made for just that purpose. Enormous, fat, soft, long, droopy, succulent, teat-ended breasts.

I can imagine sitting in a comfortable chair, quite naked, with Sheila kneeling in front of me, holding a gargantuan breast in each hand, and taking my rigid cock between them, and then masturbating me to ejaculation. Very, *very* slowly!

The ultimate fantasy would be that moment when, having masturbated me delightfully to the point where my spunk was almost ready to jet up between her huge, all-enveloping tits, she would bend her head down and take my swollen cockhead between her full, soft lips and suck me off into her mouth.

When I eventually exploded into her willing mouth, she would swallow every drop of my sticky semen and continue to suck and wank me with her tits until there was literally nothing more left to issue forth. Then she would lie on her back, open her massive thighs, and take me between her legs, for a repeat. Happy days!

F.H.S. Slough, Bucks.

What you might describe as keeping abreast of events. We hope that you are soon able to translate your fantasy into reality. But I don't think this is quite *what's meant by the phrase 'Fat is a Feminist Issue'!*

BE OF GOOD CHEER

I went to America for the first time on a business trip recently and at the weekend was taken to an American college football match. The football was a lot of fun, if slightly confusing to a Brit brought up on both soccer and rugby. But I was completely taken by the gorgeous, pretty young cheerleaders. The ones that I saw were, of course, girls from the same college as the football players, and my hosts told me that fucking the cheerleaders is one of the perks of playing for the college football team. But they also told me that, going back a few years, the finest cheerleaders in the world, bar none, used to be the Dallas Cowgirls, cheerleaders to the Dallas Cowboys, at that time the top American football team in the United States. Apparently there was some kind of scandal, and the Dallas Cowgirls were disbanded for a while.

Be that as it may, why don't we here in Britain introduce cheerleaders into British football? It's exactly what we need. Something (someone?) to amuse, excite, and encourage us to support our local football team. Those lovely, skimpy pleated skirts, those short, white frilly knickers, those tight tunic tops, and the girls' lovely long nylon-encased legs wouldn't half improve attendance at the average First Division football match. I'd love to score a goal with one of those young ladies.

D.H. Enfield, Middlesex.

Having seen the Dallas Cowgirls in action in their heyday, we entirely subscribe to your point of view. Those lovely young ladies can come and take care of our sporting tackle any time.

OBJECTIONABLE

Some girls are meant to be fallen in love with. Even to be married, perhaps. Others are for fun relationships. Friendships. Sexual relationships. Whatever. But a few – and Dorothy, in your September issue, is one of those few – are simply sex objects.

I know that's not a politically correct approach to women. Or to life. Or to anything else, for that matter. But I have to be honest. Dorothy is fantastic. She's too much. Absolutely everything about her is fantastic. She was born to fuck. To be fucked. To fellate. To have cunnilingus performed upon her gorgeous snatch. Her breasts were made to suck. Her bottom was designed for naughty things to be done to it.

Just look at her! In the first picture, at the beginning of her photographic set, she is naked, apart from a kind of cotton chemise, which she seems to have managed to get stuck up somewhere around her shoulders. And, oh yes. She's wearing shoes. White, high-heeled, fuck-me sandals. Her arse is towards the camera, and the photograph of her tanned, plump, firm, rounded buttocks leave the reader with but one thought. And yet her face, seen here side view, is totally serene. Her lips are almost virginal. Butter wouldn't melt in her mouth. (If you'll believe that, you'll believe anything!) In the next picture, she is lying on her stomach with her knees bent, her legs are up over her lovely bottom and her gloriously hairy snatch is in full view, with the lips of her vagina partly open, shining moistly at the camera. Oh, to bury my mouth and nose in that cleft! Dorothy (do her friends call her Dot?) has her face towards the lens, and her mouth is open. It's crying out for a swollen cock to be inserted between those luscious lips.

In the next shot, we get our best view so far of one of Dot's breasts. She's holding up one side of that chemise, revealing a smooth, rounded, full, firm breast, crowned with a dark-pink areola, on which is mounted a perfectly formed fully erect nipple. There are further, equally delightful variations on these pictures, but it is the final two-page spread that is the real lulu.

In this one, Dot is lying on her back with her legs apart, her knees on the bed to left and right of her, and she has her feet together, making a perfect frame for her entire genital area, closely revealed in all its perfect detail. It looks good enough to eat! And would I love to! Her arms are above her head, exposing both of her fabulous breasts. Her eyes are closed, telling you that she's thinking of sex. Her mouth is open, once more ready to take your erection between her lips, and her pussy is fully exposed, in all its mouth-watering, voluptuous desirability. This photograph would give a eunuch an erection.

It is, without doubt, the most erotic shot that you have ever published. I guarantee that every male reader who sees that picture grabs his wife or girlfriend, or failing that, his dick, and proceeds to ejaculation as quickly as possible. Dorothy's picture totally exemplifies what heterosexuality is all about. It is lasciviousness itself. It is the very stuff of carnal desire, the epitome of concupiscence. There's only one thing anyone could do to Dot, seeing her in that position, in real life. And that's fuck her brains out. Until death do you part.

P.Y. Kilrush, Co. Limerick, Republic of Ireland.

Thanks for the compliments, which we've passed on to both Dot and the photographer. Dot says you're now a friend.

TART REPLY

Why is it that, generally speaking, a man who fucks around is one of the lads, while a woman who puts it about is a whore? I'm twenty-three, single, and I love sex. An evening out isn't an evening out to me unless I end up getting shagged silly by some man with an available, firmly erect cock. (*And* the bigger the better. None of this 'It doesn't matter how big it is, it's what you do with it that matters' rubbish).

But why does that make me a whore? Why can't I be one of the girls? I'm clean. I have no nasty habits. I'm not shy, or backwards in coming forward. I'll happily suck the cock of any man who'll happily suck my cunt. But I'm not looking for emotional involvement, or a long-lasting relationship. Just for enjoyably, sexually satisfying fun.

As with many men, to me variety is the spice of life. The time may well come when I want to marry and settle down, and have kids. But until that happens, why am I not permitted, in polite society, to fuck whom I please, when I please? Why is quantity, in terms of one-night stands, frowned upon?

My fantasy, reasonably enough, has to do with fucking, and being fucked by, large groups of men. In my favourite fantasy, I'm giving a party at my place, and I'm the only woman there. The guests are all men, and naturally enough, I'm in great demand. I'm dressed only in the most divine lingerie, which reveals most of my charms, and this has the effect of causing those men who are seriously interested in me, sexually, to have erections. I move among them all, as a good hostess should, taking advantage of an erection here and there by giving some of them a good feel.

After a while, I suggest that we have a largest-cock competition, and I suggest that any men who wish to enter should line up along the wall and await my instructions. The first three places in the competition, I tell them, will all receive the same prize. Me. Any way they want me. The first prizewinner gets me first, and so on. Ten men, out of about twenty-five, line up along the wall. I am the sole judge, and my decision is final.

We start. 'Unzip your flies,' I tell them, 'but leave your cocks inside your trousers.' I start at one end of the row and put my hand inside the man's trousers. His cock is only semi-erect, but as soon as I start to handle it, it leaps to full erection. It is a good, solid, reliable cock, but not enormous. I continue down the line, and I have a lovely time playing with the ten cocks. I pretend that it is difficult to make up my mind and I go back to all of them for a second feel before I do so.

Finally, I make my decision and I announce the three winners, in reverse order of priority. I also thank the other seven for their participation. That I am enjoying myself is obvious to anyone who cares to look down at my knickers, because there is a large damp stain at the front, where my pussy juice is flowing. It is copious, and I can feel it running down my thighs.

It's always the same when I get my hands on a stiff prick. Ten stiff pricks is almost too much for a girl. I take the winner by the hand and lead him off into the bedroom. He's an attractive, dark-haired young man, in his early thirties, I would guess. I would estimate his cock at a good ten inches, and at least five inches in circumference. I'm going to enjoy myself.

I close the bedroom door, and turn to face him, in my transparent bra and knickers. I smile at him. His name is Frank. 'How would you like me, Frank?' I ask. He looks at me, and then he comes over and puts one hand around my neck and kisses me. His other hand he puts between my legs, and he feels me up.

'To start with, I'm going to bury my face in your knicker crotch,' he said, when he pulled his mouth away from mine. 'I just love sucking pussy through knickers like those, especially,' he said, 'when they are as wet as yours are.'

'No problem,' I told him. Here, thank God, was a man who liked dirty sex. I can't stand prudes. 'I'll take off my bra, if that's all right with you,' I told him.

He nodded, and I undid my bra and dropped it on the floor. My nipples were standing up stiff, like bullets. I lay on the bed and opened my legs. He stripped off, revealing his engorged ten inches. It was a beautiful sight. He was circumcised. I longed to feel it in my mouth and then in my cunt.

He knelt on the floor beside the bed, and put his head between my legs. His lips were firm, and his mouth felt hot. I could feel his tongue through the thin material of my knickers. He sucked away for about ten minutes, and then he came up for air. He put his hands on the elastic of my knickers, and slowly eased them down my thighs, and then down my legs and off. His cock, thank God, was now within reach, and I took hold of it. 'One good turn deserves another, dear Frank,' I said, and I sat up and took it in my mouth.

He stood there for a while as his rampant cock filled my mouth, and I began to fellate him, but quite quickly he said, 'Why don't we both get up onto the bed, and into the old *soixante-neuf* position? That way, we can both give and receive pleasure at the same time.'

'Great idea,' I said, and we rearranged ourselves into the position that Frank had suggested. He lay on his back and I knelt over him, with his cock directly beneath my face and with my pussy over his mouth. We got down to work with both energy and enthusiasm, and in no time at all he was spurting his semen down my throat and I was wriggling with the pleasures of a series of orgasms that built and built, until I was practically consumed by the ultimate one.

We rolled off each other, clutching at each other and kissing and laughing and talking all at once. 'That was good,' I told him.

'For me, too,' he said. 'Really terrific.'

'What would you like now?' I asked. He thought for a moment. I wondered if perhaps he was going to suggest anal sex. Frankly, I love it. But I wasn't at all sure of being able to take that giant cock up my arse. Given a choice, I'd far rather have it stretching my pussy.

'I think a good old-fashioned fuck, if I may,' he said, finally. 'Straight up and down, like mum and dad. It takes a lot of beating. What do you say?'

Saved by the bell, I thought. And then aloud, 'I can't think of anything nicer. But why don't we do it doggy fashion? They tell me that you get better penetration that way.'

'Done,' he said. 'I just love it doggy fashion. But I didn't like to ask.'

'Frank, feel free,' I told him. 'Please tell me about anything that you want. OK?'

'OK,' he said. We got down to it straight away. It, too, was good. He was a thoughtful, considerate man, who obviously loved to fuck. The sheer size of his cock, filling and distending my cunt, was enough to turn a pleasant fuck into a spectacular one. When I felt the flux of his ejaculate jetting into my womb, I came with him, passionately.

'Hey, thanks, babe,' he said afterwards. 'I've won quite a few competitions in my time, but I've never before won one with my cock, nor one with as nice a prize as you. Thank you, darling.'

I laughed and kissed him, and took him into my *en-suite* bathroom, sitting on the lavatory seat while he showered. He seemed totally relaxed, and we chattered away while he towelled himself down. When he was dressed, I asked him to give me fifteen minutes, and then send the second prize winner – Peter – in to me.

I quickly showered and dried myself, and then I douched myself, thoroughly. Clean pussy is OK pussy. Ask any man.

When Peter arrived, I was reminded that he too was a good-looking lad, but a rather younger one than Frank. Somewhere in his mid-twenties, I would say. He grinned as he came through the bedroom door. 'Hey,' he said. 'I'm ready. I've been looking forward to this for what seems like ages.'

'I'm ready too, darling,' I said. I was standing there, naked. 'How would you like me?' I asked.

He grinned again. 'How many goes am I allowed?' he asked.

'Two,' I said. Firmly. It wasn't that I was in a hurry, but it didn't seem fair to keep the third prize winner waiting all night.

'Oh, great,' Peter said. 'And can I have those two goes any way I like?'

'Absolutely, Peter darling,' I said. 'Swinging from the chandeliers, if that's what you fancy.'

He chuckled. 'Not really,' he said. 'What I would really like, first of all, is for you to wank me. You know. Toss me off. It's something I've always wanted to have done to me by a beautiful woman. I've been tossed off by a few spotty teenage girls, but it's not the same, is it?'

'I don't know,' I said. 'I never did it as a teenage girl. But I've often done it since I grew up. Usually as a special treat. Would you like me to talk dirty to you while I wank you?'

He actually blushed. But it didn't deter him. 'Oh, would you?' he said. 'That would be terrific. I'd really like that.'

'I thought you might,' I said. 'And for your second go?'

He blushed again, and looked down at his feet. 'I'd like to bugger you,' he half whispered. 'I've never buggered anyone, and I'm told it's good news. Would you mind if we did it?'

I grinned at him. 'No, I wouldn't mind at all,' I said. 'As a matter of fact, I rather like it up my arse. I find it very sexy. But buggery's a horrid word. Please don't use it again.'

He didn't know whether to laugh or cry. To put him out of his misery, I went over to him and started to undress him. It was all straightforward stuff, until I came to try and part his boxer shorts from his erection. We managed eventually, and then he was naked, his prick a wondrous sight, even after the rare majesty of Frank's Colossus.

'That's a big one,' I said. 'I bet all the girls tell you that.'

'Some of them do,' he admitted. I sat him down on the edge of the bed and I was just about to sit beside him when I saw my knickers lying on the floor where Frank had dropped them, not so long ago. I went and picked them up. If Peter wanted me to talk dirty, I'd talk dirty, I thought.

I held my knickers out to him, and he took them from me. 'You'll find those have a very damp gusset,' I told him. 'You know what a gusset is, don't you?' I didn't give him the chance to reply. 'It's that part of a woman's knickers that is lined with cotton, whatever else the rest of them is made of, so that when she dribbles things out of her cunt – you know the sort of thing? Her lover's semen. Lubricant. Whatever. The idea is that the cotton gusset absorbs the dribbles, and she doesn't go around with wet knickers on. It doesn't always work, of course. My knickers were soaking when I took them off, as you can feel.' (Poetic licence, that. I thought it more tactful to say that I'd taken them off, rather than tell him anything about what Frank and I had been doing). 'So that now, if you want to, you can sniff and lick them while I wank you. It'll be like sniffing and licking my cunt. You'll smell exactly what my cunt smells like. Because that's cunt juice right there. On the gusset.'

He raised the knickers up to his nose, and sniffed. delicately at first. 'Ooooh,' he said. 'Lovely. Is that what your . . . your . . .'

'Cunt smells like?' I finished for him. 'Yes. Exactly like that. You can suck it, a bit later on, if you'd like to. Then you can not only smell it, you can taste it. Would you like that?'

'Er,' he said. 'Er, I'm not really sure.'

'Don't worry about it,' I told him. 'Concentrate on the knickers. Sniff hard. Don't forget to lick, too.' I think I was pretty much flogging a dead horse here. I don't think Peter had yet grown out of that initial thought that all young men seem to grow up with, that pussies are things that men occasionally fuck but you don't suck them, because they're dirty. Well, mine isn't. I always keep it clean, just in case some nice gentleman comes along who wants to suck it. Meanwhile, Peter's knicker-gusset sniffing had had the obvious effect upon his tool, which now stood firmly to attention, awaiting my ministrations. His cock was of good stature, and uncircumcised. I took hold of it, and it felt as solid in my hand. I gently peeled down his foreskin, and his prick twitched, convulsively.

Then I began to pull the foreskin up and down, slowly, and

his cock began to throb rhythmically between my fingers. I quite fancied taking it in my mouth and sucking it for him, but what he wanted, he had said firmly, was a wank, so a wank was what I gave him. He was old enough to know what he wanted.

I started to talk dirty again. 'Do you like girls wanking you, Peter?' I asked him.

'Yes,' he said, breathing heavily. 'Yes, I do.'

'And do you like wanking girls?' I asked. 'Do you like getting your finger up inside their knickers, and then inside their pussies, and playing with them?'

'I've never actually done that,' he said.

'Then you can wank me, darling,' I said. 'If you would like to. Afterwards.' I could feel from the throbbing of his cock that he was about to ejaculate, so I increased the speed with which I was wanking him, and I leaned my mouth up against his ear, and whispered, 'My cunt's all wet, with excitement. Would you like to feel my wet pussy?' At which point he ejaculated, all over my hand.

I kept on wanking him until there was no more semen left, and then I let go of him and rubbed the come that was on my hands all over my tits.

Peter looked at me with astonishment. I laughed. 'It's the finest skin cream in the world,' I told him. 'Ask any woman. It's really the most wonderful treatment for a woman's skin. It keeps it firm and soft and free from blemishes. Honestly. But never mind about that. How was the wank? Where would you rate me, in tossing-you-off terms? How many marks, out of ten?' I was kidding him along, of course, but I don't think he knew that.

'Oh, just terrific,' he said. 'I enjoyed it. Twelve out of ten. Thank you. It was probably the most erotic thing I've ever done, sexually. Being tossed off by a beautiful woman. But now we're going to do something else that I've never done before. So you'll have to tell me what to do, if you don't mind.'

I allowed myself a chuckle at that particular statement, but I didn't say anything. Instead, I went through to the bathroom and found a tube of sexual lubricant. 'There's nothing to learn, really,' I told him. 'But there *are* two serious rules.' I handed him the tube. 'The first is, use plenty of lubricant.' I knelt up on the bed, and offered him my rump. 'Push as much of that as you can up my bum, as far as you can reach,' I said. 'And then rub plenty more all over your cock.'

He did as he was told. Slightly reluctantly at first, but once he stuck his fingers right up my anus he found an enthusiasm for what he was doing. In the end, I had to tell him that enough was enough. 'The other rule,' I said, 'is that if I say stop, you stop. OK?'

I looked at him over my shoulder. I meant what I said, and he could see that. 'Sure,' he mumbled.

'Right, then, baby. Let's go,' I said. I reached behind me and, taking hold of his dick, I guided it to the entrance of my bottom-hole. I placed it against my tightly closed rectum, and as I began to ease it in, I felt my hole dilate, and then he was inside me. I pushed backwards, and suddenly he was all the way in.

I took my hand away, and began to thrust back against him. I didn't think that he needed any more help. If he didn't know what to do now, God help the both of us. He grabbed me around my waist and then, realizing that he was missing out on a feel sensation, he moved his hands up to my tits and grabbed hold of those. Then he began to move his hips in the age-old motion.

I think I said earlier that I like anal sex, and this was no exception. He filled my back passage nicely, and I know that

I was feeling sexily tight to him, from the grunting noises he was making as he fucked me.

He hardly lasted any time at all, which perhaps wasn't so surprising when you remember that this was something of a memorable first for him. I felt his ejaculate spurting deep inside my bottom, but nothing that he had done so far had brought me to orgasm, so I urgently frigged myself as he groaned and spurted, and I managed to come a moment or two before he finished. He finally pulled out of me and collapsed down onto the bed with a closing moan of pleasure.

It took me a while to get him together, showered and dressed, and out of my bedroom. He was still in some kind of seventh heaven as he left. I laughed quietly to myself, wondering if his girlfriend (if he had one) would soon have a sore bottom, following his new experience this evening.

By the time the third and last prizewinner – Geoff – arrived, he'd patently spent too much time boozing while waiting for his turn to collect his prize. I couldn't blame him. He wasn't in any way unpleasant, he just wasn't up to it very much, after the amount of booze that he'd taken on board throughout the evening. He just about managed a straight fuck (with a little manual help) and retired gracefully. Me? I was still raring to go. But that's another story. Does that make me a whore? Or simply a woman who enjoys both giving and receiving sex? You tell me.

B.C. Hammersmith, London.

No, ma'am, that doesn't make you a whore. Not in our book. It makes you a lady we'd all love to meet. Please add us to the invitation list for your next party.

FANTASY UNIFORMS

As a reasonably normal woman in my mid-twenties, I'm fascinated by one of the oft-recurring themes in the fantasy letters written by men that you publish. I like sex as much as the next woman. Possibly rather more than the next woman, if I'm honest about it. And I understand some of the things that men find sexually attractive, or sexually exciting, and I'm all for them. Things like sexy lingerie. Stockings with suspenders, instead of the boring, passion-killing, useful but unattractive tights. I love giving and receiving oral sex. My only hesitation is when I'm expected to suck a cock that isn't clean, but that's basic stuff.

But why, oh why, do I keep reading about men who want their women to dress up in so much more than just sexy lingerie? They want nurses, schoolgirls, French maids, leather-clad dominatrices, or submissive women in rubber knickers. Women in all and every kind of uniform, from women in the armed services to nannies. What in God's name is that all about? Can you please explain? I've visited friends in hospital often enough to be able to tell you that all the nurses that I've seen look extremely pleasant, and very normal. What makes a nurse in uniform so sexy to the male mind? The French-maid syndrome is perhaps understandable, in that it's not an authentic vision. The skirt has to be short enough to expose the black knickers, for example. And preferably the expanse of naked thigh between stocking top and knicker bottom. Not anything I've ever seen in the many private houses I've visited in France. But I've never been in a French brothel. Or any other nationality of brothel, come to that.

Schoolgirls? Well, maybe the attraction there is youth. But a thirty-year-old woman dressed up as a schoolgirl? Where's the sexual appeal there? It completely escapes me. I've never read of women who fantasize about Boy Scouts, or bus conductors, or men wearing red boxer shorts. Can you explain this phenomenon to me, please?

J.H. Croydon, Surrey.

We're sorry to be difficult, but other than to say that a fetish is a fetish, it's actually virtually impossible to explain why. Most dictionary interpretations include the word 'irrational' in their explanations. One man's fetish is another man's bête noir. *But we've met plenty of women who are into leather, rubber, bondage and discipline, and so on. And, like the song says, all the nice girls love a sailor.*

TOY BOY DELIGHT

I read so much about male and female fantasies in your magazine – all of which I enjoy – but I do sometimes wonder whether your women readers occasionally forget one of the basic facts of life! If I may be allowed to say so, as a woman now well into her forties, I can tell you girls at least one thing about sex which I now know to be true.

At my age, sex with young men is what sex is all about. You can call them toy boys, rent boys, anything you like, but, in my considerable experience, there's nothing to compare with a young cock in an old pussy. They're harder. With a degree of experience, they last longer (and it's fun providing that experience). They become erect again after ejaculation far more quickly than, and are in every way superior to, the cocks of older men. Or, to be fair perhaps, they are certainly superior to the cocks of the older men in my life! And if they lack a little sophistication, well, what the hell. You can train them to do whatever you like done, just the way you want them to do it. Practice, as ever, makes perfect. And how!

K.O'M. Kilburn, London.

That's a difficult concept to argue with. And you know our philosophy. Whatever turns you on, dear lady.

BEAUTY IS IN THE EYE OF THE BEHOLDER . . .

What a terrific magazine. But tell me, guys, are those girls real? I mean, are they really *real*? I know they're models. But they must have private lives. I mean, apart from coming on strong in your photographs for the likes of me, they must go home to someone, and give head, spread their legs, put out, do all those lovely dirty things that all the girls I know do. Mustn't they?

So here's my only complaint about your magazine. Why don't *my* girls look like *your* girls? Why do my girls have zits, saggy tits, spotty asses, stretch marks, razor burn where they've shaved their pubes, five o'clock shadow in their armpits, cellulite, bad breath, and worse tempers? And another thing . . .

Reading the words that accompany the photographs in your delightful girl sets, all your chicks think about, all the time, seems to be fucking. Or sucking. Or taking it up the ass. All *mine* do is have hard days at the office, non-stop periods, and headaches. As to taking it up their ass, they say, 'What are you, Mac? Some kind of pervert?' So where do I go wrong? It's not that I'm short of sexual partners. Not really. It's just that I'm patently not getting my fair share of the world's most beautiful women. Take Lynne, in this month's issue. Chance would be a fine thing. I mean, just *look* at her. She's too much.

In your first shot, she's wearing a bra (well, almost) and panties, the like of which no girl I know ever wears. They're enough to make me ejaculate simply looking at them. Oh yes, and she's wearing stockings, with a tiny suspender belt. And strappy high-heeled shoes. Now, be fair. How many girls do you know . . . No. Let me start again. How many girls do *most* men know who wear stockings these days, for God's sake? Tights, yes. Stockings, no. Seamed black silk stockings? No. Lynne is beautiful. Not just pretty. Not just sexually attractive. Not just glamorous. She's all those things, of course. But she is also *beautiful.* She's movie-star beautiful. Her make-up is exquisite. Her gorgeously red-lipsticked mouth is made to suck cock. Her hands, with her long fingers and beautifully painted red nails, are made to close around cocks. I can close my eyes, and feel those cool fingers on *my* cock.

Her breasts, when she dispenses with that bra, are perfect. Simply perfect. Neither too big, nor too small. Just perfect. Her nipples, and her areolae, manage to look virginal, but they are also instantly ready to be sucked. In that first photograph, where she has dropped her panties and opened her legs, she lets us into a number of fascinating secrets. That her head hair is dyed, but that her pubic hair is not. I like that. She doesn't give a damn if you know that her hair is dyed. And why should she? Lynne has a comfortable-looking, accommodating, fleshy-lipped, pretty little pink pussy. One that I would give my eye teeth – and a fortune – to get my mouth around, and my cock into. And as for that ass, turned as it is fully towards the camera in one of the final photographs, my God! All I can say is, could he have seen it, that ass would have turned 'Duke' Wayne himself into a butt-fucker. What red-blooded man *wouldn't* want to ream that gorgeous ass?

And just to prove me wrong, with my point about the copy that accompanies the photographs of your girls emphasizing that all they think about is sex, Lynne's photographs don't have any accompanying text at all. But then, with those pictures, who needs text? It's plain to one and all that sex is a favourite subject with Lynne. So, like I said at the beginning, what am I doing wrong? While I'm not short of girls to play around with, why don't they look like Lynne? Or any of the other girls in your magazine? What do I have to do to pull girls like that?

J. McC. Washington, D.C.

Have you ever thought of publishing your own men's magazine? But seriously, you know what they say. The grass on the other side of the fence . . .

HIRSUTE HEAVEN

I'm greatly disturbed by the rapid spread among the models in men's magazines of the current fashion for trimming their pubic hair. Whilst few of the girls commit the ultimate, cardinal sin of completely shaving that area – thank God – the vast majority seem suddenly to have become infatuated with neatness, and have taken to trimming the edges, and the length and breadth, of their pubic bushes. This results in tiny, almost invisible little patches of cut-back pubes that are hardly worth the bother of looking at. I notice that having their pubes trimmed into heart shapes seems popular with these model girls currently, something first made fashionable in your magazine by the beautiful Marilyn Chambers, back in the late 1970s. But at least she had rather more going for her than a lot of these present-day girls. She was, after all, the superstar of *Behind the Green Door*, one of America's first major pornographic movies. I remember that Marilyn also had a very pretty pussy, through one labial lip of which (if I remember correctly) she used to wear a golden ring.

But where, oh where, are the gorgeous, thick, long, pubic thatches of yesteryear? Congratulations, then, to your goodselves, for running the girl set featuring Donna, and her spectacularly bearded clam, in last month's magazine. Pubic hair seriously doesn't come any hairier than that! She is magnificent. *And* she knows it! In every pose, throughout the pages, the camera focuses on her centre of attraction: her exquisite, thick-lipped, fleshy-flanged, open cunt, surrounded, as it is, by her glorious growth of long, lustrous, sensational pubic hair.

Any time the lovely Donna wants a respectful slave to brush that magnificent mane, or to lick those luscious lips clean for her – or to suck her to orgasm, should that be a requirement – I am permanently, completely available. If I could but insert my swollen penis – just once – between those hirsute, densely surrounded, dark-skinned labia, I would die a happy man. Why can't other young girls see the extraordinary strong sexual attraction of thick growths of pubic hair? What makes them think (as I must assume) that there is something unfeminine about a good, thick, heavy pubic thatch? Don't they realise that there is nothing more exciting on the beach, or in the gymnasium, than to see a woman whose pubic hairs are just peeping out from beneath the crotch of her bikini, or of her work-out body? And while I have already said that completely shaven pudenda are total anathema to me, I can at least understand something of their attraction. The way that a shaven cunt offers those pouting labia for one to suck leaves little to the imagination, but at least it is some kind of an invitation. These girls with their manicured, neat little twats are neither one thing nor the other. My respects to Donna.

D.L.O'H. Cambridge, Cambs.

We don't turn a hair at your wishing to get in Donna's hair. So, not to split hairs with you, why don't you let your *hair down, and see if you can get within a hair's breadth of those amorous tresses. Seriously, whatever turns you on is fine with us.*

THE ITALIAN JOB

My mere female fantasy may not be as horny as some of your male flights of fancy, but it's one that I always find works well for me on those evenings when, like all lonely women, I have no live male alternative to slipping my fingers between my legs to bring me the peace of orgasm. The peace that induces dreamless, much needed, restful sleep.

My fantasy takes place in Venice. I am staying – by myself – at the Gritti Palace, that lovely old-fashioned hotel on the Grand Canal, just down from the Piazza San Marco. I am sitting in the lobby, reading as best I can from the day's Italian morning newspaper (which is quite well, if I take it slowly) when this attractive man comes and sits in the chair beside mine. I can tell immediately that he is American. There are some things that a Savile Row suit, Gucci shoes, and a Nikkon camera can't disguise, and a Californian tan is one of them.

He waved at a waiter. 'Young lady,' he said, smiling at me. 'Allow me to buy you a drink. And if you don't usually speak to strange men in hotel lobbies – which I'm sure you don't – maybe if I tell you that I'm from out of town, that I don't know a soul here in Venice, and that I think that you're the prettiest lady that I've seen since I arrived in Italy, perhaps you'll make an exception. My name's Harry, by the way. Harry Steinberg. I'm on vacation.'

He was attractive. About forty, I would say. And with a Californian drawl. So I was right about the suntan. I would have accepted his invitation, even if he *wasn't* Harry Steinberg. What girl in her right mind wouldn't allow herself to be picked up by such an attractive man? The fact that he was the hottest author of the decade, with his latest novel on the bestseller lists all around the world for months now, really had nothing to do with it. I smiled back at him, accepted his offer, asked for a vodka martini, and sat back in my chair, waiting for him to make the running. He too was staying at the Gritti Palace, but we dined that evening at the Trattoria La Madonna, near the Rialto Bridge. It's one of the best seafood restaurants in a nation of good seafood restaurants. We drank Bellinis, that magical Italian drink made with champagne and fresh peach juice.

After that first drink, back at the hotel, I knew we were going to fuck. Harry was relaxed, sexual, and confident, without being chauvinistic. It became obvious that the sexy interludes that sold his books in the millions were written from real life. If I was going to be part of the research for his next book, then it was something that I was going to enjoy. We walked slowly back to the hotel through the warm June evening, arm in arm. We hadn't discussed where we were going, or what we were going to do. It wasn't necessary. We both knew. He kissed me as soon as the door was shut, his tongue probing, his right hand unzipping the Gina Fratini, his erection pressing into me.

He stepped back and lifted the dress up over my shoulders, leaving me standing there in my pale green knickers, the tiny division between the legs a darker shade from my excitement. A damp tribute to his ability to arouse me. I wondered if he too could smell the aroma of my sex, a sweet, pungent, almost musky scent.

I didn't wonder for long. He pushed me gently down upon the bed behind me, and quickly undressed himself. Then, parting my thighs, he buried his face in the fount of my sexual perfume. He tongued my pussy through the sodden silk, adding his saliva to the wetness that spread rapidly as the result of his ministrations. It was more than a month since I had received any attention down there, other than that supplied by my own fingers, and the feel of what his mouth was doing to me through the thin material quickly brought me to my first welcome orgasm.

I closed my legs around his head and writhed against his mouth, trying to get even closer to the source of my intense pleasure. I came again, and then I lay back, momentarily sexually satiated. Harry stood up and took hold of my knickers, with one hand on each side of their waistband, and started to ease them down over my hips. I lifted my bottom up off the bed to assist him, and he smiled down at me.

'I get the feeling that you may have been without a man for a while,' he said as I slipped my feet out while he held my knickers. I didn't answer him, but instead reached out and took hold of his cock. It was thick and hard, and strangely white against his tanned body. The circumcised head was swollen, the main blue vein standing out like a wire running up the side of a lamp. I leaned forward and took his cock in my mouth, just the tip at first, wetting it with my tongue, before sliding it deep into my throat. I felt it jerk as it hit the back of my throat, and I thought for a moment that he was going to ejaculate right then. But it was just a sensual spasm.

I played with it, sucking and kissing, running my tongue up and down the shaft, trying to insert the tip of my tongue into the slit at the top and then taking it all into my mouth again as Harry stood beside the bed, looking down at what I was doing to his cock. I worked hard, wanting to give him as much pleasure as he'd given me, and in a while I felt his cock start to throb, and then his hands were pulling my head into his crotch, and he was fucking my throat, the momentum all his, and he was flooding my throat, and shouting, 'Jesus Christ, yes. Fuck, fuck, fuck.'

I swallowed continuously as he thrust, his rhythm slackening off, until he was hardly moving, his cock still rigid. Then he pulled himself out of my mouth and lay down beside me on the bed. After a while, he leaned over and kissed me, and I could still taste my pussy on his lips. I wondered if he could taste his cock on mine. I reached down and took hold of him, finding him hard again in my palm. As I did so, he put his hand down to me and started fingering me, his fingers making soft squelching noises in my wetness. He next slid two fingers deep inside me and positioned the pad of his thumb over my clitoris, after which he combined a thrusting movement of his fingers with a circulatory movement with his thumb. The combination of the two activities rapidly caused me to start trying to fuck his hand.

I finally reached the point where I pulled his hand away from my pussy, pressed him down onto his back, and climbed up over the head of his straining cock. I placed a knee each side of him, and then urgently guided his shaft into my cunt with a shaking hand. He wasn't *that* long, but the thickness of him invaded me, stretching my pussy around his rampant member, my clitoris rubbing delightedly against his hardness. I rode him happily with long, slow strokes, teasing him, burying him deep, then raising myself up until just the tip of his cock was left in me, and then going down hard again, shafting myself, my eyes closed, lost in the sheer physical gratification of a long-awaited fuck.

He massaged my breasts as I rode him, squeezing them, pinching the nipples, pulling on them, rolling them, rubbing them, occasionally stretching up to suck them. As ever, I could feel the sensations in my nipples replicated in my cunt. Then, as we both approached orgasm, he let go of my now exquisitely sore breasts and grabbed my buttocks, pulling them apart, pushing them together, using them as handles with which to control the angle and depth of my strokes up and down his prick. Orgasms, they say, are all in the mind. But not this one, baby. This one was coming from my uterus, from my fallopian tubes, from my soul, by way of my cunt. It was the best ever. End of story. Rewind, and start again! Love will get you everything. What do you say, guys?

F.H. Kings Lynn, Norfolk.

We say good on yer, madam. And we thought that the only men girls got to meet in Venice were waiters. We live and learn.

TWO'S COMPANY . . .

I took part in my first three-in-a-bed session the other week. It was something that I had always wanted to experience, and my new girlfriend didn't seem too bothered about it when I first suggested it to her. In the end, it was she who persuaded one of her girlfriends to come and join us in the threesome. She was a pretty girl, and obviously into sex.

We all three went out to dinner first, and we got on like a house on fire. Neither of the girls are lesbians (more's the pity!) so when we got back to my place there was a rush for the bed from the two girls, and a lot of 'Fuck-me-first' requests. I made a joke out of it, and told them that they would have to compete for my attention.

As it happened, I fucked my usual girlfriend first, in that I felt, probably quite correctly, that it would be easier to get it up again the second time around for a new woman, rather than vice versa. The girlfriend's girlfriend – I'll call her Jennie – took quite an active part in my fucking my girlfriend (she's called Ann): she was doing all kinds of naughty things, like kissing me wetly, putting her hand down between the two of us and jacking me off as I fucked Ann (an experience, which, incidentally, I thoroughly recommend.)

Not surprisingly, I came very quickly and in no time at all I was hard again, and soon rogering Jennie. Ann entered into the spirit of the occasion, and she ended up squatting over my head, giving me oral access to her soaking pussy as I lay on my back, getting well fucked by an energetic and enthusiastic Jennie.

In fact, getting it up wasn't a problem, and we continued for a long, lascivious, sexually exhilarating night, with the girls saying the next day that they had enjoyed themselves as much as I had. My only disappointment, as I indicated earlier, was the fact that I wasn't able to watch the two girls doing naughty but nice things to each other, simply because neither of them are into other girls. Some you win . . .

But here's the snag. Both girls, the following day, voted that we repeat the exercise as quickly as possible. A suggestion which, as you can imagine, was music to my ears. Until Ann suggested to Jennie (who immediately agreed) that we should widen our sights to include another man, making it a foursome. That's something that I can't possibly argue with, for obvious reasons. But I don't think that I can cope with seeing another man take sexual liberties with my girl. I appreciate the fact that you'll tell me that I'm a chauvinist arsehole but, that aside, what advice can you give me?

P.V. Exeter, Devon.

We don't think you really spent sufficient time working out your game plan. All you can do now, we believe, is to be honest, and 'fess up. But be prepared for your popularity rating to take something of a dive.

THANKS FOR THE MAMMARIES

It seems that these days no one likes tits anymore. I read eulogies for arses, legs, pussies, mouths, hands even. But am I really the only old-fashioned tit-man left in the world?

I've always been into tits, and whilst I am an admirer of both the appearance – and the uses – of the other aforementioned attributes, breasts are what I love most of all. I love every individual breast type. Unlike many self-confessed breast-men, I'm not just into big tits, I love them all. Firm, full breasts, with rounded nipples. Tiny, pointed breasts, with longer nipples. Nipples to pull on. Full, voluptuous breasts, in their prime of life. Breasts with huge teats to suck on. I adore sucking nipples. I love feeling them through sweaters, through silk blouses, through soft, lacy bras. I like breasts with soft hairs around the areolae. I like the feel of them in my mouth. I fantasize about breasts wherever I am.

I love to have a woman with big breasts masturbate me between them. I adore the feel of my stiff cock pillowed between those soft, squashy mounds, and I delight in sitting astride a big-breasted woman, one with tits that are large enough to allow me to jack off my rampant prick between them, whilst the woman takes the tip of my prick in her mouth and sucks me. Sheer heaven!

If I am forced to take a final decision – accepting that I love *all* breasts – I would have to come down just slightly on the side of small boobs. I cherish tiny breasts, of the kind some Asian and Oriental women possess. Like small fried eggs, sitting softly but firmly on their owner's chest, and – if I'm in luck – with oversized nipples erotically attached at their centre.

So, Mr Editor, how about a breast special in your excellent magazine? How about a photographic feature that illustrates *all* of the different kinds of breasts that are out there in our great big world, even including old, worn-out, droopy, dried-up, wizened breasts? Breasts don't have to be in perfect condition to be sexy. No, sir! Not to us serious breast connoisseurs.

J.D.S. Brighton, Sussex.

We'll do our best to keep abreast of developments.

SADISTIC SEX

Whilst my real sex life is pleasantly normal (I'm into an ongoing relationship with a woman I love, and who loves me: we do most things that most young people do, and enjoy our sex enormously) all my sexual fantasies are involved with pain.

I get very excited at the idea of tying a woman up, beating her, and then subjecting her to my every sexual peccadillo. Often, when I am screwing with my girlfriend, I shut my eyes and see myself tying her to a sort of wooden frame – one made especially for the job. I tie her roughly, with cord, by her wrists and ankles, with her back and arse exposed, her face to the wall. Next, I carefully select a whip, and I then whip her back and shoulders. This gives me the most tremendous hard-on.

I next select a long, thin, supple cane from a number that are available. I try one or two of them out, caning her arse viciously, until I find the one that I feel is most suited to inflicting serious pain. By this time my girlfriend is crying, and pleading with me not to hurt her any more. When I have found the cane that is going to do the most damage, I begin to really thrash her. I cane her plump bottom until she is screaming for mercy. In between strokes, I tell her that I will stop thrashing her if she will plead with me to fuck her up her arse.

'Anything,' she cries. 'Anything at all. Just stop hurting me. Please.' I still have this tremendous hard-on, and it gets even stiffer at the thought of fucking my girlfriend in the arse. I untie her and give her a tube of lubricant, and tell her to first kneel before me and suck my cock and then – but only I when tell her that I'm ready – she is to rub the lubricant all over my cock. She must then give me the tube and turn around and offer me her arsehole, saying, 'Please fuck me up my arse,' after which I will grease her, and then I'll bugger her.

She is still crying, which helps to turn me on, and she takes my cock in her hand and puts the end in her mouth, and begins to give me a blow job. This is something that she is very expert at, and which she normally enjoys doing. Her snivelling seems to make this one all the more enjoyable, and when I feel myself ready to come, I take her head in my hands and thrust my ejaculating cock deeply down into her throat. She seems to be having trouble with this, from the choking noises and the gasping for breath that is going on, but I don't give a damn. I'm holding her head rigid, so that I can fuck her throat while I come.

When I've finished ejaculating down her throat I pull out, and she drops on the floor, choking and coughing and gasping for breath. When she is more or less back to normal, I say, 'OK, baby. Now grease my cock.' She takes my limp cock in her hands, and covers it carefully all over with lubricant. This has the effect of making it pretty much fully erect again.

I tell her, 'OK. That's enough.' She turns around on the floor, presents her arse to me, and says,' 'Please fuck me up my bottom.' I kick her. 'Not bottom, you prissy little cow. Arse. *ARSE*. Got it?' She looks over her shoulder at me and says, rather quietly, 'Please fuck me up my arse.'

'That's better,' I tell her. I take the tube of unguent from her and have a fun time greasing her anus and rectal passage. She squeezes her arsehole tightly around my finger as I grease her, and I remember hoping that she'll do the same when I fuck her there.

I next pick up a giant dildo that I have been keeping out of sight until now. 'Here, baby,' I tell her, handing over the dildo. 'Don't ever say I don't think of you. Since fucking your arsehole probably isn't seriously going to do a lot for you, you can fuck yourself with that while I'm buggering you.'

She takes it from me, but she doesn't say anything. Not even 'Thank you'.

'Let's have a little practice first,' I suggest. 'Sit up on the edge of the bed there, and open your legs.' She does as she is told. 'Now fuck yourself with it,' I command. She pushes the dildo slowly up between her legs and into her cunt, and I watch as her cunt stretches to accommodate it. It looks painful, but she doesn't complain. Finally it's in. 'Push it all the way in,' I tell her. 'Don't waste all that lovely length. You've never had that much cock in your cunt before. Now fuck yourself with it. Enjoy.'

She begins to push the dildo in and out and, as she starts to lubricate, the surface of it becomes wetter and therefore that much easier to manipulate. It really is stretching her to her limit, but after a while I can see that she is actually beginning to enjoy the sensations that it is inducing in her pussy. I've got a tremendous hard-on, watching this dirty girl wanking herself off on a huge dildo, and I'm more than anxious to get my cock up her arsehole, so I say, 'OK. That will do. Now kneel on all fours again for me.'

She does as she's told, and I take my swollen cock in my hand. I put it up against her back door. She gasps as I touch her secret entrance. Just once. And then I grab her by her hips and with one, strong, urgent thrust, I force myself up her. She is so well greased that I slide into her immediately. All the way. I begin, enthusiastically, to fuck her anally.

Her anus and her rectal muscles are in excellent condition.

She is exquisitely tight, grasping my cock like a terrified, landbound mussel, dragged from the ocean and holding tenaciously onto its meat. If this is what anal intercourse is all about, I'm a convert.

But this is entirely in my mind, remember. Does the real thing actually feel as heavenly as this? Or is this simply the never-to-be-experienced product of my cerebral fantasies? My girlfriend and I have never even discussed anal sex. She fellates me, happily, and I perform cunnilingus upon her with great pleasure. Oral sex, for us both, is a vital part of our sex life. We fuck. All the time. We masturbate, each of us the other, bestowing manual pleasures that are exceedingly well enjoyed. We masturbate ourselves, each in the other's company. We are not shy. We examine each other's sex at the closest of quarters. Fingering, kissing. Licking, sucking. I run my fingers along her anal crevice. I even finger her anus, pressing my forefinger just inside its forbidden centre. It dilates beneath my fingers.

But these are just momentary sensory delights. Neither of us has seriously contemplated anal sex. No. That is a lie. *I* seriously contemplate anal sex all the time. Neither of us has ever brought up the subject of anal sex.

That is truthful. Perhaps I should, as it were, take the bull by the horns. Maybe I should grease my forefinger, thrust it up her rectum, and say, 'Have you ever wished to be fucked up there, my darling?' Maybe I would discover that the only thing she seriously thought about, morning, noon, and night, was getting herself fucked anally. Well, you never know. Do you?

E.B. Hemel Hempstead

You most certainly don't. And you'll remember what we all used to say, all those years ago: those that don't ask, don't get.

FEMALE TURN-ON

Being what I have always regarded as a fairly normal girl, I'm amused – and intrigued – to look through the pages of your raunchy magazine, together with my current boyfriend, who introduced me to the feminine pleasures to be found between your glossy pages. But the longer I gaze upon your permissive misses, the more I realize that somewhere, deep down inside me, is a strong lesbian urge. I really want to get into these girls' laundry.

My boyfriend finds your ladies extremely sexually attractive, and gets himself off fucking me while thinking of them. My problem is, so do I. Which isn't, in itself, necessarily a bad thing. We both get some excellent fucking out of our pooled enthusiasm. But what *is* beginning to worry me is, am I actually butch? I've never been attracted to another woman in the flesh. Why, then, should I find not just some but almost *all* of your naughty girls extremely sexually attractive? Have you any advice to offer me? Is there something abnormal about me? Can I be lesbian, and not realize it? Please help me. I'm really concerned.

S.L. London, WC2

The only advice that we can offer is that you do your own thing. Whatever that might be. Lots of women find pictures of other women sexually attractive. Some of them are moved to become physically involved. Some aren't. Be yourself.

THE TENDER TOUCH

I've recently experienced something so unusual – at least within my previous sexual experience – that I felt I had to write and tell you about it. It isn't anything so amazing that you're going to say, 'Jesus, wow, my God,' or anything like that. But I believe that you will find it moderately interesting.

I was recently invited to dinner by a married couple. Old friends of mine. They have been together for about ten years now, and have a son of around seven years of age. Since they both work, the child has an *au pair,* an Italian girl of twenty-three. The evening of which I speak was the first time that I had met the Italian girl. She sat next to me at dinner, and despite a certain lack of Italian on my part, and not too much English on hers, we got on rather well.

When I rang my friend's wife the next day to thank her for an excellent meal, I asked if she would object to my inviting the Italian girl out. Absolutely not at all, she told me. But she also said that, as far as she knew, the girl was a practising Catholic and so my chances of getting her knickers down were therefore slim, in fact nil. She didn't give a damn what I did, but she didn't want me to upset the girl. This, I promised, I would not do.

I telephoned the girl later that day, and asked her if I might take her out to dinner on her next evening off. To my delight, she accepted with alacrity, and on the evening concerned I went to collect her from my friends' house. There was a great deal of jocularity about my intentions, and we all had a good laugh.

I had booked a table at a local restaurant, one I liked for its intimacy, soft lighting and romantic atmosphere, as well as for the quality of its cooking. The two of us continued to get on well, and we definitely liked each other.

We had a great meal, some amusing conversation within the limits of our mutual ignorance of each other native language, and when it was finished and I had paid the bill, I asked Amelia if she would like to come back to my place for a drink and some coffee, before I drove her back to her employers' house. (In fact, they live around the corner from me, and we would walk it in about five minutes, absolute maximum.) Amelia said that yes, she would like that.

We drove home, and I settled her in the sitting room (off which is my bedroom). I poured her a drink, and then I went off to the kitchen to make the coffee. When I took the coffee back through to the sitting room, Amelia was not to be seen anywhere.

I thought perhaps that she had taken herself off to the bathroom, but after a few minutes, when I went to check it out, the bathroom door was open and the bathroom itself empty. Further exploration revealed Amelia ensconced in my bed.

She was sitting up, to all intents and purposes naked, thumbing through a magazine and drinking her brandy. She smiled as I came through the door, but didn't say anything. I brought her coffee to her, for which she smiled, and said thanks. She had beautiful young girl's breasts, a slim, sexy body, and a lascivious little mouth.

I tore my clothes off and leapt into bed beside her. She grabbed me with apparent enthusiasm, and stuck her tongue down my throat. Just for starters.

I quickly realized that she was still wearing her knickers. Their appearance is firmly imprinted upon my memory. They were pale green, in a sort of lacy cotton material, and were minimal, rather than actually concealing anything. We kissed hungrily, and Amelia squirmed and wriggled as I began to fondle her tight little pussy through the thin material.

She didn't seem to object to my feeling her up, nor to my massaging her pussy through her knickers, but she fought strenuously against any attempt of mine to pull them down, or off, or to insinuate my fingers up beneath her knicker-leg and into her pussy. Nor would she cooperate when, realizing that whatever else happened, there was no way I was going to get my dick into her, I thought to myself that I would settle for second best and, taking Amelia's hand, tried to place it around my cock, hoping that in her kindness she might give me a quick one off the wrist. No chance. She didn't say a word, but neither would she take hold of my cock. It took me quite a while to discover what she actually *was* prepared to do for me. On her own terms.

I don't know whether young Catholic Italian girls have their own code of honour, or whatever you want to call it, but Amelia, I eventually discovered, had not the slightest objection – in fact, she joined me wholeheartedly in the activity – to my lying on top of her and rubbing my rigid cock along her open cunt through her now very wet thin knicker material, until I reached my much-needed ejaculation. She rubbed back with enthusiasm, bucking her hips, and grinding her cunt up against my cock. As far as I could tell, from her moans and groans, she too reached orgasm with this – to me – original variation upon mutual masturbation.

We repeated the exercise a number of times during the night, each time seemingly with Amelia's complete enjoyment.

During the earlier part of the night, I spent a lot of time, and my best efforts, in attempting to persuade Amelia to allow me to eat her pussy, or to get her to suck my cock. It quickly became clear that there was no way that I was going to actually touch her pussy in the raw, as it were. Nor was she going to perform any kind of sexual act with my cock, be it oral, manual or coital, other than the aforementioned frottage. That aside, I could rub myself off along the delightful, increasingly open valley of her accommodating sex as many times as I wished.

After the first couple of times, her knicker material was so wet that it might just as well have not been there. But obviously this strange performance kept us both within the house rules, as far as Amelia was concerned. We have repeated this evening many times since that first occasion, to our mutual enjoyment. My married friends tell their other friends (out of Amelia's earshot) how I am the only man in London to conquer their *au pair*'s strict no-fucking rules. I let them believe that what they say is true. Well, why should I be the one to disillusion them?

P.H.L. Golders Green, North London.

Why indeed? An interesting experience. And one that we envy.

SOMETHING OF A MOUTHFUL

At the age of nineteen, I'm becoming slightly pissed off at what – for want of a better word – you might call the men-about-town in this Godforsaken place. Where, oh where, are the MEN in Huddersfield? Yes, I can get myself laid (more or less) on a Friday or Saturday evening. As long as I'm prepared to be accepted as something that happens after the football, after the night in the pub, after far too many beers, and after the curry.

I say, 'laid, more or less' advisedly, since as often as not the gentleman of the evening either can't get it up, or can't keep it up long enough, due to the amount of alcohol consumed earlier. Sex, it would seem, is low on the list of male priorities here in Huddersfield. So you will understand that my fantasies centre entirely around men who actually enjoy fucking, and are up for it – literally – at any time of the day or night.

In my main fantasy, my girlfriends have all clubbed together to give me a surprise present on my birthday. They have been telling me for some time beforehand that the particularly nice thing about this special present is that they can all share it with me. So, after much anticipation, the big day arrives. The girls have taken a large private room at Huddersfield's most expensive hotel, and the evening starts promptly at seven-thirty p.m. with drinks at the bar which is set up in the private room.

There's champagne and everything else, so of course we all start off with the champagne. There's a small five-piece combo playing soft, gentle music in the background and after about half an hour of pleasant chatter, and the consuming of rather a lot of champagne, the maitre d' comes to ask if he may serve dinner. There are eight of us altogether, and Mary, my best friend, says yes, thank you, we're all ready for our meal.

I won't bother you with the details of what we ate and drank, except to say that it was probably the most delicious meal, with some of the finest wines, that I have ever eaten and drunk. It was mouth-wateringly delicious, and when it was almost over, and we were on the coffee and the liqueurs, I imagined that was it. But no! There was more to come, said Mary.

At that moment, the lights in the room went down, some curtains up at the far end of the room – which I had assumed were simply drapes of some kind to cover the wall – pulled apart, the combo broke into a lively melody, and eight gorgeous, hunky men came onto the stage which was revealed behind the curtains. They were very fit, very handsome, male dancers, with the emphasis on 'male', and their show was unbelievably sexy. Gay they weren't.

As the show wore on, they abandoned more and more of their costumes, until all they were wearing were what I can only describe as posing pouches. Little tiny black leather bags that *almost* covered their cocks and balls. At which point the lead dancer – Mike was his name – called a halt to the music and announced that all eight of them were here for a special occasion: my birthday! And that, as a special surprise, I could choose any one of them to fuck me! He put up a hand to stop the cheers that were sounding all around me and said that, if necessary, they would each and every one of them fuck me, one after the other, if that was what I fancied for my birthday present.

I'd had enough champagne not to be in the slightest bit embarrassed, and I went up onto the stage, took the microphone from Mike's hand and gave him a big wet kiss. I then thanked the girls for their present. And then I announced that the only way that I – or anyone else – was going to be able to choose from this band of fanciable hunks was for them to get their knickers off!

At which point the band struck up 'The Stripper', and the eight men took down their posing pouches, revealing eight rapidly stiffening rock-hard erections. 'Come along, girls,' I shouted at my friends. 'Come and get it!' They all made a dash for the stage.

By this time I was, I admit, modestly drunk. Well. A girl needs a few drinks on her birthday! I took hold of the nearest cock, which grew yet huger in my hand as I fondled it, and I said to myself, *Babs, girl, this will do you for now. Very nicely.*

And so it did. I had it in my mouth, up my pussy, was eaten out by its owner, and then I fucked it again. I was surrounded by the incredibly erotic sights and sounds of eight men and eight women fucking the bejesus out of each other. The band seemed to have gone off for a well-earned rest, but the chorus boys were earning their money in spectacular fashion.

A couple of hours later, I'd been fucked by each of the eight men. So too, I believe, had all the other girls. Whatever the score, we were fucked to a standstill. I finally scouted around the floor, searching among the slurry of abandoned knickers and skirts, blouses and dresses for anything that looked like mine.

I left to a round of applause (probably undeserved) from the girls and in the company of Mike, who kept mumbling that he had to do it again, even if it was the last thing he did. I'm happy to be able to report that it wasn't. Huddersfield will never seem the same again. Thank you, girls. And boys. It was a memorable birthday.

B.M. Huddersfield, South Yorkshire.

It sounds like a splendid rendering of Many Happy Returns!

HELP!

Please help me. I'm seventeen and have fallen in love for the first time. My girlfriend Paula is eighteen. We haven't had sex of any kind yet, and as far as I'm concerned I'm not especially in a hurry. We do, after all, have all the time in the world! But my girlfriend seems to want me to 'do it' with her. We have done a certain amount of 'If you'll show me yours, I'll show you mine' sort of games, which I thought would be interesting. But I think there's maybe something seriously wrong with my girlfriend. The thing that she's got between her legs looks more like a wound, or a sore place, than anything that is supposed to give a man pleasure. Do all girls' pussies look like this? If so, why are they so ugly? My girlfriend wants me to kiss her there, and she keeps on at me about it. Frankly, I'd rather kiss my dog. Is there something wrong with me? Am I homosexual? Please help me.

J.S. Bromley, Kent.

No, friend, there's nothing wrong with either of you. Beauty, as they say, is in the eye of the beholder. And familiarity . . . We guarantee that, pretty soon, you'll learn to love that which you find just a little bit off-putting at the moment. Since you write to us, you must read our magazine. The pictures of the girls should answer any questions that you may have. Variety, as you can see, is the spice of life. And no, we don't think you're homosexual. Neither, obviously, does your girlfriend.

RUNNING A TIGHT SHIP

I read many letters in your columns concerning the erotic excitement of stockings, as opposed to tights, and the sensual appeal of that titillating area of flesh between stocking top and knickers. Not forgetting, of course, the essential suspender belt, and the suspenders themselves. But I have yet to read a letter from anyone who, as I do, infinitely prefers the erotic appeal of tights as opposed to stockings. Surely I am not alone in this mild fetish?

Tights come in such a variety of lust-inducing forms. My particular pleasure is to see a woman, clad only in a pair of black crotchless tights, with her feet tucked up on a chair level with her bottom and her legs apart, proudly displaying her vulva and her entire vaginal, pubic and anal region through the appropriate hole in her tights. To then fuck her, doggy fashion, through this entrance, and to be able to admire her taut haunches, stretching the nylon of the tights across them, is complete heaven.

Another aspect of crotchless tights that appeals strongly to me is the chance they offer to watch a woman, sitting in a similar position to that already described, bringing herself off with her fingers through this handy gap.

And, of course, crotchless tights allow immediate access to that most private of places (assuming – reasonably, I think – the absence of knickers) in all kinds of circumstances. A hand can be slipped up underneath a skirt and instantly be welcomed into that warm, wet delight between one's companion's legs in, say, the cinema. Or beneath the table in a restaurant. On a bus, or a train. In a telephone booth, even. The possibilities are limitless.

But the real attraction isn't so much the instant access: it is the lascivious appearance of the garments, if I may call them that. Ladders in tights can be strongly erotic, depending upon where they are situated. And cutting one's way (carefully!) through a pair of ordinary tights, with a pair of blunt-ended scissors, to reach a desired objective, is an enormously erection-producing activity, if ever I knew one.

I find that coloured tights can make a welcome change from the usual run of black tights. Navy blue is a good colour for schoolgirl fantasists. Grey works wonders for visions of naughty nurses. Red, for me, conjures up images of ballet dancers, while white I always find reminiscent of nuns. Brown is for teachers, of course, while yellow puts me in mind of the kind of girls who leave their cards in telephone boxes.

Then there are the kind of tights that are, for want of a better description, constructed rather like a pair of stockings, with their own built-in suspender belt. These have the advantage of leaving the wearer's bottom bare, for those who are into spanking, flagellation and the like. Or just plain old-fashioned buggery.

But normal tights can also be tailored to this kind of fun, simply by cutting a large hole out of the seat of them, allowing the wearer's bottom to hang out in the most lasciviously appealing manner. How about a photographic feature illustrating just *some* of the delights of wearing tights?

A. McN. Glasgow, Scotland.

You've got yourself into something of a tight corner there, haven't you? We'll pass on your request to our art editor.

NURSING A GRIEVANCE

I was recently in hospital for a minor operation and, once the initial pain had diminished, I began to enjoy the almost intimate relationship that develops between nurses and their patients.

There is something rather pleasant about having an attractive young woman looking after one's every need, from feeding to inserting one's cock into the inevitable urine bottle and holding it while one pees. (The operation was on both my hands.) But, despite what you might think, I quickly discovered that it's virtually impossible to get a hard-on while urinating.

Overall, my most outstanding memory, sadly, is that of constant disappointment. Yes, I've read all those stories too, but not once did a single one of all those lovely ladies offer me a slow wank to relieve my growing frustration. Not a one of them attempted a quick blow job while giving me a blanket bath, nor did any of them creep into bed with me after lights out and gently fuck me to sleep. I guess this is why people tell me that you get looked after better in private hospitals.

But if nurses don't see the application of sexual relief of one kind or another as part of their responsibilities to their patients, then someone should stop them wearing those unbelievably sexy uniforms. Those short, crisply ironed dresses, with their starched little aprons. Those sexy black stockings. Those delightfully frilly little caps. They're all designed to titillate. Put more plainly, nurses aren't angels of mercy. They're prickteasers. But I love them all.

A.C. Camberwell, South London

Sounds like a positive lack of things that go bonk in the night.

HAND TO MOUTH

My latest girlfriend is a real lulu. She's pretty, sexy, constantly horny, and can't wait to drop her knickers each day when she gets home from work. She is also a magical cook, but that's another story.

Despite all this praise, I have one serious complaint. She loves to fuck, but she won't suck my cock. Nor does she allow me to suck her pussy. She says that the thought of oral sex disgusts her. The idea, she says, of sucking something that was made for pissing through is revolting. She won't even try, to see if she might change her mind when she has actually experienced it.

I've done all the obvious things, like suggesting that we start a gentle session of oral sex with a shared bath, during which we both wash each other's private parts, thus ensuring that nothing tastes nasty. She won't even allow me to suck her, even when I tell her that this is as much for my pleasure as for hers, and that it doesn't assume that I will expect her to do the same for me. It's like saying you shouldn't drink water because fish fuck in it.

In every other way, she's as randy as all get out, and she'll fuck morning, noon, and night. Maybe if you'll print something to the effect that cunnilingus and fellatio are considered by most people to be not only normal sexual activities but also highly enjoyable ones, perhaps she'll accept it from you and allow me to show her the delights of muff diving. (I ought to sign this Frustrated, Tunbridge Wells).

H.G. Southend, Essex.

Don't despair. There are a lot of men out there who would gladly change places with you, oral sex or no oral sex. Having said that, we also hear what you're saying. Yes, we think oral sex is very normal. Most people do. But if your lady is one of those few who do not, then that's her privilege. If she can't – or doesn't want to – change her mind, and you feel that *strongly about it, maybe you should change your girlfriend.*

PLAYTHING

As a woman I think I'm possibly sexier than most. I adore all kinds of sex. There isn't anything that I won't do for – or have done to me by – someone whom I love. But I do have one tiny little kink. At least, that's how I see it. Though my most recent man seems to take positive umbrage at it. For reasons that I don't understand, he seems to see my kink as a personal insult. It demeans him, he tells me. I don't think it does. If I tell you about it, perhaps you'll give me *your* opinion? Here goes.

Like I say, I'm dead sexy. I love it. Any way. But before I begin, I like to strip off (I'm something of an exhibitionist) and play with myself before I start to have any kind of sex with my partner.

This is not a new thing, by the way. It's something I've enjoyed doing ever since I was old enough. I like to massage my breasts, twirl my nipples, rub my body all over and, yes – of course – I like to finish off by playing with my pussy. Until I come. Call it what you like – frigging, wanking, tossing myself off, masturbating. Whatever. I enjoy it, and I enjoy doing it in front of a man. It gets me off in more ways than one. I guarantee that I'm a better fuck after I've played with my pussy than I am if I haven't.

When I've done it, I'm wet, willing and *very* able! And up until now, all the men – without exception – have found my little exhibition a tremendous turn-on, and in the past it has, without fail, got them as randy as hell and raring to go.

This new chap says that if I respected his masculinity I would get my sexual satisfaction from getting fucked by him. Not by playing with myself. What do you think?

G.J-Y. Eccles, Lancs.

We think he sounds like a very dull fellow indeed. We think you're wasting your time. And your talent.

THREE IN A BED

I was once fortunate enough to have a long-lasting relationship with a bisexual girl. After we had got to know each other really well, she began to discuss her sexual relationships with other women with me.

Largely, because I was never critical of these affairs, she slowly came to trust me, and eventually she began to share her girlfriends with me. I have to assume that she discussed these arrangements with them before bringing them home, and presumably she only brought me the ones who were agreeable in the first place. Whatever the arrangement, I have to tell you that period was the most exciting of my entire life.

The first time that this happened to me is imprinted upon my memory for ever. Jane – that was my steady girlfriend – was nineteen. She was a lovely, long-legged blonde, with a terrific figure. She also was seriously into sex. Even more so than I thought, as I was about to find out.

That first evening, she brought home a real stunner. A redhead whom she introduced to me as Susan. I put out my hand to shake hands. Susan took it, pulled me to her, put her arms around me and kissed me, with her tongue feeling as if it was halfway down my throat. 'We may as well begin as we mean to go on,' she said, smiling at my surprise. 'Janie says you're a great fuck. Now that I've seen you, I'm looking forward to it.'

I poured drinks, and then we sat down to an enjoyable dinner at which we drank a couple of bottles of good wine between the three of us. I remember the conversation well. 'Tell me, Tony, are you a tit man?' Susan asked me. 'Do you like big tits? Or pretty tits?'

'I think I'm an everything man,' I said, laughing. 'But yes, I like pretty tits. Who doesn't?'

'Janie is very much a tit girl,' said Susan. 'She loves to suck my tits. Don't you, darling? But you needn't be jealous, sweetheart,' Susan said to me. 'While Janie sucks my tits, you can suck my pussy. How about that?'

'That sounds tremendous,' I said, trying to make my erection more comfortable without letting Susan see what I was doing. But I had no chance.

'Oooh, look, Janie,' she cried, reaching out under the table and taking hold of my swollen cock in her hand, through my trousers. 'Tony's got a hard-on already, and we haven't even taken our clothes off yet. Is that a good sign?' She squeezed my cock. 'It certainly *feels* like a good sign,' she said. 'I love men with big cocks. Cocks that stretch my pussy. God, my pussy's dribbling already.' She giggled. 'Naughty pussy,' she said. 'Do you like naughty pussies, Tony? Mine's *very* naughty.'

'I love them,' I said, joining in the laughter. We finished our meal in no time at all, and Susie (as I was now calling her) stood up and peeled off her blouse and skirt to reveal herself naked apart from stockings and a pair of seriously tarty knickers. Black, lacy, crotchless ones, with tiny red bows. I could see her fluffy red pubic hair between her thighs.

'I put these on specially for you, Tony, darling,' she said, as the three of us made our way through to the bedroom, Jane and I shedding clothes as we went. 'Not forgetting the stockings,' said Susie. 'Do you like them?' They were sheer black self-supporting stockings, with lacy tops. They and the knickers, and the strip of firm, tanned flesh between the two, were making it difficult for me to walk. Susie laughed.

'The sooner you get out of those trousers, the better, darling.' she said. 'Here, let me help you.' She knelt down in front of me, and pulled down my trousers and my underpants together. My cock sprang up and out and almost whacked Susie in the face.

'My, my,' she said. She took hold of it lovingly and gave it a slow – an almost painfully slow – wank. 'Now that's what a girl can call a cock.' She then took the tip of it into her mouth and sucked. 'Mmmm,' she mumbled, over a mouthful of cock. She went on sucking, and I felt my ejaculation gathering.

'Oh, come on, Susie,' said Jane. 'Not now. Wait until we're all ready, will you?'

Susie took me out of her mouth. To my regret. She grinned up at me, then stood up and said, 'Sorry, Janie. I just got carried away.'

'Dirty cow,' Janie said, grinning back at her. 'Show her a cock, and she's anybody's.'

'True,' said Susie. 'But I've never pretended any differently, now have I?'

'You have not,' Jane agreed. Susie looked down at her knickers, and then across at me. 'Shall I keep these on, then?' she asked.

'If you're asking me, sweetheart, then no. Thank you. But let me take them off. OK?'

'Sure, she said, standing there and waiting for me. I went over to her and knelt in front of her. I put a hand each side of her waist and pulled her knickers down her legs. I could see the wetness trickling down her thighs, and I could smell the acrid scent of hot, wet, female sex. I leaned forward, my lips between her legs, and I licked her sex. Slowly.

She tasted heavenly. 'Oh God, how lovely,' she said. 'Here's a man who likes to suck pussy.'

'I told you,' said Jane. 'He takes the prize for cunt-lapping in my book.'

'What, better than me?' said Susie, pouting.

'Well, no,' agreed Jane. 'No one sucks pussy better than you. But he's the best *man* I've come across.'

'Then he can come across me any time he likes,' Susie said, laughing again. She reached down and pressed my head into her snatch, and for a wonderful moment or two my nose was buried in wet cunt.

Jane climbed up onto our king-size bed. 'Come along, then, darlings,' she said. 'Jane's ready for you now.' Susie and I joined her immediately. Susie lay beside Jane and, spreading her legs widely, at the same time she began to suckle hungrily on Jane's right breast.

I took her spread legs as an invitation and lay on my stomach with my head between her thighs. Then I began to eat her pussy. She tasted, not of sugar and spice, but of overripe tropical fruit, with perhaps just a *zest* of anchovy. Delicious. She had enormous, fleshy cunt lips. I used my fingers to spread them: they were like the heavy petals of exotic jungle flowers. Inside she was pink and wet, shading down to a kind of purply brown.

I sucked, and tongued, and licked. Susie began to wriggle her hips as I sucked her, and I felt for her clitoris with my tongue. When I found it, it was fully erect, like a tiny penis. I concentrated my efforts upon it, and Susie began to moan with pleasure. She stopped sucking Jane's nipple. 'Oh, fuck,' she said. 'I'm going to come now. Tony's sucking me, and making me come. I'm coming. *I'm coming.* Now. I'm coming NOW. Ooooh, God. NOWWWWW . . .' She was writhing about on the bed like a mad woman.

Jane grinned at me. 'I think she's coming,' she said. 'She'll be all right in a minute. She's always like this.'

We waited, patiently, and Susie slowly recovered from her orgasmic fervour. She lay on her back, breathing heavily. 'Ooooh, lovely,' she said. 'That was terrific, Tony. Thanks. I owe you.' And then, suddenly, she was totally together again and back with us.

She sat up and looked at me and then at Jane. She turned to Jane. 'Shall we do some naughty lezzie stuff, to give Tony the hots?' she asked. 'If you'd like to,' said Jane. 'Hang on, and I'll go and get the dildoes.'

I didn't know Jane had any dildoes. She'd never mentioned them. But then, why should she? She came back into the bedroom a couple of minutes later, carrying one of those bags you see sports people carrying their gear around in. She put it down on the bed and unzipped it. It was full, literally, of a selection of dildoes and vibrators. She pulled out a vicious-looking strap-on dildo and held it up for Susie.

'Shall I fuck you with this?' she asked. Susie looked at it, and licked her lips. 'Ooooh, yes, please,' she said. 'Up my arse. That should bring tears to my eyes. And while you're doing that, I'll fuck Tony with my pussy. That should give him a serious case of the hots.'

She looked at me, her eyes laughing. 'What do you say, kid? Shall we give it a whirl? I bet you've never been fucked by a girl who's being fucked in the arse by another girl, with a great big dildo. Now have you?'

I had to admit that no, I hadn't. But I couldn't wait to begin. Jane began to strap on the obscene device, and Susie went over to help her. They finally got the straps adjusted to Jane's comfort. I couldn't help but find the sight of Jane with this enormous erect pink rubber cock standing out in front of her strangely erotic.

'You'd better grease up well, darling,' said Jane to Susie. 'Otherwise I might hurt you.' Susie scrabbled around in the bag, and came up with a tube of K-Y jelly. She handed it to me.

'*You* grease me up, darling,' she said. 'It'll be so much more fun for me than if I do it myself. You might even enjoy doing it,' she said, grinning again. 'You never know.' She knelt down on the bed on all fours, and looked at me over her shoulder.

I looked at her tiny brown puckered little anus, and felt my cock begin to throb with lust. I squeezed out a big glob of the lubricant and started to grease Susie's arsehole. It was so tight around my finger when I first inserted it that I almost came on the spot. I shut my eyes, and tried not to think about forcing my prick up between those luscious full arse cheeks.

I made it last as long as I could, but finally Jane announced that she thought that Susie was probably sufficiently well greased. 'OK, baby. Here we go,' said Susie. She looked at me. 'You lie on your back,' she instructed. 'And then I'll get on top of you. While we fuck, Jane can give it to me up my arse.'

I did as I was told, and Susie clambered on top of me. She took my rampant prick in her hand and fed it into her waiting, hot, wet cunt. She felt wonderful. Tight as arseholes, as they say. She started performing sex on my mouth with hers. It was just about the sexiest thing that I have ever had done to me. She raped my mouth with hers. I loved it.

At that moment, Jane climbed up behind her, and rammed the dildo up Susie's arse. 'Oh, Jesus,' said Susie, lifting her mouth up off mine.

And don't forget that she was fucking me silly whilst all this was going on. 'Oh, God. Oh, fuck,' she groaned. 'Oh, shit. I love it up my arse. You can fuck me up my arse later, Tony darling,' she promised. Suddenly I could feel the grossness of the huge rubber prick through the thin wall of skin separating Susie's rectal passage from her cunt. I could actually feel, with my cock, Jane fucking Susie's arsehole.

Susie started humping and wriggling like a jack-in-the-box. 'Oh, yes,' she cried. 'Oh, God. I'm coming again.' And we went through the whole choral rigmarole of Susie getting her rocks off, being fucked in two places at once. *Fuck this*, I thought to myself, and I abandoned any thought of timing my ejaculation to coincide with one of Susie's orgasms.

I grabbed hold of her buttocks, well separated by Jane's assault up her anus, and pumped my semen straight up into her cunt. Delightful. I enjoyed every moment of it. Why had I wasted so much of my life believing (as I had) that fucking a pretty girl was what real life was all about when here I was, discovering that fucking *two* pretty girls was actually what real life was all about? And lovely lesbian girls, at that.

I wondered, for a moment, what Jane was getting out of this. That dildo, you'll remember, wasn't double-ended. Poor old Jane wasn't getting fucked at all. Anywhere. By anyone. *We'll have to put that right*, I thought. *Poor cow. All she's had, so far, is one tit nibbled and since then she's been working her arse off, fucking Susie up* her *arse*. That's not what I would call fair shares.

But I'd just come, and now Susie was coming again. As loudly and as violently as before. She wriggled and bounced, and thoroughly enjoyed herself. And then, again unexpectedly, it was all over. 'Oh, baby,' Susie said. 'Am I fucked. Truly fucked. Thanks, chaps.'

'Think nothing of it,' said Jane. I could see that, in desperation, her hand had just slipped down to between her legs, and she was frigging herself. She was sadly, and obviously, in need of instant sexual relief.

'Hey, come on, Susie,' I urged. 'Do something nice for our Jane. Something *dirty* and nice. It's not fair that all she's getting, right now, is a quick wank. You and me, we've had lots of fun. Make some fun for Jane. Now. OK?'

'Oh, Jane, darling. I'm so sorry,' said Susie. She leaned over and looked for something in the bag of penile goodies. 'Ah ha,' she said, obviously having found what she was looking for. Her hand emerged from the bag, grasping a huge vibrator. It was penis-shaped, but grossly over-large. 'So you can help,' Susie said to me. 'Pull Jane's pussy open for me.'

I did as I was told, and gently pulled Jane's outer labia apart, revealing her pussy, dribbling copiously with her love juices. 'Hmmmm,' said Susie. 'One very wet pussy. Well, that's OK. This will make her even wetter.'

She looked at me but didn't say anything. After a moment or two of this silent stare, she said, 'Do I really have to tell you to lick it clean?' She only had to say it once.

I sucked and licked with enthusiasm, savouring the (to me) well-known – and well-loved – flavour of Jane's love juices. I looked up at Susie, my lips wet and sticky with Jane's vaginal effluent. 'Oh, baby,' she said, and she leaned down and kissed me. Hard. She licked Jane's juices off my mouth. 'Mmmmm,' she said. 'Delicious. But that's not what we're here for, right now.'

She took the vibrator in her right hand and, with me still holding Jane's pussy lips apart, she inserted the white plastic penile-shaped weapon between them. She thrust in, hard. Jane moaned with pleasure, and wriggled her hips, closing her legs over the cock-shaped vibrator. Susie started to thrust in and out.

'Oh, yes,' Jane whispered. 'Switch it on. Fuck me with it. Make me come. Give it to me up my cunt. Now. Please. Fuck me, Susie. Fuck my wet cunt.' Susie did as she was told and switched the vibrator on at what sounded like its lowest speed. It buzzed, quietly, between Jane's legs.

I thought of what it was doing to her, and my cock started to stiffen again. I wished that it was my prick up her pussy, rather than the vibrator. But they *had* promised to show me naughty lezzie things, and these were certainly naughty lezzie things that they were doing to each other. Nice, *dirty* lezzie things.

I wondered, for a moment, whether they preferred doing lezzie things to each other, or if they actually liked hard male cock from time to time. Then I decided that I didn't actually care which they preferred so long as I could watch.

Susie was manipulating the buzzing vibrator between Jane's legs as if her life depended upon it. She was stroking Jane's inner labia and sliding the tip of the cock substitute down into Jane's open cunt, massaging her clitoris with it. Jane began to groan with ecstasy. She reached up, pulled Susie's face down to hers and began to kiss her in the most virulently sexual way that I think I've ever seen.

Up until then, I had never seen a woman kiss another woman in the way that a man will kiss a woman that he is actually fucking while he kisses her. I found it tremendously sexually exciting. Jane was getting very turned on by being fucked by the vibrator as manipulated by Susie.

'Oh God, Susie,' she said, breathlessly. 'Sit on my face while you fuck me. Let me suck your pussy while you're doing those things to my cunt. Let me suck you. Please. I want to make you come while I come. Kneel over my mouth, and let me lick your pussy. Come on, baby. Give me your wet cunt.'

Susie didn't say anything but, keeping the vibrator performing its welcome fuck job on Jane's receptive pussy, she changed her position and knelt over Jane's face. She then lowered herself down onto Jane's mouth. Jane began to eat her pussy, hungrily, while Susie ground her vagina into Jane's waiting, willing mouth.

I could see Jane's tongue darting in and out of Susie's pussy and hear the noises that the two girls were making as – in their different ways – each girl did her best to bring her girlfriend to orgasm. I was aware of the open orifices that weren't being used by the two girls, and wondered what they might think if I were to start to fuck one or other of them in these untended holes. Susie's tight arsehole was available. As was Jane's. Susie's mouth, right now, was free. Jane's mouth was occupied, sucking Susie's pussy. Jane's pussy was filled with the vibrator wielded by Susie. But Jane, I supposed, had hands available to toss me off, if that was one of her preferences.

Eventually, I was saved from having to take a decision by the fact that Jane began a whole long concentrated series of orgasms, brought to fruition by Susie's expert adminstration of the giant vibrator. This finally left the two of them gasping for breath, both giggling helplessly and completely relaxed. I assumed that Jane had also achieved orgasm, at the same time as her friend.

'OK, girls,' I said. 'So which one of you is going to fuck me?' 'I am,' they both said, together, and they then collapsed again, laughing and clutching each other and falling about on the bed.

After they had got themselves more or less together again, Jane said, 'No, go on, Susie. This is what you came for. You have him first. I've had him before. I want you to have him. Take him any way you want him. He's all yours.' What a lovely girl! What man could feel more benevolently offered by his girlfriend to her girlfriend?

'Take me, darling,' I said to Susie. 'I'm all yours. How would you like me?' I was thinking that I had already sucked her pussy, had my cock in her mouth – albeit rather briefly – been fucked by her, and been promised (but had not yet achieved) anal sex with her. She'd promised me that I could fuck her up her arsehole while Jane was shagging her anally with that huge dildo. Remember? I most certainly did. But I wasn't hung up about it. There was going to be plenty of time for us all to enjoy doing absolutely everything that any of us had ever wanted to do.

Susie finally answered my question. 'You choose, darling,' she said. 'I've been having rather a good time so far. I'm feeling decidedly generous. What would you like me to do to you? For you? Anything. Just name it.'

I looked at her gorgeous body. Her lovely auburn hair. Those fantastic tits. Her unbelievably hairy minge. I wanted to do everything to her, all at once. I wanted to fuck her mouth, her cunt, her arse, her hand. Her hand? Now there was a thought. Just imagine being slowly tossed off by that beautiful vision. Jesus. Done.

'How would you like to give me a wank, Susie?' I asked her. 'A long, slow, really dirty wank. With you talking dirty to me whilst you do it. And making it last as long as you can possibly drag it out. I'd love that.'

'Oh, wow,' she said. 'What fun. I haven't given anyone a really dirty wank for longer than I can remember. Yeah, sure. Why not? I'd enjoy that.' She looked at Jane. 'Is that OK with you, Jane darling?' she asked.

'It most certainly is,' said Jane. 'Whatever turns you both on. Just as long as I can watch you both.'

'Our pleasure,' Susie told her. 'Are you ready, sweetheart?' she asked, looking at me.

'Never readier,' I told her.

'Then come and lie down beside me, here on the bed,' she said.

I did just that. She made herself comfortable alongside me, lying back on her left elbow, and she took my cock carefully in her right hand. She began to move my foreskin up and down, lazily. There was no urgency in her manipulation. My cock sprang to attention.

'One of the things that you learn early in life,' Susie said, 'when you are a girl, is that men love to be tossed off. Depending upon the circumstances, there are times, I believe, when most men would prefer to be jacked off, rather than have to bother to get up off their backsides and fuck someone. Don't misunderstand me,' she said. 'I'm not knocking it. It's a delightful way to achieve ejaculation. And the laziest. And there's nothing wrong with that,' she said, quickly. 'It's like being sucked off, if you're a woman. I'm not convinced that women enjoy men wanking them off anything like as much as men enjoy being wanked. But women love to be sucked off. As, of course, do men,' she added. She laughed. 'Anyway, by the time you get into your late twenties, say, most girls can also give a very experienced hand job. Just like I'm going to give you now. And, I have to tell you, I love doing it. Especially because you want me to talk dirty to you. So here we go.

'I love to feel your cock growing harder and stiffer in my hand as I begin to wank you. I love the feeling of being in control of your ejaculation. As I go on wanking you, I can feel exactly when you're going to come, and I can make you come instantly, if I want to, or I can stretch it out seemingly for ever.' (*Please God*, I thought to myself). 'I love the feel of your cock throbbing as I jack you off. It always reminds me of that silly song. You know the one? "When the red, red robin goes bob, bob, bobbin' along."' She giggled. 'I guess you could call this your cock robin. And of course the other thing I like is that what I'm doing makes my pussy wet. My cunt wet. I love to say "cunt". Men usually get very excited when girls say "cunt". Do you get excited when I say "cunt"?' she asked.

I nodded. 'Yes,' I said. I almost choked from sheer sexual excitement. "Cunt" is such a lovely *dirty* word. Pussy is prissy. Cunt is dead dirty. 'Suck my cunt' is my favourite female demand. I love cunt. I love to hear them say it. And I love to suck it.

All the time Susie was talking dirty to me, she was masturbating my cock with her agile fingers in lovely long, sensual strokes. She leaned down and licked my lips. She didn't kiss me. She *licked* me. 'Are you enjoying me tossing you off?' she asked.

'Yes,' I said, slightly nervously. I wondered what was coming next.

'I love doing it,' she said. 'And I love it when you come, all over my hand. I think I shall know when you're going to come, but do me a favour and tell me, will you?'

'Sure,' I told her. 'No problem.'

'Great,' she said, 'and then I can catch it all in my mouth and swallow it. Swallow your hot spunk.' She was quiet for a moment or two, but she continued to wank me, carefully, attentively, and very, *very* expertly. If she could have been employed as a senior wanker, she would have been on a hundred and fifty thousand a year. She knew what every tiny millimetre of a man's cock did, and how she could bring about the most sensational feelings as she slowly brought him to the point of ejaculation.

'Would you like me to massage your prostate?' she suddenly asked me. I hadn't a clue. Never having had my prostate massaged, I didn't know whether I wanted her to or not.

So I said so. 'I don't know,' I told her. 'It's not anything that I've ever had done to me.'

'Oh, you'll love it,' she said. 'It's what male gays do when they fuck each other. What they're doing is massaging each other's prostates with their erect cocks.'

'Well, I'm not fucking gay, for a start,' I told her.

'Of course you're not, darling,' she said. 'I know that. But just lie back and think of England, and I'll show you what I mean.'

There didn't seem much chance of saying that I didn't want her to so I lay back, as instructed. She put her other hand down between my legs, and then I felt her begin to insinuate a finger into my rectum.

What happened next is difficult to describe, except to say that I barely had the time – remembering her request – to say, 'Jesus . . . I'm coming. NOW,' before I did exactly that. It was just about the most exciting, most needed, most anticipated ejaculation of my entire life. I'm not *really* serious, but my instant reaction was, if that's the sort of thing that you enjoy by being gay then, brothers, here I come.

What I now know I meant, looking back, was, Susie baby, whatever you did to me then, you can do to me again. Any time you like. That for sure doesn't make me gay. Not in my book, anyway.

Since that time, Jane and Susie and me have settled down happily into the most exciting, most rewarding three-way sexual relationship that it has ever been my privilege to enjoy. Long may it last.

A.F. Mousehole, Cornwall.

All we can say is that, as far as you're concerned, three's obviously company. We envy you. Enjoy.

VESTWARD HO!

I know that, to an extent, I'm something of a fetishist, in that I'm obsessed by lingerie. But I also know that it's the women wearing the lingerie, not just the lingerie itself, that attracts me. Or maybe it's the combination of both.

Whenever I see a picture in a woman's magazine, or in the fashion section of a Sunday newspaper, of a woman wearing one of those one-piece things, I get an instant hard-on. The names for the garment seem to vary: teddies, bodies, camibriefs. But the shape remains the same. Perhaps they're best described as vest-and-knickers, produced all in one piece, with a press-stud crotch fastening. They come in silk, nylon, wool, and various synthetic mixtures. All include the magical words 'cotton-lined gusset'. I simply find these one-piece outfits the sexiest form of lingerie made. They are so much more exciting to me than the usual rather old-fashioned bra-and-panties outfits that other men seem to rave about.

It's that wonderful line, stretching all the way down from the wearer's neckline with those delightfully thin little shoulder straps, down past her full breasts, over her flat stomach, and down again, past her hips, in unbroken symmetry, with those high-cut sides, and then all the way down to her moulded, pouting crotch.

And as to that line as seen from the rear view, with that fantastic shape taking in the women's trim shoulders, their slim waists, their gorgeously full bottoms, and their naked thighs . . . Well! It's almost all too much.

My fantasy is to have a house full of gorgeous women, all of whom are dressed in nothing but variations of these wonderful garments. They wander about the place, and wherever they go I'm able to feel them. *Feel* them in that wonderful old-fashioned way that we used to talk excitedly about as schoolboys. Put my hands between their legs, and feel their soft pussies, through those exciting press-stud crotch fastenings. Undo those fastenings, if I so wish, and slip my fingers into waiting tight wet receptive pussies. Feel those generous breasts. Tear down those low-cut tops and expose those breasts, naked to my fingers, my lips, my mouth.

Slowly pull the garments down from their very tops, exposing breasts, then stomachs, belly-buttons, then thighs, then hairy (or perhaps shaven) cunts. Put my fingers wherever I want. Part legs, and thrust my rigid cock into each wet gash. Spurt sticky semen into slippery, strongly-scented sex-holes.

I fantasize about selecting one of these women, one who attracts me strongly, sexually, and taking her into my bedroom. I feel her between her legs, and she gets wet as I stroke her there. I undo her press-stud fastenings, and slip two fingers into her. She moans, and, pulling away from me, she strips off the teddy. She stands there for a moment, in all her naked sensuality, and then she takes a step forward and holds the moist, cotton-lined crotch of her teddy up to my nostrils.

I can smell the scent of her pussy, feel the dampness of the material against my skin. I inhale deeply, and my erection hardens. She feels it thrusting against her. She puts the garment into my hand and kneels down in front of me and, taking my prick in her hand, she envelops my frenum with her warm, wet mouth.

I put my hands down to her breasts and feel them. I'm so horny that I have no control, and I spurt, almost instantly, into her mouth. She sucks, strongly, and swallows, until she has sucked me dry. She looks up at me, licks her lips, and smiles at me. 'Are you going to fuck me now?' she asks.

I look down at her. She's attractive enough, but there are a dozen more outside whose bodies I haven't yet seen. Whose virgin orifices I haven't yet ejaculated into. 'No,' I say. 'Perhaps another time.' I drop the teddy on the floor beside her, and leave, to go in search of new flesh.

P.T. Waterford, Republic of Ireland.

Certainly the garments that you favour in your fantasies are suggestively aphrodisiac. We are strongly partial to them ourselves.

DOUBLE ENTENDRE

I've heard of men boasting of having bedded two women at the same time and, frankly, my immediate reaction on those occasions has always been to wonder what exactly two women can do that one woman on her own can't manage. After all, a man can only fuck one woman at a time. But now I have experienced this phenomenon for myself, I have to recommend it to the many men who, I am sure, and like me until recently, haven't yet enjoyed this experience.

I was in Birmingham for an exhibition, and I had met one of my clients up there. The day had gone well, it resulted in a considerable increase in my business with that particular customer, and I took him out to dinner at the end of the day. He lives reasonably locally, and by the time he left I felt like bed, rather than getting a late train back to London. So I booked into one of the city's better hotels and went into the bar for a nightcap or two. I got talking there to a couple of attractive, youngish women, who told me that they were both business women and that they too had been visiting the exhibition. It transpired that we were all in the same business – that of information technology – and we settled down to a session of drinking and business gossip.

When the bar closed at eleven, I discovered that the girls were both staying in the hotel. I invited them up to my room, and rang room service for more booze.

To cut a long story short, the two women became very frisky

indeed, and they virtually seduced me. Not that I resisted in any way! They told me, as they proceeded to strip me, that they always hunted as a pair. They enjoyed their sex as a couple sharing the same man, and they felt safer about having sex with people (like me, let's face it) whom they didn't really know that much about.

When they got down to stripping themselves, they were wearing some very exotic lingerie indeed. Not at all the kind of thing that I was accustomed to. Matching bras and knickers, in soft, see-through materials, with flowered patterns. Sexily decorative in the extreme. Not the universal practical Marks & Spencers-type white cotton bra and panties to which I am accustomed. What these two were wearing looked as if it cost an arm and a leg. And worth every penny. The girls, by the way, were Paula and Rosie. Paula was black-haired, Rosie blonde.

After they got me down to the buff, they both lay on my bed, in their bras and knicks, and opened their legs. 'Fucking, with us two, starts with sucking pussy,' announced Rosie. 'You can choose which of us you want to begin with. We're not jealous at all.'

'Well, let the dog see the rabbit, then,' Paula said. And so saying, she pulled the crotch of her knickers aside, exposing her hairy snatch. I could see the pink gash down the centre of it, and as far as I could see, it seemed to be shining wetly.

She had nice full cunt lips, and I could imagine how they would feel, sucking them into my mouth. But then Rosie did the same with her knicker crotch, and instead of the blonde – or, to be more accurate, dyed-blonde – snatch that I was anticipating, she revealed a beautifully smooth, completely bald, naughty shaven little pussy. She too had quite big sex lips. And no razor burn.

Thinking about it, I wanted to suck them both, and I said

so. 'No problem,' said Rosie. At which she and Paula stood up, divested themselves of their up-market knickers, and lay back on the bed again, side by side, their legs open, waiting for me to get at them.

I began with Paula, since I guessed (correctly, as it turned out: they told me so, later on) that most men, given the choice, always started with Rosie, simply for the novelty of sucking bald pussy. As a matter of fact, I rather fancy myself at cunnilingus. I love it. It's my favourite thing. My very first girlfriend taught me. Slowly, and carefully. She it was who persuaded me that any man who could give good head would never be short of a pretty woman. And she was right. I owe my successful sex life to her. I'd almost rather suck than fuck.

So having two such different pussies to pleasure was both a great treat, and a fantastic opportunity for me to show off my abilities. I'm pleased to be able to say that, after a little while, I had both the girls going, wriggling about on the bed, enjoying the orgasms that my hard-working tongue, mouth, lips and fingers were inducing.

'Jesus,' said Rosie, eventually. 'That's serious cunt-lapping. What are you? Are you married to a lesbian, or something?'

'I'll second that,' said Paula. 'For what he's been doing to my pussy, may the Lord make me truly thankful.'

'Amen,' said Rosie.

'Now let's show him that we're a couple of serious cock-suckers,' said Paula.

'Me first,' said Rosie. She began to demonstrate forthwith that she was no slouch at giving head either, and for a while I lay back, with the two girls pleasurably taking turns to suck my prick.

The real fun, though, was that while Rosie sucked at my manhood, Paula sat on my face. And vice versa. It's a highly recommended variation to boring old cocksucking. The smell and taste and feel of cunt while your throbbing cock is being tongued deep in some girl's hot, wet, expert mouth is a heavenly combination.

They knew exactly what they were doing and eventually Rosie said to me, 'I can feel your ejaculation gathering. Since we've both worked hard at getting you to this stage, it's only fair that you should shoot your spunk into both of our mouths. So, if you think you're ready, we're both now going to suck you off, together. OK?'

'OK,' I said. Weakly.

And they did exactly that. I don't know quite how they managed it, but certainly both of them suddenly had their soft, wet, all-encompassing luscious lips sucking away at my pulsating prick.

It was heaven. Paradise. Valhalla. Total ecstasy. And as my ejaculate rose up from my balls and spurted its seminal message into their waiting, thirsty mouths, Rosie earned my love for her for ever by taking the base of my spasming prick in her cool, experienced fingers and milking me into their two open mouths with such grace, such skill, such aplomb, the like of which I had never before experienced. When it was finally over, I wondered what could possibly be coming next. I didn't have long to wait.

'Now, naughty boy,' said Paula. 'What would you like now? Do you want to get down and dirty? Or do you want some kind of ethereal, almost religious sexual experience?'

My response was immediate. *Fuck religious sexual experiences*, I said to myself. What could she possibly mean? That the two of them were going to dress up as nuns? Or that they would bring in a vicar to fuck me anally? The hell with that.

'Down and dirty,' I said, firmly. 'The downer and dirtier, the better.'

And then, right at that particular moment, something broke inside me. I don't know what it was. Until that moment, I had been happy to go along with these two girls. It was free, and who was I to complain? But suddenly I wanted to be in charge. In control. Be the one who decided what was going to happen.

I took hold of Rosie by her shoulders, and said to Paula, who was still sitting on the edge of the bed, 'Get out of the way, darling.' She must have heard the steel in my voice, for she leapt off the bed quicker than you could say 'Move'. I eased Rosie up to that end of the bed, and taking her two arms, I placed her hands on the edge of the headboard so that she was leaning forward with her bottom slightly raised and facing towards me. I looked at Paula.

'Go get some cream of some sort,' I said. 'Something greasy. Anything to lubricate. I'm going to fuck Rosie up her tight little arse, and I don't want to tear her arsehole. Or my cock,' I added, as an afterthought.

'Oooh,' said Rosie. 'How lovely. I just love it up my arse.'

I must admit that I was surprised. I thought she might have burst into tears and said, 'No, no. Please, not that. Please, not there. Please, not up my poor little bottom.' And here she was saying, 'Oooh, I just love it up my arse.' Dirty cow. Well, that was where she was going to get it.

Just then Paula came back from the dressing table with a jar of cold cream in her hand. 'I guess this should do the trick,' she said, unscrewing the lid and holding the jar out to me.

'You do it for me, darling,' I told her. 'Grease Rosie's naughty little bottom for me. And then you can hold her anus open while I shove my huge swollen cock up it.'

'Oooh,' said Rosie again. I couldn't believe it. Paula busied herself rubbing cold cream into Rosie's arse. She was doing it so expertly that it obviously wasn't the first time that she had performed this labour of love for her best girlfriend.

She chattered on while she was thus occupied. 'I suppose it's going to end up like it always does,' she said, more to herself than to anyone else. 'Poor little Paula's going to end up playing with herself, while her friend Rosie gets fucked from arsehole to breakfast table. Particularly arsehole,' she said, looking at me over her shoulder. 'It's not fair. It just isn't bloody fair.' I ignored her. She stood back from Rosie. 'She's well greased now,' she said. 'I'd better grease your cock while I'm at it.' I didn't argue. Well, would you?

Paula did as thorough a job of greasing me as she had with Rosie. 'Right, then,' she said, when she had finished. 'I can see that *you're* ready. Are *you* ready, Rosie, love?'

'Not half,' said Rosie, wiggling her plump bottom. Paula put her fingers each side of Rosie's brown, puckered little arsehole, and prised it open. I took my cock in my hand, put the tip up against Rosie's opening, and pressed. Hard. My cock slid in with a plop. Rosie gasped and said, 'Oh, yes. Dear God,' and I was in business.

Rosie's rectal muscles held me tightly. She felt warm inside, and, naturally enough, greasy. I began to fuck her harder, and she said, 'Oh, yes' again, and thrust her bottom back strongly against me. Paula had let go of Rosie, once I was well inside Rosie's back passage, but she now put her fingers around my swollen prick and began to masturbate me as I plunged deeply in and out of Rosie's bottom. The carnally exciting combination of the tightness and arousing feel of the inside of Rosie's arse with the skilled, titillating manipulations of Paula's fingers soon had me spurting my seed up

Rosie's arse, at which she began to move her hips about, and shout.

'Oh, yes. I can feel your hot spunk. Oh, Jesus, yes. You're shooting your spunk up my bottom.' And much more in similar vein. As she shouted, she put her right hand between her legs and began to masturbate herself furiously until she too began to orgasm, at which point she shouted out, 'Oh, fuck. I'm coming. I'm coming now. I'm coming.'

We concluded our joyous raunchy little session more or less together. Paula had continued to jack me off until all my seed was completely spent, which pretty much coincided with Rosie's orgasmic conclusion, and the two of us collapsed back down onto the bed again. I came around eventually to find Paula lovingly washing my cock, and I showed my appreciation to her by first of all regaining my erection and then by taking her and fucking her, slowly, gently, and kindly, in acknowledgement of her earlier contributions to my sexual enjoyment.

I made certain that she achieved orgasm – which she did copiously – and that, at least for the time being, was the end of my first threesome.

We discovered, the following morning, that we all live in Central London, and we took the same train down together. I look forward to my next meeting with these two ladies with enthusiasm, as you can no doubt imagine. Rosie and I have made a pact to see that the next time Paula gets her fair share of sexual activity.

F.W.S. Kensington, London.

A pigeon pair, as our grandfathers used to say. What a very fortunate chap you are.

PEEPHOLE

Ever since I was a teenager and used to spy on my sister, I've always been intrigued by the idea of spying on women in their more intimate moments, unbeknownst to them at the time.

My room at home in those days was divided from that of my sister simply by a wall made of wooden planks, and it was a simple matter, one weekend when my sister was away, to drill a spyhole through the wood, hidden by a picture on my side, and carefully arranged so as not to be easily visible on my sister's side of the wall. As far as I know, she was never aware of it, for the many happy years that I used to watch her through it.

With the opportunities provided by this medium, I watched my sister through her development from a teenager to a fully mature young woman.

I watched her through her first bra, and continued to watch as her breasts developed to the point where she actually really did need one! And of course I watched as she developed her pubic hair. At first it was hardly visible. Fair, thin, and wispy. By the time she was twenty, it was thick, black, and luxuriant. And then – joy of joys – I masturbated on my side of the wooden wall as she masturbated herself on hers.

Over the years, I saw her use anything and everything to get herself off with, from her fingers to bottles to candles, to the memorable day when she bought her first vibrator.

In all this time, I only came close to being discovered once. It was the Saturday afternoon upon which – when both our parents were out – my sister decided to stick her vibrator up her arse, as at the same time she masturbated her pussy with her fingers. I was wanking so hard as I watched that I missed my footing on my bed (which I had to stand on to reach the spyhole) and fell onto the floor.

My sister stopped what she was doing and came through to my room to see what was the reason for the sudden noise. I had the sense to grab hold of a set of weights that I used in those days for weight training, and pretended that I had dropped the bar. I had hidden my stiff prick beneath a handy towel just before she opened my door. It was all right, of course, but it was close!

I probably know my sister's cunt as well as most men know their partner's pussy, apart from the obvious fact that I have only ever looked at it. I've never even touched it, leave aside fucked it. But I must, literally, have spent some hundreds of hours studying it. My sister has one of those large-lipped, overly well developed cunts, with labia rather like the ears of a Prince Charles' spaniel. I'm a bit of a small-cunt-lips man myself these days, but it used to drive me into frenzies of masturbatory activity to watch my sister playing with herself.

She would lie back on the bed, most afternoons, hike up her skirt, pull down her knickers, and slowly start to massage herself with the flat of her hand, all over her cunt. She would gradually increase the speed with which she did this, and often – although not always – she would do this with her right hand, whilst with her left hand she would pull and twist and tweak her nipples. First the one. Then the other. I was amazed at the size her nipples would grow to, under this painful-looking treatment. But it obviously did things for her.

It was easy to see, after a while, that this flat-handed massage made her pussy very wet. When (presumably) she decided that it was wet enough, she would insert two fingers up her fanny, and start to wank herself properly. (This was in the days before she had invested in a vibrator.) For a time she would simply thrust her fingers in and out, but after a while she would start to use just her middle finger, and then she would carefully search out her clitoris and, using just that one finger, she would rapidly bring herself to orgasm. In those days, she wouldn't take her knickers off but simply pull them down around her thighs. This meant that, when she had finished masturbating herself, she would eventually pull her knickers up again, thus ensuring that her knicker-crotch was well moistened with the copious juices now flowing from her well-wanked pussy.

Knowing that at the end of the day, when she retired to bed, she would abandon the day's grubby knickers in the laundry basket in the communal bathroom, I would time my visits very carefully. Almost to the minute after she had abandoned them, I would wank myself practically to death as I sniffed the fantastic aroma from her often still moist knickers, purloined from the dirty linen basket for this very special purpose. I would not only inhale the lascivious, cock-raising odour of her cunt deeply into my nostrils, but I would slowly and meticulously lick the stained gusset of her knickers, running my tongue slowly up and down the soiled cotton, savouring not only the smell but the taste of her strongly scented, lubricious vaginal effluent.

I grew up loving the smell of my sister's cunt as I sat on the lavatory seat in the bathroom, pulling my plonker with such erotic delight. Looking back, it's a wonder to me now that I didn't pull it off. And while I wouldn't tell too many people about this next particularly disgusting childhood perversion, I must now admit, just between you and me, that in those days, when I knew my sister was out of the house for some time, I would carefully sneak into her bedroom, quietly pull out the drawer in which I knew she kept her vibrator – carefully hidden beneath a delightful pile of freshly laundered knickers – and, taking it out of the drawer, I would sneak it back to my bedroom next door, and wank myself silly whilst I sucked and licked it, remembering with swollen prick how I had last seen it.

So you can see from the above that I have a big thing about observing girls in what they believe to be their completely private, most intimate moments. You will therefore understand when I tell you that my most erotic fantasies centre around this naughty concept.

I imagine myself the owner of a block of flats in the West End of London, letting exclusively to the well-off single daughters of rich and hopefully upper-class parents. I interview all applicants, so I am able to select only those whom I find sexually attractive. The flats have been built to my own specification, which means that I have video cameras installed in each room of every flat, completely hidden from view, but also situated so that I am able to observe every corner of every room. I can zoom in for seriously close close-ups.

In my control room – a special room in my own apartment in the block – I can manoeuvre each and every camera, bringing anything that I wish into immediate focus. It's a terrific turn-on. You should try it some time. These girls are delightful. Pretty, sexy, and single. And raring to go. And *dirty*. Seriously down and dirty. They fuck, suck, toss men off, play with themselves. Whatever. You name it, they do it. But mostly when they think they're on their own.

All of them, for example, have vibrators. *All* of them. And they use them. All the time. They come home from the office, knowing that they have a date in a couple of hours' time, but they'll frig themselves off thoroughly with a vibrator first. Before they have a shower and change to go out on their date. And I watch. And wank. I love it. All of it.

Some of these girls have those double-ended vibrators. Do you know the sort? With a normal large end, with which to vibrate their fannys, but with the addition of a smaller, slimmer end, which vibrates and throbs at the same time, to fit up their rectal passages, whilst they frig their cunts. It certainly gets them off, that's for sure.

Sometimes I wonder if I should volunteer to go up – or down – to their apartments and fuck them. Or suck their pussies. Science – even Hong Kong science – hasn't, as far as I know, yet invented a plastic substitute that will suck a woman's pussy. The day that they do, we men can forget about sex, that's for sure.

But then, if you think about it, if I were to do that, how do I introduce myself? 'Excuse me, miss, but I notice that you wank yourself off with a vibrator most evenings. Could I perhaps pop in and fuck you? Or suck you off?' I mean, it's not on, is it? Sadly. If only it were. We'd all be happier people, that's for sure.

But if they knew that I knew, then they would probably say yes. Even yes, please. Well, wouldn't they? I mean, they jack off, all the time. Regularly. If some lovely girl came up to me one day and said, 'Don't ask me how, but I watch you jack off every evening, and I frig myself off while I watch you doing it. Why, for God's sake, don't we get together, and jack each other off? Or fuck? Or suck? Or whatever?' I mean, do you think I'm going to say, 'How dare you?' No way. I'm going unzip my fly, pull out my stiff cock, and say, 'Here it is darling. Do what you like with it. And please drop your panties, while I suck you or fuck you and do dirty things to your cunt. Oh, baby. Here I am.'

I must digress long enough to tell you that I love to read those advertisements in the down-market mens' magazines, offering ladies' (*ladies*'?) worn/used/dirty knickers for sale. 'Smelling the way you like them,' say the ads. 'Worn for one day, £10. Worn for seven days, £15.' Magic.

But to get back to my main fantasy. All these sexy single girls, doing themselves mischief with vibrators and the like. I mean, we chauvinist men sometimes describe plain girls as 'brown-paper-bag jobs', don't we? As you know, this means that we are not particularly attracted to them, but at the same time, we'd give them one. Preferably with a paper bag over their heads. Well, there must be women who feel the same way about men, mustn't there? I wouldn't at all mind being a brown-paper-bag job for any woman who fancies a quick shag. I don't give a damn if she isn't actually attracted to me. That she just wants a fuck. She's more than welcome. Are you listening, girls?

But back to my main fantasy. It's difficult to concentrate when there're so many sexy subjects to contemplate. The girls in the block of flats. Join me in my secret room at around five in the afternoon. From now on, the girls will be coming home from work – the ones that work, that is – and either settling down for the evening or getting themselves ready to go out. Some of them, of course, will be entertaining guests at home. Let's start with Sheila, on the third floor. Ah, yes. There she is. She's just going into the bathroom.

I cut to Lynda, in one of the two top-floor penthouses. Lynda's daddy is rich, and gives her an allowance. It must be a generous one, for it's obvious that she doesn't need to work. What's she up to this early evening? There she is. She's in her sitting room. She's just putting a video on her video machine. I think we're in luck. Lynda loves porno videos, and she puts them on when she's got boyfriends there, and they toss each other off for hours, and then they finally fuck. If she's on her own (let's have a quick look: I switch from one to another of the various cameras around her penthouse – yes, she's on her own) she usually stimulates herself with one of her seemingly vast collection of vibrators. Yes, we *are* in luck.

The porno video's just starting. Two almost-naked girls are *soixante-neuf*ing each other. One's a white girl, the other black. Jesus. I wouldn't mind changing places with either one of those. But look! That drawer over there that Lynda's just opening is the one she keeps her vibrators in. See? Lynda opens the drawer, and I can see twenty or so vibrators of different shapes and sizes, all made of different materials. She picks up a largish white plastic one, looks at it closely and weighs it in her hand. She licks the end of it, thoughtfully.

No! That's not the one. Back into the drawer it goes. She scrabbles around in the drawer for a moment or two, and then comes up with an even larger pink rubber one. She examines this one for longer. What's she doing now? She puts the vibrator down on top of the cupboard, lifts up her skirt, and pulls down her knickers below her knees. They're black and tiny, and look obscenely sexy, stretched between her legs. More of a G-string than proper knickers. She picks up the vibrator and squats down on the floor. Yes! This is it! She uses one hand to spread her cuntlips, and with the other she starts to feed the vibrator up herself. Suddenly she stops. What's wrong? Is it too big? No. She's forgotten the lubricant.

She opens another, smaller drawer and takes out a tube, squeezes some of its contents onto her fingers, and then rubs them all over the vibrator. Sensible girl. Now she squats down again, and this time the vibrator slides in without too much trouble. She stands up and, carefully manipulating her G-string panties over the end of the vibrator that is sticking out of her pussy, she takes them off.

She throws them into a corner. Next she unzips her skirt, steps out of it and throws it after her panties. Then she walks – 'waddles' is a more accurate description, because of the vibrator in her pussy – back over to the video machine and sits down in an easy chair in front of it. She's naked from the waist down and is wearing a blouse, beneath which she is patently also naked. Her nipples are erect. She spread her legs wide, and reaches down and switches on the vibrator. From the buzzing that I can clearly hear, she's got it on high speed.

The black girl we saw earlier is now being fucked anally by a white guy with a huge prong, and the white girl is sucking off a black guy, similarly well endowed who, as we watch, starts deep-throating the white girl. This obviously strikes a chord with our Lynda who reaches down again and starts to push and pull the giant vibrating vibrator rapidly in and out of her pussy.

I can see the wetness dribbling from her pussy through her thick pubic hair and down her thighs. The pink rubber of the penis substitute is shining wetly with her juices, and I can actually hear the little squelching noises that it is making as she wanks it in and out of herself. I'd love to go down there and stick another of those huge vibrators up her arse, switch it on and then tie her up and fuck her mouth. But that's just a momentary distraction. I'm seriously enjoying watching her vibrate herself to orgasm. It shouldn't be too long now. And it isn't.

As I watch, the two guys in the video change partners, and each now does to his new girl that which was previously being done to her by the other man, so that the white guy who was fucking the black girl's arse is now deep-throating the white girl, and the black guy now has his well-sucked prong up the black girl's arse.

It all looks pretty unhygienic to me but all concerned seem to be enjoying themselves, and it's obviously doing things for Lynda who is bouncing around in her armchair, wanking the vibrator in and out at a great pace and shouting, 'Oh, wow. Oh, yes. Give it to me now. Fuck me like there's no tomorrow. Oh, baby. Oh, yes. Oh, shit.' At which point she begins to orgasm.

It's beautifully timed for, as she does so, the black guy pulls out of the black girl's arse and, wanking himself with his hand, he spurts his load all over her buttocks. The white guy pulls out of the white girl's mouth, and shoots his spunk all over her face and tits. Lynda eventually comes down from her series of orgasms as they build to a peak, then get smaller and smaller, and finally stop. She subsides, pulling the vibrator out of herself. Then, switching it off, she gets up, shuts off the video and goes through to the bathroom.

She doesn't hang about but, as I watch, she rinses the vibrator, dries it and returns it to its drawer. She takes a quick shower, dresses, makes up, and is out of her penthouse less than twenty minutes after she has finished frigging herself silly. She takes the lift down to the basement garage, and I take a final glance as she drives out in her black 5-series BMW. Sexy little cow.

I won't bore you with running through the whole of my fantasy apartment block, but I'll just mention one of the other pleasures to be found there on occasion.

There's Frieda, up on the fourth floor, who's bisexual. With careful timing, you can either watch her being fucked by one of her four regular boyfriends or, if you prefer, you can contemplate her activities with one or other of her two regular lesbian girlfriends. I've seen her at play with both sexes on the same day. She's very into oral sex, seeming to enjoy giving head to her men friends as much as she does lapping pussy in lengthy cunnilingual sessions with the girls.

I've always wanted to catch her with both of her girlfriends together, indulging in a threesome, but so far – sadly – I've had no success. You can imagine them, can't you, all three of them naked on Frieda's great big bed, lying in a circle, each girl with her head between one of the other girls' legs. What a fantastic sight that would be!

But enough. You can see how my misspent youth, spying upon my sister, has grown into what is now a full-time perversion. Long may it last!

L.G. Newton Abbot, Devon.

It sure beats collecting butterflies as a hobby. But we wonder if you may perhaps have lost out somewhere along the way. For example, do you, these days, ever actually have sex with women?

CLEAN SWEEP

My partner loves me to shave my pussy, so that he can spend hours sucking the clean-shaven end result. But he won't do as I ask and shave it for me. It would turn me on no end to have him shave my pussy – carefully, of course – but he simply won't agree. His pleasure, he says, is in sucking and licking and kissing my hairless pudendum. As far as he's concerned, he says that I can get my pleasure from him doing that. Well, I do, of course. I love having my pussy sucked. But since my shaven cunt gives him so much pleasure, why shouldn't he add to mine by shaving it for me? What's your opinion, gentlemen?

P.G. Lee-on-Solent, Hants.

We think that your gentleman isn't one, ma'am. If he still refuses to oblige you, come and see us. Any day. It will be our pleasure. We promise.

SISTERS UNDER THE SKIN

At the age of nineteen, I'm having my first sexual relationship with a black woman. It's opened up a whole new perspective upon things sexual for me. She too is nineteen. She's called Gina, and she's of Afro–Caribbean descent, although born here in Britain.

Everything, absolutely *everything,* is so much better with her than with any of my earlier experiences with white women. Gina is, first of all, intensely sexual. She's up for it, any time. And the sooner – and more often – the better. She isn't doing me a favour. She's just loves to fuck and be fucked. She has no sexual reservations whatsoever. She'll take it anywhere, do anything. She loves it all. She never, ever has what I now think of as a white girl's headache.

Her body is so much more beautiful than that of any white girl I know. Fuller, more rounded. Her breasts are bigger. Her nipples fatter. Her arse is out of this world. Sexier. Her skin is softer. Smoother. She smells nicer. More sexy! Her tongue is softer, silkier, her lips fuller, her mouth an additional sexual orifice. One that she loves me to use.

Her pussy is delightful. Whilst her actual cunt is tighter than any cunt I've ever fucked before, the rest of her pussy is much bigger, and considerably better than your average white girl's pussy. Her labia are wonderfully big. Soft and fleshy. They're purplish-black on the outside (pink on the inside, she says, all same Princess Margaret, as the old joke goes.) And she has a lovely sense of humour. Sex, to her, is fun, as well as sexy. After this eulogistic letter, I do, however, have just one small complaint. Her pubic hair is of the texture of barbed wire. Are all black girls' pubes as scratchy?

L.B. Notting Hill Gate, London.

No, sir. As with Rosie O'Grady and the colonel's lady, women's pubic hair, like everything else about women, varies as much with black girls as it does with those who are white. Some black girls have the strong, tightly curled short pubic hair to which you refer. Other black women have long, soft, silken pubic hair. Others have all the stages of pubic hair in between. Maybe, as in the letter above this one, you should – with your lady's unqualified agreement – shave off the cause of your very minor problem. She sounds like quite a girl. Enjoy her while you can.

GLOVES OFF!

One of the small idiosyncrasies in my current ongoing sexual relationship, which is otherwise stress-free, is that – only as a small part of our total catalogue of sexual preferences – I enjoy being masturbated by my girlfriend while she wears soft white cotton gloves. I'm not sure that I can even explain why I find this an intensely erotic experience, but I do.

I like it when she masturbates me while wearing a white brassiere, white stockings with lacy tops, a white suspender belt and white, lacy knickers. Plus, of course, the gloves. I don't suppose I've asked her to provide this small pleasure more than half a dozen times in all the time that I've known her. Other men, I read in your columns, make far more demanding – and, in some cases, quite outrageous (and sometimes painful) – demands.

Why, then, do you suppose that my girlfriend finds it so difficult to fall in with my occasional requests for this small fetish? I've asked her to try and explain her dislike of it to me, and she says that it is the fact that it's not her but the gloves, etc that are providing the sexual pleasure. I should add that she doesn't mind tossing me off in other, perhaps more normal circumstances, i.e. without the white lingerie and gloves.

I should also add that she likes me to spank her, something that, frankly, I find moderately distasteful but which I do whenever I am asked, simply on the basis of believing that one good (sexual) turn deserves another. It's not as if I'm asking her to allow me to sodomize her (a practice which, strangely in the circumstances, she thoroughly enjoys) or indulge in water sports (something we both utterly dislike).

She enjoys all our other sexual activities, and provided that I start our sessions by giving her the good spanking that she always asks for, she will do anything and everything that I wish – apart from the gloves bit. I cannot be alone in my modest fetish, for I see that in some of the more expensive lingerie departments of stores here in London these days many lingerie manufacturers are now offering gloves to match their bra-and-knickers and suspender-belt-and-stocking sets. Many of these, I note, are in white.

Please help. If only to agree that my need is harmless.

J.McT. Harringay, London.

We wish we could *be of help. But if the lady doesn't want to, she actually doesn't want to. In our book, that means that she doesn't have to do that which you are requesting, harmless as it may seem to you. Sorry.*

BOTTOM LINE

May I please put in an urgent plea for the better representation of an area of erotic interest that I feel is badly neglected by your magazine?

As a diehard bottom man, I am of course aware of the fact that you publish photographs of girls' bare bottoms. (Or should that be bare girls' bottoms? Whichever.) And very nice they are too. But I refer to the lack of the proper pictorial representation of girls with *enormous* bottoms. *Gargantuan* bottoms. *Huge* bottoms.

There must surely be many of your male readers who, like me, worship at the altar of elephantine female *derrieres.* But please don't misunderstand me. I'm not a pervert. I'm not into fucking bottoms. I'm strictly a normal sex man. I know where I like to put my dick, and it's not up bottoms. Female or otherwise.

It is the sheer erotic sight of those huge buttocks, preferably wobbling naked in their sexually arousing enormity, that so strongly attracts me. I love to stroke them, feel them, hold them while I fuck their owner, doggy fashion.

Stretch marks? I love them. Huge white buttocks that have never been exposed to the sun? Magic! Buttocks so large that they stretch their owners' outsize panties so taut that the panties look as if they are about to split? Let me at them.

I beg you to start printing at least one girl set per issue showing a real woman, one with a gigantic arse. Show her bending over, with her gorgeous, naked bottom facing the camera. Choose a girl with thick tufts of hair between her legs. And preferably one who has taken her tight knickers off only moments before your photographer points his camera, so that we may still see the red lines indented in her white flesh, the lines where her knicker elastic has been cutting into her waist and thighs.

Another delightful shot would be with the woman standing halfway up a stepladder, with the camera focusing from below, up her fat thighs to her naked bottom. This would look particularly good if the girl was wearing black stockings supported by a black silk suspender belt, thus framing her huge, undraped cheeks.

My fantasy is to follow an obese woman whom I see in the street. I'm walking behind her, revelling in the way her enormous buttocks are swaying and wobbling as she walks. It is summer, and she is wearing a thin summer dress through which I can see the outline of her panties.

She goes into a pub and I follow her in there and sit next to her in the bar. It is a simple matter to get talking to her, and she seems to return my interest. After a while, she turns the conversation to, first of all, the loneliness of living as a single person in London (with which I can quite honestly concur) and then – joy of joys – to her problems finding sexual partners, due to her being overweight.

'But you're worth your weight in gold to the right person, darling,' I tell her. 'And I'm that right person!' I quickly tell her of the erotic delights, to me, of sex with ladies with large bottoms, and within moments she is inviting me back to her place which is, she says, no more than fifteen minutes' walk away from the pub.

As we talk, she pulls her bar stool nearer to mine and, taking my hand, she puts it on her thigh. 'Feel that, darling,' she says. 'That should give you some indication of how my bottom will feel when you take a handful of it and squeeze it.' I practically fall off my stool with excitement, and I have difficulty in arranging my erection so that the entire pub is not aware of it. We quickly finish our drinks and leave the pub.

It takes us rather longer than the fifteen minutes to get to her place, largely due to the fact that we can't keep our hands off each other on the way there, and also the fact that we keep stopping, in doorways, on street corners – anywhere we can stick our tongues down each other's throats and stick our inquisitive fingers between each other's thighs without bringing the traffic to a stop. She's so wet between her legs, long before we have completed her journey, that I have made a great damp patch at the front of her dress, immediately over her groin, where I have been rubbing her dress and her knickers against her damp quim as I feel her up.

Eventually we get to her place, a small three-room flat on the third floor of a converted house in a pleasant, tree-lined street. As she closes her door behind us, she says, 'I can't wait to feel that great cock of yours rogering me. Do you want a drink to take with you into the bedroom?' I grab her and stick my hand up underneath her skirt, and frig her sticky cunt through her knickers.

'No, thank you,' I say, between her wet kisses. 'Just get your knickers off and let me fuck you.' She takes my hand, and leads me through to her bedroom. She has a big bed, thank God. I tear my clothes off and sit naked on the bed, my cock standing up erectly and throbbing as I watch her expose her huge, obese body.

Her breasts are gigantic. Larger than her head. They're in reasonable shape, allowing for their size, and are tipped by enormous teats, like a cow's udders, which I can see are rigidly erect. I've seen smaller cocks in men's changing rooms than those erect teats. She could fuck girls with them.

My cock throbs even harder at the thought. She's got her dress off, and she's down to her knickers. She isn't wearing any stockings. Her knickers are stretched tightly over her huge arse, and she deliberately turns her back towards me as she starts to peel them down her fat thighs. Her knickers are black, semi-transparent nylon, and her white fleshy buttocks shine through the tightly stretched material like giant moons on a cloudy night. I can smell the unmistakeable aroma of aroused cunt as she pulls them down. She pulls them over her haunches slowly, revealing her giant arse-cheeks gradually. They are wondrous. It's the only word. Fat. Gross. Dead white. With stretch marks lining them everywhere, just like her tits.

She has an enormous thick black hairy growth between her legs which, from the rear, completely hides both her pussy and her anus. She is so grossly fat between her legs that, even when she turns around and faces me, her cunt is hidden between folds of flesh.

'Is this what you like, baby?' she asks me. She looks a little uncertain. She lifts an arm, unconsciously, to touch a breast, and I see – further joy of joys – that she has a huge bush of unshaven hair in her armpit. I am so highly sexually excited by all that my eyes are trying to take in that my cock suddenly spurts a jet of semen high up into the air.

I looked down at it. My hands weren't anywhere near it. No one's hands were anywhere near it. 'Does that answer your question?' I asked her, laughing. She joined in with my laughter.

'Actually, it's just as well that happened,' I tell her. 'Otherwise I was going to shoot my load the moment I got anywhere near you. At least now I might last a minute or two. But if you want a reasonable fuck, I strongly recommend that you wank me off at least a couple of times before we get down to any serious kind of fucking. I really do. Otherwise, I'm afraid you'll be cross with me again.'

'That'll be my pleasure, sweetheart,' she said. 'Come over here.' She led me over to the bed. 'Unless you're particularly into being tossed off,' she said, 'I think we can probably do rather better than that.' She pushed me gently down onto the bed on my back, and then took my once more stiff cock in her hand. She gave it a leisurely wanking stroke or two.

'Is that what you want?' she asked. And then she leant down and sucked my cock into her mouth. Her lips were soft, her mouth was warm, her tongue was busy. She explored the tip of my cock for a pleasurable few moments, and then took it out of her mouth. 'Or would you prefer that?' she asked, grinning hugely at me as she did.

'No contest,' I said. 'Thank you.' And I lay back, and thought of England. This was going to be a great relationship.

'Do you want to suck my pussy while I suck you off?' she asked. 'Or would you rather leave that for another time?'

Jesus, I thought. *Suck that lovely fat cunt! My God.* How could I not have thought of that? 'Oh, wow,' I said. 'Forgive me. I simply wasn't thinking. Let me at it, baby. Pussy, here I come!'

She had the sense to lie on her back, open her legs, and let me mount her so that my cock was over her open mouth and I was lying on her huge stomach, with her fat, wet pussy lips within reach of my hungry mouth.

I couldn't believe the sight of her cunt. It was huge. A positive thicket of pubic hair grew around what, as I pried it apart with my fingers, revealed itself to be enormous outer labia containing almost equally enormous inner labia. The flesh of both pairs of lips was a dark purplish-brown in colour, and both were the largest examples of their ilk that it has ever been my pleasure to see.

She smelt strongly of her own sexual effluent, a perfume that had me fully erect in seconds. I love the taste of pussy that smells like that. Having pulled her cunt open with my fingers, I delved deep down inside it to see what other excitements I could discover.

What I did discover, to my delight, was a tiny, tight, virginal little vagina It clung to my fingers like a sea urchin to a small fish. It felt hot, wet, and gloriously tight. I moved my fingers around until I found her clitoris, which sprang to attention as I rubbed it. I then drew my fingers out, and began to kiss, suck and lick. She tasted divine, as I knew she would.

As I began to suck her, so she began to fellate me. Short of sexual partners she may have been, but there was little she didn't know about cock-sucking. Perhaps they do mail-order courses in it these days?

Wherever she got her experience, I didn't care. She was a past-mistress at the art of sucking men off. I seriously started to think about marriage. And we hadn't even fucked yet! I knew that I was going to spurt my seed again shortly, and so I concentrated my tongue on her now swollen clitoris, and felt her starting to move her gigantic hips as a result of my efforts. Her cunt was releasing so much lubricious juice, it reminded me of how that dreadful expression 'cunt-lapping' came into being.

And that was exactly what I was doing. Lapping up her pungent vaginal emission. Swallowing it, in what seemed like generous mouthfuls. While I was thus occupied, she was sucking my cock with both skill and enthusiasm, and very soon – it might have been within only seconds – we both came.

I swear that she actually ejaculated. I know it's not possible. But I also swear it happened. As I sucked her and tongued her clitoris, and as she lay back and moaned – breathing heavily the while – I'll guarantee that she spent an eggcupful of liquid down my throat. That it's not possible, I know. But I promise you, this fat goddess really did jet her orgasmic discharge down my neck. I took it as a compliment.

But suddenly all this preamble, all this instant ejaculation, all this jacking off, sucking off, was over. I came in her mouth, quickly and efficiently. I enjoyed it. I shot my sperm down her throat and she swallowed all of it. And then I was seriously ready to go. I had this giant lady, with her goddess-like, carnality-inspiring, totally voluptuous magical fat buttocks. And I wanted to fuck her.

I wanted to hold those great globes, those mountains of fat, in both of my hands, whilst I rammed my rampant cock up her tiny, tight little cunt. Was that too much to ask? After what I'd been through, no. It was not.

'Baby,' I said.

'Yes' she answered.

'I'm going to fuck you now. OK?'

There was a short pause. And then, 'That's very OK with me, darling,' she said. 'Very OK indeed. I'm ready for you. Ready, willing, and anxious. Fuck me now. Ram your stiff tool up my hot, wet cunt. Rape me. Sodomize me. Fuck me. Do dirty things to me. Do anything you like to me. But do it now. Make me come.'

'Don't worry about a thing, darling,' I said. I pulled back from her, took hold of her huge hips, and helped her to turn over. 'Now get up on all fours,' I told her, 'and offer those gorgeous buttocks to me.'

She did as she was told. My prick felt two feet long. I took two handfuls of those gross, elephantine buttocks and pulled them apart, far enough to see roughly where, underneath that thicket of heavy pubic hair, the entrance to her cunt should be.

'Let me help you, darling,' she said, and she put both her hands behind her and pulled her arse cheeks widely apart.

With both of my hands free, I was now able to dig down into the mass of those delightfully obscene folds of flesh, and, digging around with my fingers, I once more found that tiny aperture, hidden within their midst. I thrust two fingers up it to find that it was still as well lubricated as before. The sticky, glutinous liquid running copiously out of it allowed me to force my stiff prick straight into her, without any kind of a preamble.

Her vaginal muscles closed around me instantly, holding me tightly. This was it. This was the heaven that I had been dreaming of for years, and working up to for what seemed like a week, although a quick glance at my watch told me that it was only a couple of hours.

She looked back at me over her shoulder. Almost proudly. 'Oh, darling,' she said. 'You're fucking me. Please God, you're fucking me. And you're enjoying it. I think I love you. I really think I love you.' Of such delights are fantasies made!

O W. Lancaster Gate, London.

You're very up front about your preferences. You've obviously got right to the bottom of things. We regret your tastes are too specialized for us to publish the photographs you request.

WIFELY WISHES

As an ordinary married woman, I enjoy looking through my husband's copy of your magazine. You certainly know where to find some attractive-looking women. And your photographs have, over the years, provided me with some original ideas, many of which have contributed to my ongoing, happy sexual relationship with my husband. We both thank you.

Sadly, I'm unaware of any kind of similar publication for women. The only magazines showing naked men, with or without erect penises, are patently aimed at homosexuals, and – with the very occasional exception – they do not show the kind of men that I find sexually attractive.

Don't misunderstand me. I have no wish to be unfaithful to my husband, or to have sexual relations with other men. But I *would* like to be able to indulge my fantasies. Particularly my masturbatory fantasies. All of which revolve around a male brothel, staffed by the male equivalent of the girls in your publication. That's right! Young, fit, attractive, tanned, available, *sexy* men!

As I lie on my bed, playing with myself, I close my eyes and dream up my favourite establishment. It is a discreet establishment, and from the outside looks like any other office. Its reception is manned by an attractive woman who, when I enter, hands me a folder containing photographs and details of the available men on any given day. One can select certain preferences. For example, circumcised or not circumcised. My personal preference is for not circumcised. I love looking at a man's cock immediately in front of my face as I slowly pull down his foreskin prior to taking him in my mouth.

Other specialities that can be requested are men with exceptionally large cocks, men who specialize in various sexual acts (oral sex, anal sex with women, manual stimulation, and so on), black men, men who like to be treated as sexual slaves, and (one of my many favourites) men who can fuck for long periods without ejaculating.

My personal fantasies are more for variety than for any one particular act, and in my male brothel I always line up at least half a dozen men to service me, one after the other. As I begin to masturbate myself, I will fantasize the first man, who will fuck me with his huge cock. I will suck it for a while to begin with, in order to get my juices flowing well between my legs. When I'm really wet, he'll fuck me long and hard, and when he comes, he'll spurt his come up inside me. I *always* want to feel their spunk, wherever they are fucking me.

When I've been well fucked by this first man, I will have arranged for him to be followed by an attractive young black man, who will also have a good-size cock. I'll suck him off until he comes in my mouth and will swallow everything he can give me. I love the salty flavour and the gooey feel of his semen as it pulses thickly down my receptive throat.

I will have come a couple of times myself by now – in reality, this is – and at this stage I will probably stop using my fingers to pleasure myself and resort either to a vibrator or to one of the small selection of dildos that I have for this purpose. Whichever I choose, I will make certain that I use it with a generous coating of lubricant. Well, I don't want to get a sore pussy, now do I?

In my fantasy, my black lover, having come in my mouth,

then fucks me in the more usual manner, before taking himself off. It may surprise some of your readers to know that next I take the final three men whom I have ordered all at once.

This is because I always end up my masturbatory sessions by imagining myself being gang-raped. In my fantasy, one man takes me roughly but normally, i.e. vaginally. At the same time the second man takes me brutally and anally, and the third man rapes my mouth.

I help these fantasies along by having one vibrator in my pussy, one (from choice, a much smaller one!) up my bottom, and I suck on a realistically-shaped rubber cock complete with moulded frenum, thick veins, and an authentic-looking scrotum. It is the kind of dildo that one can fill with warm water and when you squeeze the balls, it ejaculates. Whatever will those Japanese think of next?

If I'm feeling really raunchy, I'll repeat the gang-raping session a number of times over, changing the three men about, so that each of them will fuck each of my orifices in turn. And, of course, I help my orgasms along by increasing the speed at which the vibrators vibrate.

By the end of one of these marathon sessions I am, literally, really well-fucked. I'll then have a long, lazy bath, select some of my most sexy lingerie, and get myself ready for my dear husband, who will fuck me silly when I tell him what I've been doing all afternoon!

So come on, fellas. How about showing us girls a few naked male hunks, sporting their equipment the way we girls most like to see it? Long, thick, strong, and erect!

J.McD. Fort William, Scotland.

Much as we admit that life without you ladies would be tantamount to no life at all, we also need to remember that our prime purpose is the entertainment of our male readership. For that reason, we regret we must refuse your request. But should you ever need volunteers for your male fantasy brothel, feel free to call upon us. We'll be happy to oblige you there.

NUN BUT THE LONELY HEART . . .

I don't know if you would describe my sexual fantasy as a perversion, in that I find it quite difficult to draw a line between the two words, other than to appreciate, as my dictionary tells me, that a fantasy is retained strictly in the mind whereas a perversion is actually physically performed and is preferred to 'normal' sex (whatever that might be). But here goes. Tell me what you think.

I have amazing sexual fantasies about nuns. I have only to see that instantly recognizable black outfit in the distance, with its white headgear, to get a screaming erection. I think it has something to do with having read somewhere, many years ago, that some of the sexiest underwear in the world is hand-made by nuns in convents, who sew these nicely salacious undergarments in order to raise money.

If I'm standing near a nun, in the street, say, at a bus stop, or on a railway platform, I have an almost uncontrollable desire to kneel down in front of her, lift up her habit (if that is what it is called) and press my nose and mouth between her legs. My dirty mind imagines her wearing the sexy, skimpy knickers of my uncertain memory. I want to bury my nose into her scented, flimsy, sexy, wet knickers, which are covering her gorgeously hairy cunt. I want to pull those gossamer, sacrilegious knickers down. I want to suck her off. Feel her pussy. Fuck her. Stick my finger up her arse. I don't know what it is that brings out this disgusting need, this lust, this wish to ravage, to desecrate, deflower. It's a conditioned reflex.

I see the habits. I feel the urge. So much so that, from time to time, I have to pay prostitutes to dress up as nuns for me and allow me to defile them. I pay them to wear the sexy underwear, with the added erotic addition of black silk stockings and black, lacy suspenders. I pull their habits off, tear their naughty knickers down (that costs me extra, as you can imagine!) I rip their stockings off. And then I fuck them. I pretend to force them to suck me off. Then I make them wank me. And, finally, I shag their not-so-tight little arses. (Well, they *are* prostitutes. You can't have everything in this world, can you?)

I've got one special prostitute now, she's my favourite. She's not young. She must be in her late forties. Well past her prime. But I think she enjoys dressing up for me as much as I enjoy doing what I do to her. She even bought herself a silver crucifix. She is the epitome of a Holy Mother. That's what I call her.

'Holy Mother,' I say to her, 'I'm going to fuck your dirty, holy cunt. I'm going to suck your smelly, dirty, hairy pussy, and frig it for you, and then I'm going to fuck you. How do you feel about *that*?'

'Hail Mary, Mother of God,' she says, crossing herself furiously. 'God protect me from this rapist. God preserve my virginity.' *Virginity.* That's a laugh, if ever I heard one. She must have been fucked by half of London in her day. But, I must say, she enters into the spirit of the thing. She screams and pretends to cry when I fuck her. And she pretends to be offended when I do dirty things to her. (She also makes me wear French letters when I fuck her up her arse, but that's something else.) 'I don't want your filthy spunk up my arsehole, thank you very much,' she says.

That's a bit out of character, of course, for a nun, but there you go.

So, gentlemen: what do you think? Is it fantasy, or perversion?

L.J.T. South Lambeth, London.

Well, taking your initial premise – with which, basically, we agree, despite its slightly simplistic approach – your fantasies are far from being confined to your mind. You are very actively acting them out. Which should answer your question for you. But you know our overview of sexuality: provided that everyone taking part is in agreement, and that no one gets physically or emotionally hurt, then it's OK with us. Is that OK with you?

SWING LOW . . .

I changed my job recently and am slowly making friends, as one does, with some of my new colleagues. My position is a promotion for me, both in terms of seniority and salary. I'm now part of my new company's senior management. One of the guys there (who in fact is marginally senior to me) seems to have taken a shine to me.

My problem is, first of all, that I don't really take to him, although I'm not absolutely certain why. But, far more importantly, other men in the office tell me that this chap is a real swinger, sexually speaking. Apparently he gives parties that are literally orgies. All the male participants contribute to the cost of the parties. The women go free. I'm told by colleagues who have attended these orgies that they think nothing of having sex with half a dozen different women during the course of an evening.

Now this man has approached me, described to me what goes on at these events, and invited me to attend the next one. First of all, I'm not a swinger. I like sex, naturally. But sex to me is a private thing, between me and a woman. One woman. (Well, one woman at a time.) I have no desire at all to have group sex, or screw a number of different women over an evening.

A lesser point, but still one that worries me, is that if I were to accept this invitation, I'm not at all sure that I would even be able to get it up in the company of a crowd of people, never mind get it up often enough to fuck a number of different women in succession. Will you advise me, please? I'm worried sick about this problem.

D.I. Orpington, Kent.

There seem to us to be two quite separate issues here. One, the question of whether or not you wish to participate in this happening. It would seem that you don't, since your sexual preferences are not aligned to swinging. There's nothing to be ashamed of there. If you don't want to attend the party, then the solution is quite simple. Say so. Politely refuse the invitation. Whether or not this refusal will affect your future with your new company only you can judge. The second issue – which may or may not be relevant – would seem to be concern over whether or not you can raise an erection (or a number of erections) in public. The point here, surely, is that if you don't want to, don't try. We hope this is helpful.

CORPS DE BALLET!

How kind of you to provide those wonderful pictures of two girls acting out my favourite fantasy! How did you know that I go out of my mind at the thought of lesbian girls dressed as ballet dancers having their naughty way with each other? And what a fabulous thought (and fabulous pictures) having the girls wearing their tu-tus, bodices, white stockings, and satin ballet pumps, but having forgotten their knickers, or panties, or whatever ballerinas call those garments that they wear under their skirts.

How amazingly sexy it is to gaze at them while they are still dancing, with their carefully coiffed hair, their immaculate make-up, their elegant positions, but also to be able to see their exquisite pubic hair, their little pussy lips and, later on, their pinkly open pussies beneath those formal outfits. It brings a whole new, exciting meaning to the phrase *pas de deux*.

How wonderful it would be if one could only go and see the corps de ballet of, say, the Royal Ballet, dressed (perhaps I should say *un*dressed) in this manner. Imagine the entire chorus dancing one of those lovely scenes from *Swan Lake*, fully dressed, in a long line, but totally naked between their lovely legs. It would perhaps produce rather more realistic bulges than are normally to be seen under the tights of the *male* ballet dancers.

And then those fantastic shots where the two girls are still dancing, but they are progressively undressing each other as they dance. First a glimpse of a tiny, budlike, small-nippled breast behind an open vest. Then two breasts. Suddenly a naked bottom, its utterly erotic nudity emphasized by the loose-fitting cotton top and the coarse woollen leg-warmers worn by one of the two girls, contrasting so exquisitely with the soft, nude flesh of her smooth athletic thighs.

The curvaceous buttocks are beautifully, firmly taut as the dancer holds her position, with the tresses of her partner's pubic hair a furry, golden, crowning glory to her plump pudendum. And then the girls start to get to know each other rather better, and there are those sensual pictures of them kissing each other's breasts, their nipples stiffening almost as we watch, their lips wet with saliva as they drink, sweetly, from each other's mouths.

And then that shot of a gentle hand caressing a naked buttock. In a different picture another hand, this time oh, so close to heaven between her partner's legs. Sadly, one has to imagine the natural progression that patently follows on from there. But it is a rewarding scene to fantasize.

A pair of carmined lips upon another, softer pair of lips, amidst those golden pubic locks. A tongue parts them, and searches, gently, for an aroused clitoris. The juices flow as the kisses strengthen, and slowly transform into loving, drawn-out, passionate cunnilingus.

And then, perhaps, the final surrender, as our matched pair of girls – dominant and submissive – join, the one to the other, entwined in their own romantic ode to *soixante-neuf*. And now those powerful dancers' legs and thighs are spread widely for each other, as they each kiss their partner's sex to orgasm. The ultimate gift, the final sexual pleasure.

When that is finally spent, they uncoil their tangled limbs, and then each kiss the other's mouth once more, savouring the exotic, strongly-flavoured tastes of just-slaked sapphist lust. Encore, I say! Encore!

F.B.S. Stoke-on-Trent, Staffs.

An eloquently imagined conclusion to the young ladies' pas de deux, *if we may say so, sir. Thank you.*

A NEW EXPERIENCE

Your excellent magazine has long been acknowledged as a champion of the beauty of the female form. And I have no quarrel with that. Far from it. It is also an obvious fact that your staff – writers, photographers and editors – are strong supporters of the joys of sex, in all its varied forms. Again, no quarrel. But why, oh why don't you occasionally show us the bodies of women who are somewhat older than the dolly girls who seem to be your speciality?

In my experience, older women are sexually so much more satisfying than younger ones. Your average eighteen-year-old is almost always a totally selfish lover, who only wants to be sexually satisfied herself, without any thought about her partner's wants or needs. She probably only allows sex straight up and down, like mum and dad, as the saying goes.

The chances are that she finds oral sex 'disgusting', whether you want to do it for her or you want her to do it for you. She certainly won't want sex more than once on any given evening, and even then she'll need to be in the mood for it. She'll complain if you want to shag her doggy fashion, and tell you you're a filthy pervert if you want to fuck her anally. So what *has* your younger girl actually got going for her?

Let me try and be fair. She probably looks terrific. Her body will be at its absolute peak of perfection. Firm breasts. Nothing is drooping. No need for a bra. Her boobs will stick out straight in front of her. Terrific legs. All the way up to her bottom. And she'll have a gorgeously firm bottom. No need for 'control' panties. Not a sign of cellulite anywhere. No stretch marks. She'll enjoy showing her body off with the latest, most revealing fashions.

But not just to you. She'll want everyone to see it. Her tits are probably practically poking out of her dress/blouse/swimsuit. Her short skirts probably show her knickers when she sits down, and they undoubtedly will when she bends down to pick something up off the floor, or goes to the bottom drawer of the filing cabinets in her office.

When she goes to the local pub with her girlfriends after work she's there for one reason, and one reason only. She's on the pull. But not for sex. Or, at least, only as a loss leader. No. What she's there for, mate, is *marriage.* Got it? MARRIAGE. And don't you forget it.

Now, for a complete contrast, take your average woman in, let's say, her middle-to-late forties. First of all, she been around the houses a few times. She knows what sex is, and she has become accustomed to it. She probably even enjoys it. She loves having her pussy sucked, and she probably doesn't get too many offers these days. So when you get down to it for her, she's grateful. Bloody grateful. Right? Which also means that she takes the view that one good turn deserves another, and she's guaranteed to suck your cock for you morning, noon and night.

She'll never have a headache. Or if she does, she won't tell you about it. She'll shag you silly, any time you like, day or night. You want to fuck her anally, she'll say, 'Oooh, you naughty man. Hang on a second, darling. I'll just go and get some cold cream/K-Y jelly/butter/something to use as a lubricant.' If you want to shag her doggy fashion, as you do, she'll put her hand around behind her and give you a lovely wank with one hand while you're fucking her, and she'll toss herself off with the other hand. She's learned about life, is what it's all about. So she's got a few stretch marks. So what?

And speaking of wanking, if you've been out with the lads for a few pints, and you get home and you're feeling randy but you don't really want to be bothered with all that making love nonsense, all you want is a quick one off the wrist from the girlfriend while she talks dirty to you, she'll understand that. And she'll oblige. Of course she will.

Her tits might sag a bit, but her nipples will come up like bullets when you suck them. Her pussy might be just marginally slacker than your average eighteen-year-old's, but it will get much wetter, much more quickly. And it will always be available. You won't have to plead for it.

And if it's something tight you're after, she'll love it up her arse. Honestly. Ask her. Her bum might not be as firm and muscled as it was a few years earlier, but will you really care, as you grasp hold of it and do that which your dolly girlfriend thinks is dirty?

And she'll wear sexy gear for you, too, if that's what you like. You name it, she'll wear it. Stockings, suspenders, basques, naughty knickers. Whatever. Because she wants to *please* you sexually. That's the vital difference, you see. She actually (a) likes sex (b) wants to please you and (c) will do anything to achieve that end. QED. She'll shave her pussy, if that turns you on. Or she'll let you shave it for her, if that's your bag. You can come in her mouth, and she'll swallow your ejaculate. All of it. And enjoy doing it. And on top of all that (as if that isn't enough!) she'll wash and iron your shirts, do all the weekly shopping, pay her share of the rent, and have your meal waiting for you every evening when you get home. Now what more could any man want? I ask you. Who wants dolly birds?

D.R. Hendon, Middx.

That's a very strong case you put forward there. But suppose, my friend, just suppose *that you found a fantastic-looking eighteen-year-old dolly, with all the advantages of the lady whom you describe so convincingly above? No contest. Agreed?*

ADDRESSING THE QUESTION

I've been living with my boyfriend for about six months now and, as far as it goes, it's been a pleasant relationship. Our sex is unexciting, but fun. Neither of us wants to rape the other the moment we get home. But we have sex two or three times a week, and we both seem to enjoy it. I know I do. It's just that it seems to lack, what shall I say? *Ooomph*? But how many people do you know whose sex lives have *ooomph*? Well, there you go.

And then, one evening recently, I came home much earlier than usual. I suppose I must have let myself in fairly quietly. There was no sign of my boyfriend downstairs, so I went straight up to our bedroom. I was going to strip off, have a bath and make myself look nice for him when he came home. So imagine my surprise when I opened the bedroom door and there he was, naked apart from one of my pantie-girdles. He was standing in front of the mirror, sporting a huge erection, and playing with himself. You know? Tossing himself off.

I'm not sure who was the most shocked. It was something of a surprise, I can tell you. But at the same time, I found myself sexually very excited at the sight of his enormous erection. I just grabbed hold of it and we made fantastic love, right there on the bedroom floor, with him wearing my girdle and me still with all my clothes on, except of course that I'd pulled my skirt up and my knickers down. It was really good sex.

Afterwards, he explained to me that he'd always had a thing

about being turned on by wearing women's underwear, ever since he could remember. Apparently, when he was a teenager at home, he used to take his mother's knickers out of the dirty laundry basket in the bathroom, and wear them while he masturbated himself silly.

The entire episode and the events that it led to and our conversation afterwards gave me a great deal to think about, as you can probably imagine. But after a while, after I'd thought about it quite seriously, I decided that, what the hell? He wasn't doing anyone any harm. He wasn't being unfaithful to me. He wasn't going with other women. Nothing like that. It might seem strange to me, but if he enjoyed it, if it excited him, and if it satisfied him sexually, and if – as it seemed – it had such a good effect on our mutual sex lives, then why not?

So I told him, eventually, that as far as I was concerned he could dress up in my underwear as much as he liked. But I also said that, if he agreed, I'd rather do it with him, I'd rather try and share it with him, than have him do it alone when I wasn't there. Since when our sex lives have all the *ooomph* that I, for one, can possibly manage. He agreed with everything I said.

So these days, when I'm buying sexy lingerie, I buy it in two sizes: one for me, another for him. And I'm getting the best sexual seeing-to that I've ever had in my life. It's a funny old world, isn't it? But at least it's a happy one!

K.L. Brighton, Sussex.

That's a very sophisticated approach you're taking there, ma'am. And, if we may say so, a very sensible one. Long may your happy and fruitful relationship last.

LAURA

I've been taking your magazine for something like twenty years now and I thought that, through your good offices, I had seen almost all of the most erotically dressed – or undressed – and most beautiful girls in the world. I now know (after this month's issue) that there was just one more to go before I could claim a full set. And that's one of those lovely pictures of Laura, taken by Fred Enke.

It's the one where she's kneeling down, naked apart from her skimpy lacy black knickers, pulled tightly down and stretched across the underneath of her bottom, and her sheer black stockings and her unbelievably high-heeled black patent leather shoes. The photograph is taken from her side view, with her looking directly at the camera, her brown eyes sparkling with who knows what naughtiness. Her short blonde hair is swept back and her arms are outstretched. That fantastic globular bottom, with its deep cleavage, is raised slightly towards the camera. 'Offered' is probably a better word. Her beautiful firm thighs are naked down to the tops of her stockings. Her perfect full breasts hang down, entirely unencumbered, her nipples tiny but erect.

Her whole attitude, her total pose, is a plea for someone to pull those black tightly stretched knickers down and fuck her. It excites me, too, that her tightly curled pubes are black, as distinct from her pale blonde tresses. In my fantasy, I am able to take Laura much farther down the road to total sensuality than do you.

It is my fantasy to imagine a university of sexuality. A place where one can devote oneself to learning all there is to know about sex. One can take whatever kind of degree one wishes. I'm studying for a Master's in Heterosexual Intercourse. Today, Laura is my professor, and we are having a tutorial, a period of individual instruction. My last paper, I'm told, shows a lack of sufficiently detailed knowledge of the female sexual organ. Laura is the college Senior Professor of Female Sexuality, and is about to instruct me. She is dressed today in a tight, low-cut white blouse with narrow straps – rather like a swimsuit – and large buttons down the front.

The top button is undone, exposing the upper half of her generous breasts. I don't know if it is wishful thinking, or if I can really see just a glimpse of the top of each of her areolae. She is wearing a knitted grey wool skirt, with silver threads in the wool, and she is also wearing silver stockings and silver court shoes.

Right now she is standing up. Her skirt is tight, and I can see the line of her knickers when she turns away from me for a moment. I begin to get a hard-on. 'Well, Peter,' she says, turning back to face me. 'I gather that your tutor thinks that you need a little personal tuition. Don't worry about a thing. By the time I have finished with you, you'll be top of your class. But before we start, let's get one or two things clear. You've been to a number of my lectures, I know. You therefore know already that I use the words that we all use when we fuck. I say fuck and cunt and cock and come and so on, instead of intercourse and vagina and penis and ejaculate or orgasm. I use spunk instead of semen, and suck instead of fellate, or cunnilingus.' She stopped for a moment, and looked down at my swelling fly. 'One of my favourite words,' she said. 'Suck.'

She reached out and stroked my erection through my trousers.

'Mmmm,' she said. Then she deftly unzipped my fly, put a hand inside my trousers, and expertly found my rigid cock, which was strangling itself in a knot made by my shirt and my underpants. She pulled it out and released it.

'Since an erection is a vital part of what we are here for today,' she said, still smiling, 'I suggest that you let it all hang out.' She took hold of my cock again, and pulled and squeezed it, and then went through a couple of what I can only describe as wanking strokes.

'Hmmm,' she said this time. 'Nice one.'

'Thank you, ma'am,' I said.

'Oh, call me Laura, for now,' she instructed me. 'You can call me darling later. Now then, you're in your fifth week, this semester. Is that right?'

'Yes, er, Laura,' I said.

'Have you fucked many of the college practice girls yet?' she asked. The college thoughtfully supplied about thirty girls, all of whom were paid handsomely by the college to allow the male undergraduates to fuck them. They didn't attempt to teach, but were there simply to make themselves available for physical practice. I understand that they sometimes made confidential reports to the college staff if they thought there was a problem of any kind.

There was also a similar number of men available to the women undergraduates. I had to admit that lack of confidence had meant that I had only fucked two of the girls so far. I had enjoyed myself both times, but I was conscious of my tendency towards premature ejaculation. I admitted my inadequacies to Laura.

'Just don't worry,' she said. 'That's par for the course at this stage of your studies. Worrying will only make it worse. Now then, did you get my note about hygiene?'

I had. She'd sent me a memo, prior to this meeting, instructing me to make certain that I either bathed or showered thoroughly before our session, paying particular attention to my genital areas. I had done exactly that, and I said so.

'Good,' she said. 'Now then, this is, of course, a study session. But we may as well enjoy ourselves. Learning to relax with your sexual partners is a lot of what successful sex is all about. So let's try and have some fun, while we're learning,' she said, smiling her naughty smile.

Not bloody half, I thought, but I kept it to myself.

'Right, then. I think that covers the preliminaries. Let's get at it.' She unhooked her skirt, let it drop around her feet, and stepped out of it. She kicked it to one side and stood there. 'What do you think?' she asked, doing a twirl to let me see her sexy little knickers from every angle. 'Do you like them? Do you think they're sexy?'

They were exactly like the ones in the magazine; black, lacy, tiny, and dead sexy. 'I love them,' I told her. 'They're as sexy as hell.'

'Great,' she said. 'You take them off. And remember, we're supposed to be lovers. You're supposed to be making me want you to tear my knickers off. *Want* you to fuck me. OK?'

I looked at her, I hope not quite as nervously as I felt. But I was determined to enter into the spirit of the session. So I didn't just pull her knickers down. I knelt down on the carpet in front of her, and leaned forward and kissed her, hard, right where I reckoned her cunt was, underneath her knickers. Then I put my hand between her legs, and massaged her cunt with two fingers for a little while.

'Oh, yes,' she said, opening her legs. 'That's good. I like that.'

I could feel the crotch of her little black knickers getting wet, so I rubbed even harder and she began to move her hips in time with my fingers.

'Oh, yes,' she said again.

I put my hands up to the top of her knickers, beneath the elastic, and I slowly pulled them down over her hips. They got to a stage where the waistband was down around her upper thighs, but the crotch, because of my fingering her there, was still stuck up in between her cunt lips. I could see that the gusset of her knickers was lined with white cotton, now discoloured grey with her moisture. She looked down.

'I know,' she said. 'My knicks are stuck up in my cunt. Tell me about it. But that means that I'm getting wet from what you're doing to me, so that's an excellent start.'

She put a hand down and carefully pulled the sticky gusset out from between her legs. 'Ooh,' she said, as it slowly withdrew. 'That feels nice.'

I could now see her snatch and I wasn't listening too hard to what she was saying. Her pubic hair, as in your magazine, contrasted blackly with her dyed-blonde hair. Her thatch was really thick. Thick and curly, and quite long.

'Now then, Peter,' she said. 'This is where the work starts. OK? I'm going to sit up on that stool there' (pointing to a high sort of bar stool, standing up at the other end of the room) 'and spread my legs for you, and tell you what this cunt of mine is all about.' So saying, she went over to the stool, sat upon it – which put her cunt on about a level with my face – and opened her legs.

The first surprise was the thickness, seen close to, and the sheer abundance of her pubic growth. The second surprise was that everything about her cunt – *everything* – seemed larger than life. It was akin to looking at a target in a shooting gallery. Her bush of pubic hair, seen from where I was standing, formed a hirsute circle around her cunt, running at its thickest across the top of it, but continuing along down the sides, and then again across the bottom of her cunt, then across her lower buttocks, meeting over her anal crack and completely hiding her anus, which I knew must be nearby.

'Here it is, baby,' she said. 'Take a good look. You can see my hairy snatch, with its lips closed. Here are my outer lips – see? Right here. And then my inner lips. Look.' She put her hands down, one each side of her hairy pussy, and pulled the outer lips open. With her outer lips gaping widely, she exposed her inner lips. In between the two pairs of lips, the skin stretched tightly and pinkly, and shone wetly. Her inner lips were fat, looking almost as if swollen.

Now she moved her fingers once more, and spread her inner lips for me. 'And now you're looking right up my cunt,' she said. 'The font of all pleasure. For you and me both.'

I was suddenly aware of the eroticism of the visual contrasts. Her rough, coarse pubic hair. Her fleshy inner and outer labia, and the smooth, tight skin between the two. The inner, moist, darker pink of her actual cunt, shading down to what looked like an almost purple colour deep inside. Her tanned legs, with the pale, totally white, never-seen-by-the-sun flesh of her buttocks.

Now use your hands and your fingers,' she said, 'and feel me. Push your fingers up inside me. Accustom yourself to the layout, the physical ramifications. And don't worry. I'm good and wet. You won't hurt me. Use your fingers to explore. Pull my inner and outer lips apart for yourself. She how they function. That's what I'm here for.' She giggled. 'Enjoy.'

So I did. First I did that thing that all men want to do, given the opportunity. I thrust my middle finger all the way up her delightfully tight, slippery cunt, until my largest knuckle was flush with the lips of her sex. When I was all the way in, she started to use her vaginal muscles on my finger, squeezing me surprisingly hard with them.

'Just imagine that on your cock, Peter,' she said. My cock stiffened up again at the very idea of it. I pulled, prodded, stroked, opened, and felt all and every part of her. I was leaning forward so that I might see closely everything that I was doing, and the strong scent of aroused pussy filled my nostrils.

My God, I thought. *And to think that some chaps are studying electronics.* She was the most erotic thing that had ever happened to me, leaning back there on her stool, her legs spread, totally relaxed, while I probed her cunt. It was very wet indeed now, the juices beginning to run down her thighs and to disappear into the thick bush at the join of her buttocks.

After some considerable time, Laura asked me if I thought that I now knew the physical composition of her cunt. I replied that yes, I thought that I did. 'Right,' she said. 'Then it's time to move on to the next stage. Have you ever sucked pussy, as yet?'

Jesus, I thought. No, I hadn't. But I'd spent my teenage years masturbating myself while I imagined doing exactly that. 'No, Laura,' I said. 'No such luck.'

'But you know the theory?' she asked.

'Well, I *think* so,' I told her. 'I've read all about it, and seen pornographic illustrations and photographs.'

'Great,' she said. 'Then now it's time to put the theory into practice. So suck my pussy. Now. Please. But take it in stages. Have a little lick first. Just run your tongue gently up and down the length of it. See what you think. See if you like the taste. There's absolutely no hurry. Tell me if you have any problems.'

I put a hand on each of her firm thighs and then I bent forward and did as I was instructed. I ran my tongue from the top of her open pussy all the way down to the bottom. And then from the very bottom right the way back up to the top. And I was instantly hooked. From the very first taste. They tell me that taste is actually ninety per cent smell. I wouldn't argue with that. For I found that I loved the smell of wet pussy, as well as the taste.

I began to lick her more seriously and then, suddenly, I was sucking and licking and tonguing her cunt with everything that I had. I would have dived inside it, were that possible.

'Oh, yes,' she said, putting a hand down onto the top of my bowed head, and pressing my mouth even more firmly down upon her cunt. 'Oh, yes. That's a good boy. That's a *very* good boy. Very well done.' She seemed to tense up for a moment, and then she relaxed. 'Mmmm, nice,' she said. 'I had a sneaky little come there. Thank you.' She smiled at me.

I must have looked a little taken aback, for then she said, 'Don't worry, baby. You'll get yours. But later. This is where you learn where girls keep their clitoris. You know what a clitoris *is,* don't you?'

I admitted that I did.

'Good. So hang on a second, whilst I just frig mine up to its fully erect state.' She slipped her middle finger into her cunt, felt around for a second, found what she was looking for, and began to frig herself. 'Oooh,' she said. 'Maybe this is where we should stop. I could go on doing this all day.' She looked at me, and laughed. 'Just a joke, Peter,' she said. 'Take no notice.' She pulled her wet finger out of herself, and held it out to me. 'Do you want to lick that clean for me?' she asked.

'Please,' I said, and did as she asked. Afterwards, I licked my lips.

'There's a naughty boy,' she said. 'You're a fast learner. Now give me your right hand.'

I did as she asked, and she separated my forefinger from my other digits and guided it up between her legs. Once it was inside her, she moved it around for a moment and then she stroked it across what felt like a small knob or knurl.

'There it is, Peter,' she said. 'That's it. That's my clitoris. Generally speaking, all girls have them, although they vary in size and shape and – just a little bit – in where they are. But now you've found mine, feel around down there for a bit. Take your finger out, and then put it back, and see of you can find it again, without any help from me.'

I did as I was instructed, and quite soon I was able to find her clitoris without any trouble. As I touched it, so it slowly swelled, until it was standing up quite erectly, like a miniature penis.

'That, basically, is what makes women come,' Laura told me. 'The stimulation of the clitoris by the man's erect cock is what female orgasm is all about. And, of course, that's also how women masturbate. Shall I show you?' she asked. 'Would you like to see me masturbate?'

'Yes,' I said. 'I would. Very much.'

It was something that I used to imagine when I was tossing myself off: watching a girl masturbate. When she began, it was the sexiest thing I've ever seen. She pulled her cunt open, slid in her middle finger, and began to rub herself. It was an intensely erotic sight, and I found my hand straying down, almost without thinking, to my cock, which I began to wank as I watched Laura playing with herself.

'Naughty boy,' she said, smiling at me. And then, 'Why not? Is it turning you on, watching me frig myself, and wanking while you watch?

I nodded, wanking myself harder and faster. We came almost together, just a matter of seconds later. Just as I was about to ejaculate, Laura held out her left hand (the fingers of her other hand were still busy) and said, 'Come in my hand. Spurt your come on my hand. Please.'

I directed my spurting cock as instructed and she took her fingers out of her cunt and began to wank me herself, until all my come was finished. She then licked it off her hand, and swallowed it.

'Mmmm,' she said. 'I love swallowing come. Most of all, I like to swallow it when I'm sucking someone's cock and they come in my mouth and spurt it down my throat. Would you like to do that, Peter?'

'Would I?' I said. 'Just try me.'

Laura looked at her watch. 'I'm going to miss my next lecture,' she said. 'But we're having such fun. Hang on, while I make a quick phone call.' She went over to her desk, picked up the phone, and called the common room. She got someone to take her students, claiming not to feel well. 'I've never felt better in my life,' she said, laughing. 'Just make sure you keep this a secret between the two of us. OK?'

'OK,' I said. 'No problem.'

'Right,' she said. 'Lesson number two. Oral sex. I think this one will be better undertaken in the bedroom.' She opened a door on the far side of the room and I followed her through it, into her bedroom. She had a double bed and she lay down upon it and patted the duvet beside her.

'Let's first finish our anatomy lesson,' she said. 'So far, you've done your homework on my cunt, and now you know where my clitoris is. But women have three orifices, and those of us who are sexually liberated enough use all three of them, on occasion, for sex. I don't have to tell you where my mouth is, and in any case we're going to study that rather more closely in a little while. But you may as well familiarize yourself with my arsehole, while you're here.'

She knelt up on the bed and turned her back to me, presenting me with her well-formed buttocks. In between them, her thick pubic hair stretched up into the lower part of the small of her back, in a triangular shape surrounding her anus.

'That's my arsehole,' she said. 'That's the word I use. 'Anus' sounds prissy. When I'm extremely fond of someone, and I've got to the stage where I trust them implicitly, I let them fuck my arsehole. You're obviously not at that stage, but at least examine it. Feel it. Kiss it, if you like. I assure you it's clean. Always think of it as part of every woman's sexual paraphernalia. If you get to know me well enough, then, eventually, you'll understand why I regard it that way. But remember, too, that some women don't. Does thinking of its sexual uses appal you?'

I wasn't too sure how to answer her. I must admit that, up to now, if I'd thought about it at all, I had always thought that buggery was for queers. But then, I can remember a time when I used to think my cock was just for pissing through. 'No,' I said. 'Not really. But I haven't actually given it a lot of thought.'

'Well, Peter,' she said. 'If you take my advice, now's the time to start giving it some.'

'Right,' I said, and I put my hand out, tentatively, and touched it. It was surprisingly soft. Almost as if it was covered in velvet. She clenched it as my finger touched it, and then relaxed it. I looked at it, closely.

It wasn't exactly pretty, but then, cunts aren't exactly pretty, even though I love them. It looked almost like a misplaced umbilicus, with puckered edges. It looked far too small too take an erect prick up it. The skin was brown in colour, shading to pink at its core. I bent down, and kissed it. It felt exactly like a mouth. I kissed it again, and licked it with the very tip of my tongue. It tasted quite different from cunt. Reasonably enough, I suppose. Rather like dark chocolate, mixed with a touch of, what was it? Mango? Something jungly. But not unpleasant. I put a finger centrally on to it, and pressed, gently. Nothing much happened.

'Put a gob of spit there,' Laura said. 'And rub it in. It needs something greasy, ideally. I've got some jelly somewhere, but spit will do for what you're doing.'

I spat onto my fingers and carefully rubbed it well into her arsehole. Then I pressed again. This time it dilated, and my finger sank in with a slight sort of plopping noise. She felt hot inside and – to my surprise – quite wet.

'Push it in as far as you can,' she said.

I did, and then she clenched my finger – hard – with her rectal muscles.

'How does that feel?' she asked. 'Think of me doing that to your cock. You'll love it, when it happens, I promise you.'

'Jesus,' I said, involuntarily. It was the thought of her kneeling down like that, but me with my rampant cock up her arsehole instead of my finger. Suddenly, the one thing that I really wanted to do was fuck Laura's arse. I pushed my finger into her, as deeply as I could. All the way up to my knuckle. Then I shut my eyes, and tried to imagine that was where my cock was.

'That's probably enough exploring of my bottom for now,' said Laura. 'But just remember what I've been telling you.'

I pulled my finger out of her. Slowly. Then I bent down and kissed it once more. 'Goodbye, little arsehole,' I said. 'Nice to meet you.'

She laughed. 'Somehow,' she said, 'I think I've got a convert to anal sex here. Now then. Oral sex. Right. Well, you said hello to my pussy a little while ago, but now you're going to get to know it rather better.' She lay on her back, and opened her legs. 'I'll suck you off later on, Peter,' she said. 'So don't waste any time wondering what's happening. But I want you to become accustomed to sucking pussy before I start sucking you. OK?'

'Surely,' I said. 'That's perfectly OK.'

'So, off you go,' she said. 'Just help yourself. Do whatever you feel like doing. Suck me. Kiss me. Lick me. Finger me. Anything. And don't forget, it's my clitoris, mostly, that makes me come.'

I began by kissing her cunt. It was open now, and really wet, and it tasted delightfully of what pussy should taste of. Sugar and spice, and all things nice. I went from kissing to licking, and then to a combination of sucking and thrusting my tongue deeply inside her and tonguing her clitoris. I slipped my hands underneath her buttocks, and pressed my face hard down onto her.

She moaned, and began to move her hips beneath me. 'Oh, Peter,' she said, her voice suddenly deeply, huskily passionate. 'Oh, yes. Oh, God. That's good. Oh, Jesus. Oh, yes. I'm going to come.'

I'm not sure why, because it wasn't anything that I had ever done before in my entire life until today, but I suddenly had an uncontrollable desire to stick my finger up Laura's arse. So I did.

'Oh, God,' she shouted. 'Oh, yes.' And she started to orgasm. A huge, big, series of orgasms, which slowly built up to a crescendo, and then as slowly died away. I pulled my finger out of her arse, and she shuddered and opened her eyes. She grinned at me as I lifted my face up from between her legs.

'I've said it before, and I guess I'll say it again,' she said, still grinning at me. 'You are a *very* naughty boy. I really ought to spank you.' She hesitated, and then said, 'Would you like that?'

'What?' I said.

'For me to spank you,' she said.

'Christ, no,' I said. 'Pain and sex are in no way connected, in my book. Spanking is out. Definitely, positively out. Sorry.' And then I wondered. So I asked her. 'But tell me,' I said. 'Do *you* like being spanked? Caned? Any of those S&M things?'

She giggled. 'No, not really,' she said. 'The nearest I get to S&M is letting the occasional boyfriend fuck me with a dildo. Or a vibrator. Strictly penis substitutes. I'm not into pain either. Just sex.' She giggled again. 'Come here, darling,' she said. 'Let me suck your lovely cock.'

I climbed up onto the bed beside her and lay down on my back, my throbbing cock sticking up like a miniature flagpole. She gripped it with the fingers of her right hand, and then she leaned down and kissed me. I felt her tongue in my mouth as she began to wank me. I wondered – just for a moment – if this was the standard tutorial, or whether she was going rather farther than was usual. And then I realized that it didn't actually matter. All that really mattered was that she was doing it. And doing it to me.

'Mmmm,' she said. 'Your mouth tastes of cunt. My cunt. I love to taste my cunt on men's lips. It shows that they've been paying lip service to me.' It was an old joke at the university, but I giggled dutifully.

'I've often wondered if I would enjoy sucking another woman's cunt,' she said, still wanking me slowly. 'It might surprise you to know that I've never had a lesbian affair. Never ever. I've often thought about it, but I've never done anything about it.' She paused. 'I used to quite fancy that Angela Dartford. Do you know her? She's one of the practice girls. She's rather pretty.' I didn't, and I said so.

'I was thinking of asking her up here for a drink, and seeing if it developed into anything,' she continued. 'But one of my students told me that she wears dirty knickers, and that put me off. I can't stand the thought of smelly knickers. Knickers that smell of cunt, yes. That's one thing. But knickers that just smell, no. That's something else. But enough. Let me get down to business.'

She stopped her wanking movements and slowly took my cockhead into her warm, wet mouth. She wet my cock, all over, with her saliva and then took it out of her mouth and blew on it, making it deliciously cold. Her lips were full, and generously painted with sticky-looking, dark-pink lipstick.

I looked at my cock, out of curiosity, to discover that she had left a ring of pink lipstick around the circumference of it, about halfway down the shaft. Laura's was the kind of mouth that you wanted to fuck. I suddenly realized what people meant when they described girls' mouths as 'cocksucking' mouths. Laura's certainly was. She saw me looking at her mouth and made pouting, gobbling noises with it before returning my cock to its warm, moist embrace. She began doing unimaginable things to my cock with her tongue. If I didn't know that it simply wasn't possible, I would have thought that she had penetrated the tip of it with her tongue. At least, that was what it felt like. Fantastic.

I reached up and began to pull on one of her tiny nipples, and then I used her whole breast to pull her down to me. Her nipples may be small, but they're hard, like bullets. I pulled at one and she groaned, her mouth satisfyingly full of cock.

I was enjoying what she was doing to me. What man

wouldn't? Here I was, being sucked off by the Senior Professor of Female Sexuality at a university specializing in sex. I mean, who could possibly be better qualified? But something was missing. I looked at her, watching my cock disappearing almost completely then reappearing from between those luscious, full lips. And then I realized. 'Laura,' I said.

'Mmmm?' she said, with her mouth full.

'Do me a favour,' I said. 'Move yourself around a bit, and kneel over my face, so that I can suck you. I can't just lie here doing nothing, with your gorgeous wet pussy ready, willing and able. Come on,' I said. 'Sit on my face, please, there's a good girl.'

She actually took the time to take my cock out of her mouth for just a moment. 'Oh, how lovely,' she said. 'That will be my pleasure.' And, popping my cock back into her mouth, she did the necessary, carefully lowering her still moist cunt down onto my appreciative lips.

I can't think of anything nicer than lying on your back, having a woman who is an expert sucking your cock with loving attention, while you hold her plump buttocks and suck her wet, open pussy. I allowed my tongue to stray to her sphincter just occasionally, getting a delightful reaction from her every time I did so. I wondered how long it would be before she allowed me to fuck her there.

As I continued to suck her cunt, I slowly and carefully – and lasciviously – thrust a finger up her gloriously tight arsehole, and then I finger-fucked it while I sucked her. I could feel her reaction as she thrust down against both my mouth and my finger. Her thick thatch of hair tickled my face as I sucked happily away at her, and I could feel the increase in her flow of vaginal juices as I continued to play with her arse.

It suddenly struck me, in the midst of all this energetic

sexual activity, that attending one of Laura's lectures would never be quite the same again. And then I could suddenly feel my moment of truth rapidly approaching. I was going to come. I could feel it, urgently, somewhere way down in my loins. I didn't feel the need to tell her, for she had already announced her love of swallowing semen, but she obviously knew anyway, or could feel it gathering, just as I could, for she suddenly thrust a finger deep into *my* arsehole, massaging my prostate, thus causing instant ejaculation.

I spurted my seed down her throat in long, throbbing jets which she swallowed, sucking hard as she did so.

So there you have it. In my fantasy, I study hard (working long into the night!) and get a first class honours degree, mainly due to the enthusiastic assistance of Laura, plus the energetic practice girls. Is this what they mean by higher education?

P.A. Yeovil, Somerset.

It's all a matter of degree. Or 'Tell Laura I Love Her', as the song says. Whatever do you get up to in the holidays?

THAI ONE ON . . .

I was fortunate enough, on a visit to London recently, to be recommended by a friend of mine to a particular so-called sauna club, in the West End. What I am going to describe all actually happened to me, despite the fact that it reads more like one of the fantasy letters that I enjoy reading so much in your columns.

I telephoned beforehand to make an appointment, mentioning my friend's name, and I agreed to take out an annual subscription, which would cost £50. I visit London often enough to make it worthwhile, and in any case, my friends's recommendation told me that I wouldn't be disappointed. I arrived in the club's reception to be greeted by an attractive, pleasant young woman, who took me through the membership process and made out my membership card. She then pressed a button, and an exquisitely beautiful young Thai girl appeared, and greeted me.

'Welcome to the club, Mr Saunders,' she said. 'My name is Chana. May I show you the way?' I followed her down a corridor, and she guided me through an open door. We went into a large room, furnished in what I would call hospital style. There was a bath and shower, a massage couch, and a small sauna cabinet of the kind that you sit in and the front is then folded down over your chest and knees.

Chana smiled at me. 'First a bath,' she said. 'Let me help you undress.' Chana herself was dressed in a very respectable white overall, apart from the fact that the skirt was considerably shorter than those normally seen in medical establishments. My friend had told me simply to relax, and whatever I wanted to happen would happen, he said, without any need for prompting from me. He had telephoned the club to arrange for my membership, and had assured them that they could trust me.

Chana undressed me as I stood there, a new experience for me. The last garment was, naturally enough, my underpants, which she simply slid down my legs and held there while I stepped out of them. She then held a towelling bathrobe for me to slip on and sat me in an easy chair with a selection of newspapers and magazines while she ran a bath.

'How do you like your bath, Mr Saunders?' she asked. 'Hot? Medium hot? Cool? Cold?'

I shivered at the thought of a cold bath, and told her that medium hot was my choice.

Then, 'Bath ready now,' she said. 'You come this way, please.' She helped me out of the robe and into the bath, where she washed me all over, very thoroughly. And I do mean everywhere. She carefully washed my by then erect cock, seemingly ignoring that fact, pulling back my foreskin and soaping it well before rinsing it with a flannel.

She finally had me stand up in the bath and spread my legs, whereupon she soaped my arsehole, inserting a long, slim, soapy finger deep inside, to ensure that I really *was* clean all over. I then stepped out of the bath, and she dried me as thoroughly with a huge, soft, fluffy bath towel.

She next took me over to the sauna cabinet and sat me in it. She made sure that I was comfortable, closed it down, put a towel around my neck to keep the heat in, and left me to it. She stayed in the room and was very attentive, adjusting the heat up and down as I wished, and mopping my sweating brow with an orange-scented cloth every few minutes.

When I eventually said that yes, thank you, I'd had enough, she released me and led me to the shower where, to my amazement, she stripped off and joined me. But nothing that could faintly be described as sexual took place there, unless you count my once more rampant prick, which Chana completely ignored.

She again soaped me, then rinsed me down, took me out of the shower and towelled me dry again before drying herself. She had worn a little plastic shower cap to keep her hair dry. Her wet, brown, naked body was something else. I know that Eastern girls look younger for their years than Western girls, but this was ridiculous. She had a slim waist, long, black hair, abundant black pubic hair, small but prettily-formed breasts with hard little nipples, slim, well-shaped legs, and gorgeously slim, tight buttocks. When I was dry again, she led me over to the massage couch and laid me down upon it.

She then proceeded to give me probably the best all-over body massage that I have ever had. This wasn't one of your English massage parlour girls' 'strokings', by a tart who only wanted to get it over with and get down to the 'extras' that were probably the only part of the exercise that she had any experience in. This was an expert, deep, professional, full body massage, perfectly performed.

I am ashamed to say that I maintained my involuntary erection all the way through the massage. It was the proximity of this gorgeous little Thai girl, who (whether deliberately or because she had simply forgotten, I do not know) was still naked from our shower. She had to bend over me to massage me, and from time to time her hard nipples would brush against my chest. I looked at her mouth from just a few inches away, and every time she caught me looking at her she smiled at me. From time to time, she licked her lips. And the feel of her supple fingers, manipulating my body, led my dirty mind to all kinds of sexual fantasies as I lay there.

Thank God, she finally got around to it. She finished my massage by trailing her hand all the way down my body, from my chest to . . . YES. You've got it. My cock. She took its rigid length into her warm hand and played with it. Masturbating it, lazily. Expertly.

'You like some sex now, Mr Saunders?' she asked, smiling down at me.

'Yes, please,' I said, weakly, trying to fuck her hand.

'What you like?' she asked.

'What you got?' I said.

She went on wanking me. 'I can give you hand relief,' she said, still smiling. 'I can gobble you. Like this.' She bent down, and enveloped the end of my prick with her soft lips. I felt her tongue doing lovely, dirty things to me. She took me out of her mouth. 'You can fuck me,' she said. 'But Chana not take it up arse. Find other girl, take it up arse. Not Chana.'

I almost came in her hand at the very thought of anal sex with her. Or another of these delightful young Asian women. We spoke of money for a moment, and I settled for a fuck. She asked me how I would like it, and I said that I would just like to lie there on my back while she fucked me. She said that for what I was paying for a fuck, I could suck her pussy too, if I wanted to. I ask you. If I wanted to! I nearly shot my load again.

I then had the sense to add a wank to the bill and I had her toss me off, solely in order that I could enjoy my forthcoming fuck rather better. Otherwise I would have shot my load into her the moment my cock delved into her tight little Thai cunt.

She wanked me off as I lay there, her slim brown fingers deftly masturbating me with God knew how many years of expertise. I swear she jacked me off better than I do it for myself. Praise doesn't come any higher than that.

As she wanked me, she bent down and kissed me, her warm pink tongue thrusting into my mouth. When I ejaculated, she did things to my cock that made my ejaculation a thousand times more enjoyable, last a thousand times longer. She kept at it until there was nothing left, and then she leaned down once more and sucked and licked my cock clean. She was too much. I considered proposing.

We relaxed for a while. She didn't hurry me at any time. In any way. When I was ready, I got her to straddle me and then kneel over my face and lower her delightful little pussy down to my mouth. She tasted of heaven. Of paradise. Her cunt was tiny. The skin of it was dark brown, and her cunt lips were tiny too. Almost negligible. She spread them for me with her fingers, and inside she was the prettiest pink I've seen for ages. She was wet, too.

I slurped my tongue up and down the length of her and sucked her juices into my mouth. I pushed my tongue up her, and she was so tight that I had a job to actually get my tongue up into her. Imagine how that was going to feel around my cock!

She moved herself about on my mouth, fucking it with her gentle, strong-tasting pussy, until my cock was almost exploding.

'Chana can tell you like to suck pussy,' she said. 'Chana is going to come now.' She ground her pussy hard down onto my mouth, rubbing it against me. As I licked and sucked, I could feel the orgasm pulsating through her cunt as she came.

She hardly stopped. Just paused for a moment. And then she said, 'Are you ready for Chana to fuck you now, Mr Saunders?'

'Yes, darling,' I said. 'I'm ready.'

She climbed off me, took my rigid cock in her hand, and examined it. 'Nice cock,' she said. 'Good fucking cock. Good for woman. Chana enjoy this.' She gave my cock what seemed to be becoming an almost compulsory wank or two, and then she climbed back up onto the massage couch.

This time she was further back, down my body. She squatted over me and took my cock in her hand again and drew the top of it along the length of her cunt. It felt hot, wet, and sticky. 'Chana going to fuck you now,' she said. 'You will remember.'

I bet I will, I thought. She held me at the entrance to her sex and eased herself down onto me. She was tight. Really tight. She had to grip me firmly, to get my frenum past her entrance. Once in, she felt terrific.

'You can play with my tits, if you like,' she said, looking down at me. 'Chana like tits felt.' She began to ride me. She pressed herself down onto me, hard, so that my cock was deep inside her. She was tighter than any woman I've known, before or since. And then she drew herself up, slowly, carefully, until only the tip of my cock was still inside her compact cunt, and then she thrust down onto me again, hard and firm. She did this with increasing speed, so that, quite quickly, she was fucking me with the speed with which I would toss myself off. But instead of my sweaty fingers clutching my rigid cock, it was thrusting into her incredibly tight, hot, wet, wonderful little cunt. 'You like?' she asked, bouncing around on me as if she was on a trampoline. 'You like Chana's cunt?'

I watched, fascinated, the sight of my swollen cock disappearing deep down into her brown cunt-lips, then reappearing again, wet with her emanations, swollen with my lust. She was using muscles that I didn't know girls had, squeezing and pulling at my cock as she enveloped it on her downward strokes, grasping it firmly on her upward cycle.

'You come now, Mr Saunders,' she said, suddenly. 'Chana feel it coming. Chana like spunk up her cunt. You come now.'

Obediently, I jetted my semen up into her as she squeezed every last drop of it out of me. As with her earlier masturbation of me, she seemed to manage to make my ejaculation last for ever.

After it was all over, she said 'Finish now?' politely, before lifting herself off me and climbing down from the massage table. 'You like, Mr Saunders?' she asked, seeming to be genuinely interested to know whether or not I had actually enjoyed the experience.

Mere words simply couldn't do justice to the way I felt. 'I like,' I said, truthfully. 'I really like.'

'You come back?' she asked. 'You come fuck Chanda again? Maybe?'

I laughed, and grabbed her around the waist, pulled her to me, and gave her a big wet kiss. 'There's no maybe about it,' I told her. 'I shall be back. Probably tomorrow.'

She had the grace to laugh with me. Then she said, 'Chana pleased. Chana enjoy too. Chana like to fuck. Be pleased to see you. Any time.'

B.D.S. Liverpool, Merseyside.

It certainly sounds as if it beats the usual office Christmas party. Did you meet any members of the Jockey Club there?

TELEPHONE SEX

We recently acquired a new telephonist at the company where I work. She's a pretty young girl, and there was much conversation among the male employees about who was going to score with her first. You can imagine my delight, therefore, when it became obvious to me that, when putting callers through to my extension or getting long-distance calls for me, this young lady was actually chatting me up. Not one to let an opportunity slip by, I was quick to invite her out.

We had a few drinks in a pub beforehand, and then I took her to a quite decent restaurant, where we had a most enjoyable meal. We both took to each other quite naturally and when I asked her if she would like to come back to my place for a drink she accepted with some alacrity. Naturally enough, I was led by this to believe that the evening would end in the normal, happy, traditional way. In bed.

You can imagine my chagrin, then, when, after pouring the young lady a large one, she announced that, while she would be more than happy to stay the night with me and cope with my sexual needs by giving me one off the wrist, there was no question of my fucking her. She was, she told me, a virgin, and she had every intention of staying that way. She also announced that she would be more than happy for me to masturbate her. But fucking, she repeated, was out.

Some you win, some you lose, so I agreed on that occasion to her stipulations, partly from urgent need and partly in the hope that time would resolve the problem. But it was not to be.

This relationship has been going on for some time now and, while I'm happy to tell you that I am the fortunate recipient of some of the best hand jobs it has ever been my pleasure to enjoy, the lady insists upon remaining a virgin. Oral sex – in either direction – is also banned. She'll toss me off night and day, and allow me to do the same to her, but that is it. Full stop. What can I do to persuade her to change her mind?

C.U. Cardiff, Wales.

It sounds as if you've got a bit of a faulty connection there. But if that is what the lady wants, it's pretty much a case of take it or leave it. You'll just have to take matters in hand.

MAKING A BOOB

When I was younger, I was delighted when my breasts started developing earlier than those of the other girls in my class at school. By the time that I was in my mid-teens, I was secretly pleased that my breasts were larger than those of any of the other girls at school or, later still, at college. It ensured that, while I was no raving beauty, I had a constant supply of male admirers and I was able to pick and choose, while many of my contemporaries had to make do with my rejects.

Now that I'm in my mid-twenties, I'm seriously considering an operation to have my breasts made smaller. Why, I hear you ask? For what seems to me to be one very good reason. Now that I have progressed from the schoolgirl excitements of letting boys feel my breasts to the pleasures of proper, adult sexual intercourse, I find that the men who are attracted to me are still fascinated by the size of my breasts, to the exclusion of practically everything else.

For the record, I am a 44D, but they're in good shape, if I say so myself. And every single man I have taken to my bed wants only one thing. He wants to toss off between my tits. Nobody wants to fuck *me*.

I don't mind giving any man the occasional tit wank. For obvious reasons, I'm something of an expert. But why, oh why do grown men want to behave like small schoolboys, obsessed by any girl who's got big breasts?

N.C. Haslemere, Surrey.

Don't knock those big knockers, darling. Most of the girls in the office here tell us that they'd kill for well-shaped 44D breasts. We'd advise you to think long and hard before deciding to go ahead with plastic surgery. Can't you and your boyfriends take it in turns to decide who does what to whom, and with what?

HAND IN HAND

I read much in your magazine about the masturbatory fantasies of your male readers, but what about us poor girls? We have fantasies too, you know.

I was taught to masturbate at boarding school by one of the older girls, and our main pastime in our dormitories, when we first went to bed at night, was either masturbating ourselves or each other. Almost all of the girls at school masturbated, all the time, and we all looked upon it as a perfectly normal thing to do. A pleasant way of releasing our sexual tentions. I don't think that we were in any way really lesbian, even when masturbating each other. I think it was simply companionship, and friendship. As far as I know, none of us grew up to be serious dykes.

Our mistresses were something else, of course. A number of them were raving lesbians, although, to be fair, they didn't bother us. They seemed too busy being involved with each other. But I suspect that some of them at least enjoyed being surrounded by nubile young ladies, often (in dorm, at gym, or in the changing rooms, or at bath time) quite naked. But I digress.

I still masturbate frequently, although I really have as much sex as I want or need, being single and living in my own flat in London. The great thing about frigging myself is that I don't have anyone else to think about. That might perhaps sound silly to you, but when two people are fucking each other, it's only natural to be concerned about the other person's feelings. And let's face it, what gives them *their* jollies may not necessarily be what gets *your* rocks off. Playing with myself, I can fantasize absolutely anything that I wish, without having to give a damn for anyone else.

My favourite fantasy is being raped by huge Japanese Sumo wrestlers. They take me and strip me, and throw my down on the floor. They then rape me, continually. They rape me vaginally and anally. And they make me take them in my mouth. They all have huge cocks, on a par with their huge bodies, and they pass me on, from one to another, so that someone is always raping me, in one or more orifice, absolutely non-stop. Sometimes two of them rape me at once, in two of my entrances. Their enormous, swollen cocks stretch my poor little pussy and my poor little bottom until I'm screaming. But I'm screaming with pleasure. With fulfilled lust. And I'm coming all the time. While all this is happening in my mind, my fingers are working overtime between my legs, like the proverbial fiddler's elbow.

In another fantasy, I'm a slave to a whole tribe of Africans. They're giants. Blue-black. Masai, probably. I live in a native village, in the jungle, and I'm there to be taken sexually by any one of therm, at any time. I'm the village bicycle. They most of them have wives, apart from the youngsters (who use me to practise on). But if any of the adult males' wives has a headache, or her period, or she simply doesn't feel like it, there's always me. I'm permanently, totally available. And I love it!

As with my Sumo wrestlers, my male Africans are all blessed with giant cocks with which they penetrate my every orifice. Their cocks are so big that, when they force me to take them in my mouth, I don't so much suck them off – it simply isn't physically possible – they just plain fuck my mouth. They hold my head down in between their legs, and fuck my mouth until they come, spurting their thick, creamy seed down my throat.

When they sodomize me, I make them grease my bottom with palm oil. Without which, with the size of their massive cocks, they would split me in two. But much of my favourite sexual exercise, in my African fantasy, comes from my hours spent with the young men. Those who are too young to marry. Those who are still learning what sex is about. The ones who use me to practise on. They come to me on the advice of their elders and betters, and they tell me that they do not know about women, but that they are keen to learn. And I teach them everything. I massage their little cocks into huge erections. And over a period of time, I massage their sexual egos into something appropriate to their proud African heritage. In between, I get fucked a lot.

Thank you for allowing me to share my phallic fantasies with your other women readers. Writing about them has made my panties very wet. I must stop and take myself in hand.

J.C. Belfast, Northern Ireland.

You're more than welcome, ma'am. While we sometimes need to remind ourselves that our prime target is men, we are always ready to print anything as delightful as your female fantasies.

SECOND BEST?

As a single woman in my middle forties, I have, for some time now, accepted the sad fact that I'm unlikely to get married. I'm seldom lonely (at least in the early evenings) and I get plenty of good sex. My complaint is that I'm a substitute, rather than being desired for what I am.

You must know a hundred women like me. We work in offices, and we supply the sex to their husbands that married women don't seem to want to know about. We never, ever have headaches. You want to fuck us, we're ready. You can take us home and fuck us in our solitary little spinster flats. You don't even have to buy us a drink on the way there. You certainly don't need to buy us dinner. If you want to give us a quick one in the stationery cupboard, or lock your own office door and have us across your desk, we'll drop our knickers for you whenever and wherever you wish.

We're grateful for what we can get, you see. We know our place. And you know our place. And you can stick your prick up our place any time you like. We'll suck your cock, and swallow your come, without the least complaint. You can suck our pussies whenever you want. Two things, these last, that your wives often don't want to know about. They tell you that you're dirty – perverted, even – when you ask them to suck you off. We love it. And if you *really* want to be dirty, or perverted, well, of course, we don't mind that too much, either. Provided that you don't go *too* far.

A little flagellation – given or received – isn't entirely out of bounds. If you want to tie us up, well, OK. But not too tight, mind you. You can wear our knickers while you fuck us, if that's what turns you on. You can have anal sex with most of us. These days, we quite enjoy it.

We'll talk dirty to you, if that excites you. ('Tell me what I'm doing to you, darling.' 'You're making love to me, darling.' 'No. No. I'm fucking you. Say it.' Pause. Then, 'You're fucking me, darling.' 'Where am I fucking you?' Excitedly, this. Another pause. Oh yes. Of course. 'You're fucking my cunt, darling. With your big, stiff cock. Your cock's in my cunt. My tiny, wet cunt. And you're fucking me.' Silent pause for ejaculation. Three minutes later. 'Forgive me, sweetheart, but I've got to dash tonight. The old girl's got some friends coming to dinner. I mustn't be late. Goodnight, darling. See you in the office tomorrow.' 'Goodnight, darling.')

And, of course, if it's after a late office meeting and you've had a few too many with your male colleagues in the pub before getting yourself round to us for a quick one on the way home, or if you're quite simply feeling lazy and all you fancy is lying there while we give you the long, slow, expert wank that your wife always refuses to give you, well, it's all understandable. Isn't it? Darling? We office girls are so lucky. No, really.

P.T-H. Notting Hill Gate, London.

We don't know about 'second best'. We would have thought that 'first choice' was a better, more accurate description. At the very least for the sexual services. But we have to accept the sad facts concerning some people's marriages and their so-called marital relationships. In the scenario that you describe, there are not too many options, are there? Accept the situation, or be lonely. That's not really much of a choice, is it?

ALL GIRLS TOGETHER

My husband doesn't normally have the kind of job where he ever needs to be away overnight. But recently, due to his firm taking over another company, he's been sent to America for three months, to help train staff over there. We've been married for four years, and we have what I would call a good sex life. It's regular, and we both enjoy it, and there's plenty of variety in it. We're never short of ideas, thanks, in part, to your publication. But while my husband's been away a girlfriend that I see all the time, even when my husband is at home, has been spending a lot of time with me.

At first I thought that she was just being thoughtful and keeping me company. But not so long ago she confessed to me that she was essentially a lesbian, and that she was in love with me and wanted to *make* love with me. In my book, that means she was either wanting to suck my pussy or fuck me with a strap-on dildo. It turns out that I was right, on both counts!

But here's the problem. I loved every minute of it, and I can't wait for her to come stay overnight with me again. What that girl can do to my pussy with her tongue is nobody's business. My husband sucks my pussy, and I love him doing it, but he could certainly take lessons from this lady. And she's extremely expert with her dildo.

Now, I'm not saying that I don't love my husband any more. Nor that I *prefer* this lady's attentions to his. It's simply that I enjoy them as an adjunct to sex with my husband. I've suggested to my new lover that she might like to become a threesome with my husband and me, once he returns from America. I just know he'd love to watch us getting it on and even join in, if she were agreeable. But she says she's not into men in any way. What shall I do? I don't want to give either of them up.

K.L. Luton, Bedfordshire.

Some bisexuals manage to keep all their balls in the air, if you know what we mean. But this is usually either because everyone involved knows their proclivities beforehand and is happy to accept them, or because the two different ends of the sexual spectrum are unaware of the other's involvement. We suspect that your husband might find your new relationship difficult to cope with, were he aware of it, especially since it would seem to exclude him. Only you can decide how to handle this problem.

JUNGLE JOYS

My favourite fantasy has always involved generous numbers of African women. A veritable tribe of black Amazons. Tall, long-legged, full-breasted, and all with insatiable sexual appetites.

I am walking in the jungle when I fall into a trap set for me by these lovely women. However much I try, I cannot climb out, and have to sit and await my fate. Quite soon, two nubile young members of the tribe arrive and let down a rope, which I tie around my waist, and they then haul me out. The girls are that wonderful blue-black of the real African native. They are naked, apart from tiny, apron-style pieces of cotton, which do little to hide their sex. They have magnificent breasts and attractive facial features, a mixture of African and European.

As soon as I am back up at ground level once more, I realize that the women are armed. They are carrying spears, bows and arrows, and hunting knives. One woman holds a knife at my throat, while the other cuts off my safari suit and underwear, leaving me standing there naked. Both girls look at my prick, and smile at each other. One girl takes hold of it and quickly masturbates it to full erection. They smile at each other again, and then they take it in turns for one of them to hold the knife while the other one rapes me. Except, naturally, that I am only too pleased to be fucked by these two girls. Rape it isn't.

After both of them have fucked me, one of them kneels in front of me and takes my penis in her mouth. She sucks me off, expertly, quickly, and with apparent enthusiasm, swallowing my semen as I ejaculate in her mouth. She then lies down on the ground, the other girl watching with interest (and with her knife still handy, just in case, although I think that they have now both realized that I am enjoying that which they are doing to me and I to them).

The girl on the ground then opens her legs and, lifting her little apron once more, she points at her pussy, then at my mouth, and pokes her tongue out, which she then waggles in an excellent imitation of what she has just been doing to me. I understand immediately. She wants me to suck her pussy.

'My pleasure, darling,' I told her, smiling at her. She said something and smiled back at me, but neither of us knew the other's language. I got down between her legs and lifted the apron out of the way. During our earlier intercourse, I hadn't had too much of an opportunity to examine the source of my pleasure, but this time I could see her sex at close quarters.

Her pubic hair was coarse and luxuriant. It was thick, black and tightly curled. Her outer vaginal lips were full and almost black in colour, as were her nipples and their surrounding areolae. As I looked at her nipples she took them, one in each hand and, smiling down at me from where I was looking up from between her legs, she pulled and twirled her teats until they were startlingly erect. Raising her arms to do this, she revealed thick growths of underarm hair. It was longer and straighter than her pubic hair.

I reached out and gently pulled her vaginal lips open to expose her inner lips and the moist gash of her vaginal orifice. Down inside her sex, the black faded to a dark purple which, as I looked farther inside, became a darkish pink.

She was wet, and her vaginal odour was strong and gamy. Her juices were running down the insides of both her thighs. Obviously these women were highly sexed. I held her labia apart and took an exploratory lick, the full length of her open pussy.

Then I began to kiss and suck in earnest, and she started to make soft grunting noises. She tasted strongly. Much more strongly than a European woman. It wasn't unpleasant. Nor was it in any way unhygienic. Her intimate parts were clean. They tasted of her vaginal juices, and a trace of my own semen. It was an exotic, slightly jungly flavour. I thrust deeply into her with my tongue, and, to my relief, found her clitoris. Some African tribes indulge in clitoral circumcision, but it seemed logical in a tribe where the women were obviously the warriors that they kept their clitorises for the pleasures for which they were intended.

The woman's grunts soon became louder and more frequent, and she suddenly took my head in her hands and began to hump my mouth with her sex, a sort of fucking motion. Soon after that she held herself pressed tightly against my mouth and put her head back, making a noise that I can only compare to that of an animal howling, as if in pain.

I could feel her orgasms as she held herself against my mouth and after they had slowly died away she relaxed, released my head, smiled down at me, and said something in her strange tongue which, from her tone of voice, I took to be 'Thank you'.

I looked up at the other woman and was amused to see her with her knife abandoned down on the ground beside her. She had her right hand delving beneath her apron which, from the movements of it, indicated that she was masturbating herself rhythmically. Her eyes were shut, and she had a half-smile upon her face. As I watched, she too came, with much grunting and an increase in the speed with which she was manipulating herself. When she had finished, she opened her eyes to see me gazing at her.

My prick was once more fully erect, despite the sterling work that it had performed earlier. The second woman said something to her colleague, and they both looked at my swollen penis. One of them said something else, which made both of them laugh. The one who had been masturbating put her fingers to my lips, from which I could smell the scent of her pussy juices. She pressed her fingers against my mouth, and I took the hint and licked and sucked them clean for her. They were wet and sticky, and she tasted sensational. If she was endeavouring to whet my appetite for more of the same, she succeeded. But she had a more friendly exercise in mind than the one her friend had initiated, in that she was wanting to give as well as to receive. She indicated that I should lie on the ground on my back, which I did, my prick standing up like a like a small flagpole between my thighs.

The second girl then knelt over my face, lowering her wet black pussy down onto my mouth, where I began at once to eat her. At the same time she took my prick into her right hand and, holding it by its base, she started to fellate me. A classic *soixante-neuf.* As a result of her playing with herself just prior to my sucking her, the woman's pussy was creamy with her nectar and she tasted as strongly as did her colleague, although the actual flavour was quite different in itself. Her pussy was similar to the other girl's in colour and shape, although her labia were slightly smaller.

She worked hard and conscientiously at her fellatio, and like her sister under the skin, she was obviously greatly experienced at oral sex. In return, I did my best for her, and quite soon she and I were coming together, enjoying our mutual orgasms. When it was all over, this girl also repeated whatever it was that the other girl had said, after my session of cunnilingus with her. The phrase that I took to be 'Thank you'.

After a short period in which we lay quietly on the jungle floor, resting, the girls spoke to each other for a moment, and then got themselves up off the ground, collected their weapons, and adjusted their minuscule aprons. They then indicated to me that I should join them. When I attempted to dress, they both shouted at me, and one of them leaned forward, and gave my prick a couple of wanking motions. I think that they were trying to say that they didn't want me to dress, for they liked being able to see my prick. It obligingly stood to attention from the fingering that it was getting, at which they both giggled and clapped their hands. I supposed that they too were very nearly almost as naked as they insisted that I remain. We took off in single file, me in the middle, with one native girl in front of me, leading the way, and the other one behind, bringing up the rear.

After what seemed like a long time, mostly because of the heat, we arrived at a native village where my captors announced their arrival by beating a gong hanging from a tree branch at the entrance to the village. This brought a horde of similar tall Amazon-like women out of the various huts, all naked except for the now familiar small aprons. There were no men in sight. The two girls who I was with engaged the others in an intense conversation which I could tell was largely comcerned with my prick, since both of the two girls took hold of it in their fingers and held it, from time to time, to demonstrate something. At one point, one of them masturbated it to erection again, as she had done before earlier in the day.

They were also – from the way in which they used their tongues to demonstrate – describing in detail my efforts at cunnilingus. Both descriptions brought a series of what sounded like 'ooohs' and 'aaahs' from the assembled company, and one or two of the girls began playing with themselves beneath their aprons. Others came and handled my now rigid cock, making kissing *moues* at me, licking their lips in an exaggerated way and making sibilant, unmistakable sucking noises.

Finally, one young girl knelt before me and took my prick in her mouth, as one of the two girls who brought me in from the jungle had done earlier in the day. I came fairly quickly, for she, like the others, had a very practised mouth. When I finally came in it, in concentrated spurts, she swallowed my ejaculate, as the other girls had done.

When she had finished, she got a round of applause from the assembled crowd and she smiled, first at me, then at her audience. The two who had brought me into the village then spoke to each other in whispers, after which one of them turned and made a short speech to the assembled crowd. There were one or two comments from different people, and then my two girls indicated that I should follow them. They took me off with them, ending up beckoning me to follow them into the interior of one of the huts.

It was the usual mud-walled, thatch-roofed kind of native hut, and the interior was simply one big round room. There were no windows, and the only light came from the doorway. There wasn't much furniture, either. A large but simple bed, a table, two chairs, rugs here and there, and in one corner a fireplace with a few pots, pans and cooking utensils on the floor beside.

I stood there, naked as the day I was born. My clothes had been left in the jungle clearing, where they had been cut off me. Moments later, a youngish girl came in with a pail of water that she put down on the floor beside me. She rummaged about in a corner and came back with soap and a small cloth. She then proceeded to wash me, all over. She tended my cock lovingly, peeling back my foreskin and rinsing my prick carefully, after which, looking first carefully over her shoulder to see that the other two women were preoccupied with talking in low tones to each other, she bent down and licked it for a moment or two, her tongue tickling the end of it erotically.

She then looked up at me and smiled and, letting go of my cock, she joined her thumb and forefinger together and then thrust the forefinger of her other hand backwards and forwards through the circle, in the age-old sign for sexual intercourse.

I began to get the idea that this tribe must in some way worship male sexual organs, or fucking, or all forms of sex. The total lack of any sign of males about the place, together with the seeming preoccupation of all of the women with matters sexual, seemed to point to it. But I wasn't sure exactly what this girl was suggesting, or trying to tell me, by her sign language. Was she suggesting that we fuck? If she was, she was a lot more subtle about it than her tribal sisters. Or was she saying that, in an ideal situation, she would *like* to fuck?

She stood up from the kneeling position that she had been in and, standing in front of me so that my body hid hers from the others, she took the fingers of my right hand and placed them beneath her apron into what I could immediately feel was her soaking wet pussy.

Having got them positioned to her satisfaction, she then began to move my fingers up and down, leaving me in no doubt about what she wanted me to do. I felt for and found her clitoris, which was rigid with excitement, and quickly frigged it for her until she came, which was literally within only a few seconds. She managed, successfully, to endure her orgasms without making a sound and when she had finished she took my fingers out of her pussy and kissed them clean and dry before letting go of them.

She smiled, and said something which, for a change, didn't

sound like the thank you to which I was becoming accustomed. Perhaps she was saying goodbye, for she put the cloth back from whence she had brought it, picked up her pail, and took herself off, a happy smile upon her face as she departed.

But the three of us weren't alone for long. About ten minutes after the girl who had washed me left, a line began to form outside the hut. I was very quickly made aware that this queue – for that was what it was – was made up of sex-hungry women, all of whom wanted my body.

I began immediately, and managed to fuck the first three women before I indicated, by sign language, that I needed a rest before I would be able to continue.

In my fantasy, I slowly work my way through the seemingly never-ending queue of women, over a period of many days. I am helped by the fact that a new woman is in herself the greatest of all aphrodisiacs, plus the fact that these women were expert at raising erections in sexually exhausted males.

Not all of them wanted intercourse. There were a number who were keen to be brought to orgasm by oral means, and these became welcome interludes. In my fantasy, I never did discover what had happened to the original men of the tribe, but it was their disappearance that had led to my subsequently happy duties.

L.J. Ealing, London.

What you might describe as a new – and pleasurable – African tribal dance!

COMING TO THE POINT

Three of my girlfriends and I were sitting around the other evening, having a quiet drink and talking about the kind of things that girls talk about when they are on their own and, reasonably enough, the conversation finally got around to sex. Well, it does seem to, somehow, doesn't it? Our main topic that evening was female orgasm, and whether or not the average man really knew very much about it. I thought that the outcome of that conversation might be of interest to your male readers.

Most of the girls (all single, all between the ages of twenty-five and thirty-two) confessed that the most usual way of their achieving orgasm after sex with their menfolk was either by getting their man to masturbate them, or by masturbating themselves. One of the four of us was lucky. She has, she tells us, a boyfriend with an enormous cock, who is always concerned that she enjoys her sex with him, and apparently he takes the time and trouble to make certain that she achieves orgasm before he ejaculates. She says that the size of his cock makes this a fairly simple matter for him, for when erect it rubs really hard against her clitoris, whatever sexual position they are using.

All four of us agreed that our very first orgasms, as teenagers, came from masturbation, and one of us said that masturbation was still the only way that she could achieve orgasm. All four of us admitted that we masturbated ourselves frequently, for the sheer pleasure of it, not necessarily because we were short of sexual relations with a male. All of us agreed that none of us had achieved orgasm in our early sexual relationships.

One girl advanced the theory that female orgasms were in the head, in the mind, rather than achieved by stimulation of the clitoris, but the girl with the boyfriend with the large cock violently disagreed with this suggestion.

Strangely, all four of us found that we always achieved orgasm when having cunnilingus performed upon us, but we also all agreed that it was quite difficult to find men who wanted to suck pussy and who had much idea of how to do it successfully. We all agreed, at the end of the conversation, that we would happily volunteer to form a membership club, specifically for readers of your magazine, to coach male readers in the gentle art of cunnilingus. In return, we would pay for these services by providing some of the finest fellatio available in the United Kingdom. Any offers? We're ready, willing, and able!

S.R., D.C., V.P., and K.L. Purley, Surrey.

Feel free, girls, to come up to the office, and see us, sometime. We'll road test all four of you, gratis. That's a promise.

A DIFFERENT KIND OF BLOW-UP DOLL . . .

What with interactive CDs and videos, virtual reality, and all the rest of the high-tech world that we live in, surely it can't be beyond the abilities of those clever Japanese to invent a programmable female robot? One that could be tuned to look like any woman in the world, from Marilyn Monroe to Princess Di? Literally any woman you have ever fancied. The girl next door, if that's who turns you on. A robot that looked, smelt, tasted, felt, and fucked like a real human woman. But one that never had a headache, always wanted to fellate you (*and* swallow your come) and who took it up her ass whenever you felt like it.

With the right programming, your robot could be an eighteen-year-old virgin one night, a nun the next, a whore when you felt like one. Think of the fun you could have dressing up a pretty nun in naughty knickers! Or it could be any woman from history. You could resurrect Veronica Lake, Mata Hari, or that girl who used to live down the road, who would let you fuck her when you were teenagers. Nell Gwynne. Joan of Arc.

It could look and feel like real, live people from contemporary life. Your wife's sister. Any of the strippers from your favourite club. That tarty barmaid from the Red Lion. You could do all the naughty illegal things to it (or have it do them to you) because it is, after all, only a robot. But it would be so realistic that no one would ever know the difference. You could do all the dirty sexual things to it that you've always wanted to do, and never dared to ask for.

You could pull its knickers down and spank it. You could have it fellate you while you watched *Newsnight*. You could get it to give you a quick wank before you got out of bed in the morning. Or you could fuck it while you watched *EastEnders*. You could program it to behave like an expensive French tart. You could turn it into Queen Victoria, if that was your bag. Or reproduce your boss's wife, and then be beastly to her. Or make her perform perverted sexual acts.

There is almost no end to the possibilities. One thing for certain: you'd never be short of any sexual act that you wished for. And when you felt like a quiet half-hour with a good book, you could simply switch it off.

J.D. Swansea, South Wales.

But what if she/it fell in love with your best friend? What if someone wanted to borrow her? Or if someone stole her? What if she/it was unfaithful to you? But joking apart, yes, what a boon she/it would be. We wonder where she would position her control panel . . . And on second thoughts, why only one? Why not two? They could do naughty things together. Three? A dozen?

DICK ROGERS

SUMMER SCHOOL

Life is hectic on the British Riviera, where the local girls will do anything – but anything – to get what they want, and the co-eds at the Summer School lap up the sun . . .

HODDER AND STOUGHTON PAPERBACKS

RAY GORDON

SEX THIEF

. . . And the suit comes off.

By day, Jade Kimberly is an unimposing secretary, but by night she runs amok as a gorgeous cat-burglar, raiding the country pads of the rich and famous. Everything is fine until she is caught 'red-handed' by a wealthy businessman. She quickly realises that she is not cut out for a life 'inside' and after peeling off her skin-tight black cat-suit, she 'persuades' him to let her go. But that is only the beginning of her nocturnal fun . . .

RAY GORDON

SUBMISSION

WOULD THEY TAKE IT LYING DOWN?

The time: early in the next century. There's been a massive backlash against the domination of society by women. Special 'correction centres' have been set up by the brutal new male dictatorship to bring militant female liberationists into line.

Most feared of the custody officers are Fowler and his sadistic lesbian sidekick Swain. Their lustful treatment of attractive female prisoners is legendary among the members of the resistance movement. When Fowler is captured by resistance leader Hanna Kelley, the jackboot is on the other foot – for a while. But Fowler escapes and takes Hanna captive in turn. Now she's at his mercy. Not that he's inclined to show her any . . .

SUBMISSION
is another outstandingly inventive novel of the wilder shores of lust by one of the most powerful talents on today's erotic fiction scene.

HODDER AND STOUGHTON PAPERBACKS

RAY GORDON

NAKED LIES

Shafted . . .

Gorgeous young housewife Jane Daniels is in a bit of a bind. Her next door neighbour seems to have found rather attractive photos of her as a teenager in one of his hard-core porn mags. And he wants paying off. And not with money either. But as he forces her into performing a series of sordid sex acts for him, and she realises she has been well and truly set-up, she is planning her revenge in quite the most pleasurable way possible . . .

HODDER AND STOUGHTON PAPERBACKS